When Summer Ends

By Isabelle Rae

ISBN -10: 1479325295
ISBN-13: 978-1479325290

Acknowledgements

Special thanks must go to Mollie Wilson who made the adorable cover for this book.

This book is dedicated to my mum, and my older sister. I love you both dearly.

Chapter One

My vision was a little blurry as I continued to dance. My head was just that little bit fuzzy from the alcohol. My legs had that rubbery feeling, like I wasn't quite in full control of myself. "Shall we drink some more?" my best friend, Amy, shouted to me over the music.

I shook my head. "I can't drink anymore, I'll be sick," I answered, turning my nose up.

"You've only had four drinks," she teased, laughing hysterically at me. She always did think I was a little bit pathetic because I couldn't hold my drink at all.

"You can have one. I'll come to the bar with you," I shouted back, grabbing her hand so we didn't get separated in the packed club. My other two friends didn't want a drink, so we left them dancing.

Amy led me to the bar so I stood behind her as she waited for the barman to notice her. After about five minutes she still hadn't been served. She turned back to me with an apologetic smile. "I desperately need to pee, can you keep my place? The guy hasn't even looked down this end yet," she said, nodding to the barman who was serving up the other end of the busy bar with his back to us. The place was packed, and he was on his own, he must have been a little stressed.

"Yeah, okay," I agreed, moving into her space quickly. I leant over the bar a little so I could see if the barman was coming up this end. I watched his back; he was wearing nicely fitted jeans and a black T-shirt with the club's logo on the back. He looked pretty toned from what I could tell, and his ass was edible. I was happily watching his ass when he turned around so I accidentally looked at his crotch. I blushed and looked away quickly, grateful that he hadn't caught me.

Suddenly, he was walking towards me; horrified, I quickly shot my eyes up to his face. He was so handsome that my mouth started to water. His brown hair was messy and swept to one side, his mouth twisted into a smirk as he walked right up and stopped in front of me. He was tall, probably about six foot one. I felt my breath catch in my throat as I looked into his eyes. I couldn't quite make out the colour because the club was dark, but they were fairly light, so clearly not brown. He was looking at me so intently that it made my heart start to race.

"Hi. Do you want a drink, or are you happy looking at the scenery?" he asked, smirking at me.

Damn, he's got a sexy voice. I laughed. "Well the scenery's pretty good in this club," I replied, nodding, raising an eyebrow trying to look sexy. I had no idea why I was flirting with him. If he worked here then that meant he was over twenty-one, and he'd probably assumed I was too, considering I'd used a fake ID to get in the club.

He grinned. "Yeah, my views pretty good too," he flirted, looking me over slowly. I grinned and leant back slightly so he could get a view of the bottom of my dress. It was pretty short, not my usual type of dress at all, but I thought I would go for something different tonight.

"Hey can we get some service down here? We've been waiting ten minutes," some guy shouted, waving his hard around angrily.

The barman looked at me apologetically. "I'll be right back." He walked off to serve the angry looking guy. I couldn't stop myself from glancing at his ass again. It certainly was a pleasant view, I wasn't joking.

After serving Mr Angry, he came back to me. "So, have you decided what you want?" he asked, running a hand through his tousled hair.

"Um, yeah. Can I get a rum and coke?" I asked, trying to think about what Amy would want. He poured the drink and put it down on the counter in front of me before smiling and walking off to serve some other people. I watched him, confused. How much was the drink? He'd walked off before I paid for it. "Hey, you didn't charge me," I called to his back.

"It's on me," he replied, not looking at me. Around me, people continued to shout their orders at him while he struggled to keep up.

The guy next to me slammed his hand down on the bar and growled in frustration. "Seriously, how fucking long does it take to get a drink in this place?" he shouted angrily.

Wow, there's going to be a riot soon. Why isn't there someone else to help him run the bar? "Why are you on your own?" I shouted, waving to get the barman's attention.

"We're short tonight, so I'm on my own until Kane comes back from his break." He shrugged, continuing to serve. *Well that isn't fair, people are being so rude to him as he serves them and it isn't even his fault!* I turned around and boosted myself up onto the bar, swinging my legs over the other side, and dropping down. "Hey! What the hell are you doing? Get back the other side, no customers are allowed back here!" he instructed, frowning at me angrily.

I waved my hand dismissively and turned to the nearest man that was shouting abuse. "What can I get you, handsome?" I asked, smiling sweetly.

"Four bottles of bud and four shots of vodka," he answered, leaning in, smiling now.

2

"Sure." I gave him a flirtatious smile before turning back to the barman who was staring at me, a shocked expression on his face. "Well don't just stand there looking at me, get to serving!" I teased. "And how much does that order come to?" I asked, grabbing four beer bottles from the fridge behind me.

"Er, we have a special on bud with a shot for the next hour. It's four bucks each, so sixteen bucks in total. Most people will be ordering that," he stated, still looking at me shocked.

I nodded and grabbed four shot glasses from the side, looking around for the vodka. He pointed to the wall where the bottles where hanging. "Thanks."

"Thanks for this. I'm Will, by the way," he said, walking off to the next customer.

"Chloe."

I finished serving the guy and took his money. I had no idea how to work the cash register though. I was standing there looking at it confused; it was one of those electronic ones with a touch screen. I had no idea what I was supposed to do to make it open. I winced and raised a tentative hand, deciding some button mashing was in order.

Just as I was about to start a long sequence of button pressing in the hope that something would happen, two arms shot around me from behind, making me jump. Will took hold of my hand, guiding it towards the screen. "Touch here," he instructed, tapping my hand on the screen at the top right. A menu appeared with little boxes with the names of the drinks. I felt a blush creep up on my face at how close he was. His hard, toned body was pressed against my back; his breath blew across my cheek making me hot and bothered. "Just tap the drink you made. You made four happy hours," he continued, tapping my hand on the 'special offer' icon four times. "Then click total. Then cash," he stated, moving my hand to the right places. The cash drawer shot out at me quickly. His other arm went across my waist, pulling me back into his body so the drawer didn't hit me in the stomach. "You might want to be careful, a pretty little thing like you could get hurt by the big bad register," he whispered in my ear, making me shiver. Then he was gone, leaving me there, my whole body tingling, my mouth slightly open, and my breathing coming out in uneven gasps. My mind was whirling with thoughts of how hot he was.

After regaining my composure I served a couple of other people, when I suddenly spotted Amy looking around for me. "Amy!" I shouted. She didn't respond and carried on looking around for me worriedly. "Amy!" I grabbed an ice cube and threw it at her. Her head shot up in surprise as it hit her on the shoulder.

She gasped and looked at me, confused, before shaking her head and walking over to me, grinning. "What on earth are you doing?" she asked, laughing.

I gave her a little twirl. "New job. Do I make a convincing bartender?" I asked, winking at her.

She laughed harder. "Seriously, Chloe, what are you doing behind the bar?"

I went to serve the guy standing next to her so that I could talk to her. "Will was on his own, people were getting annoyed so I thought I'd help him out." I shrugged.

"And who's Will?" she asked, raising an eyebrow at me. I nodded over my shoulder at his back. Amy looked over at him. "Wow, nice ass," she complimented, giggling.

"I'm going to help him until the other guy comes back from his break, then I'll come and find you," I called over my shoulder as I went to serve someone else.

"Sure, have fun," she replied, winking at me.

I was actually having a lot of fun; the guys were flirting with me like crazy. I refused to serve people unless they were singing and dancing, so people were having a lot of fun waiting to be served, which made Will laugh. I'd been told to keep the change loads of times and had about forty bucks tucked in a glass under the bar. Not that I could keep it though, it should be Will's really. I didn't get a chance to speak to Will much because it was too busy, but I brushed past him a few times, sending him flirtatious smiles. I was trying not to though; he was too old for me and probably thought I was twenty-one instead of seventeen, so I certainly shouldn't be lusting after him like I was.

After about half an hour the rush started to slow down because the happy hour finished. Will came over and stood next to me. "Thanks for this, I really appreciate your help," he said, handing me a glass which contained a white creamy looking drink.

"What's that?" I frowned at it. It didn't look too appealing.

He grinned. "It's called a Screaming Orgasm. I thought I'd give you one as a thanks," he stated, smirking at me.

I blushed like crazy and giggled. "It's not called that."

"It is. You've never had one?" he asked, raising his eyebrows innocently, even though his smirk clearly showed there was nothing innocent about it at all.

Okay, well I guess I can flirt with him, that's harmless after all. "A screaming one?" I asked, narrowing my eyes, pretending to think. "No actually I don't think I have, you'll be giving me my first," I stated, trying not to blush when I said it.

"Well then I'm honoured." He flicked me on the nose as he walked off to serve someone else. I took a hefty swig of the drink and almost gagged; it was disgusting and had so much alcohol in it that it burnt my throat. "You don't like it?" he asked, faking hurt.

"Sorry, I guess you have too much confidence in your ability," I replied, handing it back to him, still wincing as I rubbed my mouth with the back of my hand.

4

He laughed and knocked the drink back as he leant against the bar, watching me. Taio Cruz; Dynamite, started, and I squealed excitedly. "I love this song!" I chirped, dancing and singing along with the lyrics.

He just watched me with an amused smile on his face. "Wow, you're a terrible singer." He laughed.

I rolled my eyes and grabbed his hand, pulling him towards me. "Dance with me, payback seeing as the orgasm you gave me was a let-down," I teased.

He laughed and put his hands on my hips, pulling me closer to him as we started to dance. I put one hand on his hard chest as we were grinding against each other, making my whole body burn and tingle with need. *Damn, he is so hot.* My breathing was coming out in pants. I desperately wanted him to kiss me even though I was clearly too young for him.

"I get off in another hour when the other two staff get here, how about I buy you a drink or some food as a real thanks," he suggested, brushing my hair away from my face with his fingertips.

I didn't want to drink anymore, but I was actually quite hungry and could really go for a pizza or something right about now. "I am quite hungry," I admitted, biting my lip, thinking. *I really shouldn't go with him, I don't even know the guy, I shouldn't go off with him, I should just stay with my friends...*

"Great." He smiled a dazzling smile, his eyes twinkling. I desperately wished they would turn up the lights so I could see the colour of them, they must be blue or green, they were too light for brown, definitely.

Just then a man wearing a black T-shirt the same as Will's, lifted one side of the bar and walked in, looking at me shocked. "What the hell are you doing letting a customer back here?" he asked, shaking his head, but smirking at Will. He obviously thought we were getting it on or something.

"Chloe was helping with the happy hour rush," Will explained, shrugging easily, his eyes not leaving mine. "So, can I get your number so I can give you a call when I'm done?" he asked, looking at me hopefully as he pulled out his cell phone, holding it out to me. I nodded and punched in my number excitedly. "I'll be about an hour then," he said, leading me over to the gap in the bar. Just as I was about to walk off he caught my hand, making me stop. "Wait, I forgot to give you something." He stepped closer to me, a smile tugging at the corners of his mouth.

I looked at him curiously. *What have I forgotten?*

He bent his head quickly and kissed me lightly, just for a second. His soft lips seemed to match mine perfectly. I was actually too shocked to kiss him back. When he pulled away he was smirking at me, so obviously I looked a little shocked. My whole body was screaming for more and I wanted to grab him and rip his clothes off and have him take me in the middle of the bar.

"Er... right... well... I'll... um... yeah," I stuttered, feeling a blush creep up onto my face again.

He flicked my nose again. "You honestly are too cute." He laughed and turned back to the bar, closing it behind him and walking off without a second glance at me. I sighed happily and made my way over to my friends who were

5

still dancing. I spotted Amy's back, she was making out with some random guy. I rolled my eyes and went to my other two friends, Emily and Catherine.

"Where were you? Amy said you were helping behind the bar?" Emily asked, looking confused, as if she thought maybe Amy was drunk or something.

"Yeah I was, they were short staffed," I confirmed, nodding. "And now I have a plans with an extremely hot bartender in an hour," I added, waggling my eyebrows.

Emily and Catherine laughed. "You're such a slut," Emily teased.

"I know," I joked. That wasn't true though, we both knew it. I'd only dated two guys before, and both of those had been serious boyfriends. Well, at the time they were serious anyway, but they didn't work out. I'd split up with my boyfriend of six months, Nick, at the beginning of the summer and hadn't even had a date since then because I just wasn't interested in anyone.

As we danced and I told them every single detail about Will, the kiss, and the flirting. After a little while my phone rang in my little clutch purse. I answered it nervously, knowing it must be him because it was an unknown number.

"Hey, Chloe, I'm now finished. Do you still want to go and get something to eat?" he asked.

"Yeah okay," I agreed, swallowing my nervous excitement.

"I'll meet you by the front door then."

"Okay." I turned to my friends. Amy was practically jumping up and down with excitement, she was probably thinking of all the gossip she would get tomorrow. "Right guys, if I get killed then tell my parents that I love them, and you guys can fight over my iPod," I teased.

Amy pulled me into a hug. "Make sure you tell him that we know you're with him, then he won't try anything. Tell him that we know he was the last one you were with, and we'll be able to tell the cops if he murders you. Promise me you'll tell him," she said, looking at me seriously.

Wow, maybe this isn't such a brilliant idea at all. "Um, Amy, please don't say things like that, you're scaring me." *Maybe I should call him and tell him I've changed my mind or something.*

She giggled drunkenly. "Just go. You said he was hot. All I saw was the ass and that was scrumptious," she instructed, giving me a little push in the direction of the door. "Call me or text me when you get home so I know you're safe. And tell him what I said!" she ordered, sounding like a mother hen even though she was drunk.

"I will, and you guys be safe too." I blew them all air kisses as I made my way to the exit.

He was standing there leaning against the wall casually; he looked so handsome it made my heart speed up. "Hey, you have a jacket?" he asked, nodding at the coat desk. I shook my head in answer. We came here in a cab so I hadn't even thought about a jacket earlier, maybe I should have done, it was

6

almost midnight now and looked quite windy outside. "Here, you can have my sweater," he offered, putting a blue hoodie in my hands.

"But then you'll be cold," I protested, shaking my head and pushing it back to him. He took it out of my hands and rolled his eyes, fiddling with it. Suddenly he pulled it down over my head. It smelt amazing, just like he did. I smiled and slipped my arms through the sleeves. He laughed.

"It's a little big, maybe you'll grow into it," he teased. I pushed the sleeves up, and he nodded towards the door signalling for us to leave.

I grabbed his hand making him stop. "Wait, my friends made me promise that I would tell you something," I mumbled, slightly embarrassed. He looked at me curiously, waiting for me to say it. "They know I'm with you, and if you murder me that they'll tell the cops you were the last one to see me," I rushed out, blushing at how stupid that sounded. *Damn it, Amy, I just made myself look like an idiot.*

He burst out laughing and pulled me towards the door again. "I'll try my best not to murder you then. I wouldn't want to be in trouble with the cops," he replied with mock horror. I giggled, chewing on my lip.

He pulled me over to a silver jeep; I had no idea about cars so I didn't know what type it was. He pressed his keys, unlocking the car. As soon as the door mechanism clicked, he opened my door for me. I looked in and laughed. There was trash everywhere, all in the footwell and all over the seat. Newspapers, candy wrappers, empty soda cans just scattered around carelessly.

"Oh shit, er, I should have cleaned the car out then called you. Whoops," he muttered, grinning sheepishly as he grabbed all of the clutter and threw it into the back seat.

"Thanks." I smirked at him as I got in. I watched him walk round the car, noticing the muscles in his arms, and how the wind blew the T-shirt against his chest showing how flat it was. *I bet he would look incredible shirtless.*

He climbed in interrupting my ogling. "So, what do you like to eat?" he asked, starting the car.

"I don't care. Whatever you want. I eat anything." I shrugged, unconcerned.

"Pizza?" he suggested. I grinned and nodded, I was secretly hoping for that.

He smiled and drove down the road, pulling up outside a little late night pizza place not too far away. I climbed out and walked to his side. As we passed a group of guys that were sitting around, laughing loudly and genuinely being rowdy, he pulled me somewhat closer to him. *Damn, he's sweet.*

"Any preference?" he asked as we looked over the menu board.

"Anything without anchovies, I'm allergic."

"Pepperoni?" he suggested, rubbing his hand up and down my back lightly, making me shiver. I nodded, biting my lip, trying not to show him his casual touch was affecting me.

He ordered the food and bought us two cans of Coke. There was a little plastic table and chairs off to one side so we sat down to wait. I looked up at him and saw his eyes properly for the first time. They were beautiful. A light grey colour with a slight hint of blue, they were captivating, and I couldn't look away. My whole body started to tingle. I couldn't sit still. He smirked at me and looked down at his drink, releasing me from his intense gaze and those beautiful eyes. I breathed a sigh of relief.

"So, have you done bar work before? You seemed to know what you were doing," he asked, leaning in over the table.

"My uncle has a bar. I've been behind one a few times, but I've never actually served until tonight." I shrugged.

"You make a decent bartender, the customers liked you. Oh, by the way, I grabbed your tips for you." He reached into his pocket, pulling out a handful of money and offering it to me.

"I don't want it, you keep it, it's your job not mine," I refused, shaking my head.

"Chloe, you earned it, you get to keep your tips. You made like fifty-two dollars in just under an hour, imagine how much you would earn working all night." He raised his eyebrows, looking impressed.

"Yeah, maybe you should get me a job there then," I joked.

"I can put in a good word if you're serious," he offered, flicking his head to the side so his hair moved out of his eyes.

I laughed and shook my head. "I don't think I could stand that every weekend. It must get boring, I bet?" I asked curiously. It had been fun tonight, but doing that all the time would get a little tedious, watching everyone around you get drunk while you're working would get a little annoying after a while.

"Yeah having girls throw themselves at you all the time definitely gets irritating after a little while," he said, laughing. *Oh right, I get it, he's a player and uses the bar to meet girls. Nice one, Chloe, you just got picked up as his easy lay for the night.*

"Yeah, I would imagine it would," I muttered sarcastically. I was annoyed at myself for even thinking any different. *What the heck would a guy like him see in me anyway? Why on earth did I agree to this? He thinks I'm the kind of girl to put out on a one night stand. Great, just great.*

"Yeah, you only had an hour of the guys drooling over you, imagine if you had that every weekend for the last year," he stated, turning his nose up. *Wait, was he actually being serious when he said it gets irritating? Oh crap, now I'm just confused.*

Luckily the pizza came over then, so that interrupted our conversation. "We're now closing, guys," the man said, plopping the box down on the table.

"Oh, I thought we could eat in," Will replied, looking at him confused.

"Usually yeah, but I need to get home early. There's a sign on the door." The guy nodded at the piece of paper taped to the inside of the door.

"Oh right okay, thanks." Will stood up and grabbing the box and turned to me. "Sorry, I thought we could eat in. If you want we could eat it at my place, it's just around the corner," he suggested as we walked to the door.

"Is it cleaner than your car?" I teased.

8

He laughed and shook his head sheepishly. "No actually."

"Okay well I guess I need to put up with it so I can eat my pizza." I rolled my eyes playfully. He laughed and opened the passenger door for me, waiting until I was buckled in before putting the box on my lap.

He drove us down the road for a few minutes before pulling up outside an apartment building. He took the box off of my lap and climbed out, while I scrambled along behind him and up to the second floor, stopping outside his door. He fumbled with the keys while I took off my shoes. My feet were killing me from wearing high heels all night, I would undoubtedly have blisters. He let the door swing open and looked at me apologetically. I walked in and stopped, my mouth dropping open in shock. His place was a tip. There were empty takeout cartons and soda cans everywhere. Dirty dishes scattered around the place, and random clothes on the floor.

Wow, he's a slob! "Oh crap, have you been robbed?" I joked, trying not to laugh.

"Ha ha," he replied as he walked past, grabbing my hand and pulling me further into the lounge. I looked down at the sofa; it was littered with magazines and clothes, a half drunk mug of what could have been week old coffee was sitting there.

I burst out laughing. "Will, this place is disgusting! Maybe we should have just sat on the floor in the street it would have been healthier."

"Stop whining and suck it up," he stated, taking the cup off of the seat and brushing everything else onto the floor, making me laugh harder. *Wow, his idea of tidying up blows big time.* "Sit and eat," he ordered.

I sat down on the sofa, which was actually surprisingly comfortable. He put the box on my lap then walked off into another room; I pulled out a piece of pizza and started munching on it. When I looked down I realised I had my feet on a load of his papers so I pulled them up, tucking them underneath me.

He came back a minute later with two cans of Pepsi. "I didn't have anything else. I would offer you juice, but you'd have to drink it straight from the carton because I have no clean glasses," he said, laughing sheepishly.

"You're disgusting. I bet the bedroom's worse," I mused, shaking my head and laughing.

"Want to go check it out?" he asked, raising an eyebrow at me looking incredibly sexy. My food got stuck halfway down my throat so I choked. *Oh man, does he think I'm here to have sex with him?* He laughed and patted me on the back, handing me the can of drink. "I was kidding... well, maybe I was kidding," he teased, smirking at me.

"If you think I'm going anywhere near a bed in your place, you're very much mistaken. When was the last time you changed your sheets?" I joked.

"You have to change your sheets?" he asked, looking shocked. *Oh my God, is he serious? Yuck!* I looked at him disgusted and shocked. He burst out laughing. "Oh, Chloe, you are too funny." He shook his head, laughing so hard that he had tears in his eyes. I laughed too, but my laughter was more out of relief. *I can't believe I actually thought he was serious. Damn, I am so gullible.*

"So, tell me some more about you," he encouraged, going for his fifth slice of pizza.

"Um, like what?"

"You got any brothers or sisters, do you have any hobbies, where do you work. That kind of thing," he replied, shrugging.

"Okay, well, I don't work, I go to school. I don't really have any hobbies, I like to swim and read, and I'm an only child. What about you?" I answered, watching his reaction to my answers.

He smiled so I felt myself relax. He obviously wasn't bothered about the fact that I was still in school, which meant he knew I was under eighteen. "Well you know where I work. I like to play pool, but that's just for fun with the boys, and I have an older sister and younger brother."

"Yeah? How old?" I asked, finishing my drink and looking around for a trashcan or something to put it in.

He grinned and took the can off of me, putting it on the floor. I rolled my eyes. "My brother, Sam, is nineteen, and my sister, Kaitlin, is twenty-five. Um hey, this might be a little forward so you can say no if you want to…" he trailed off looking embarrassed. I looked at him curiously waiting for him to continue. "Well… er… my sister's getting married tomorrow. I was planning on going on my own, but I was wondering if you wanted to come with me?" he asked, looking at me hopefully.

Holy crap, he wants me to go on a date to a family wedding? That's a little awkward! "Umm…" I mumbled, biting my lip, thinking; on the one hand I would like to spend more time with him. He seemed incredibly sweet but, on the other hand, what if it was awkward? I couldn't exactly leave if I was bored. It was a wedding which would mean dinner and then a party after, it was an all-day thing probably.

He smiled awkwardly. "You have a think about it. The wedding's at two o'clock tomorrow, if you want to come you can call me. I mean, it's just a thought, I told them I would go on my own because I don't have a girlfriend, so my plus one's going empty. My sister said something about setting me up with some of her single friends in the evening." He winced which made me laugh.

"Right, and you don't want that because you have enough with girls flirting with you at work," I teased.

"Exactly! Wow, you can listen. Maybe I had you pegged all wrong," he mused, grinning.

"Yeah? You thought I was an airhead who would put out in your dirty bed?" I asked, sticking my tongue out at him. He didn't say anything; he just leant forward and kissed me lightly. For the second time I was too shocked to do anything.

He pulled away before I'd recovered. "I didn't think you were an airhead."

"But you did think I'd put out in your dirty bed," I retorted sarcastically.

He laughed wickedly. "Come on, I'll drive you home if you've finished insulting my place," he suggested, standing up and holding out a hand to help me up. I stood up and held out the pizza box to him, he laughed and threw it on the couch, waving a hand at it dismissively. "I'll sort it later."

"You truly are gross."

He made a small bow as if it was a compliment and grabbed my shoes off of the floor. "Come on then, Cutie, let's get you home," he said, heading towards the door. He put my shoes down and waited while I slid my sore feet into them. We chatted easily as he drove me home; he was surprisingly easy to talk to. When we pulled up outside my house, he jumped out and came around to my side, opening the door just as I was about to, so I pushed against fresh air, almost falling out of the car. He laughed but stopped immediately when I glared at him.

"Sorry," he muttered, trying to stifle his laughs. I slapped his chest as I stepped out of the car; it was so hard that I immediately started to think lustful thoughts. I blushed and looked away from his smirk; he looked like he knew what I was thinking. He followed behind me and walked me to the door. "So, yeah, you have my number from where I called you, if you want to come tomorrow then call me. The latest I'll be able to pick you up is one thirty I guess, so yeah…" he trailed off looking uncomfortable.

Jeez, he is really sweet. I gripped the front of his T-shirt and pulled him closer to me, going up on tiptoes and pressing my lips to his. He wasn't shocked like I was when he kissed me. He kissed me back immediately, one hand going up to the side of my neck. He pulled back and I was a little giddy. The kiss was so sweet and soft that it made my insides do a little flip. He licked his lip lightly, his eyes locked on mine, the beautiful shade of grey making me a little light headed.

"I'd better go. Thanks again for helping me tonight," he said, letting me go and turning to leave.

As I watched him walk down the path towards his car, I realised that I didn't want him to go. I definitely wanted to see him again, kiss him again, and have him wrap his arms around me. "Will?" I called, making him stop halfway up the path. "Pick me up at half past one then."

He grinned. "Great, okay. I'll see you tomorrow, Chloe." He looked so happy that it made my heart beat a little faster.

I quietly let myself into the house and crept upstairs. Once in the solitude of my bedroom I flopped on the bed and let out a little sigh. I sent a text to Amy telling her that I was home safely, and then pushed myself up off of the bed and grabbed my pyjamas. I pulled off his hoodie and looked at it with wide eyes because I'd forgotten to give it back to him. I'd just have to give it to him tomorrow instead. I smiled at the thought of seeing him again, I could hardly wait. I pulled on my pyjamas and slipped into bed, I couldn't keep the happy smile off of my face as I drifted off to sleep.

Chapter Two

When I woke up I immediately remembered last night. Images of meeting Will and us flirting washed over me leaving a warm sensation in the pit of my stomach. I smiled when I thought about seeing him again today. I was actually pretty excited to see him again, even though it was with all of his family there. I rolled over to look at the time and gasped. *Holy crap, it's after twelve, he'll be here in under an hour and a half!* I jumped out of the bed and dashed down the stairs looking for my mom. I had no idea what to wear to a wedding; I was assuming that jeans and a tank top were out of the question.

"Mom, I'm going to a wedding this afternoon, what should I wear?" I cried as I burst into the kitchen at full speed.

My parents both smiled and looked at me, confused. "Good morning to you too, Pumpkin," my dad laughed.

"Right sorry, morning guys. Mom, what should I wear?" I repeated, looking at her pleadingly.

"You're going to a wedding? Who's is it? I don't know of anyone getting married." She frowned and looked at me as if I had lost my mind.

"A friend's sister is getting married. His date backed out at the last minute, so he asked if I would go with him instead," I lied, shrugging. I couldn't exactly tell them that it was the bartender I met at the club I snuck out to last night while they thought I was at a movie marathon at Amy's.

"Oh, okay. Well, how about you borrow my strapless dress, the one with the pink roses on it that I wore to Kara's Christening," she offered.

I gasped and looked at her with wide eyes. *Wow, that dress is beautiful.* "Really? I would love that," I gushed, trying not to jump up and down on the spot. I was pretty sure that I had the best parents in the world. My mom's dress sense was awesome. I thanked my lucky stars that we were the same size, because more often than not, I wore her clothes rather than mine.

"Go get ready. I'll sort it out for you. What time are you going?" she questioned, getting up from the table. My dad got up too and poured a glass of juice, holding it out to me as he walked past, kissing my forehead.

"Thanks, Dad." I turned back to my mom. "Will's coming here to pick me up at half past one." I chugged the glass of juice as fast as possible, eager to go and shower so I would have time to do something nice with my hair.

I rushed a shower and dried my hair quickly, pulling it up in an elegant twist and straightening the loose bits around my face and my bangs. Once I was done beautifying myself, I pulled on the dress and looked in the mirror. I smiled, happy with the result. My dark blonde hair looked better than I thought it would, and my brown eyes were sparkling with excitement. The little make-up that I had put on complemented my complexion perfectly. The dress was beautiful, and clung to me in all of the right places, showing off just the right amount of cleavage. I sighed happily and grabbed my shoes and purse, heading downstairs as I pulled them on. My parents had already left; they were going to visit some old friends and wouldn't be back until late.

I paced around the kitchen nervously until the doorbell rang. I practically skipped to the door, straightening my dress and taking a deep breath before pulling it open. My breath caught in my throat when I saw him. He looked incredible in a black tux, white shirt with a pale blue tie.

I ran my eyes down his body slowly, taking every part of him in before dragging my eyes back to his face. His hair was styled but yet still managed to look messy and like he'd been running his hands through it. His eyes were still raking down my body, his mouth open slightly. I smiled to myself. *He likes what he sees!* I cleared my throat dramatically to get his attention. His eyes snapped to mine and he smiled at me, his grey eyes boring into mine again.

"Finished undressing me with your eyes or do you need a few more minutes?" I teased, leaning against the door frame, trying to look sexy.

"Sorry, I was just trying to work out how the hell I'm going to keep my hands off of you in front of my family today," he replied, shaking his head, looking me over again.

I giggled and grabbed his tie, pulling him into the house, shutting the door behind him. "I'm sure you'll manage somehow," I stated, rolling my eyes and patting his tie back down in the right place, discretely loving the feel of his chest under my hand. *Actually I'm not sure how I'm going to keep my hands off of him either.* He looked so handsome he was making my mouth water.

"I'll have to I guess," he said, blowing out a breath and flicking his head to get his hair from his eyes. *Wow, that's so sexy when he does that.*

"I'll just get my purse, then I'm ready." I slipped off to the kitchen, checking to make sure I had my keys, cell phone, and money. As I turned back around I didn't realise he'd followed me in there and I walked straight into his hard chest and almost fell over. His hands shot out to steady me, gripping my waist tightly.

"Whoa, easy, I know I look hot in my tux but you don't have to fall at my feet," he teased, bending a little to look into my eyes. I felt the heat creep up onto my cheeks because I'd made a fool of myself in front of him. He hadn't let go of me. We were just looking at each other, making my breathing speed up. I couldn't drag my eyes away from his face. After what felt like an

13

eternity he looked away first and stepped back. "You look extremely beautiful, Chloe." He smiled his sexy little smile making my face heat up even more.

"Thanks, you just look okay," I joked, waving a hand at him dismissively. He chuckled at my remark. I stuck my tongue out and walked past him to the front door, waiting for him to come out before locking up.

When we got to his car, I laughed in disbelief. He'd cleaned out all of the clutter and empty takeout cartons from the car. It even smelled nice inside.

"Wow, did you do this for me?" I asked, shocked.

He grinned and shrugged. "Well, I didn't want you thinking I was some kind of slob who couldn't clean up after himself."

A smile tugged at my mouth because he'd gone to so much effort. "Yeah? How long did this take?"

He laughed wickedly. "No idea. I paid my neighbours kid five bucks to do it for me."

I gasped. "Five bucks? Jeez, Will, that's just cruel, that's like slave labour, this car was disgusting. I hope the kid had his TB jab before he touched anything." I laughed.

"Yeah, I checked with his mom and made sure he was up to date with his shots before I set him loose," he joked, winking at me.

On the way to the church he preceded to tell me everything I needed to know about his family before I met them. His parent's names were William and Angela, his sister was getting married to a guy named Andrew, and I was to stay away from his perverted Uncle Chris, who would undoubtedly like a 'pretty young thing' like me apparently. By the time we pulled up at the church I was wringing my hands nervously. *This is a really terrible idea. I mean, who on earth comes on a first date to a family wedding?* He jumped out and came round to my side, holding out a hand to help me out of the car.

When I was out he leant in and grabbed something from the glove compartment. He turned to me and held out a little corsage. "I got this for you."

Aww, that's so pretty. "Thanks, Will." I took it and looked it over. It was one of the ones that pinned on your dress; it had a little white flowers in the middle with green leaves behind. It was lovely.

"Want me to put it on for you?" he asked, raising one eyebrow cockily.

I laughed and shook my head. "I think I've got it, pervert," I answered, giggling and pinning it on the front of my dress as we walked to the church.

When we got to the door he took my hand and pulled me to a stop. "Thanks for coming, Chloe. If at any point you want to leave then tell me and I'll drive you home. I mean, this is a terrible first date." He looked at me apologetically, as if expecting me to run away any second.

"Oh crap, you think this is a date? Will, I only came for the free food," I teased, pulling him forward into the church. He was laughing as we walked through the doors. The people in the back turned to watch us walk in, obviously wondering what all the commotion was. I blushed and dropped my eyes to the floor letting him lead me over to a pew near the front. He was saying 'hello' and 'nice to see you' left right and centre. I put on a fake smile and followed behind him uncomfortably. When we got the second row, he gestured for me to go in first. I smiled as I sat in next to a guy who looked like Will but just not quite as handsome and a little younger; his eyes were brown instead of grey. He was totally checking me out, and not even bothering to be discreet either. *This is obviously his little brother.*

"You must be Sam, right?" I asked, grinning.

The guy smirked back at me, his eyes twinkling with mischievousness. "Yeah, and you must be the girl I'll be waking up with tomorrow."

I giggled quietly. "Wow, cockiness runs in your family, huh?"

Will reached over and punched his brother in the arm, making me laugh harder. "Rein it in, dipshit, that's my date," he growled.

"Shh, you can't swear in a church!" I hissed, giggling again.

Will rolled his eyes as the lady in the front row turned round. She was very pretty and had the same grey-blue eyes as Will. "Can't you boys cut it out for one day?" she scolded, shaking her head, obviously trying to sound stern but the smile on her face kind of ruined the effect. Her gaze locked on me, and her smile got even bigger. "Oh, Will, are you going to introduce us?" she cooed excitedly. I sat up straighter. *That's his mom and I'm sitting here giggling in a church. Wow, great first impression, Chloe.*

Will nodded. "Mom, this is Chloe. Chloe, my mom, Angela," he introduced, "and that's my dad there," he added, pointing to a man who was standing up talking to a couple of people at the front of the other aisle.

"I'm so pleased to meet you," Angela gushed, holding out a hand to me.

I shook it uncomfortably, feeling my face heat up. "You too, Angela. I love your hat," I said, smiling. She looked extremely cute in a little cream suit and matching hat with a little netting on it, my mom have totally bought that hat too.

"Thank you, honey." She smiled happily, touching the top of it.

The guy that Will had pointed out as his dad, came over and sat down, before turning in his seat to talk to us too. He shook Will's hand in a very grown up gesture. I could see they had a close relationship; his parents doted on him, I could tell just by looking at them.

"William, this is Will's girlfriend, Chloe," Angela chirped, looking at me proudly.

Girlfriend? Wow, okay, jumping the gun there, Angela. It's not my place to put them straight though. I glanced at Will, waiting for him to say something, but he just slipped his arm across the back of the pew, resting along my back, making me shiver slightly.

"Yeah? Nice to meet you, Chloe," his dad greeted, grinning and looking proudly at Will.

"You too," I muttered, embarrassed by all the attention.

"So, how's Andrew doing?" Will asked, glancing over at a nervous looking guy standing up the front. He looked extremely cute in his tux, but was wringing his hands together, watching the door.

15

William chuckled to himself quietly. "He's fine. I think he'll feel a lot better when Kaitlin shows her face. He's somehow got it into his head she's going to stand him up at the altar," he replied, laughing.

"Why does he think that?" I asked, frowning, a little concerned. *That will be awful if she doesn't turn up. Poor guy.*

William laughed harder, which earned him an elbow to the ribs from Angela. "I told him that she would. I was just joking around this morning, but I think the poor guy's taken it to heart," he replied wickedly. Will and Sam both started laughing. "It would have all been fine if the wedding planner hadn't just dragged Kaitlin off to fix a problem with her dress. When he saw me on my own, I think he thought she wasn't coming."

Angela shook her head and looked at them all disapprovingly. "You three are mean! Seriously, like father like sons, you all have the same warped sense of humour," she scolded. "Chloe, I would think twice about having children with Will. You should look at his father to see what he'll be like in twenty years." She rolled her eyes playfully.

I blushed like crazy and giggled, looking at Will and waiting for him to say something to his mother about this being our first date. He didn't. Instead, he smirked at me and leant in, kissing my burning cheek. "You are way too cute," he whispered in my ear as his hand traced patterns across my bare shoulder.

My skin prickled where he touched me. "And you are way too confident," I whispered back, making him laugh.

A little while later a pretty lady in a business suit came to collect William so they both disappeared off. A few minutes later the organ music started. People stood up, turning around to watch the bride's entrance. Will took my hand, interlacing our fingers, and I must admit, I really liked it. His hand seemed to fit mine perfectly, making my whole body feel warmer.

I looked back to see his sister and his dad walk up the aisle, but quickly realised that I couldn't see over the sea of people, so I turned back to the front and watched the groom instead. He was watching the back of the church, all signs of nervousness gone now. A huge, proud smile was stretched across his face. I felt my heart skip a beat. I would love someone to look at me like that one day, I could only hope for that level of devotion that was clear across his face in that moment. He was watching her entrance like she was the only girl in the world, like she was the most beautiful thing he had ever seen. It was so romantic that my eyes prickled with tears, which was silly because I didn't even know the couple.

After the ceremony we headed to the churchyard for the photos. I stood with Will and Sam while their sister had all manner of family photos done in various positions, with all sort of people. Will and Sam had a photo done with their sister. Kaitlin was really pretty, and her dress was beautiful. She had the same colour hair as the rest of the family, but brown eyes the same as her dad and Sam. They were all so attractive; the photos would be really nice.

Will came over and grabbed me, pulling me over to the photographer. "What are we doing? Are you done?" I asked as he wrapped his arm around my waist.

"No, I need to have my photo done with my date, apparently," he explained, taking hold of my chin and turning my head towards the guy. "Smile," he whispered. *Oh man, I hate having my photo taken!* "Smile, Chloe. Stop panicking," he instructed, laughing quietly. I took a deep breath and smiled, hearing the sound of the camera going crazy in front of me while I blushed and tried not to blink.

"Thanks guys, you two are done. Okay, can I get Aunts and Uncles with the bride and groom?" the photographer shouted, waving around.

I breathed a sigh of relief as Will led me off to one side again. As we were walking I noticed he hadn't taken his arm from around my waist, and I also noticed I didn't want him to.

"There now, that wasn't too bad was it?" he teased, bending to look into my eyes, a smirk across his face.

"As long as you didn't smile like that," I retorted, putting my hand over his mouth. He laughed and bit the palm of my hand lightly making me giggle and pull my hand away quickly, wiping my hand across his shirt.

After another few minutes of flirting and joking around, we were all dismissed to go to the reception. "Hope you have your dancing shoes on," Will chirped, grinning happily as we drove to the hotel where it was being held.

"Why, you going to bust a few moves?"

"I've been known to in my time." He smirked at me, making me laugh.

When we got to the hotel, he took my hand again, leading me through to the function room at the back. It was beautifully done out. Round tables were dotted around the room, each covered by a blue table cloth and matching napkins. Set on the centre of every table was a little blue and white flower arrangement. It was perfect.

"Looks like we're early," Will mused. "Let's go check out where we're sitting and pray that it's not near Uncle Chris." He looked at me with mock horror as he led us over to a seating plan. He stood close behind me as we scanned it over, looking for his name. His breath blew across my shoulders making my body almost tremble with excitement. "Oh dammit, we're sitting with Aunt Lucy and Uncle Ronald," he muttered under his breath.

I turned to face him, smiling. "More perverts?"

He grinned and shook his head. "No, but if you want to hear stories of what I was like as a child and see naked baby pictures, then we're sitting in the right place." He closed his eyes and shook his head, looking like he was in pain. I burst out laughing. *This dinner is going to be awesome.*

Will was incredibly funny during dinner. His aunt was one of those cute ones that pinches cheeks and pulls out the photos from the back of her purse to show you. During the three course meal, I heard all manner of stories about him and his brother from their childhood. Some good, some bad. Will was a pretty naughty child by the sounds of it.

17

When he was younger he gave Aunt Lucy's cat a haircut with electric clippers, painted her living room furniture with gloss paint that he found in her shed, smashed windows with footballs, and I even found out that he wet the bed until he was five. As he got older he crashed her car into a lamppost, got up drunk one night when he was staying at her house and went for a pee in her closet because he thought he was in the bathroom. One time he even put an egg in a pan, then went to watch football on the TV and burnt half of her kitchen down.

Every single story she told was said with a big grin on her face though. She absolutely adored Will, that much was glaringly obvious. He just sat there like a good sport the whole time, he didn't complain once even though I was teasing the life out of him all evening.

When the music finally started up he immediately jumped out of his chair and dragged me over to the dance floor. "Damn, that was embarrassing, any chance you can forget you heard any of that?" he pleaded, pulling me close to him as the first slow song started.

I grinned and shook my head slowly. "Oh no, I won't be forgetting any of that for a while," I teased. He laughed dejectedly and cringed.

The DJ announced the bride and groom's first dance so I pulled Will off of the dance floor, much to his disappointment it seemed. I watched the happy couple dancing. They looked so cute and in love that I was actually a little jealous of their relationship.

Suddenly Will's arms went around me, pulling me close to his chest as a guy walked over. He was probably in his mid-forties. He looked me over slowly with a sly grin on his face. I smiled back nervously, wondering what was going on.

Will held out his hand to him. "Hey, how are you? Long time no see," he said politely as they shook hands.

"I'm great, son, you look like you're doing good," the guy answered, nodding at me as his eyes wandered down my body again.

"Yeah. Chris, this is Chloe, my girlfriend. Chloe, this is my Uncle Chris," Will introduced, looking at me with one eyebrow raised. My heart thumped in my chest when he said the G word. *Girlfriend? Oh wait I get it; this is the pervert Uncle I'm supposed to stay away from.*

"Hi, Chris, it's nice to meet you." I shook his outstretched hand and he brought it to his lips, kissing the back gently. Will's arms tightened on me again as he pulled me back into his chest, making me giggle at how protective he was.

Another arm snaked around my shoulder. "Come dance with me, Chloe," Sam instructed, winking at his brother. Will immediately let go of me and smiled at Sam gratefully. I glanced at Will to see if this was okay and he nodded in prompt, stepping away from me. I didn't actually want to dance with Sam, but Will seemed a little relieved to see me go. More people were dancing now. The cheesy wedding songs were out in force, eighties and nineties music to get people up off of their seats.

"So, what's up with that guy then? Will doesn't seem to like him," I observed, frowning as I watched them talking. Will looked decidedly uncomfortable, and also a little annoyed.

Sam snorted, looking distastefully in their direction. "Chris is an ass. He hits on everything that moves, it's gross. Will probably doesn't like him looking at you like that. He asked me to keep an eye on you too," Sam replied, leaning in to talk into my ear over the music.

"Ew, he's like forty, that's gross. Wait… when did Will ask you that?" I asked, confused. He'd barely left my side the whole time.

"When we had our photos done," he answered, shrugging. "So, Will's never mentioned you before. I actually didn't know he was dating anyone. How long have you been together?" he asked, moving closer to me.

I grinned. "We're not together, we only met last night."

He laughed and put his hands on my hips, pulling me closer to him. "Oh really? So if you're not dating, maybe I could ask you out?" he flirted, winking at me suggestively.

I rolled my eyes and put my hand on his chest, pushing him away from me. "Seriously, you two are so alike, cocky and overconfident. Maybe I'm not interested in seeing either of you again after meeting the uncle," I joked.

"You'll see me again," Will purred confidently in my ear. I jumped as his arm snaked around my waist, pulling me against his hard body as we continued to dance. "Thanks for that, Sam." He held out a fist to his brother, who immediately did one of those cheesy punch things.

"Wow, you two are nerds," I joked, making them both laugh.

The rest of the night passed without incident. We laughed and danced. I chatted easily to his family, other than his uncle they all seemed genuinely nice. Every time his mom looked at us flirting and dancing I would see a little satisfied smile creep across her face.

During the slow dances at the end of the night, Will didn't let go of me once. One of his hands rested on the small of my back, the other on the nape of my neck. His eyes were locked on mine, making my body tingle and my stomach get butterflies. He was so close that there was barely an inch of space between us and it made my heart race uncontrollably. He didn't kiss me though, he looked like he wanted to and I would imagine that my face looked exactly the same, because I certainly wanted him to kiss me.

At eleven thirty the music finished, and the lights came back on. We said our goodbyes to his family and he led me out to his car. We drove me home in comfortable silence, it was sweet. I'd had an extremely nice time, and I really hoped he did too. I was seriously hoping he would want to see me again.

When we pulled up outside my house, he walked me to my door. I noticed that my parents' car wasn't in the drive, signalling that they weren't home yet. Based on prior experience, the monthly friends reunions lasted until around one or two in the morning so I had a while before they'd be home.

"You want to come in for a coffee or something?" I asked. Immediately I mentally slapped myself for adding the 'or something' on the end. *Wow, that sounds like I'm offering him 'something', meaning sex! Damn it, Chloe!*

"Yeah? Your parents won't mind if I come in for coffee?" he asked, looking at me hopefully. I shook my head and unlocked the door heading in leaving the door open for him. I slipped my shoes off and headed for the kitchen, flicking on the kettle.

"This is a nice place," he complimented, looking around and leaning on the kitchen island.

"Yeah, we've always lived here, I love this house," I replied, grabbing some mugs and making coffee. I knew how he took it; I'd watched him make one after the meal tonight. He was leaning against the counter watching me, smiling. "Your family is cute."

He laughed uncomfortably. "Yeah, most of them. My mom's a pain in the butt sometimes. Sorry she kept looking at you like that all night. I've never taken a girl to meet the parents before, I guess she got a little excited," he explained, shrugging.

"Really, you haven't? Why not?" I asked as I poured the coffees out.

"I've never really had a serious girlfriend that I wanted to take to meet them."

"Yeah? Are you a player?" I teased.

"What do you think?" he asked, smirking at me. He looked so sexy that my mouth started to water.

He is unquestionably a player; he's too freaking hot not to sleep around. "Absolutely." I grabbed the coffees and headed into the lounge, switching on the lights and putting the drinks down on the side table. "So, Will, this is what a carpet looks like," I joked, gesturing to the clean floor.

He grinned. "Wow, I've not seen one of these since I moved out of my parents' house," he replied, faking shock. I burst out laughing and sat down on the sofa, looking at him expectantly.

He sat next to me. He was so close that I could barely sit still. "Thanks for asking me to come with you today; I had a really nice time," I said honestly.

"Well, thank you for coming with me," he whispered as he inched his head closer to mine. I held my breath, knowing he was going to kiss me again. My heart was thumping in my chest as the hair on the nape of my neck prickled with excitement.

His lips touched mine for the fourth time in two days, and I felt as if my whole body was on fire. I wrapped my arms around his neck, pulling him closer. He traced his tongue along my bottom lip so I opened my mouth eagerly. His tongue slipped in my mouth massaging mine. The kiss was beautiful, perfect even. It made my whole body tingle. He moved forward more, making me lay down on the sofa; he hovered above me, kissing me deeply. His hands trailed down my body as he pressed himself to me closer. He pulled out of the kiss just as I was getting a little dizzy, and started kissing down the side of my neck and across my bare shoulders. I ran my hands down his back, clutching him to me.

Wait, this is way too fast.

"Will, stop," I mumbled breathlessly. I was so excited that I could barely force the words out.

He stopped immediately and pulled himself back up, putting his forehead to mine. "Sorry, I got carried away," he apologised.

"That's okay. I'm just not the type of girl who puts out on a first date," I replied, blushing.

He laughed and reached behind his back, taking my hands and pinning them above my head. "And what makes you think that I'm the type of guy that puts out on a first date?" he asked, smirking at me.

I giggled, looking at him challengingly. "I can tell you are."

Will laughed and shook his head. "You have me pegged all wrong, I'm not that type of guy at all," he said innocently.

Yeah right, I don't believe that for a second. "You're not, huh? So if I asked you to carry me upstairs and screw me on my parents' bed, you'd say no?" I challenged, raising one eyebrow teasingly.

He groaned and shook his head. "No, I wouldn't say no," he admitted, kissing me again. I tangled my hands in the back of his hair. He pulled away a minute later. "I should probably go before I start begging you for sex," he said, smirking at me and making me blush again.

I burst out laughing and nodded in agreement. "Good idea."

Immediately, he pushed himself up off of me. I stood up too; we hadn't even touched the now cold coffees on the side. "So, can I take you out again?" he questioned, smiling his sexy little smile.

"Nah, that kiss just didn't do it for me, sorry," I teased.

His eyes went a little wide, his body seemed to tense up. "Oh right, yeah okay, that's fine," he muttered uncomfortably.

I burst out laughing and stepped closer to him, pressing my lips to his again. He moaned in the back of his throat as I pulled away. "The kiss did it for me, don't worry. And I'd love to see you again," I said, gripping his tie pulling on it gently.

His body visibly relaxed. "That was mean," he scolded.

"Yeah, I am mean; you'll find that out the more you get to know me. Now get out of my house," I instructed, smirking at him.

"Yes, Ma'am." He kissed me again and headed for the front door. I followed him out into the hallway and leant against the door frame. "I'll pick you up at seven tomorrow." He pecked me on the lips again before stepping out of the house.

"And what if I have plans tomorrow night?" I asked, laughing.

He waved his hand dismissively. "You'll cancel them," he called over his shoulder as he walked back to his car, laughing. The cocky overconfidence was back again now. I laughed quietly. *He's right; I would cancel them if I did have any plans.* I closed the door and leant against it, touching my finger to my lips. They were still tingling from his kiss. I knew I would be dreaming about him tonight.

Chapter Three

"So where are you actually going?" Amy asked, lying on my bed while I looked through my closet.

"I have no idea, he didn't say." I looked back over my shoulder at her, shooting her a hopeless look. Amy and I had been trying to choose something for me to wear for the last hour; I was getting more and more stressed with each passing minute.

"Well, first date to a wedding, second date maybe the opera?" she offered, laughing.

"You're no help at all! Amy, seriously, if you're going to be sitting there making stupid comments then what was the point of you coming over to help me?" I whined, throwing a pair of socks at her.

She caught them and threw them back at me. "Stop stressing, it's just a guy," she replied, rolling her eyes.

I sighed and closed my eyes. *She's right. I'm getting myself worked up other nothing. Sure, he seems nice, and damn he's hot, but I actually know nothing about him at all.* I took a deep breath and slumped onto the bed on my back. "You're right, I'm just going to wear the black pants and red shirt," I decided, fed up with thinking about it. I'd had hardly any sleep last night because I was so excited about the date, and every second of today had dragged because of it. I still had an hour and a half to wait until he'd be picking me up.

Amy nodded. "Good idea. Wear the shirt open at the bottom so he'll catch a glimpse of the navel piercing," she instructed, winking at me. "You know a guy can't resist that."

I nodded and headed into the shower. When I was out, Amy helped me do my hair, straightening it all. Once I was dressed, I looked at her and did a little twirl, waiting for her approval. "What do you think?" I asked, biting my lip.

"I'd do you," she replied, narrowing her eyes at me playfully. "Wait, another button at the bottom." She leant forward, unfastening another button so I literally only had two buttons done up now, just about covering my breasts.

I scoffed and batted her hands away. "Amy, seriously, I don't want to give him the wrong impression. He's probably already thinking I'm going to be putting out tonight, I don't want to shove it in his face," I protested, doing it back up.

She sighed. "Fine, but I don't know why you're so dead set against sleeping with him though. You need to get laid. It'll loosen you up and put a smile on your face." The doorbell rang before I could answer. I looked at her nervously, my heart leaping in my chest. She grinned and shoved my purse and black jacket into my hands. "Go. Have fun, and don't do anything I wouldn't do," she encouraged, winking at me.

"Is there anything you wouldn't do?" I joked.

"No," she replied, laughing and heading over to my window. "I'm going to watch from the window. He can't be as hot as you say he is." She shook her head and pulled the drapes aside, peering out, trying to sneak a peek at Will. I smiled, knowing she wouldn't be able to see him at the moment; he'd be under the porch, waiting at the front door.

"All right. Lock the door on your way out okay?" I called as I skipped down the stairs to the front door. My parents were out again tonight which I was secretly glad about. I'd met his parents already, but I definitely wasn't ready for the whole introducing him to my dad thing. My dad was embarrassingly protective when it came to guys, and he also wasn't shy with making threats of castration for taking advantage or hurting me. That usually happened while I was standing there too, which was indubitably horrifying for all parties involved.

I pulled the door open and there he stood, looking impossibly hot in a pair of ripped jeans and a white fitted T-shirt with a checked blue shirt over the top. He wore it unbuttoned so you could see how the T-shirt clung to his toned body. I could barely breathe; I was so excited that I shifted from one foot to the other, not knowing what to say.

"Wow you look incredible," he complimented, looking me over slowly. "I got you these." He held out a bunch of assorted multi-coloured flowers.

Flowers? This is already the best date ever. "Thanks, Will, that's incredibly sweet, you shouldn't have." I took them from him, smelling them and smiling gratefully.

"I didn't know what your favourite flower or colour was so I went for one of each," he admitted, laughing.

Aww, could he get any better? "Thank you. Let me just put them in some water and then I'll be ready." I opened the door wider, motioning for him to come in. I headed to the kitchen and grabbed a vase, putting them in and filling with water. I'd arrange them properly when I got home. Will was leaning against the counter, watching me. "So where are we going anyway?"

"Well, I thought we could go for dinner, and then maybe, if you're up for it, we could go and do my favourite thing in the world," he replied, smirking at me.

24

I gasped, looking at him shocked that he would be that blunt. "I'm not having sex with you after dinner!"

He grinned and came closer to me, putting his hands on the counter either side of my body, leaning in and pressing his body against mine. My breath caught in my throat as he inched his head closer to mine. I could smell his aftershave. The spicy, masculine scent filled my lungs and made me lean in unconsciously. My whole body was trembling with excitement, waiting for him to kiss me. I closed my eyes when his mouth was barely an inch from mine. His minty breath blew across my lips. Time seemed to stand still as I waited and waited for his lips to connect with mine.

Finally, his lips brushed against mine, so softly that I could barely feel it. "You really have a dirty mind, Chloe, now why would you instantly think about sex?" he whispered, moving away quickly and flicking my nose.

My eyes snapped open as he stepped back laughing wickedly. I blushed like crazy and slapped his chest. "That was teasing." I frowned and pouted.

He grinned, shrugging. "Sorry I couldn't resist. Honestly though, you're such a pervert, your mind snapped straight to that. I bet you even dreamt about me last night, didn't you?" he inquired.

Actually, yes I did but I'm not admitting that to you, buster! I made a scoffing noise and shook my head. "Will, do you want to go out tonight or not? At the moment I'm considering changing my mind." I raised one eyebrow challengingly, hoping that would change the subject before he figured out that he had hit the nail on the head with his line of questioning.

"Way to avoid the question, Chloe," he teased. "And yes, I want to go out with you tonight. Now that I know what a pervert you are I'm eager for the end of the night," he added, winking at me.

I gasped and giggled. "I'll tell you right now I'm not the type of girl who puts out on a second date."

"What a coincidence, I'm not that type of girl either." He grinned, his eyes sparkling with humour. I laughed and rolled my eyes. "Anyway, come on, pervert, before they give our table away," he suggested, holding out a hand for me to take.

I waved it off and smirked at him. "You'll need to get back in my good books before any form of physical contact happens again. Punishment for teasing me," I rejected, walking to the door and laughing at his pout.

He followed behind and waited while I locked the door. We walked to his car in silence. I stole a glance at him only to see he was already looking at me. When our eyes met, he smiled his beautiful smile making my heart speed up. As we approached the car he opened the door for me. "My lady," he said in a fake British accent, doing a little bow.

I smiled and laughed as I climbed in. While he walked around to the driver's side, I waved to Amy who was watching from my bedroom window. She didn't wave back so I assumed she couldn't see very well into the dark night.

Will climbed in the other side and buckled his seatbelt. "Do you like Mexican food? If not then we can go somewhere else," he suggested, starting the car, looking at me worriedly.

"Seriously? I love Mexican food," I exclaimed. I was even more excited now. Mexican was my all-time favourite.

We drove to the restaurant he chose. It was an extremely cute little rustic place. There was only one other couple in there. "This is my favourite restaurant ever," he told me as we looked over the menus.

"Yeah? So what's good here?" I asked, scanning the menu. My mouth was already watering at the thought of enchiladas and tortilla chips with sour cream dip.

"Everything's good so order whatever you want," he replied, grinning and putting his menu down barely even glancing at it.

"What are you having?" I asked a couple of minutes later, still undecided.

"Cheese and tomato quesadillas for starters, then chicken fajitas," he answered, grinning happily.

Finally, the waiter came over to take our order. He was fairly young and was flirting shamelessly with me the whole time he stood there. At one point Will had to clear his throat dramatically to divert the waiter's attention from my chest. The guy eventually scurried off. I laughed wickedly.

"Was that really necessary?" Will asked, grinning.

"Was *what* necessary?" I asked, pretending to be confused.

He sighed and shook his head. "I can see you're a handful. I've got my work cut out for me to bag you, haven't I?" he stated, leaning back in his chair, narrowing his eyes at me.

"Bag me? Is this some kind of kinky term I've not heard of?" I asked, confused.

He laughed and shook his head. "No, pervert, it means you're going to make it hard for me to win you over and make you fall for me," he explained, smirking at me.

I smiled, taking a sip of my coke. "Well if something's worth having, it's worth working for."

"I like a challenge. Once I see something I want, I don't quit until I have it," he warned.

I leant forward, looking at him curiously. "You're not a hit it and quit it kind of guy then, like I thought?"

"You want me to answer that honestly?" he asked, raising an eyebrow. I nodded. I genuinely wanted to know if he was player or not, because sometimes I thought he definitely was, and other times he seemed really sweet and genuine. "I've never had a serious girlfriend, and yeah I've played the field quite a bit. I just never met anyone I wanted to be exclusive with before." He seemed to be watching my reaction as he spoke.

I was a little shocked at his answer. I never expected him to admit that to me. He surely must know he'd just made it harder for himself now. "And

26

with that little speech you've just made it harder for yourself to *bag me*, as you called it," I said confidently. All thoughts of putting out were entirely gone from my mind now. I would certainly make him work for it.

He smiled, seeming unconcerned. "I thought it would, but you wanted me to be honest so I didn't lie like I normally would have done if a girl had asked me that question." He leant forward and cocked his head to the side, obviously waiting for my reaction.

I didn't know how to react. Yes, he'd just admitted he was a player, but, on the other hand, he also told me the truth knowing I would react badly to it. So what did that mean exactly? *Damn, this boy is just confusing!*

"Well I guess we'll see how hard you're willing to work now then," I said, grinning. He seemed to relax a little when I said that, maybe he was expecting I demand he take me home or something. "Besides, I'm interested to see what your favourite thing to do is, if it's not women," I added, smirking at him.

He laughed. "Hopefully you'll like it; if not then we can go see a movie or something."

Thankfully the food came over then which gave us something else to talk about. We talked and flirted over dinner. We talked about movies, music, and random likes and dislikes. I'd actually had an extremely enjoyable time with him. Plus the food was incredible; I would undoubtedly come back to this place again.

When we were done eating, he led me to his car, pulling out of the restaurant parking lot with a big grin on his face. He was obviously excited about whatever we were going to do now. When the car stopped I looked up at the building shocked. "An indoor ski slope?" I mused, looking at it nervously. I was more than a little intimidated by the vastness of the building, and that was only the outside.

He laughed and climbed out of the car, walking round and opening my door for me before heading to the trunk. He pulled out a thick black fleece sweater and held it out to me. "It gets a little cold in there," he said, nodding at the building. I took if and pulled it on, swallowing loudly. *I'm so going to break my leg I can just see it happening.* I silently thanked Amy for suggesting I go for flat shoes tonight in case we were walking anywhere.

I watched as he pulled on a sweater and held out a hand to me. I looked at it and smirked at him. "Oh no, you've still not made up for teasing me," I declined, crossing my arms. He laughed and put his hands on my shoulders instead, pushing me towards the building. My nerves grew more pronounced with each step.

Once inside, he led us past the counter. "Hey, Mac, we're going on for a while okay," he called as he led me through the 'staff only' door.

I glanced at him confused. "Do you work here?" I asked, looking around nervously. No one seemed to be yelling us to get out of the staff area so he must.

He nodded. "Yeah, I give lessons."

Lessons? "Really? What sort?" I questioned as he walked us past a huge rack of snowboards.

He shrugged casually. "Skiing, snowboarding, and I also supervise the tubing sessions, which is what we're doing tonight." He waggled his eyebrows at me. *Okay, what the heck is tubing? Sounds kind of painful.* He grinned at my obviously concerned face. "Don't worry, Cutie, I'll look after you," he vowed, smirking at me as he flicked my nose. He turned and walked over to a huge stack of black rubber rings.

"Oh man, really?" I muttered, turning my nose up at them.

He laughed and grabbed two rings, nodding towards another door. I opened the door and walked through; cold immediately attacked my system making me draw in a sharp breath and pull my elbows in against my side, hunching my shoulders. I thanked him silently with my eyes for giving me the fleece.

He nodded around the corner so I walked in that direction. As I turned the corner, I stopped again, my mouth popping open in awe. There was a huge hill of snow, people were skiing and snowboarding down it. There was a snow blower going at the top making it look like it was snowing inside. It was beautiful.

"Holy crap, I didn't even know this place was here!" I cried excitedly. "Is it real snow?" I immediately bent down, grabbing a handful, expecting it to be that fake plastic snowflake stuff they use in the movies. It wasn't though, it was real powdery snow and it instantly made my fingers cold. I laughed and squeezed it into a ball throwing it at his back as he walked past me.

"Er, Chloe, no throwing snowballs or I'll have to ask you to leave," he scolded, nodding at a large sign that was mounted on the wall. It had pictures of all the prohibited things on it. Right at the top was snowball throwing, second was snow angels.

"Oh man, you can't even make an angel?" I pouted. *Shoot, I was just about to do that!*

He shook his head sternly. "Rules of the house. Come on." He grinned and stepped onto an escalator that was slowly moving up the hill. I jumped on behind him, rolling snow around in my hands, resisting the urge to throw it at his edible little behind.

When we reached the top he set the rings down. I looked down the hill immediately hit by a wave of vertigo. We were so high that my stomach seemed to quiver. I was the type of person that could break bones in the most unlikely events like dancing, so this was just tempting fate. "Um, this is really high, I don't think I can," I whimpered, backing away from the edge, shaking my head.

"Chloe, I promise you'll love it, you just need to try. If you don't love it then we'll leave," he persuaded, walking up to me and bending to look into my eyes. His beautiful grey eyes were boring into mine, it was as if he was trying to hypnotise me or something.

"I can't," I whispered, looking back in the direction of the hill. *I can't sit in a ring filled with air and push myself off that hill, no way.*

He smiled reassuringly. "I give lessons to kids as young as six. Everyone loves tubing. Come on, I promise you'll be fine. You just need to trust me." He took my hand and pulled me closer to his chest. Oddly, his smell was somewhat calming. "You can trust me," he whispered, cupping my cheek with the other hand.

Oh man up, Chloe, you're making yourself look like a wimp! "Kids really do this?" I asked, watching his face to see if he was lying.

He nodded. "Kids do it all the time." He leant in closer to me. His eyes flicking down to my lips made his intention clear. Just as his lips were about to touch mine I turned my head so he kissed my cheek. He laughed and shook his head. "Still not made up for the teasing, huh?"

"Damn right."

"Come on, Cutie, let's give it a try. Want to go together? You can sit in my lap if you don't want to go on your own," he offered, raising an eyebrow. He looked so sexy that my insides did a little dance.

"Don't push your luck, Will," I scoffed. "Come on let's get this done before I change my mind. If I don't like it then we go watch a movie, deal?" I bargained.

He nodded and held the smaller of the two rings still for me to climb in. "Stand at the front and open your legs, relax, and then kind of sit back onto it," he instructed.

I laughed wickedly. "Right, and you say that to all of the girls I bet."

He laughed. "Only the beautiful ones," he replied, winking slyly at me.

I lowered myself into the ring gripping the handles for dear life. "Oh crap," I muttered over and over. I tried to ignore Will chuckling at me. He was just about to push me off the edge when I screamed, grabbing hold of the leg of his jeans. "No! Aren't you coming too?" I squealed, giving him my begging face.

"Damn, that's a cute face," he said, laughing and shaking his head at me.

"Please! Can't we go at the same time?" I begged, struggling to get out of my ring. I frowned. *Wow, getting out of one of these isn't the easiest thing to do in the world.*

Will put his hand on my shoulder, pushing me back down into the ring. He leant over me, smiling wickedly. "It'll cost you," he whispered. His face was inches from mine, his eyes flicked down to my lips for a split second. I nodded quickly and grabbed the front of his sweater, pulling him forwards so his lips crashed to mine. He smiled against my lips and pulled away smirking at me. "I was thinking more like five bucks but hey that works too," he joked, laughing. He pressed his lips to mine again for a second and then stood back up.

I watched as he settled himself into his ring, using his foot to stop him from going over the edge. He grabbed my hand, interlacing our fingers. "Ready?" he asked. I nodded. Immediately he lifted his foot. His hand jerked against mine and suddenly we were both hurtling down the hill. We were going so fast I could barely breathe, but I couldn't stop laughing with that amused fright that you get on roller coasters. I probably hurt his hand because of how tight I gripped it, but he didn't complain.

Within a few seconds we were at the bottom. I couldn't stop laughing. *That was awesome!* I clambered awkwardly out of my ring, jumping up and down, squealing excitedly. "Oh God, I want to go again! Can we go again?" I asked, giggling and turning back to him. As soon as I turned, a snowball smacked me right in the leg. I squeaked from the shock of it and looked up at Will, confused. *Did he just throw that at me?* "I thought you said it wasn't allowed?" As soon as the words left my mouth another snowball sped towards me. I barely had time to turn around and cover my face before it smacked into my back. "Oh game on!" I called, grabbing a load of snow and lobbing it at him.

We had a huge snowball fight at the bottom of the hill. One of my throws hurtled straight past him and smacked straight into a young kid on skis. The kid looked up shocked; I giggled and pointed at Will, blushing like crazy, trying to look innocent. Will was laughing his ass off. The kid started to laugh as he kicked off his skis and joined in the fight. After that almost everyone in the whole place joined in, taking off skis and snowboards, running around trying to pelt each other with snow.

We quickly divided into two teams, boys verses girls, which I must say was pretty fair in my book considering there were almost twice as many girls. I threw a couple at the kids and a few at the dads, but my attention was firmly fixed on Will - who actually seemed happy just to hit as many people as possible, boys or girls, he didn't seem to care.

I crept up behind him and tapped his shoulder. He turned back to me, laughing. "Hey," I whispered, biting my lip trying to look sexy. My plan must have worked as his eyes flicked down to my lips. I raised one eyebrow and he grinned before bending down and placing his lips against mine softly. I almost forgot what I was trying to do because the kiss was so sweet.

When I regained my composure, I grinned against his lips and pulled away quickly, smashing my handful of snow on the back of his head. I giggled uncontrollably when the snow started to fall down the back of his sweater. He gasped and jerked forward. His wide eyes held a mixture of accusation and amusement. The shocked look on his face made me laugh so hard I could barely breathe.

He composed himself quickly and grabbed me, tackling me to the ground gently. His body pressed against mine as he pinned me down with his weight. I tried to wriggle out from underneath him, but he just held me still easily, grabbing my arms and pinning them above my head. He freed one of his hands and scooped up a handful of snow. Still pinning my hands down, he bent his head, pulling the fleece up with his teeth, exposing my stomach.

I squealed and laughed like a lunatic as his hand rubbed the cold snow onto my stomach. "Stop, stop!" I squeaked breathlessly.

He did stop, but not because I asked him to. His hand stopped moving and I felt him fingering my belly button, looking at me a little shocked. "You have a piercing?" he inquired, letting go of my hands and pushing himself up so he was straddling me still pinning my legs to the freezing floor. I could feel the wet seeping into my clothes, but I didn't care, all I could focus on was the lustful expression on his face as he lifted my top higher to have a look at the platinum bar I had through my navel. He definitely liked it, and I liked him liking it. My whole body was starting to get warm as my mouth started to water; he still hadn't taken his eyes, or fingers, off of it.

I took advantage of his distraction and twisted to the side, throwing him off of me. I squealed and jumped up, running as fast as possible to the little group of girls off to one side. I could hear him laughing behind me.

After another half an hour my hands were stinging with the cold. I could see Will crouched down with a group of boys and their dads on the other side of the arena. There were about fifty snowballs all made ready in front of them, just waiting to pounce.

Oh man, I've really had enough. My whole body was shaking with the cold, my clothes were soaked, my perfectly straightened hair was now dripping wet and hanging in rats tails around my face. *I must look extremely attractive!*

"Will, I've had enough!" I shouted. I purposefully stayed hidden in my little safe spot where I was crouched behind one of the fences at the side of the slope.

"Okay, come on then, let's go," he shouted back. His voice had an amused, yet challenging twang to it.

He doesn't mean that at all, he just wants me out of my safe place. Damn competitive boy. "Seriously, I've had enough, I'm cold." I turned and peeked out, looking in the direction he was hidden. A snowball whizzed in my direction. I just managed to get my head back in behind the fence in time. *Jeez, he's a good throw.*

"Will, please, can we leave? I promise I've had enough," I begged.

"Is this a trick?"

"No, I promise," I vowed. "I'm now stepping out." I pushed myself out, stepping out with my hands up in surrender. Almost immediately about ten snowballs all flew over towards me. I screamed and jumped back behind the fence. I groaned. *I don't want to stay here all night!* "Will, I need to pee!" I whined.

I could hear him laughing and talking to the boys on his team. "Okay come on then, come out and we'll leave," he called, sounding more genuine this time. I chanced a peek over the fence. Nothing flew in my direction so I pushed myself up slowly. I breathed a sigh of relief when nothing happened, and smiled as I walked over to him. He was standing on the side waiting for me by the staff door.

I was half way across the slope when the boys team let rip. There was no cover at all. All I could do was turn my back and cover my head as I was pelted all over with snow. Suddenly arms wrapped around me, turning me to the side. I turned my head to see that Will had wrapped himself around me so the snow missiles were hitting him instead. He was laughing which made his chest vibrate against my back as he pressed his cheek to the top of my head, covering me completely.

"It'll stop in a minute, they'll run out then we'll make a run for it," he assured me, still laughing.

"Was this your plan? Get me out in the open?" I accused playfully, pressing into him further, loving the feel of his warmth against my cold body.

"No, I told them we were stopping now, we agreed, then they all started throwing when you got halfway," he replied, shaking his head. "It's slowing down; get ready to run for the staff door." After another few seconds he pulled away from me and grabbed my hand dragging me along at full speed towards the exit. "Same time next week, guys," he shouted as we got to the door. He pushed me in first and slammed the door shut as a few snowballs hit the door causing loud bangs.

I burst out laughing. "That was seriously fun," I admitted, shaking my hands, trying to get them warmer.

He walked up to me and cupped my face in his chilly hands. "You look like you have frost bite."

"I feel like I've got frost bite. My fingers are numb," I pouted.

He smiled and took hold of one of my red hands, raising it to his lips, putting two fingers into his mouth. It was so warm that I gasped in shock. His eyes never left mine as he pulled them out and inserted another two. I had another idea about how to warm the other hand so I pushed my hand up his shirt, putting it on his stomach, trying desperately not to show any reaction to the muscles I could feel there. He grunted and his body stiffened, his eyes went a little wider as I warmed my hand on his body while he sucked on my fingers. I could feel my body starting to warm up, the trembling easing up a little.

He pulled my hand away from his mouth. "Better?" he asked. His voice was so husky and sexy that my body immediately started to tremble again, but it wasn't from the cold this time.

I nodded. "My lips are a little cold," I teased.

He smiled. "Really? Mine too," he whispered, bending his head and pressing his lips to mine. I wrapped my arms around his neck, gripping my hands into his wet and icy hair, pressing my body to his. He pushed me against the wall gently, kissing me deeply. His kissing was so beautiful that it almost made me lose myself in it. One of his cold hands found its way under my top, his fingers playing with my belly button again.

I smiled against his lips and he pulled away, pressing his forehead to mine. His eyes were shining with lust and passion. I could tell it was hard for him to stop, but he was probably trying not to rush me after what I said about him being a player. "I should probably get you home before you catch pneumonia, your clothes are soaked," he suggested, looking me over slowly.

"You're wet too," I commented, brushing some ice from his shoulder.

"That's what she said."

I rolled my eyes and tried not to smile. "I hate those jokes."

"Yeah so do I, I actually can't believe I just said that." He shook his head, laughing. When he stepped back, he held out a hand out to me again, looking hopeful. I smiled and placed my hand in his. "So you've forgiven me

32

for the teasing now?" he asked as we walked out of the building into the cold night.

I narrowed my eyes at him jokingly. "Not really, you still have some making up to do."

"Awesome. That's what I was hoping you'd say," he replied, grinning as he opened the car door for me to get in.

"Yeah? What does that mean?"

"Means you have to see me again." His cocky smirk was back again in full force as he started the engine, turning the heat up to full blast and aiming both of the air vents at me. I chewed on my lip because that was a sweet little move he'd made. On the drive home I warmed my hands and melted the ice crystals from my hair.

He pulled up outside and cut the engine. "Are you going to invite me in to warm me up?" he flirted.

"Sure why not. My parents are home so as long as you're okay with getting warmed up with them there," I agreed, nodding to their car in the drive.

He smiled and unbuckled his seatbelt reaching for the door handle. *Wait, what? Is he serious?* I started to panic. I couldn't have my dad scare him off yet. "Whoa, bit early for meet the parents," I said quickly.

He laughed incredulously. "You met mine yesterday," he countered, shrugging easily, not looking phased by meeting my parents at all.

I gulped and nodded. "Yeah but your parents didn't threaten to cut my genitalia off like my dad will," I stated, watching as that sank in.

His hand moved back off of the door handle as he grinned sheepishly. "Okay fine, we'll leave it for tonight then."

I giggled. "Wimp," I joked, leaning over and pressing my lips to his again. He tangled his hand into the back of my hair making my whole body burn and thrum with excitement. *Jeez how the hell is he doing this to me? How can he just waltz into my life and make me feel like this? This isn't fair.*

"So... tomorrow night?" he asked hopefully as I pulled away.

I nodded grinning as I jumped out of his jeep and practically skipped up the drive to my house. I turned at the door and waved before letting myself in the house. I sighed contentedly as I heard his car pull away. A happy smile was painted on my face as I skipped into the kitchen to arrange my flowers.

My mom came into the kitchen while I was putting the finishing touches to my flowers. "What on earth happened to you?" she asked with wide eyes as she took in my dishevelled and icy form.

I sighed dreamily. "I had the best date ever, that's what happened," I gushed, smiling. I picked up the vase and headed towards my room, kissing her cheek on the way past. "Goodnight. Love you, Mom," I said before dancing up the stairs.

Chapter Four

Over the course of a week and a half I saw Will every single night, apart from Friday and Saturday because he worked at the club those nights. On those two days we went out for lunch instead as he said he still wanted to see me.

It had honestly been the best ten days of my life. Every date he had taken me out on had been different. There were some traditional things like the movies and dinner or picnics in the park. He'd introduced me to his friends at a house party; they were all really nice and easy to get along with, even though they were all man-whore flirts from what I could tell.

There were also some not so traditional dates. He took me to a football game. To the batting cages, but personally I think that one was just an excuse to wrap his arms around me while he taught me how to bat correctly. We went for a walk along the beach; we even went to the stock car races. The best night by far was when he drove us to an empty field and left the headlights of the car on, turning the radio up to some cheesy love song station while we danced under the stars. That one was last night and was so romantic it made me want to cry.

Will was honestly incredible and he hadn't once put pressure on me to sleep with him, which made me even crazier about him. Today was Tuesday so he was due here any minute. I had thrown on a little denim skirt, and plain black V neck top making sure to put on my sexiest underwear. I had definitely made him, and myself, wait long enough. Every time he kissed me my body just craved more and more so I knew tonight was the night.

When he pulled up outside my house, I skipped out to him before he even got fully out of the car. "Hey, handsome," I flirted as I climbed in the passenger side.

Hi mouth dropped open with an audible pop. "Damn, you look so hot," he complimented, looking me over slowly.

A blush crept up on my face as I settled myself in the seat. "That was a nice hello," I teased.

He grinned sheepishly. "Right yeah sorry. Hi, Cutie," he corrected, leaning over to kiss me. I tangled my hands in the back of his hair and kissed him hungrily. The little moan that he made in the back of his throat seemed to make my skin come alive. "So where to tonight? You said tonight was your choice," he asked as he pulled away from me and started the car.

I shrugged. "Takeout pizza."

He frowned, pulling the car out and heading down the road. "Well that's not very romantic. Where are we eating it? In the park or something?"

"No." I grinned teasingly. He looked at me expectantly, but I shook my head. "Just drive to the takeout place, I'll tell you after." Nervous excitement was bubbling up inside me, and I was starting to chicken out.

Will drove us to the same takeout that we went to after the club the first night we met. While it was cooking he held my hand and kissed around my neck, making goosebumps break out all over my body.

Finally, just as I was about to say to hell with the pizza, it was cooked. Will took the box and walked me back to the car. "So where to?" he asked again.

"Your apartment," I answered, shrugging. He looked at me with wide eyes, seeming a little taken aback. I shrugged. "I thought we could have a night in with a movie for a change," I lied. He nodded, frowning, seeming apprehensive. *Wait, does he not want to sleep with me or something? Does he understand what I'm offering or does he think I really just want to watch a movie?* "You don't want to?" I asked worriedly.

His face softened instantly. "It's not that. I just wish you'd told me, that's all. I could have paid my neighbours kid to come in and tidy up," he replied, grinning. I burst out laughing, shaking my head in amusement. "My place is a mess, Chloe." He winced and looked at me, his grey eyes apologetic.

"That's okay, but maybe you need to start keeping it a little cleaner in case you have company," I teased.

After a couple of minutes he pulled up outside his building. I climbed out and walked around to where he was waiting for me. His arm wrapped around my waist tightly as he kissed the side of my head. My nerves disappeared as I remembered how easy it was being in his company. It was like I didn't have to think, everything just came naturally with Will. I slipped my hand into his back pocket squeezing his ass gently as we walked up the stairs to his place.

When I stepped into his apartment, I stifled a laugh. It wasn't as awful as last time, but it was still a mess. He shot me an apologetic look and watched as I walked into the lounge, sitting on the sofa and kicking my shoes off. He went to the kitchen and came out with two bottles of flavoured water. "This okay? Or I have Pepsi," he offered, shrugging.

I smiled and took the bottle out of his hand. "That's good for me, thanks."

We chatted while we ate and then he put on a movie. He didn't have much choice and mostly they were your typical guy's film - violence, blood and guns. We finally agreed on Die Hard 4.0 and settled onto the sofa to watch it.

I snuggled into him, hooking my legs over his, practically sitting in his lap. His hand rested just above my knee making my whole body a couple of degrees hotter. I could barely even concentrate on the movie.

After about an hour I turned my head and pressed my face into the crook of his neck, breathing in his delicious smell. He literally smelt good enough to eat. I pressed my lips to his skin. His hold on me tightened as he moaned quietly making me even more excited.

I kissed up his neck slowly and along his jaw line, nibbling on the skin lightly. *Okay, time to make the first move, Chloe!* I moved my legs and pushed myself up so I was straddling him as I gripped my hands in the back of his hair. His eyes were burning into mine making my whole body tingle and my heart beat erratically in my chest. He moved his hands and put them on the small of my back, pressing lightly making my chest press against his.

I kissed him long and deep, loving the soft feel of his lips against mine. His hands gripped fistfuls of my top at my back as he kissed me so passionately that it felt like my world was spinning slightly too fast. He pulled away just as I was getting a little dizzy. Little kisses were planted down the side of my neck making me close my eyes and just enjoy the sensation. Everything felt so right that I could barely keep the euphoric smile off of my face. As his hands slid up the back of my top, tickling my skin, his hot tongue traced the V at the front. I gasped, fisting my hands into his hair.

I couldn't keep still, I wanted more, but I didn't want this to happen on the sofa. I pushed myself off of him quickly. His eyes snapped up to meet mine, an apologetic look crossed his face. "Sorry, I got carried away again," he mumbled. I shook my head and took his hand, pulling gently. He frowned, looking at me confused. "Chloe?"

I smiled, pulling him to his feet. "Shh, it's time to stop talking now." I gave him a little tug towards what I assumed was his bedroom because it was the only other door in the apartment.

He groaned and followed me, looking ridiculously eager. Once we were in his room he pushed the door shut behind us. I looked around quickly, taking in the clean brown carpet, the well-made bed, the well organised dresser. *Hmm, maybe he doesn't like to sleep with a mess around.*

He crashed his lips back to mine, continuing to walk forwards, making me walk backwards to the bed. When my legs hit the side of it I lowered myself down onto it. He didn't. Instead, he stayed standing up and just looked at me. His face was so lustful I could barely stand it. "Chloe, you are so beautiful," he cooed, looking me over from my head to my toes and back again. I sat up quickly and gripped his shirt, pulling him roughly down on top of me. He laughed wickedly. "And there was me wanting to take it slow," he mumbled against my lips.

36

I giggled guiltily and gripped the bottom of his T-shirt, pulling it off over his head and tossing it on the floor. He'd barely moved yet my whole body was starting to ache with anticipation. "Will, please, if you don't take me soon I'm gonna die," I whined.

He smiled, his grey eyes sparkling as he brushed my hair back from my face. "Well I definitely don't want that," he whispered, bending his head and kissing me. But it wasn't the passionate 'I'm about to make love to you' kiss; it was a chaste kiss that lasted a split second before he broke it and looked down at me again. "I have something I want to do before this happens," he said, shifting his weight so he hovered above me, barely touching me.

"What's that?" I asked breathlessly, gripping his hips with my knees so he couldn't pull back any further.

He blew out a big breath as his eyebrows knitted together. "I want to ask you this before we sleep together so you know I'm not just asking because I have to or anything. I was actually going to ask you tonight anyway," he rambled. I smiled reassuringly, nodding in prompt, silently wondering what this was about. "Okay, well, I know it's maybe a little fast and we've not known each other for very long. You can say no if this is too fast for you, it's fine." He squeezed his eyes shut and shook his head, seeming frustrated as he struggled with his words.

What's got him all nervous and fluttery? He's never like this usually. "Will, what's wrong?"

He groaned and then opened his eyes, looking down at me with a pleading expression. "Will you be exclusive with me? Be mine?" he asked quietly. My mouth popped open in shock. He smiled weakly. "I really am crazy about you. Every second I spend with you is better than the one before, but I honestly don't know how that works, because how the hell can you improve on perfection? But you do all the time. You just amaze me." A subtle blush coloured his cheeks as he spoke.

I chewed on my lip as my insides seemed to melt into a puddle because of how cute that little speech was and how insecure he looked. *Oh my days, he wants to be exclusive with me? He's never had a girlfriend before, but he wants me?* My eyes prickled with happy tears. I felt so special just because the incredible boy wanted me and thought our time together was perfection. My mouth was so dry that I knew I wouldn't be able to speak, so instead I just nodded in acceptance.

His eyes widened, a smile twitched at the corner of his full pink lips. "Is that a yes?" Hope coloured his voice as he spoke.

"Yes," I croaked.

He made a little growl of victory and crashed his lips back to mine again. The kiss was different this time. Maybe it was because I was now officially his girlfriend, or maybe it was because we were spread on his bed and both knew what was about to happen. Whatever the reason, the kiss was full of fire and passion, but yet still so sweet and intimate that it made my insides tremble with happiness.

37

After, we lay in a tangled mess, our bodies slick against the other. I closed my eyes contentedly, just lying in his arms, resting my head on his chest. That experience had been beautiful. He was incredible, patient, passionate, caring, and yet still so mind numbingly good that even now, after a couple of minutes, I was still trying to catch my breath and calm my body. It hadn't been my first time, I'd been sexually active with my ex-boyfriend, Nick, but because of the emotions and feelings that went into it, it kind of felt like it was my first time. It had been a life altering experience, and I knew that if for whatever reason this didn't work out with him, he would always be the one I compared everyone else to. He would always be the one that totally rocked my world.

The thought of it not working out made my stomach ache. As I listened to his heart slowly returning to normal, I silently prayed I was enough to keep him interested. He blew out a big breath so I looked up at him, resting my chin on his chest. He smiled down at me, tracing one finger across my face, down the line of my nose and across my cheekbone. I wasn't sure what my face looked like, but I would bet my bottom dollar that my expression mirrored his in that moment. He looked enthralled, satisfied and contented.

"So that's what that feels like," he said quietly, gripping my waist and pulling me up so my face was level with his.

I looked at him quizzically. He raised his head, peppering little kisses on my face where his finger had been seconds before. I closed my eyes, smiling happily as he clamped me to him. "That's what *what* feels like?" I asked breathlessly, realising that I didn't actually understand what he meant.

He lowered his head back to the pillow. His hand came up to the back of my head, tangling in my hair. "Making love to your girlfriend," he answered, guiding my mouth back down to his, stealing my breath.

Will honestly was the best boyfriend ever. He was incredibly sweet and attentive, buying me little things and calling and texting me all the time. I was seriously falling hard for him. It had been almost two weeks since he asked me to be exclusive with him and every day just seemed to get better and better. I had spent quite a few nights at his place, which he even cleaned for me, a proper clean too, not just a simple throw the vacuum around type of clean. He didn't even pay the neighbours kid to come and do it, he did it himself. He continued to take me on inventive dates, each one surpassing the one before in the fun stakes. The passion between us was out of this world too which just seemed like the cherry on top of an extremely well frosted cake.

I was actually pretty sad today. School reopened today and it was my first day as a senior. I didn't want to go though, this summer had been amazing, and I didn't want to go back to a normal life of sitting in class all day and having homework assignments at night. I wanted to spend time with Will. Before I even got out of bed I grabbed my phone and checked to see I had a new message from him:

'Hey Cutie, missed U last night x'

38

I grinned and text him back that I'd missed him too. We hadn't spoken much yesterday, actually, we'd spent almost the whole afternoon in his bed, barely saying a word to each other.

I pushed myself up out of the bed reluctantly and took a long shower. My day got even more glum as I remembered I couldn't even see him tonight as he was going out with his brother, so I would have to wait a full thirty-six hours and see him tomorrow night instead. I sighed and pulled on a pair of high waist Miss Sixty jeans and a black short sleeve top which I tucked in, I pulled on a pair of red ankle boots with an open toe and looked at myself in the mirror, smiling my the outfit choice. I wasn't really one that fussed about my appearance that much, so didn't bother with any make-up. I left my hair down, platting my bangs and clipping them to the side. Once I was satisfied that I was as good as I was going to look, I headed downstairs for breakfast. My mom was cooking waffles and bacon the same as she did on the first day of every school year.

"Hey, honey, oh you look beautiful," she gushed, smiling at me happily.

I laughed uncomfortably. 'Beautiful' wasn't exactly a term that I applied to myself; though lately I had started to feel prettier all because of the way Will seemed to view me. When he looked at me with those adoring eyes, it was very hard not to feel special. He'd definitely boosted my self-confidence up a few levels.

"You have to say that, you're my mom," I replied.

She smiled and set down a plate of waffles. "No I don't," she rebutted. "Anyway, here, I made waffles as per tradition."

I forced a smile, pulling out a stool from under the counter and sitting. I tried not to groan when I looked down at the mountain of food. I wasn't even remotely hungry. I held in my heavy sigh and picked up my knife and fork. I resisted the urge to pout as I pushed the food round on my plate like a lovesick puppy, pining for my boyfriend that I wouldn't see for a day and a half. It didn't sound a terribly long time when said that way, but it was actually the longest time I had spent away from him since we met.

My mom sat down next to me with her breakfast. "So, are you still bringing Will to meet us on Saturday?" she asked, smiling happily.

I felt a little thrill go through me at the mere mention of his name. I nodded, grinning. Will had finally plucked up the courage to want to meet my dad, so we had arranged for him to come over for a barbeque on Saturday afternoon. My friends were coming too; they still hadn't even met him because I wanted to keep him all to myself for a little while before we integrated into the social network of my friends. I also didn't want them to embarrass me and say something that would make him run away from me screaming.

A horn blasted from out the front. I smiled, grateful for the fact that I didn't have to force down the rest of my waffles. I jumped up quickly, scraping my plate into the trash before kissing my mom on the cheek. "See you after school," I called over my shoulder, grabbing my bag and running from the house to Amy's waiting car.

As soon as I was inside, she was talking. She was ridiculously eager for school to start again; she wanted to find a new boyfriend. "So what do you think, will there be any hot transfer students this year?" she asked excitedly as she drove the fifteen minutes to school.

I shrugged. "I don't know, maybe. If there is you'd better get in there quick before I do," I joked, winking at her.

She smirked at me. "And what would Mr Perfect say if he heard you talking like that?"

I grinned, I didn't even need to think about how to answer that question, I already knew what his answer would be. "He'd say; *'damn, Cutie, I must need to step up my game if you're looking at other guys'* or something like that anyway," I said, grinning as I tried to do an impression of his silky voice.

Amy laughed and shook her head. "I can't wait to meet him. I love that he calls you Cutie, that's so sweet." She sighed dreamily. "I want my own Mr Perfect."

"Maybe you'll meet yours today," I suggested as we pulled into the parking lot.

"I hope so." She cut the engine, grabbed her bag from the back and swung her long legs out of the car. As soon as we were out we were both attacked into hugs by friends and people that we hadn't seen for weeks. Excited chatter started as everyone exchanged summer stories.

After a few minutes, Amy and I excused ourselves and went to get our schedules from the office. I cast my eyes over mine quickly. Everything looked all right, apart from the fact that I had gym first and calculus last, which totally sucked. I hated calculus and was seriously failing last year, actually to the point where I had to be buddied with someone to help me. To say that was an embarrassing experience would be a massive understatement. Some people just weren't meant to learn math, and I was undeniably one of them.

A quick glance at Amy's schedule showed that we had exactly the same. I squealed with excitement that I would at least have her there too. *Hmm, maybe she can help me with the stupid math.* "We have the exact same schedule!" I cried.

She grinned. "Awesome! See, senior year is going to be great, I can feel it." She linked her arm through mine as we made our way to the gym.

Luckily, as it was our first day and no one had their gym uniform, we were to 'discuss our expectations of the subject and what we wanted to achieve this year in gym class' which essentially meant a free period to hang out and catch up with all of the gossip over the summer.

At lunchtime, I headed over to the table of my friends and spotted Nick, my ex-boyfriend, standing there chatting to Matt, one of my other friends. Nick had gotten cuter over the summer; his face had lost some of the roundness. He looked like he'd grown up a lot. His light brown hair was longer and a little scruffy around the neck, but looked stylishly messy. His brown eyes still held that little twinkle that I remembered so well. If I hadn't met Will, I would totally be thinking twice about breaking up with him at the start of the summer.

"Hey, Chloe," he greeted, pulling me into a hug. "You look good," he said as he pulled back, letting his eyes drag down me slowly.

I shifted uncomfortably on my feet. "Hey, Nick. How was your summer?"

He shrugged, a frown lining his forehead. "It was okay, you know," he replied, seeming a little sad.

Guilt flowed through my body because I was obviously responsible for his sad expression. Nick was a genuinely nice guy, but he just wasn't right for me. We'd been friends for a few years, then started dating last year. The relationship lasted just over six months before I realised it wasn't working for me and broke it off at the start of summer. He was actually extremely upset about it at the time, and obviously still was.

"Yeah," I gulped. *Man this is awkward. Please let us get past this uncomfortable stage!* "We can sit together, right?" I asked, hoping he would say yes. I didn't want to chase him off out of our group of friends, and I didn't want to have to leave either.

He nodded quickly, pulling out a chair for me, and then sitting in the one next to it. "Yeah, of course," he answered. I smiled and felt my body relax. "I was just telling Matt about my disastrous morning," he stated, turning his nose up distastefully.

I sat down in the chair he'd pulled out for me, ripping open my sandwich. "What's so bad about it?" I asked, eating quickly.

He sighed dramatically. "My schedule sucks big time. I went to the office to try and change it, which made me late for Biology, so I now have a detention after school. I forgot my locker combination so I didn't take the right books to English, so now I have to do an essay tonight about 'the importance of bringing the right reading materials to class'," he grumbled, crossing his arms in frustration.

I smiled. "You got a detention from your first class? Surely that's some type of record for the school," I teased. "Maybe you'll have your name immortalised in the book of delinquents. You should be proud."

He made a scoffing noise in the back of his throat. "Ha ha. I forgot how funny you were... not." He jabbed his finger into my ribs playfully. I squealed and jerked away quickly. "At least calculus was okay, we didn't do anything at all. The new teacher is pretty cool, even though all the girls were drooling over him instead of me," he said, looking a little put out.

"Oh are you talking about the new calculus teacher?" Emily interjected. A dreamy expression crossed her face. "Oh my goodness he is so hot I swear I almost climaxed just listening to him talk," she gushed, fanning her face dramatically. Practically every boy at the table puffed out their chests unconsciously.

I burst out laughing as other girls started joining in with the hot comments, gossiping about how calculus was now their new favourite subject.

Some of the sluttier girls were planning how they could get themselves in trouble just so they could hear him shout at them in his sexy voice. *Pathetic.*

Amy groaned. "Oh man, and we don't have it until the end of the day! I want to look at him too," she whined, standing up and grabbing her empty food cartons.

I linked my arm through hers. "Come on, the bells about to ring and I need to get my Spanish books from my locker. You can see the hot new teacher in two classes' time," I insisted, rolling my eyes and pulling her away from the table, throwing my bottle and sandwich wrapper in the trash can on the way past.

The rest of the afternoon passed the same, people were gossiping in the hallways, fantasising about the hot young teacher falling in love with them. I didn't join in with it, to be honest it all seemed a little ridiculous to me. But then again, maybe I would have been joining in with them if I didn't have the perfect boyfriend already. I had gotten a little homework already but not too much, so I would still be able to spend an hour on the phone with Will tonight before he met up with Sam.

For the last lesson of the day, I made my way to calculus and sat in the middle row with Amy. She was practically bouncing in her seat with excitement. I looked around the room, noticing that girls were fixing their hair and applying fresh lipstick. I sighed, slumped down in my seat and waited for the most painful hour of my life to start. Hopefully he wouldn't single me out for any answers and then I could just speak to him after class about how disastrous this subject was for me. If he was nice, then maybe he would be a little lenient this year.

After a couple of minutes, the door opened. Immediately the girls in the room sat up straighter, smirking at each other with wide hungry eyes, whispering and giggling. Amy elbowed me roughly in the ribs making me hiss through my teeth at the sudden pain.

I looked up to the front of the classroom, curious to see what all the fuss was about. My curious eyes landed on Will. He was standing there, smiling, seeming a little nervous. He looked handsome as ever in black pants and a short sleeve white button down shirt.

Panic rose in my chest. *Why the hell is he here? Has something horrible happened to my parents, and he's come to collect me and take me to the hospital?*

Just as I started to stand, he spoke. "Okay class, settle down and let's get this show on the road so you can all go home," he said in his sexy voice.

I looked at him, shocked. *Class? What the hell?* I was half out of my seat, frozen in place as realisation suddenly washed over me like a bucket of cold water. My boyfriend was the hot new teacher that everyone was swooning over. I couldn't breathe. His eyes roamed the room and met mine. I saw his easy smile fall from his lips. His eyes widened in shock as his whole body tensed up.

Chapter Five

I stood there looking at him for hours, well, it felt like hours, but in reality, it was probably only a couple of seconds. *This has to be some kind of sick joke or something. He's a bartender and works as a ski instructor, he isn't a teacher. He especially can't be my teacher, that's impossible.* I still hadn't taken a breath and my lungs started to burn.

"What are you doing?" Amy hissed, grabbing my hand and pulling me back into my chair, giggling.

I couldn't look away from him; he was just staring at me with wide eyes. Suddenly his face tightened, his eyebrows knitted together and his teeth snapped together with an audible click. His eyes turned hard, his stare boring into me making my blood seem to turn to ice in my veins. I flinched. *Is he angry at me? What possible reason does he have for being mad at me? This isn't my fault.*

He composed himself a lot quicker than I did. He looked away from me, moving to his desk. "So I'm Mr Morris, I'll be taking over from Ms Patterson this year," he said confidently as he looked over the class. I noticed his eyes skipped over me without so much as a hint of recognition. It made my heart race.

This really can't be happening to me, I knew this was too perfect, I knew something would come along to ruin it.

"Obviously with me being new here, and this being your first day back, we don't want to actually do any work today, right?" he asked, smirking at the class. Everyone nodded eagerly. The girls were watching him with dreamy expressions, the boys slapping each other high fives. "So, how about we play a little getting to know you game? You each get one question for me, and I get one question for you," he suggested, perching on the edge of his desk, flicking his head to get his hair away from his eyes. "So who wants to go first, or should we just start at the front and work our way through?" He smiled his sexy little smile, gaining him flirtatious smiles in return. He nodded to a girl who was sitting in the front row who immediately blushed and smiled. I shifted on my seat, fighting the urge to go and rip her head off. "Just tell me your name then ask your question."

43

"I'm Jessica Edmunds, um... where were you teaching before?" she asked, chewing on her lip and looking at him through her eyelashes.

Slut! Stop looking at him like that.

Will smiled. "I wasn't. This is my first teaching job. I graduated college this year and was lucky enough to be offered this position immediately," he replied. "What's your favourite movie, Miss Edmunds?"

I didn't listen to her answer; I was watching him so intently that it was actually making my eyes sting. *What the hell are we going to do? Maybe I'll have to transfer schools or something or he'll have to quit his job. Jeez he would be in so much trouble if people find out he's dating a student.*

I listened to his answers of the class's questions as they asked them. He was twenty two, he lived alone, his favourite book was sports illustrated - which earned a laugh from the class. His favourite movie was Halloween, the original version. His favourite sport and pastime. The list went on and on of trivial facts that I mostly already knew about him and his family. The class seemed to be hanging on his every word.

When he got to me, I noticed that his hands gripped the edge of his desk making his muscles in his arms tense. His jaw was tight. He was looking at me angrily but was obviously trying to hide it with a polite smile. "Name?" he asked.

I shifted in my seat knowing I needed to play along with the whole, 'I don't know who you are' thing. "Chloe Henderson. And um, I don't have a question," I mumbled, squirming under his intense gaze.

He raised one eyebrow. "Okay, well I have one for you, Miss Henderson. Do you like to lie?" he asked. His beautiful grey eyes were hard and burning into mine.

Do I like to lie? What the hell have I lied about to make him ask that? "No, I don't lie," I answered, shaking my head in confusion.

"Really? Never lied about your age or anything?" he prompted. His voice was tight and harsh. The class had gone quiet and was watching the exchange, obviously interested in where this line of inquiry was going.

He thinks I've lied about how old I was? I've never lied to him, ever. "No, I've never lied about my age," I replied confidently as I frowned at him. *Why the hell is he looking at me like that? This it isn't my fault!* His hands seemed to tighten on the desk edge as he looked like he wanted to say something else. Instead, he looked away from me, turning his attention to Amy who sat next to me. He nodded for her to ask her question.

She leant forward in her chair, obviously excited to get her turn at asking him a question. "Okay so I'm Amy Clarke, and I wondered if you had a girlfriend." Her voice sounded seductive even to my ears.

His eyes tightened, his whole body tensed he didn't even look at me as he spoke. "No I don't. What's your favourite colour?"

I felt my heart break at his words. *No? How can he say no?* My eyes prickled with tears. I couldn't be here; I couldn't sit here any longer and

44

pretend like I wasn't dying inside. I stood up quickly and grabbed my bag from the floor, throwing my books in it angrily. Class was almost over now anyway.

"And where exactly are you going, Miss Henderson?" he questioned, sounding so much like a teacher that it hurt my insides.

"I need to be excused," I croaked as I walked to the door. I could practically feel everyone's eyes on me. Shocked silence filled the room.

"Sit down, Miss Henderson," Will barked.

I ignored him as the tears started to flow down my face. I swiped them angrily and threw the door open. As soon as I was in the hallway I ran, not knowing where I was going but just needing to be away from here and alone before I broke down completely. Suddenly fingers wrapped around my hand, and I was yanked to a rough stop. I looked around to see Will standing there. His expression was incredibly angry.

"Where the hell are you going? You can't just run out of a class like that! I'll have to give you a detention or something for that," he berated, shaking his head and letting go of me as he stepped back and ran a hand through his hair.

I was still hurting from the 'I don't have a girlfriend' answer in class, and I could feel the tears trying to force themselves out again. I knew I needed to get away from here quickly. "Just do whatever you want," I muttered, shrugging, trying to appear unconcerned. I turned to walk away, but his words stopped me.

"For fuck sake, Chloe, what the hell else am I supposed to do? Let you walk all over me in class?" he spat venomously.

That's all that's bothering him? The fact that I'd made him look like a pushover by walking out of his class? Nothing else about this whole situation is affecting him at all?

I turned round and gave him my best drop dead glare. "If you're that worried about what your precious class think of you, then give me a month of detentions; make me scrub whiteboards for the rest of the school year, see if I care. Do whatever you want, just don't ever talk to me again," I growled angrily.

The bell rang signalling the end of class. He grabbed my arm and pushed me into the nearest bathrooms roughly, locking the door behind him. "You think all I'm bothered about is my reputation for being a soft teacher? Trust me that's the least of my worries," he snapped. "I slept with a fucking minor! Do you know how much trouble I'm in right now? Do you know how freaking long I'm going to jail for because you lied to me?" His hands gripped into his hair roughly as he glared at me accusingly.

"I didn't lie to you. You knew how old I was." I lost my battle against the tears and slumped down to the floor, sobbing and hugging my hugging my knees to my chest.

He made an angry snorting sound in his throat. "I met you in a club, Chloe! How am I supposed to gain that you're a minor from that?" he countered, kicking the wall in frustration.

I shook my head. "I told you that night that I was in school." This wasn't my fault, I definitely told him.

"I thought you meant college not pissing high school! You have to be twenty-one to get into the club! You should have told me. Damn it, Chloe, I've been sleeping with you for two weeks!" he raged, looking at me disgusted.

I pressed my face into my knees and sobbed until I couldn't breathe. This was my fault he was right. I could see his point, I was underage in a club, and I'd never specifically told him how old I was, I just assumed he was all right with it. We'd never specifically spoken about school or his jobs or anything because we always had better things to talk about.

"I'm sorry," I croaked. "I thought you knew, I honestly thought you knew and didn't care."

He groaned. "How the hell could I not care that I was raping a minor? Is that the type of guy you think I am? A paedophile?" he asked angrily. He slid down the wall next to me and put his head in his hands. I could feel his body heat crashing into me and his aftershave filling my lungs.

"It wasn't rape," I correct adamantly, shaking my head, raising my eyes to look at him. He was pale and clearly shocked. His whole body looked defeated and sad. His shoulders were slumped forwards; his perfect angels face tight with worry and stress.

He sighed sadly. "Yes it was. I took advantage of you. I'm an adult, and you're a minor, that's how it works." He rested his head back against the wall and closed his eyes.

Took advantage? Is that some kind of joke? "Are you kidding me? Do you have any idea how much I wanted you? How much I still want you?" I asked, frowning. I was incredibly angry at him for cheapening what happened between us by making it sound like it was wrong and dirty.

"You need to go to the Principal and report it. I'll come with you," he croaked, pushing himself up and walking over to the door. His hand was just about to flick the lock before I grabbed it, stopping him.

I shook my head fiercely. "I'm not telling anyone, I don't want you in trouble because of something that I did wrong. This is my fault, you're right. I should have made sure you understood. I'm so sorry. You're not a paedophile, please don't think that," I begged, stepping closed to him and wrapping my arms around his waist. I buried my face into the side of his neck, breathing him in. He was trembling, I could feel it.

"You need to report this, Chloe, or I will. It'll look better on you if you do it," he countered, taking my arms from around his waist and stepping back from me. He looked like he was in pain.

"No, I won't do it," I refused. "And if you do, I'll tell them you made it all up." I looked at him warningly. I wasn't allowing him to get into trouble because of this. We'd get through it and work something out.

He shrugged. "If you have to."

"Don't do this, no one needs to know, please, Will," I begged. My tears were falling again as I pressed my back against the door, gripping the lock tightly so he couldn't get out.

He sighed and stepped forward, wiping my tears away with his thumbs. "Please don't cry." His voice broke as he spoke and it made my heart clench in my chest.

We were quiet for a little while; the only sounds were my ragged breathing as I struggled to stop crying. He just stood there staring at his feet looking pale and scared.

"How old are you anyway?" he asked quietly, still not glancing up from his feet.

"Seventeen. I'll be eighteen in eight months."

He groaned and nodded. "And you don't want to report me?" he asked. I shook my head fiercely. "Thank you," he said gratefully.

"You don't need to thank me. You didn't do anything wrong," I whispered, stepping closer to him and wrapping my arms around him again. He hugged me back this time and I pressed my face into the side of his neck loving the feel of his body against mine.

His breath blew into my hair as he held me against him. "We just need to pretend like this never happened, like we just met in the classroom," he said quietly. His arms tightened on me as I went to jerk back to look at him.

What the heck does that mean? He doesn't want to be with me? I opened my mouth to beg him, but nothing came out. Deep down I knew we couldn't be together, not only was it illegal because of my age, but he was also my teacher now so we would both be in a lot of trouble if this came out. He would lose his job and probably go to jail, and I would be expelled.

"I don't want to do that," I whispered, trying desperately not to cry again.

"Well we don't have a choice. Thank you for not reporting me, which you have every right to do, but I can't be anything other than a teacher to you. We need to stay away from each other. It's just lucky that this has all come out now instead of further down the line when we had any feelings for each other," he said, pulling away from me.

Any feelings for each other? Does that mean he doesn't feel anything for me already? Wow that hurts so much. I knew I was falling for him, another couple of weeks and I would have been head of heels in love. I thought he felt the same, but he must have just been using me all along. I really had him all wrong.

He bent his head and kissed my forehead softly, his lips lingering on my skin. It was a sweet kiss, a goodbye kiss. He stepped away and flicked the lock on the door and walked out quickly. As soon as I was on my own my heart seemed to shatter. My chest tightened, and my breathing hitched before I finally gave in and succumbed to the devastated and rejected tears.

Chapter Six

I stood there for ages not knowing what to do. Could I pretend that nothing happened like he said? Sure it was probably easy for him if he didn't feel anything for me, but I was totally crazy about him. How was I supposed to sit in his class everyday knowing that? I took a deep breath and splashed some water on my face. My skin felt tight from all the crying, my eyes were sore, and I was starting to get a tension headache.

When I was composed again, I walked out of the bathroom, keeping my eyes firmly on the floor, not wanting people to see me and know I had been crying. I couldn't tell anyone. I couldn't talk about it at all. I had no one to rant to and help me mend my breaking heart because I couldn't get Will in trouble. I silently thanked my lucky stars that he hadn't met any of my friends as they would have known who he was today.

The hallway was abnormally quiet for the end of school. I raised my head and risked a glance to see the hall empty of people. *Where the hell is everyone? Surely people should be messing around in the hall getting their things from their lockers before heading home.*

"Chloe!"

I turned round to see Nick walking towards me smiling. "Hey," I muttered, turning my body so he wouldn't get a clear look at my face that was sure to be puffy and red.

"What are you still doing here? Amy was looking for you earlier, she's gone home now," he said, stopping at my side.

I looked down at his feet letting my hair fall over my face. "She left? What time is it?" I asked, confused.

"It's almost four."

Almost four? Was I in the bathroom for that long?

"Where were you anyway? Amy said you jumped up and ran out of class like a bomb went off and then she couldn't find you." He put his hand on my shoulder, squeezing gently. The warmth of his hand seeped through my shirt and into my skin. I turned my head and put my cheek on the back of his hand needing comfort as my eyes started to fill up again. "Are you okay?" he asked quietly. I shook my head in response. He pulled me into a hug, stroking his hands down my back as I sobbed on his shoulder. When my tears finally dried up he pulled back and cupped my face in his hands. "What happened?"

I sniffed loudly, swiping at my nose. "I don't want to talk about it. Thank you for the hug, I seriously needed that." I forced a fake smile and stepped back.

He smiled warmly. "Anytime, I'll always be here for you." Nick really was a really sweet person. We were friends before we dated, not best friends or anything, but we were fairly close. He was always someone I could talk to. When we broke up we promised we would go back to that and still be friends. I really hoped we could. "Come on I'll drive you home," he stated, putting his arm around my shoulder and taking my bag in his other hand as he led me towards his car. "You know, you look so attractive right now, Chloe. Puffy definitely suits you," he joked, smirking at me.

I laughed and slapped his chest with the back of my hand. Nick always could lighten the mood. He grinned looking a little proud of himself as he opened the car door for me, throwing my bag in the back seat. I climbed in, and as he shut the door, I spotted Will standing by his car watching me. He was frowning angrily about something. He climbed in his car and slammed the door so hard I was surprised it didn't smash the glass. He sped out of the parking lot a split second later and Nick climbed in the driver's side.

"Was that the new calculus teacher in that car? Damn, that dude drives like a maniac," he mused, laughing as he pulled out at a more reasonable speed. He turned right heading towards my house. *Oh no! I can't go home yet. My parents will know I've been crying, and my mom won't let up until I tell her what happened. I'm not ready to talk about the break up yet!*

"Nick, do you think I could come to yours for a little while?" I pleaded, knowing his house would be empty. His dad worked a late shift and didn't get home until ten at night, and his mom had died about three years ago of cancer. That was actually when we met, I found him crying in the hallway after her death and we'd been friends ever since.

He glanced at me from the corner of his eye. "Let me guess, you don't want to talk to your mom yet. Am I right?" He didn't wait for an answer; he just pulled into a side road and turned the car around, heading back in the other direction, towards his house.

I smiled gratefully. Nick always had known me well. "Not yet. I just need to forget about it for a little while. Are you sure this is okay?"

He nodded easily. "Sure, you can cook me some food. You know I'm a terrible cook," he confirmed, grinning. I laughed thinking about all the times he had cooked for me when I went to his house after school. He wasn't just a terrible cook, he was disastrous.

"I guess that's a deal." I pulled my cell phone out of my pocket, noticing that it was on silent. As I looked at my screen, I saw that I had nine missed calls and two texts, all from Amy. I opened the texts:

'Where the hell are you? Is everything okay? Answer your phone or call me!'

'I can't find you, I assume you went home. I'll talk to you later. Call me as soon as you get this message!'

I sighed and sent a text back to her telling her that I was fine but that I couldn't talk right now. I promised to call her tonight instead. Then I sent a text to my mom, telling her I was having dinner at Nick's but wouldn't be late.

We pulled up at Nick's house, and I climbed out, watching as he grabbed our bags from the bag seat. "Come on then, master chef, let's go eat I'm starved," he teased, heading towards the front door.

I smiled and followed behind him. I felt a little weird as I walked in. I hadn't been to his house since we broke up. I sighed and forced myself not to think about it. I used to hang out here with him before he asked me out so we really needed to get used to it again if we were to be friends. He dumped the bags down and led us over to the kitchen, pushing me towards the fridge gently as he stood behind me, resting his chin on my shoulder. I winced when I looked in his almost bare fridge. A lonely pack of ground beef sat at the bottom, luckily it was still in date.

"Spaghetti bolognaise?" I offered, grabbing it. I could probably whip that up with what he had in his cupboards.

"Awesome!" he chirped, grinning happily.

While I set to work cooking, he put on the sports channel. We didn't speak apart from polite conversation. He didn't push me for any details; he didn't ask me why I was crying or anything, which I was grateful for. When it was done, I dished it up, also putting a plate on the side for his dad ready for when he got home.

We took the food into the lounge, watching some crappy sitcom on the TV while we ate. After, we did our homework and then chatted a little about his summer. He told me how his dad had taken two weeks off so they went to visit some family in California. Apparently Nick had learnt to surf. It was easy and comfortable, and actually managed to keep my mind off of Will for a little while.

After a couple of hours he drove me home. "Thanks for letting me come round, I really appreciate it," I said, hugging him tightly as we pulled up outside my house.

"No probs, it was fun and thanks for cooking I haven't eaten like that since we broke up," he replied. His smile turned a little sad and I felt awful for hurting such a lovely person.

"I'm so sorry about that, Nick, honestly I am." I swallowed the lump in my throat. We hadn't actually spoken much over the summer, the occasional friendly text but nothing else, so we hadn't really spoken about the break up.

He nodded. "Yeah me too. You think maybe I could get another chance?" he asked, looking at me hopefully.

"Nick, I'm sorry I…" I trailed off, lost for words. I wanted to tell him that I had a boyfriend, but that wasn't true anymore so I couldn't say that. I wanted to tell him that I was crazy about our new calculus teacher, but I couldn't do that either. So I just sat there looking at him with my mouth open probably looking like a complete moron.

He smiled, putting his finger under my chin and closing my mouth. He leant in and pressed a soft kiss to my cheek. "It's okay, forget I said anything." He leant further forward, gripping the handle of my door and pushing it open for me.

I laughed at his obvious prompt for me to leave the car. "I get the hint; I'll get out the car now. Thanks again, see you tomorrow."

"Night, Chloe," he called as I walked up the drive. I waved as I let myself in the house.

"Chloe? Is that you?" my mom called from the lounge.

"Yep," I confirmed, tossing my keys on the sideboard and walking into the lounge. Both of my parents we sitting there watching TV.

"How was your first day, pumpkin?" Dad asked.

I shrugged noncommittally. "It was all right I guess," I replied dismissively, not wanting to talk about it because I knew it would make me cry again.

My dad cocked his head to the side, looking at me curiously. "How come you went to Nick's? I thought you were with this new guy, Will," he asked, frowning. I smiled weakly at the casual mention of his name. My dad didn't mind Nick, but he was a little apprehensive about meeting Will. That was probably what his frown was for; he hadn't had his chance to threaten him yet.

"Nick and I are friends," I replied. I took a deep breath before continuing, knowing I needed to say it out loud for the first time. "And Will and I broke up today." I shrugged, trying to pretend I was fine even though my voice broke slightly as I said his name.

My mom gasped, immediately springing up from the sofa. "You broke up?" she repeated, heading over to hug me.

I held up a hand to tell her to stop. "I'm okay, it's fine," I lied. "I'm going to bed. See you in the morning." I turned on my heel and quickly headed out of the room, making a break for the stairs and the safety of my room. When I got there, I flopped down on the bed face first, crying uncontrollably again.

I couldn't speak to Amy, I didn't want to talk about it again so I text her instead telling her about the split, but that I didn't want to talk about it and that I'd just see her as usual in the morning.

I turned my cell phone off knowing she would try to call me back anyway even though I said I didn't want to talk. Zombielike, I stripped out of my clothes and headed to the shower, letting my tears mingle with the spray as I let the water calm my tight and stressed body.

By the time I got out and headed back to my bedroom, Amy was sitting on my bed. I jumped and squeaked from the shock. She just smiled sadly. "Your mom let me up," she explained, shooting me a sympathetic look. I nodded and silently went to sit next to her; she grabbed the brown bag from the floor and put it in my lap. I opened it to see about thirty bucks' worth of different candies and ice creams.

She held out a spoon to me. I smiled gratefully. "You know you're the best friend ever, right?" I asked, pulling out a carton and holding it out to her.

We sat up eating ice cream until both of us felt sick then she finally fell asleep just after midnight. I closed my eyes too and prayed for sleep, but it didn't come easily. All I could think about was Will and how handsome he was. When I finally fell asleep at about four in the morning all I dreamed about was him and the fun we had, how he could make me laugh and feel special.

By the time morning came my head was pounding, and I felt like death warmed up. Amy was trying to brighten me up by doing my hair for me, straightening it and pulling it half up. I plastered on a fake smile even though I kind of felt dead inside. She already knew I didn't want to talk about it so she didn't ask at all which I loved her for.

The drive to school was awful. With every passing second I got closer and closer to seeing him again. I just prayed I could hold it together for his class and not burst out crying in front of everyone.

When we pulled into the parking lot, I spotted his car immediately. As I walked past it, I had the strong urge to kick it or throw a stone through his windshield as payback. *But for what? What had he actually done wrong, apart from not having feelings for me? Nothing.*

I sighed and went to my locker, storing my books as if on autopilot. I nodded along with the conversations going on around me, pretending I was listening and interested.

"Mr Morris!" Emily suddenly called excitedly from my right.

My breath caught in my throat as I glanced in the direction that she was looking in. He was walking towards us looking so handsome I could cry. He had on jeans and black T-shirt with a cream shirt over the top, left unbuttoned. I bit my tongue hard enough to draw blood. I hadn't prepared myself for this; yes I expected to see him in his class, but not just randomly popping up in the middle of the hallway.

He stopped when he got to us and gave everyone his trademark smirk; I noticed his eyes didn't even pass in my direction. "Morning, girls."

I swallowed the blood in my mouth and forced myself not to cry. Emily twirled her hair around her finger as she looked at him. "I listened to that song you said was your favourite. I'd never heard of One Republic before, but that song was amazing," she gushed, fluttering her eyelashes.

Will nodded. "Yeah it's a good song; you should listen to some of their other stuff too." He smiled back at her and I was suddenly unsure of which one I wanted to punch the most, Emily for flirting with him, or Will just because he was my teacher and had ruined everything we had going over the summer.

I looked down at my feet trying not to let the tone of his voice affect me. They carried on talking about some stupid group that I'd never even heard of. Unable to stop myself from looking, I dragged my eyes off of the floor to see that Emily had moved slightly closer and had her hand on his arm.

Oh crap, this is killing me. Why can't he just go away? Why is he standing there talking to my friends about music? Does he not know how much this is hurting me?

"Chloe, there you are!" someone called.

My head snapped up in the direction of the voice and I saw Nick walking towards me, grinning. "Hey," I mumbled as he stopped at my side.

"You left your notebook at mine last night," he told me, digging in his bag and pulling it out for me.

As I took it I noticed that Will's hands were in tight fists for some reason. "Thanks. Wouldn't have been too smart of me to go to class without that would it?" I joked, shrugging and smiling weakly at Nick.

"Want to go out and get some lunch offsite today?" he asked.

I thought about it. *At least if I'm not here I won't be running into Will all the time.* "Yeah sure, sounds good, but you're buying."

He rolled his eyes. "Don't I always? Surely it's your turn."

I shook my head. "You buy, I cook, that was always the deal," I countered, sticking out my tongue at him.

"Miss Henderson, you can't leave site today," Will stated, looking at me annoyed.

I frowned. "Why not?" I asked confused. *I'm a senior, I don't need permission to leave site for lunch.*

"You have detention at lunchtime."

I gasped. *What the heck is that about?* "No way! Why? What am I supposed to have done?" I challenged, glaring at him.

Will raised one eyebrow, seeming unaffected by my angry glare. "For leaving my class without permission yesterday," he stated. "And if you keep disrespecting me like you are right now it'll be lunchtime detentions for the rest of the week too."

Oh my goodness, what an asshole! He knows why I left his class yesterday, and he can't cut me a little slack? What did I even see in him anyway? He turned on his heel and walked off. "Son of a bitch! What a freaking asshole," I ranted, throwing my bag down roughly thinking he was out of earshot.

He stopped and looked back over his shoulder. "All week it is then, Miss Henderson." I heard him chuckle as he walked off again.

My mouth popped open in shock as I tried, and failed, to shoot lasers out of my eyes and somehow set him on fire. When I turned back to my friends, I was greeted by a sea of shocked expressions. Not wanting to talk about it, I sighed and threw the rest of my books in my locker angrily, ignoring how all the pages got bent up. I slammed the door shut harder than necessary.

From the corner of my eye I saw Emily shake her head in disapproval. "Wow, what was that? Why did you speak to him like that, Chloe? Seriously, I've never seen you talk back to a teacher even once," she scolded.

Is she defending him? Is she annoyed with me because I called him an asshole? Wow I have some annoying friends.

I ignored her question. "Looks like I can't come to lunch today, Nick, sorry. Thanks for the notebook," I muttered as I turned on my heel and stormed off towards the gym.

Chapter Seven

We were playing soccer today so I changed into sweats and a T-shirt, pulling on some sneakers and heading out with the rest of the students to the hard courts that were situated around the back of the school.

I didn't like sports; I was a little accident prone. I wasn't clumsy or anything, I didn't fall over all the time, but I usually ended up getting hurt if there was any sort of physical game being played. Today was no exception. I went in for a tackle at the same time as a guy from my class, and ended up going face first into the ground. Luckily I got my hands up so I didn't totally face plant, but I ended up scraping both of my palms pretty badly. I hissed in pain and pushed myself up to sitting.

Oliver, the guy that I tackled, came over immediately, crouching down next to me. "Dammit! Are you okay, Chloe?" he asked, looking at me apologetically.

I nodded and let him pull me up to standing. My hands were burning. I turned them over to see they were bleeding from lots of little cuts and scratches, there was dirt all mixing in with the blood and what looked like a couple of little stones under the skin too.

"I'm fine, Olly, don't worry this is a regular thing for me," I said dismissively as I used my T-shirt to brush some of the dirt from my hands.

Mr Andrews, the gym teacher, came over and restarted the game to stop people gawking at me "Go wash your hands, Chloe, maybe you should see the nurse to check all the dirt comes out," he suggested, wincing at my palms.

I nodded and headed to the nurses office, sitting there as she cleaned my hands with cotton wool and used tweezers to pull out a couple of little stones before rubbing some foul smelling pink antiseptic cream over my palms. After she was finished I went straight back to the locker room, changing out of my gym clothes instead of going back out to play.

The rest of the morning passed so fast I could barely keep up. *Why is it when you're eager for something, the time takes forever to pass, but when you don't want something to come, it takes no time at all. It's like time is torturing me or something.*

55

When the lunch bell rang I grabbed my bag and headed to Will's classroom. The door was already open, but thankfully he wasn't there yet. I let myself in and wandered to the desks at the back of the room. I chose the one next to the window and pulled out my iPod. I forced my mind on to anything other than him. I shut my eyes and put my hands on the desk, palms up, hoping that they would stop stinging soon.

A couple of songs later my music stopped unexpectedly. I snapped my eyes open to see Will hovering in front of me, frowning.

I scoffed and ripped my headphones from my ears, throwing them on the desk angrily. "Don't tell me, I'm not allowed to listen to music in your detentions," I spat sarcastically.

He smiled sadly. "You can listen to music. I just wanted to know what happened to your hands," he said softly, nodding down at them.

I clenched my hands in fists. *Why is he suddenly being nice to me? He can't be all 'this never happened' and shouting at me one minute, then acting nice again the next. That's not fair.*

"That's none of your concern, Mr Morris." I shoved my headphones back into my ears, a little too harshly to be comfortable, and turned up the music so loud that it made my ears ring. We glared at each other for a few seconds then he looked away and put something down on my desk, before walking off to the front of the room and plopping himself in his chair. I watched as he pulled out a file and started to write, ignoring me entirely.

I looked down at what he had put on my desk to see it was a cheese and pickled onion sandwich, a bottle of orange juice, and a peach. My favourites. *Damn it! Why is he doing this to me? If I can't be with him then he just needs to be the asshole so I can get over him. If he keeps being nice to me, I'm never going to be able to move on.* I looked back at him to say thanks, but he wasn't even looking in my direction as he sat stiffly, scribbling in his folder.

I turned the music down slightly and grabbed the food, eating it quickly. I looked at the peach and sighed. You couldn't buy them from the cafeteria so he must have brought this in from his place. I stared the clock, watching the second hand go round so slowly that it looked like it was going backwards. *Damn stupid time! The morning went too fast because I didn't want to come here and now it's taking forever to end.*

Finally the bell rang. He still didn't look up as I put my iPod back in my bag and grabbed my empty sandwich carton. I walked to his desk and threw it in the trash. His hand was a tight fist, but he didn't look up at me as I stood there.

"How much do I owe you for the food?" I asked quietly when it was clear that he wasn't going to acknowledge me. I wished he would look at me; I desperately wanted to see his beautiful eyes.

"Nothing, forget it." He shook his head and continued with his lesson plans that he had scattered across his desk. *Wow, two days and he's already made a messy desk…*

"Oh, well, um… thanks," I muttered uncomfortably. "You know, you should try and keep your desk a little tidier, people will think you're a slob. Maybe you could pay a freshman to keep it clean for you." I turned to walk off, listening to him laugh quietly behind me. I didn't stop; I just walked out and headed to my next class.

When I got to my Spanish class I slipped into the seat next to Amy. "Hey, how'd detention go with Mr Hottie?" she asked, looking at me jealously.

I shrugged and slumped down in my seat, wishing this day was over already. This morning I prepared myself for one meeting with him, I'd already had two and had a whole hour of my worst subject to come. Life was cruel.

Two hours later I was being blindly led down the hall by Amy. "Seriously, come drool over the hot new teacher. It'll take your mind off of that ass of an ex you have," she insisted. I sighed, wishing I could tell her and have her understand that was exactly the reason I didn't want to go to calculus.

I stopped outside his classroom. "No, I'm going to skip, I have a headache. Just get me any assignments I miss, okay?" I said, shaking my head. I couldn't cope with seeing him anymore; I was physically and emotionally exhausted already. My lack of sleep last night was catching up on me making my eyes sting.

"You're not sick, you just want to go home and pout over that ass that didn't deserve you anyway. Well screw him; you can do better than a waster bartender. A little dose of Mr Hottie teacher will perk you up no ends. And if the sound of his sexy voice doesn't do it then I bet he could make your headache disappear with one of those sexy little smiles." She waggled her eyebrows at me playfully.

I groaned and shook my head in protest. "Definitely skipping."

Someone cleared their throat behind us. I jumped, quickly looking back to see Will standing behind us with an amused expression on his face. "Ladies, is this a private discussion about how hot I am or can anyone join in?" he asked, smirking as Amy blushed tomato red and giggled. "And no skipping, Miss Henderson," he added. His beautiful eyes met mine seeming to trap me in his gaze. I couldn't look away as my breath caught in my throat. His eyes were warm and playful and so much like my Will that it actually hurt my insides.

Amy grabbed my arm and yanked me into the room before I could say anything at all. "That was so embarrassing, I can't believe he heard all of that!" she hissed in my ear. I chuckled darkly. Knowing Will he probably liked hearing that people thought he was hot. I flicked my eyes back to him to see a small smile on his face as he headed to his desk.

We were last in because of the whole discussion outside the door so the tables were pretty full. There were two empty seats, one on the front row next to Oliver, and the other on the back row next to a girl that honestly didn't smell very pleasant. I weighed my options and decided I would go to the back so I wouldn't have such a good view of Will.

"I'm going for the back," Amy said quickly as she almost ran away from me, her face still burning with embarrassment.

I groaned quietly and headed over to sit next to Oliver at the front. He smiled at me warmly. I pulled out my notebook and pen, slyly watching Will as he sat on the front of his desk looking all sexy and alluring without even trying.

"Right then, boys and girls, yesterday you all had a free pass but today you need to do some work I'm afraid." He grinned wickedly as he got up and walked over to the laptop on his desk. After pressing a few buttons a series of complicated equations popped up on the electronic board.

"Alright, so obviously I have Ms Patterson's notes on what you were learning last semester, but I don't know what stage you're all at because everyone learns differently. On the board you'll see some equations. I want you to find the domains of the functions. Have a go at the problems at the board, don't forget to show your workings, and then I'll have a look and see where we need to go from there," he instructed. "Take as long as you need. Please don't help each other though; I need to know each person's stage so that I can give them the right amount of help." He looked around sternly at the class.

I groaned and opened my notebook looking at the board. *I have to find the domain of what? Damn, why wasn't I listening properly?* I turned to Oliver who was already scribbling on the first equation.

"Olly, we have to find the domain of what?" I whispered, giving him my I'm lost face.

He chuckled and leant over. "Functions, it's like the answer to the question. So take the first one, for example, you have to find the value of F. Ignore all the other stuff after it, the actual question is 'F' equals? Then do the equation to find what the answer is." He shrugged as if that made perfect sense. I tried my hardest not to stare at him and ask him if he was speaking English.

Yep, I'm totally lost and utterly screwed! "Oh right, yeah I get ya, thanks," I lied, nodding slowly and turning back to my blank notepad, now even more confused.

"No problem. By the way, how are the hands?" he whispered.

I held them up to show him. "Fine really, they look worse than they feel."

He leant in further and took hold of my hand, looking at it closely. "I feel really bad about it. Hey, know what, maybe I could take you out on Friday night and make it up to you," he suggested, looking a little uncomfortable.

I squirmed in my seat. "Er, Olly, that's sweet but honestly my hands are fine. You don't need to make up for anything, besides, it was an accident."

He laughed quietly. "Okay, so that wasn't the real reason I asked, I actually just wanted to ask you out and thought that would be a good excuse," he admitted, grinning sheepishly.

Oh no! How can I say no nicely? "Umm... I'm er... I..." I stammered.

"Mr Hawk, maybe you could pick up girls after my class?" Will snapped from in front of us.

Olly jerked back to his seat, dropping my hand like it was a hot coal. "Right yeah, sorry, sir." He grabbed his pen and started writing again.

I glanced up at Will and smiled gratefully. He didn't smile back, he just walked off and sat at his desk, leaning back on his chair and pushing it back onto two legs with his hands behind his head. I had a sudden urge to throw something at him so that he would jump and fall back on the chair. It would be incredibly funny, and I was pretty sure he would laugh - well, if we were on our own he would laugh, but probably not in front of a class full of his students.

I sighed and looked back at the board, deciding to make a start. The equations just looked like complete gibberish to me though, and was actually making my headache worse. I closed my eyes and rubbed my forehead, wondering if I actually needed to finish high school or if I could just drop out and never look at another equation again. Maybe get a job as a cleaner or something.

Something slammed down on the front of my desk making a loud crash. I jerked my head up, my heart thumped in my chest. "Shit!" I shouted, shocked.

I looked up to see Will standing there laughing hysterically, his fist on my desk. *What on earth?* I could hear other people laughing so I looked around to see the whole class was laughing at me. *Oh my gosh, was I asleep?*

"Am I boring you, Miss Henderson?" Will asked, raising one eyebrow at me teasingly. He turned and walked off, slapping Tom a high five on the way past. "And watch your language," he added, still laughing.

What a jerk! "Yeah laugh it up. That was just hysterical, good job," I shot back sarcastically.

He turned and grinned at me, the playful, boyish grin that I knew so well. "I know, I really crack me up sometimes. Maybe I need to up my game and make my class more interesting to keep you awake," he mused, smirking at me.

"You could always do it shirtless," a girl called from the back. Everyone except me laughed.

"Nah, because then none of the girls would do any work," Will joked, shrugging cockily, earning another high five from the guy next to him.

I rolled my eyes and looked down at my notebook; I hadn't even done the first problem on the board. I groaned and scribbled down a load of letters and numbers so I would have something to hand in. Oliver handed me five other pieces of paper, obviously belonging to the other people on my row. I shoved mine in the middle of the pile and put it to the edge of my desk so I could hand them in at the end of class.

As soon as the bell rang people started getting up. "Guys, if you could all read chapter one of your textbooks for tomorrow, please," Will called as people started filing out of the room.

Amy came down to my desk, giggling wickedly. "I can't believe you fell asleep. How the hell can you fall asleep in his class? Just looking at him is enough to keep you awake surely. He is so funny." She sighed, looking at him with that daydreamer look in her eye. I frowned. It was slowly killing me to see all of the girls looking at him like that. *Why the hell can't they just back off?*

"Freaking hilarious," I mumbled, grabbing the assignments and heading over to Will's desk so I could put them in his tray.

"Miss Henderson, may I have a word?" he requested.

I looked at Amy who gave me a sympathetic look and headed out. Hopefully she would wait for me by my locker and give me a ride home because I genuinely didn't have the energy for the forty five minute walk today.

Will watched her leave. As soon as the door closed he looked at me with concern. "You okay?" he asked quietly.

I nodded and shifted my heavy bag on my shoulder. "Yeah I'm perfect."

"You look tired."

"Wow, thanks, I used to get 'you look beautiful', now I just look tired. That's real nice, thanks," I snapped angrily.

He sighed and shook his head, clearly annoyed. "I was just worried that's all, no need to be bitchy about it."

"Are we done with the concern now? Can I go?" I looked at the door hopefully.

"Yeah go," he said dismissively.

As I turned to leave he grabbed my wrist making me stop, he turned my hand over and looked at my palm. "Please tell me what happened," he said quietly, looking up at me with the puppy dog face that always seemed to work on me. His eyes locked on mine making me feel slightly weightless.

"I fell playing soccer, no big deal," I said, shrugging. My whole body was tingling with the need for him to hold me, and kiss me, and tell me everything would be fine, and that he wanted me.

He nodded, seeming to digest that information for a couple of seconds. "Okay, thanks. You should go," he stated, letting go of my wrist. I stood there looking at him for a few seconds before I felt my eyes starting to prickle with tears so I turned and practically ran out of the room.

I ran down the hallway to my locker. Amy was waiting there for me, smiling sympathetically. "Another detention?" she asked, turning her nose up.

Another detention? What's that about? "No, why would I get a detention?"

"You fell asleep in his class then gave him some sarcastic comment and didn't even apologise," she explained, looking at me as if I was stupid.

Oh. Actually, yeah, I guess I should have gotten a detention for that. Hmm, maybe he felt that lunchtime detentions for the first week of the semester were enough. I shrugged. "I got a lecture about it but no detentions," I lied.

She linked her arm through mine. "Well that's too bad; I would love detention with him, more chance to stare at that face." She fanned her face dramatically. My rage spiked immediately because yet another person was attracted to my ex-boyfriend.

"He's not that freaking hot!" I snapped angrily.

A hurt expression crossed her face so I immediately felt terrible. I knew I shouldn't be taking this out on her; she was being a loyal friend and trying to take my mind off of my ex-boyfriend. It wasn't her fault she was just rubbing it in my face how hot that ex-boyfriend was.

"I'm sorry, Amy, I shouldn't keep taking this out on you. I just don't want to keep talking about hot guys, it reminds me of Will," I lied, hoping that made sense.

She smiled sadly. "Okay it's no problem," she dismissed. "Right then, missy, we're going for some retail therapy and then I'm going to buy you the biggest, most sickly piece of chocolate cake I can find." She grinned wickedly and pulled me out of the school towards her car.

Chapter Eight

Almost two hours later we were done shopping and went to get some dessert from the café in the middle of the shopping mall. I'd honestly tried not to think about Will as I was browsing the stores, but he just kept popping back into my mind. Every time I saw a nice shirt I thought about buying it for him, or when a guy walked past with brown hair I would check to make sure it wasn't him. I really was obsessed.

Just as we were done with our cake, someone tapped me on the shoulder. My eyes flicked to Amy who was looking behind me with a flirtatious smile. I turned in my seat, looking behind me, seeing that Sam, Will's brother, was standing there grinning at me.

"Hey, Chloe."

"Oh… um hey, Sam," I greeted uncomfortably. My eyes flicking back to Amy as I tried to hide my worry. *Does Sam know that Will and I have broken up? What if he accidentally says something about him being a teacher in front of Amy?*

"How have you been? Long time no see." He smiled his cheeky, make all the girls melt smile. It reminded me so much of Will's smile that it made my stomach ache.

"I've been good," I lied. "Er, Sam, this is Amy. We go to school together," I introduced, putting plenty of emphasis around the word school, secretly trying to tell him not to mention anything in front of her. "Amy, this is Sam, he's Will's brother." I waved a hand between them both.

"Hey, nice to meet you," Amy said, smiling flirtily.

Sam turned on the killer charm, his eyes seeming to sparkle as he regarded her with barely contained interest. "And it is definitely nice to meet you," he replied, winking at her. "So, are you going to leave me standing here all day, or ask me to sit down?"

I sucked in a ragged breath, already wishing this meeting was over. It was like walking on eggshells.

"Sure, sit down," Amy offered, patting the seat next to her.

He smirked at her and went to sit there before turning back to me. "So you and Will broke up, huh?" he mused, cocking his head to the side, looking at me curiously.

I gulped. "Yep," I confirmed, shrugging, trying to pretend it didn't feel like he was killing me with a plastic spork.

He frowned. "It's a shame, you two were cute together."

"Can we not talk about it?" I snapped. I instantly regretted it. *There I go taking it out on others again!* "Sorry, I'm being all snappy and bitchy today; I didn't sleep very well last night so I'm taking it out on everyone."

"You didn't? You need someone to volunteer to rock you to sleep? Because I'm definitely up for that," he teased, smirking and waggling his eyebrows at me suggestively.

I laughed despite the awkwardness of the situation. "Shut up, flirt, I just broke up with your brother. I don't think I'll be as quick to take up with another cocky, overconfident, brown haired pervert." I stuck out my tongue at him. He laughed quietly.

Amy bent down, picking up her purse and shopping bags from the floor at her feet. "Chloe, we'd better go, I need to get home, I'm babysitting for my brother tonight," she interrupted, shooting me a regretful look.

I nodded and stood up grabbing my purse too. "Nice to see you again, Sam."

He nodded. "Yeah, listen, you want to hang out sometime? As friends? Catch a movie or something?" he asked, smiling sympathetically.

I looked at Amy for help, but she wasn't that much use because she was nodding vigorously, telling me to accept. I pondered on it for a few seconds. Sam was a nice guy, I'd met up with him a few times with Will and we got on well. It wouldn't make much difference being friends with him. At least I would have someone to talk to about the fact that Will is my teacher. Sam was the only one I would be able to talk to about it, actually.

"Um, yeah okay. Just as friends though, I'm not interested in anything else," I clarified.

He snorted and rolled his eyes. "What makes you think I'm interested in anything? Jeez, you've got Will cooties all over you. Gross," he scoffed, looking me over with a mock disgusted face as he faked a shudder.

I burst out laughing. He reminded me so much of Will - they had the same humour. Sam grinned and pulled out his cell phone, passing it to me. I typed in my number and handed it back. "Come on then, Amy. See you around, Sam."

As we walked off, Amy looked at me with wide eyes. "Wow, he's so hot! Seriously yummy," she gushed. I nodded and shrugged. Sam was really cute, even I could see that though I didn't look at him like that. "Does he look like Will?" she asked flatly as we weaved past people towards the pay machines for the parking lot.

I took out a deep breath and blew it out loudly. "Yeah a little, Will's better looking though, annoying as that is to admit." I shrugged. My cell phone beeped in my purse. I pulled it out to see I had a text from an unknown number:

'Just 2 let U know U can talk 2 me about Will if U need 2. I'll call U later in the week and we can catch a movie. Sam'

I smiled and messaged back a thank you. Amy was watching me curiously. "My mom wondering what time I'll be home," I lied, slipping my phone back into my pocket.

That night I flopped on my bed doing my homework. I'd deliberately left calculus until last so I could take my time with the chapter we were supposed to read so I could let it sink in. I read the whole thing three times, but it still didn't make much sense to me. I fell asleep with the book on my chest.

The next day I didn't see Will all morning which I was grateful for, but I still had the lunchtime detention to get through. Hopefully, like yesterday, he would ignore me and that would make it easier. I'd brought a book to read today so at least I wouldn't have to watch the clock. When the bell rang at the end of the morning, I said bye to my friends and reluctantly trudged off to his classroom. Again he wasn't there, so I made my way to the back and pulled out my iPod and book.

A little while later I saw movement from in front of me and looked up just as Will was turning the chair around from the desk in front of mine. He settled himself in the chair and looked at me expectantly.

I reluctantly turned off my iPod. "I thought you said I could listen to music," I muttered, frowning.

"Yeah you can, I just wanted to talk to you about the assignment you did in class yesterday." He shrugged, his eyes not leaving my face.

I groaned. "I was asleep; I didn't do any of them so I scribbled some stuff down so I had something to hand in," I said defensively. "They were all wrong I'm guessing."

He shook his head, his eyes sparkling. "No actually, every single one of them was right, and I wanted to talk to you about joining the Mathlete team."

"Holy crud, really?" I cried, shocked.

"No, they were all wrong," he stated, laughing. "You're so gullible."

I laughed and blushed at my stupidity. "Not funny."

"Seriously though, last semester you were buddied with someone. Do you have a problem with calculus?" he asked, snapping his teacher head back.

I groaned. "Yeah, I honestly just can't do it. You could just fail me now to save us both the effort," I suggested hopefully. *Then I won't have to come to his class at all!*

He shook his head firmly. "How about you get a tutor? I would offer to do it, but I don't think that's appropriate." He frowned, seeming to think. "Looking at the work from yesterday there's a girl called Erika Dennison who's pretty good." He flicked his head to get the hair from his eyes. I chewed on my lip so I didn't make a sound. I loved it when he did that, it was sexy as hell.

Suddenly it dawned on me what he'd just said. Erika Dennison tutoring me? I hated her. She'd picked on both me and Amy when we first started school. She was a bitch who liked to make people's lives hell. I couldn't have her do it and know I was bad at something; she would make sure everyone knew how terrible I was at it. She'd embarrass the heck out of me on purpose.

"No not her, please," I begged.

He puffed out a big breath. "Well the only other one I would recommend from your class would be Oliver Hawk, but I don't think that's a good idea either." He frowned, looking a little annoyed about something.

Why is that not a good idea? "I'd definitely prefer Oliver, but he tried to explain it to me yesterday, and I still didn't get it." A wave of humiliation hit me. *Jeez, I'm so stupid! Why does my worst subject have to be the one he teaches? I bet he's wondering what he even saw in me in the first place... but then again he didn't have any feelings for me so all he probably saw in me was an easy lay.*

"Well, seeing as we already have a week of detentions I can help you for this week, and then we can see how you go okay?" he offered, smiling kindly.

"Actually, I'd rather just fail." I shook my head in rejection. I couldn't be that close to him, it was too painful.

"What does that mean?"

I sighed. "I just need you to stay away from me; I can't be talking to you all the time. Just leave me to get on with it and I'll struggle through somehow. I don't need your help," I replied, putting my headphones back in.

He looked a little hurt as I turned the music up full blast. Without trying to talk to me again, he stood up and set a little brown paper bag on my desk, before storming back to his desk not looking back at me.

Hesitantly, I looked in the little bag. In there sat a chicken salad wrap, tortilla chips, and a pot of sour cream dip that had the name 'Old Giuseppe' on the side. That was the name of the Mexican restaurant he took me to on our first real date. *Damn, he is so freaking adorable! Did he bring this in for me? Maybe this is his lunch.* I glanced up to see him eating a wrap of his own so it obviously wasn't his. *Why is he being like this? He wouldn't buy lunch for another student, so why do it for me?*

I sighed and pulled open the wrap, just wishing that things were different, that either I was older, or he was younger. Anything. Whatever would make this painful situation better. The only thing that I didn't wish was that I had never met him. I would never wish that, I had the perfect summer with him, and I was grateful for every second of it.

My pocket vibrated so I pulled out my cell phone to see an unknown number flashing on my screen. I snuck a glance at Will wondering what he would do if I answered my phone. *Screw it, what more can he do?*

I answered it quickly. "Hello?" I whispered, sinking lower into my seat trying to go unnoticed.

"Hey, Chloe. It's Sam."

"Oh hi, um, this isn't a good time," I whispered, closing my eyes.

"Really? I thought it would be your lunchtime," he replied, sounding a little bemused.

"It is, but I have detention."

He laughed. "Oh I knew you were a bad girl," he teased. "But wait, who the hell gives a lunchtime detention on the first week of school? That's just cruel."

Cruel is right! "Your brother does. I have one every day this week."

He burst out laughing. "You're in there with him right now? That's too funny. Wow, talk about awkward."

A scowl lined my forehead. "Screw you, there's nothing even remotely funny about this situation," I snapped angrily.

"Whoa, Chloe, chill! I'm sorry, I was just kidding around. Listen, I just called to arrange that movie." His voice was apologetic so I felt my annoyance ebbing away.

"If you're going to keep making these lame ass remarks then I'm not even sure I want to go with you anymore," I countered, pouting even though he couldn't see me.

"Well that's too bad. I'll pick you up from school Friday. You finish at three o'clock, right?" he asked.

Friday? I'm not ready to go out yet. I would rather curl in bed and eat chocolate all weekend. "What? No, I don't want to go Friday."

He chuckled darkly. "Well it needs to be Friday because I'll be getting laid on Saturday."

"You're such a man-whore," I teased.

"Yeah, but being a man-whore is so much fun. Right then, I'll be there at three o'clock Friday."

"Sam, no," I hissed as the line disconnected. "Damn it!" I groaned and dropped my phone on the table roughly, wishing the ground would just open up and swallow me, putting me out of my misery.

"Was that an emergency call?" Will asked, his voice harsh.

"No it was a booty call," I teased, expecting him to laugh. He didn't. Instead, he got up from his desk and walked over to me, snatching my cell phone from the table and slipping it into his pocket.

"No personal calls allowed in school unless they're an emergency," he snapped, shrugging and walking back to his desk. "You can get it back at the end of the day."

"Are you kidding me? Do you enjoy annoying me? Why are you doing this, Will? Seriously, you've turned into a freaking jerk!" I cried, jumping out of my seat and throwing my stuff into my bag angrily. I pulled out ten dollars from my pocket, walked up to his desk and slammed it down. "That's for the lunch."

He glared at me. "You have half an hour of detention left."

"So go freaking report me," I spat, glaring back at him. He didn't say anything so I turned on my heel and walked out, marching to the cafeteria, spotting my friends sitting there still chatting over lunch.

Amy looked at me confused as I walked up to them. "What are you doing here? Shouldn't you be in detention?"

"I feel sick, I'm going home," I lied, shrugging. There was no way I was going to see that ass again today, if I did then I'd probably slap his face, either that or kiss it. I couldn't exactly do either of those things in a class full of students.

"You feel sick? You're not pregnant are you?" Amy joked, looking at me with a mock horror face.

"Yeah, how on earth did you guess that? I'm only three months, I shouldn't be showing already," I joked, playing along and rubbing my stomach. I saw Nick jerk in his seat, his whole body tensed up as he looked at me with wide eyes. I burst out laughing. "Relax, I was kidding." I winked at him playfully.

He blew out a big breath and rubbed the back of his neck. "Christ that scared me."

"Sorry, Nick." I laughed. "Amy, can you get anything I need from this afternoon? I don't have my cell phone it's been confiscated so don't bother texting me or anything." I shrugged and shifted my heavy bag on my shoulder.

"Who confiscated it?" Emily asked, frowning and clutching her cell for dear life. Emily was someone who believed that you were helpless without a phone. She would probably have a mild heart attack if she didn't have it on her at all times.

"The new guy," I muttered, not wanting to say his name.

The table of people all laughed. Emily looked at me with narrowed eyes. "What's up with you? That guy is awesome, funny, smart, and he's a fair too, but you just seem to rub each other up the wrong way. Everyone else loves him; he's the best thing to happen to this school since they got rid of the Thursday meatloaf," she mused, shaking her head, looking a little baffled.

And there she goes defending him again. "Really? Wow, you should tell him that, I'm sure that'll earn you one of those oh so sexy smiles," I replied sarcastically, rolling my eyes. How could he come in here and have everyone eating out of the palm of his hand so quickly? It was just plain annoying. "I'll see you tomorrow," I called over my shoulder as I turned to walk out.

Just as I got to the front door someone grabbed my hand, making it hurt a little from the scratches yesterday. I turned back angrily, expecting to see Will there telling me I had to get back in detention or something. It wasn't him though, it was Nick.

"How are you getting home?" he asked, looking at me worriedly.

I shrugged in response. "I'm walking."

He sighed and slung his arm around my shoulder. "I'll drive you. You can't walk home if you're sick." He led me towards his car. I smiled, not wanting to admit I was faking. I didn't want to walk home. I knew it was selfish but I liked his company, he took my mind off Will for a little while because he wasn't talking about how hot he was all the time like Amy did.

He drove me home in silence. When he pulled up he looked at me curiously. "You're not really pregnant are you?" he asked, wincing.

I smiled and rolled my eyes. "Nick, I'm not pregnant, that was a joke, not a particularly funny one but a joke nonetheless. Stop stressing," I assured him, smiling apologetically. "Want to come in and keep me company?" I asked hopefully. Otherwise I'd have to go in and find some other way of distracting myself.

"As long as you promise not to throw up on me like that other time." He turned his nose up in disgust.

I burst out laughing. On our third date I wasn't feeling particularly well but didn't want to cancel so I still went, and ended up vomiting on his foot in the middle of a busy movie theatre.

"Oh, Nick, I'm surprised you still talk to me," I mused, still giggling.

"Me too sometimes." He rolled his eyes and climbed out of the car, waiting for me to get round to his side before slipping his arm back around my shoulders and leading me inside.

My mom wasn't home yet. She worked until four o'clock so we had the house to ourselves. Nick pulled me over to the couch and made me sit down. "I'll go make you some tea or something, and then we can watch a movie," he said, smiling and walking into the kitchen like he owned the place.

I laid my head back on the sofa, silently counting just to stop my mind from wandering to Will again. After a couple of minutes Nick came in and set some toast and a cup of peppermint tea in front of me before he headed to the DVD player.

"Thanks." I smiled.

He plopped down on the sofa next to me while I nibbled on the toast, not really wanting it, but not wanting to offend him after he went to the trouble of making it for me. When the movie started I smiled. It was 'Love Actually', my favourite. I snuggled against his side and sighed. *Why can't I just fall in love with someone like Nick? A sweet and adorable guy who is crazy about me, and more importantly, my age.*

After the movie we talked easily for a bit. When talk turned to my classes my heart sank, knowing he would soon mention Will. "So how are you getting on in calculus this semester? Think you'll get buddied again?" he asked. He knew I hated it last time; I'd ranted about it enough to him.

"I don't think so; the new guy said I should get a tutor. He suggested Erika, can you believe that? Her of all people," I griped, annoyed at the thought of her again.

"If you need a tutor I can help you. I mean, I'm not a complete whiz or anything, but I get by easily enough," he offered, shrugging casually.

"You're kidding me! You'd do that for me?" I asked, looking at him hopefully.

He grinned, holding up one finger. "On one condition."

I held my breath, praying he wasn't going to ask me out again or something. I really liked us being friends again and didn't want things to get awkward. "Okay, what's that?" I inquired nervously.

He smirked at me confidently. "We do it at my house, and as payment you can cook for me on those nights. At least twice a week."

I grinned and threw my arms around his neck, hugging him tightly; I would have cooked for him if he asked me to even without the tutoring. "Deal definitely," I agreed happily. He hugged me back and suddenly there was a knock at the door. I glanced at the clock to see it was just after three. *Who the heck is that? I'm not expecting anyone.*

I jumped up, but Nick instantly pulled me back to the sofa, tickling my sides. I squealed and giggled as I tried to fight him off me. He laughed and finally stopped, leaving me gasping for breath. "I'll get the door. You're supposed to be sick, remember? I knew you were faking," he said, narrowing his eyes at me playfully.

I laughed as he pushed himself up and went to get the door. I rested my head back and listened to see who it was and what they wanted. "Oh hey, sir, um… What are you doing here?" Nick asked, sounding confused.

Sir? What's that about? I stood up and walked towards the door. Just as I got to the corner, I heard his voice.

"Well, I have Miss Henderson's cell phone. I said she could have it back at the end of the day, but her friends said she went home, sick. I know how important a cell is to a girl," Will replied. His voice sounded extremely uncomfortable and a little annoyed.

Oh my days, he came to my house? What the heck is he doing? I turned the corner to see Nick standing there half blocking the doorway, his arm on the frame as he looked out at Will. His body language wasn't very welcoming. They seemed to be looking at each other strangely. Will was definitely pissed; I could tell by the clenched jaw.

"She's sick; I'll give it to her," Nick said, holding out his hand for the phone.

"I'd just rather check she's okay. She came over a little funny in detention," Will replied sternly, using a teacher tone of voice that I didn't even realise he had.

I took a deep breath and walked up behind Nick, lifting his arm and stepping in front of him. Will's face softened as he saw me. Nick stepped closer to me and pressed his chest against my back, his hands resting on my shoulders. Will's posture seemed to change instantly, his shoulders tightening again. The air was thick with awkwardness as we just gazed at each other, not speaking.

Nick broke the silence. "Mr Morris was bringing your cell phone back."

I nodded and held my hand out for it. "That's really nice of you, sir, but you could have kept it until tomorrow." I tried to keep my voice light and friendly in front of Nick.

Will placed the phone in my hand, cocking his head to the side, looking at me intently. "I also wanted to check you were okay after lunchtime."

"I'm fine." I turned to Nick. "Um, do you think you could make some more tea? I'm pretty thirsty," I asked uncomfortably. He frowned and nodded, walking off. I looked back to Will to see a smirk on his face as he watched Nick's retreating back. "What do you really want?" I asked quietly, pulling the door close behind me so that it would muffle the conversation from Nick.

"Like I said, I just wanted to give you your phone and check you were okay. You looked pretty upset when you stormed off," he said quietly, cocking his head to the side and watching me avidly.

"I'm fine." I shrugged nonchalantly. "As you can see, I have company, so thanks for returning my phone, Mr Morris, and I'll see you tomorrow in detention," I said in my bitchiest voice.

He snorted, his eyes tightening. "Yeah I noticed you had company. Replaced me already?" he asked, raising an eyebrow at me challengingly.

I gasped. *Man, he's just starting to piss me off more and more!* "Is that some kind of joke?" I snapped, clenching my fists and ignoring the stinging from the little scratches on my palms as the skin stretched slightly, probably starting them bleeding again.

"Just an observation."

"Nick and I are friends, not that it's any of your business anyway." I looked back into the hallway quickly, making sure Nick wasn't there listening to any of this.

"Yeah? That's not what I heard, I heard that you two used to date but broke up at the start of the summer," Will retorted. His jaw tightened as his piercing grey eyes hardened accusingly.

What the hell is he looking at me like that for? This is none of his damn business even if I did start to date Nick again! He's the one that broke up with me, not the other way around. "That has nothing to do with anything; we were friends before we got together. Where are you getting this crap from anyway?" I asked annoyed.

He shrugged, his jaw relaxing now. "I hear stuff. You weren't in class so people started speculating because you were seen leaving school with your ex-boyfriend."

"Well like I said, it's none of your business anyway. Thanks for the phone." I stepped back, starting to close the door in his face.

Before it even got half way he stuck his foot out, holding the door open. "I'm sorry I'm hurting you," he said quietly, looking at his hands.

I scoffed at that. "You're not sorry at all. It's no skin off your nose. You're probably just pissed that you'll have to work a little harder for sex from now on. No longer on tap when you want it. Oh, and by the way, I've sorted my tutor issues; Nick's offered to help me." I kicked his foot making him pull it back. I slammed the door in his face, ignoring his shocked expression.

I leant against it barely able to breathe. He hissed a cuss word from the other side of the door, and then a few seconds later a car door slammed. I pushed myself away from the door and headed to the kitchen. Nick was leaning against the counter waiting for the kettle to boil. His back was to me so I went and pressed my face between his shoulder blades, fighting the urge to cry again.

"Okay?" he asked, turning awkwardly and wrapping me into a hug.

I nodded, hoping my voice would work. "Yeah I'm good. Want to stay for dinner tonight?" I asked hopefully.

He grinned. "Hell yeah, your mom's cooking is even better than yours, no offence," he replied, pulling back and smirking at me. I slapped his arm, faking hurt. "Ouch, easy with the right hook, Rocky Balboa," he teased.

Chapter Nine

The rest of the week passed much the same. I tried to avoid Will whenever possible. If I saw him coming down the hallway or anything I excused myself to the nearest restroom or classroom. The lunchtime detentions were okay, he didn't let me off of them so I just sat at the back of the room listening to music and reading. I ignored him completely, as he did me. He didn't buy me lunch again; I purposefully made myself a sandwich so I could turn him down even if he did anyway.

His classes were awful. I had no idea what I was doing. I barely understood anything and sat there on edge the whole time while the girls all drooled and flirted with him like crazy. He didn't single me out, and he didn't ignore me, he just treated me like any other student in his class. Except maybe I got fewer smiles. Actually, come to think of it, I got no smiles at all, but that was probably because I didn't give him any either. Nick and I were meeting up on Saturday so he could help me study.

Today was Friday, and I was due to meet Sam any minute. As the bell sounded signalling the end of the day, I packed up my books and stood there waiting as Amy pulled her hair into a loose ponytail.

"So tonight's the big date," she gushed excitedly, waggling her eyebrows.

I could practically feel Will's stare boring into the side of my head. From the corner of my eye I could see him standing there watching me. His whole body seemed tense.

"It's not a date," I reply flatly. My hands were starting to get sweaty because Will was staring at me so intently.

"You're going to the movies with a boy, it's a date," Amy countered, waving her hand dismissively. I shook my head and opened my mouth to protest, but she spoke again cutting me off. "It should be a date anyway, because damn, I would screw that boy senseless, and you should too. It'll help you get over Mr Perfect if you jump his brother. It'll stop you pouting so much," she teased.

I gasped. "Amy!" I hissed, grabbing her arm and dragging her closer to me giving her the shut the hell up face. Too late. I heard a loud crash from

Will's direction and looked over to see he had walked into a desk, knocking the chairs over and dropping the stack of books he was carrying. His jaw was tight, he looked furiously angry.

"Are you all right, Mr Morris? You need a hand?" Amy offered, smiling seductively.

"Er... it's... no it's fine. Thanks for the offer, Miss Clarke," he rejected politely.

I decided I needed to leave before he could pull me to one side. "I gotta go," I muttered looking only at Amy. "I'll call you and we'll meet up Sunday." I hugged her quickly, before turning for the door leaving her to finish packing up her books.

"Chloe, wait!" Will called.

I stopped dead in my tracks. That was the first time he'd called me Chloe since we found out he was my teacher. The sound of it made my stomach get all fluttery even though I was angry at myself for still letting him have power over me. I turned back to look at him, not really wanting to see his angry face again.

"I could actually use some help, maybe you could give me a hand?" he requested, though his eyes were saying something different entirely.

"I'll help you, Mr Morris," Amy interjected. "Chloe has a hot date." She shoved me towards the door with a sly grin and a wink. No doubt she was excited for a few minutes alone with Will.

Will frowned. "But I... I... right, okay yeah thanks, Miss Clarke."

I waved to Amy and headed through the door. I felt guilty for not staying and clarifying to Will that it wasn't a date and that I wasn't going to 'jump his brother' like Amy had made it seem. But then again, he should know that I wouldn't sleep with his brother anyway. He should know that because firstly, I wasn't the type of girl to go sleeping with someone on a first date, and secondly, we'd only just broken up, therefore I wouldn't do that anyway, especially not with his brother.

I headed to my locker quickly grabbing the rest of the books I would need so I could do my homework over the weekend. I lingered near my locker, wasting time. When I could put it off no longer, I walked out of the front doors, silently wishing I hadn't agreed to this. I just wanted to go home and change into sweats and chill. *Hopefully Sam won't even show up...*

My hope of that faded as soon as I looked up and saw a black jeep parked right at the edge of the walkway. My heart sank as I spotted him perched behind the wheel. He grinned as he saw me and started the car up; I plastered on a fake smile and opened the door.

"Hey," I greeted with forced happiness, slinging my bag into the backseat.

"Hey, Chloe, good day? Uh-oh, big brother alert," he said, looking over my shoulder as I was just about to get in. I turned back to see Will walking out of the building. I could see the barely contained fury building with each step he took towards us.

He stopped right behind me. "Chloe, I'd like a quick word with my brother, please," he growled, not even looking at me. He was glaring at Sam with so much anger that I'm surprised he hadn't died from the venom alone.

I gripped his arm tightly making him look at me. His eyes met mine. I flinched a little from the hardness of them. "Just leave it. Ignore Amy, it's not a date," I assured him. I looked around seeing that most people had left already so luckily there was hardly anyone around.

He didn't answer; instead he gripped my upper arm and pulled me behind his body, putting himself between me and the car as he leant in to speak to his brother. "Don't you fucking dare. I'm warning you, Sam. You need to drive away right now," he spat angrily; his whole body tense and alert.

Sam just laughed. "Relax, I don't want your sloppy seconds." He rolled his eyes.

"Sam," Will said his name as a warning, his hands clenching into fists.

Dammit, is Will going to hit his brother? I grabbed his wrist quickly, pulling him back out of the car. "Stop this! We're going out as friends. Not that it's any of your damn business anyway, but I have no interest in your brother at all. You're behaving like a spoilt child, arguing over a toy that you don't even want to play with anymore!" I chastised. I could feel my eyes prickling and I knew I would cry soon. I needed to go.

His face softened as he looked at me pleadingly. "Chloe," he whispered. His eyes bored into mine making my heart beat faster.

I shook my head. "I'm going out with a friend; you have a good weekend, Mr Morris," I said acidly as I climbed in the car.

Just as I went to slam the door and make a dramatic exit he caught it, pulling it open again looking at Sam warningly. "You keep in mind that she's a minor, Sam," he warned.

Sam laughed. "Like you did you mean?" he teased. Will opened his mouth, probably for an angry retort based on the look on his face, so I held up a hand and cut him off.

"For goodness sake, you both need to chill out, or I'm just going home. I'm not in the mood for this right now. Just grow up both of you," I scolded, crossing my arms over my chest, staring out of the windscreen.

"Fine," Will huffed. "Have a nice time, Miss Henderson. We'll talk later, Sam." Will slammed the door with so much force that it made the whole car shake.

"Wow, someone's jealous," Sam muttered, chuckling to himself as he waved teasingly at Will.

"He's not jealous; he just doesn't like the thought of someone touching something that he's had. What a jerk! What the hell did I see in him anyway? He doesn't want me, but I can't go and have fun? Damn he's so... so... ugh; I don't even have the right word! Annoying will have to do for now until I can think of something stronger," I ranted. Sam laughed at me as he pulled out of the parking lot, heading in the direction of the movie theatre.

I couldn't stop thinking about him all the way there. *Will's reaction was so annoying. Where the hell does he get off telling me who I can go out with? And that little comment to Sam about keeping in mind that I was a minor, jeez, does he actually think I'm going to sleep with someone? What kind of person does he think I am? He really doesn't know me at all.* That last thought hurt me more than anything.

"Earth to Chloe," Sam teased, laughing and waving a hand in front of my face.

I snapped back to reality. *Oops, had he been talking to me?* "Sorry, Sam, what?" I asked, smiling apologetically.

He sighed and shook his head in exasperation. "I said; are you planning on getting out of the car or do I need to find a drive-in movie or something?"

I looked around to see we were parked outside the movie theatre. I laughed sheepishly because I was so lost in thought that he'd driven the whole way there already. I rolled my eyes, grabbing the door handle and climbing out of the car.

Sam walked around to my side and slung his arm round my shoulder. "Come on then, let's get you cheered up. I've not seen a real smile from you since you two broke up," he suggested, looking a little sad about it.

As we walked into the foyer, he stopped and cursed under his breath. An angry looking bleached blonde girl in a tight and very short skirt was walking towards us, glaring at him. *Hmm, what's this about?*

"Sam Morris! You were supposed to call me three weeks ago. What happened? Were you too busy with a new slut?" she spat angrily. Her voice was a little screechy and made me wince at how loud she was. Her hateful glare turned to me so I stepped away from him quickly making his arm drop down off of my shoulder.

Sam shrugged. "I lost your number."

"You lost my number? I stored it in your cell!" she countered, her nostrils flaring as her voice somehow got even higher pitched.

"Oh, well in that case maybe I lost my cell," Sam replied, laughing quietly.

Holy monkey-butt, he really is a man-whore!

She scowled at him. "You had no intention of calling me did you?"

Sam shrugged, seeming unconcerned. "I told you beforehand that I wasn't interested in anything. You were the one that said I'd call, not the other way around."

She stepped forward quickly and before I realised what was happening, her palm connected with the side of his face. A resounding crack drew the gaze of every single person in the foyer. I gasped. I'd never seen anyone do that in real life, only in the movies. It was actually pretty funny and a lot louder than I thought it would be. She turned to me and raised her hand again, going to hit me too. *Oh hell no!*

"If you touch me I'm going to rip your cheap extensions out with my bare hands," I warned.

75

She scowled at me again and I could practically see her brain ticking over. Obviously she was weighing her options as to whether she wanted to take the risk of it or not. "Whatever, he'll hurt you more than I can anyway," she snapped, sneering at Sam again before storming out of the front door, dramatically flicking her hair over her shoulder. A couple of girls quickly ran out after her, already telling her what a hoe I was and what a waste of space Sam was.

I looked at Sam with my mouth open in shock. He raised a hand and rubbed his face lightly, and I burst out laughing. I laughed so hard that I had tears in my eyes. He was laughing too as he continued to rub his face wincing.

"You know what? That was almost worth getting slapped for. Cheered you up no end, huh?" he said, waggling his eyebrows at me when I finally calmed down.

Sam took my hand, pulling me over to the ticket desk, buying two tickets for the next movie that was playing. He was right. That had definitely cheered me up... and so did the reddish tinge to the side of his face.

"Are you okay, Sam?" I asked, trying not to laugh again.

He nodded and rolled his eyes. "Thanks for your concern, though maybe it should have come before the hysterical laughter to actually mean something."

I choked back another laugh. "Yeah maybe you're right. Who the heck was that girl anyway? Seriously, *that's* the type of girl you pick up?" I turned my nose up. She wasn't exactly a class act or anything. Her skin had a nasty orange tinge to it and her hair was bleached to the point of looking like it would snap in a strong wind.

He shrugged. "Someone I met at a party," he answered. "And no, that's not usually my type, but it was slim pickings that night. I didn't want to go home on my lonesome, that's no fun." He winked at me playfully, grinning.

"You really are a slut," I scolded. "I hope you use protection because seriously, she was... yuck."

"Jealous?" he asked, smirking at me.

I nodded and stepped closer to him, putting my hand on the opposite side of his face to her slap mark. "Absolutely I'm jealous. My hand fits pretty good here; it'll leave a nice print. I bet I slap harder than her." I was overcome by another fit of giggles as I remembered the sound and the shocked expression on Sam's face as her hand connected with his cheek.

He laughed, and we went to get some popcorn and a drink before heading into the screen. The movie wasn't very good, but I still managed to enjoy it. Sam and I were throwing popcorn at each other and behaving like kids, gaining us glares from the people around us. I was definitely glad that he made me come with him.

After it finished we had a pizza before he dropped me home. It was nice. Relaxed, and actually quite fun. We didn't talk about Will at all which I was grateful for. We talked about other stuff like his college and his family, just easy stuff.

"So, maybe next week we can meet up again?" he suggested as we pulled up outside my house.

I smiled. "Sure, if you want to." Sam was actually an exceptionally nice guy, and I could definitely see us being great friends.

"Okay, well maybe next time we could do something a little less public, there's less chance of me getting slapped again then," he said, grinning wickedly and making me laugh again.

"Maybe if you stopped sleeping around and not calling girls back then you wouldn't get slapped," I countered as I hopped out of his car.

"Nah, a slap now and again is totally worth it." He waggled his eyebrows.

"Whatever, slut, call me then okay?" I laughed. He nodded in agreement so I shut the door, turning to go inside the house.

He unrolled his window. "You know, that's the first time I've ever agreed to call a girl and actually meant it," he mused, laughing as I walked up the path to the door.

I turned to look at him and smiled. "Well then I'm honoured," I replied sarcastically. I waved and went inside. My parents were sitting on the sofa watching TV; I flopped down next to my mom.

"Hey, honey, you have a nice time?" she asked, smiling.

I shrugged. "Yeah it was good."

Her smile got broader. "That's great, Chloe. It's nice to see you smile again. You've been so down all week."

"Yeah I guess," I muttered uncomfortably. I didn't want to talk about Will, and she was going to bring it up I could tell. I stood up quickly. "I'm a little tired. I'm going to bed, night guys. Oh, Nick's coming to pick me up in the morning and I'm going to his to study for the day," I told them, changing the subject before she mentioned Will.

"Okay, honey, see you tomorrow then."

I kissed both of my parents on the cheek before heading upstairs. I pulled on my nightshirt and slipped into bed. Turning my iPod on quietly, I decided to ignore Amy's text's that had been buzzing on my cell phone all night asking how I was getting on with the 'hottie brother'. I'd talk to her tomorrow; I couldn't deal with her tonight. She seemed desperate for me to hook up with someone. That was her answer to everything, when you break up, you move onto someone else to take the pain away, but it just didn't work like that for me. I wish it did, that would be a lot easier.

Chapter Ten

A drip of something cold dropped onto my cheek. I squeezed my eyes shut tighter, swiping at my face. Another drop landed on my forehead, then another on my nose. I gasped, suddenly having a thought that the roof was leaking or something. I sat up so fast that my head started to spin. Hysterical laughter came from my right making me jump and squeal from the shock. I turned to see Nick sitting on the edge of my bed, a glass of water in his hand.

"Morning, sleeping beauty," he chirped happily.

I groaned as I slowly worked it out. "Did you put water on me?" I accused, wiping my face again.

He laughed. "Don't start being all dramatic, it was five drops of water."

I rolled my eyes. "What are you doing here anyway? And how did you get in?" I asked, stifling a yawn.

"We said ten, and your mom let me up," he explained, nodding at my alarm clock. I blinked a couple of times then gasped as the red glowing numbers came into focus. 10:06.

"Oh crap! I'm sorry," I apologised, quickly climbing out of the bed and heading over to my drawers to get some clothes for the day.

I glanced back to Nick to see he was looking anywhere but me and was sitting a little uncomfortably on my bed. I frowned, wondering what that was about, and then realised that I was only wearing one of his T-shirts that he'd left it at my house before we'd broken up. I quite often slept in it, but I guess it barely covered my butt.

"Nick, it's nothing you haven't seen before," I said, shaking my head and chuckling.

"Yeah well it's a little different now though. I mean, I'm not supposed to look now," he countered, blushing slightly.

I rolled my eyes and carried on grabbing some clothes. "Do I have time for a shower?" I asked, shooting him a puppy dog face complete with pouty lip.

He sighed dramatically. "Yeah, whatever. I knew I should have just come at half past. There was me thinking you'd changed and would manage to be ready on time for once," he teased. His gaze was firmly fixed on his nails as if they were the most important thing he'd ever seen in his life.

"You never know, there's a first time for everything." I shrugged and headed into my bathroom for the quickest shower ever.

Fifteen minutes later I was dressed and ready. I pulled my wet hair up into a messy twist and then we headed out. We chatted easily while he drove. Nick always had something to talk about, that was one of the things I loved about him. He pulled into the parking lot of the supermarket and grinned at me.

I looked around, confused. "What are we doing here? I thought we were studying."

"We are, but you're cooking. I want something good, so you can come and tell me what to buy." He slid out of the car and headed around to my side, opening my door for me.

I followed him into the supermarket and grabbed a shopping cart. "So what do you want to eat?" I asked.

"I don't know. How about chilli or something?" he suggested excitedly. I grinned and nodded. He always chose that, I should have known.

I followed him up and down the aisles while he grabbed random things from the shelves: shampoo, deodorant, everyday stuff. I was totally bored. The next time he stopped I grinned and swung my leg up over the side of the cart, climbing in quickly. He used to do this all the time to me, push me around in the cart, racing down the aisles, well, until we'd get caught by the security staff that was.

"You're such a child," he scolded, laughing.

I nodded, grinning unashamedly. He smiled wickedly and pushed the cart forward making us hurtle down the aisle. Nick jumped on the back, both of us laughing hysterically. As we neared the end he got off and stopped us well before the end in case someone came round the corner. Safety first, as always with Nick.

We got the rest of the supplies in a flash. Nick named what he wanted from each aisle, and I tried to grab it as we whizzed past it. Most of the time resulting in knocking things off of the shelves though. The whole time I was giggling like crazy.

"Hey stop that!" someone shouted angrily.

Nick immediately pulled the cart to a stop. "Oops, well that fun didn't last long," he mused, chuckling and shaking his head.

I grinned and stood up in the cart as a security guard came walking up the aisle, glaring at us. "What on earth are you two doing? I've told you about this before," he accused, pointing at the cart.

Nick nodded, looking at him apologetically as he put one arm around the top of my thighs and the other around my back, lifting me out of the cart and setting me back on my feet. "I'm sorry, sir. Won't happen again," he said, looking extremely reproachful.

The guy's face softened. Nick had that kind of face that you just couldn't get mad at. When he wanted to, he could look just like a little lost boy and you literally felt your anger melting away. It would be like beating a sick puppy or something. It had gotten him out of some arguments with me in the past. He was a damn good actor.

"Okay, well don't let me see you do it again," the guy scolded, shaking his head disapprovingly.

"Absolutely, you won't, sir," Nick promised, still doing the face.

I bit my lip and tried to copy his expression. I obviously didn't manage to pull it off though because the guy's face hardened as he looked at me. "And you, Miss, don't climb into the cart. It's dangerous among other things, you could hurt yourself or someone else," he chastised.

Whoa, why am I getting all the blame? I really need to learn Nick's face! "Yes, sir, I'm sorry," I apologised. He nodded and walked off, looking extremely pleased with himself that he'd sorted out a problem.

As soon as he rounded the corner Nick burst out laughing. "Every freaking time we come to the store you get us in trouble," he accused, digging his finger into my ribs.

I giggled and pushed him away. "You need to teach me that face, I swear it's the best face in the world." I shook my head, looking at him in awe.

He laughed wickedly. "Oh no. That's my trademark getting out of trouble face. Took me a long time to master." He slipped his arm around my shoulders, leading us through the store again so we could finish getting the things he needed.

Half an hour later we finally pulled into his drive. As we carried all of the groceries in I spotted his dad sitting at the counter eating his breakfast. His face lit up when he saw me. "Hey, Chloe, long time no see, sweetie." He grinned happily.

I hugged him in greeting. "Hey there, Trevor." I loved Nick's dad, he was a really nice guy. I didn't get to see him that much though, only really at the weekends. He worked a lot because he was the only earner in their house.

"Chloe's cooking tonight," Nick announced excitedly.

A grin split Trevor's face. "You always were a good girl." He patted me on the head teasingly as he grabbed a can of soda and headed to the lounge.

I rolled my eyes and boosted myself up onto the counter watching as Nick emptied the bags of groceries putting them away. He threw a pack of sugar into my lap. "Empty that into the sugar pot."

I snorted. "What am I your slave or something?" I joked, faking annoyance as I put it down on the counter and crossed my arms theatrically.

I saw a smile twitch at the edge of his lips. "Do you want tutoring or not?" he blackmailed, raising on eyebrow cockily at me.

I raised one eyebrow back. "Do you want chilli or not?" I countered.

He laughed. "Chloe, I could buy chilli from down the road if you refuse to make it. If I refuse to tutor you, you'd have to go crawling to Erika." He smirked at me confidently.

Damn it, he's right! I guess he wins this round. "Fine, but just so you know, I'll be spitting in your food," I joked.

He laughed and shrugged. "Awesome, it always tastes best when you do that."

I laughed and tipped the sugar into the pot while he put away everything else. He grabbed two glasses and a carton of juice and nodded towards the hallway. I grabbed two apples from the bag he'd just bought and jumped down from the counter.

As I made my way to his room I started feeling a little nervous. It was all right being back in his house again, but going into his bedroom would be a little weird for me. We spent a lot of time in there because his dad was hardly ever here. His bedroom held a lot of memories for both of us.

I pretended I didn't care as I walked into his room. Heat crept up on to my face as I looked at his double bed. *Damn it, Chloe, stop blushing!*

"Want to do it on the bed or at the desk?" he asked, shrugging.

I giggled. "Wherever is good for me from what I remember," I joked, then immediately wished I hadn't.

He burst out laughing and shook his head. "That's filth, Chloe, and I'm ashamed to say I dated you." He turned his nose up making me laugh even more. "Come on let's go for the bed so I don't get a numb ass tutoring you."

I grinned and headed over to the bed, sitting cross-legged and munching on my apple as he pulled out his books, paper and pens. He settled himself down on his stomach, flicking through his text book.

"So what is it that you have a problem with?" he asked, skimming through the pages.

I shrugged. "Calculus."

He grinned. "I know that, obviously, but what part of it?"

"Nick, just the whole stupid thing. I just don't get it." I looked at him hopelessly. He sighed and gripped my hand pulling me down next to him; he took my apple out of my hand and threw it in the trash. "Hey, I wasn't done with that!" I whined, pouting.

"Chloe, if we need to go over the whole thing then we need to get started; otherwise we're going to be here all night long," he explained, pushing a pencil and stack of paper in my direction.

Three and a half hours later and I had my forehead pressed against my arms. "I can't do anymore! My eyes hurt, my hand hurts, and my brain hurts!" I whined.

"Come on, you're doing awesome. Just two left to go," Nick prompted, elbowing me in the ribs for the hundredth time.

"Please?" I begged, turning my head and looking at him giving him my puppy dog face.

"You've really had enough?" He sighed, looking a little defeated.

"Oh hell yeah, I can't look at another equation without screaming," I confirmed, nodding enthusiastically.

He frowned but pushed himself up to sitting. "Fine then, let's leave the last two. You can do them after dinner. We still need to go over the homework assignment; we've barely even covered what's been happening in class all week." He looked at me warningly so I let out a long groan of frustration.

"Oh man, seriously? I thought we were nearly done." I wanted to cry. It was actually making sense the way he was explaining it to me, but I just couldn't cope with doing anymore. This was just too much all in one go.

He smiled apologetically. "Nowhere near done. There's a couple of hours left easily."

I sighed. "Thank you so much for doing this for me. You've wasted your whole Saturday to help me, and I really appreciate it." I hugged him tightly. He really was adorable. I was lucky to have him as a friend. I was so glad that we seemed to be able to move back into the friend zone after dating; otherwise I would really miss him.

"You're welcome. Anyway, how about you pay for it now? I'm starving." He scrambled to his feet, taking my hands and pulling me up too.

I laughed and followed him to the kitchen, both of us stretching our muscles as we went. Trevor smirked at us as we walked through the lounge. "Get much studying done?" he asked.

"Yeah, loads actually. We're nowhere near done though," Nick answered, ignoring his dad's obvious disbelief; clearly he didn't think we were studying in there.

"Okay that's good," Trevor replied, taking another sip of his drink. "Hey, Chloe, your shirt's on inside out," he called just as I got to the kitchen door.

I gasped and looked down, mortified that I'd been out in public with my clothes on the wrong way. I could hear Trevor laughing his ass off as I realised my shirt was fine. "Studying… right," he mocked sarcastically, shaking his head and rolling his eyes. I looked at him with wide eyes, squirming with embarrassment as my face seemed like it had burst into flames.

Nick shook his head and grabbed my hand, pulling me the last few steps into the kitchen. "Ignore him."

I blushed even more. "Ignore him? Nick, he thinks we were in there having sex!" I hissed, trying to hide around the corner so Trevor couldn't see me.

Nick shrugged. "A couple of months ago we would have been, that's all he's basing it on. Why the hell are you blushing so hard? You didn't seem to care that he thought we were having sex when we actually were," he said, chuckling.

"Yeah but he didn't know we were then!" I countered.

"Oh he knew, trust me. I got a lecture about safe sex almost every night." He nodded slowly, watching as I digested that information.

I can't believe that whole time we told his dad that we were listening to music, or watching TV, or doing homework when we were dating, that he knew what we were actually doing! Oh God, how am I going to look him in the eye from now on?

"Calm down, Chloe! You're being stupid. We were actually studying just now. You have no reason to be embarrassed." He rolled his eyes and headed to the fridge, pulling out the ground beef and tossing it in my direction. I came back to reality just in time to catch the packet before it hit the ground. "Good catch. Now come on, stick to your end of the bargain and make me some food. I could eat a horse." He rubbed his stomach as if it was hurting.

I laughed. *He is so silly sometimes.* "Right, I guess. Just make sure you tell him after that we weren't doing anything okay?"

He nodded. "Whatever makes you happy."

After dinner we went straight back to studying again. I was so bored I could cry. *How on earth could Will study this at college? He doesn't even strike me as the calculus kind of guy, he's too… fun.* By the time we'd gotten through the homework assignment it was almost midnight and my eyes were stinging from the effort.

"Want to stay here tonight?" Nick offered, shrugging and packing up his books we'd been using.

I smiled. "Sure, if that's all right with your dad." We'd arranged to go out in the morning anyway as he wanted to get a new pair of sneakers, so it seemed silly me going home only to be picked up again in a few hours anyway.

"I'll go ask. He won't mind though, you know that." He shrugged as he headed out of the room. I knew he was right, his dad wouldn't mind at all. Trevor was always easy going like that and adored Nick. He trusted him completely. While we were dating I'd stayed over a few times - though my parents thought I slept in the spare bedroom of course.

I pulled out my cell phone and called my mom to let her know. I knew she'd be awake still, waiting for me to get home. My parents were night owls at the weekends staying up late. Nick came back in while I was still on the phone to my mom and nodded signalling that his dad said yes. He pulled out a T-shirt and threw it into my lap for me to wear. I smiled gratefully and finished talking to my mom.

Once she'd agreed, and I'd assured her that we were just friends, I disconnected the call. I smiled at Nick. "Thanks, you know I'm keeping this though, right?" I asked, waving the T-shirt at him. I loved to wear a T-shirt to bed and the couple that he'd left at my house we getting a little worn out now. He sighed and took the shirt from my hands, pulling out a different one and handing that to me instead. "What's wrong with that one?" I asked, laughing.

"That's my lucky shirt. I can't give that away, it helps me get girls." He smirked at me.

I laughed and looked at it as he folded it and stuffed it into a drawer. "Weren't you wearing that shirt when you asked me out?" I asked curiously. He was definitely wearing sky blue that day, I remembered specifically because that was the first time I ever looked at him as anything other than a friend. It was sort of engrained in my memory.

He grinned. "Yep. Lucky T-shirt," he confirmed.

I shook my head and walked to his bathroom to get changed. When I went back into his room he was making up a bed on the floor with spare sheets and pillows. I smiled guiltily because he was planning on sleeping on the floor in his own house. I knew he wouldn't let me sleep on the floor - that just wasn't his style.

"You can sleep in bed with me if you want, I trust you," I offered, laughing as I climbed into his cold bed.

He frowned uncomfortably. "Umm... won't that be a little weird?"

I shrugged. "Only if we make it weird. It's not like anything's going to happen, we're just sharing a bed that's all. I share a bed with Amy all the time," I said casually. I knew it was different but I didn't want him to sleep on the floor. I was completely fine with it; it was just sleeping after all.

"It's a little different with two girls sharing a bed," he mumbled, picking up his pillow from the floor still looking a little undecided.

"I don't mind. If you think it's weird then I'll sleep on the floor."

He sighed and threw his pillow at me. I giggled as it hit me in the face. "Okay fine, but don't grope me in the night," he teased, looking at me warningly.

I grinned. "I'll try my hardest not to."

He laughed and went to turn out the light; I settled down into the bed, hugging myself against the cool night. I felt the bed dip and knew he was in, but he was staying on the other side, not making any moves to come near me, just like I knew he wouldn't. He always was adorable like that, not like most seventeen year old hormonal boys would be if they were in a bed with a girl.

I was shivering lightly so I scooted closer to him, pressing against his side and using his body heat to warm myself up. He laughed. "I thought we agreed on no groping," he said playfully. I laughed and pressed my cold nose against his shoulder. "You cold?" he asked, turning and lifting his arm so I could snuggle closer against him.

"Yeah," I mumbled.

He wrapped his arm around me and hugged me close to his body. I was warming up now so I started to get comfy.

"Chloe?" he whispered after a couple of minutes.

"Yeah?"

"It's the anniversary of my mom's death next week..." he trailed off, his voice wavering with sadness.

I hugged him tightly. I already knew that but I didn't want to bring it up unless he did. I didn't want to upset him. His whole body was tense and stiff. "I know it is," I said quietly.

"I was wondering if, when I got to the cemetery, whether you would come with me?" he asked hopefully.

84

I smiled sadly. Nick hated to go to the cemetery. He got really upset there so he only went on the anniversary of her passing, or on her birthday. Each time I had gone with him and held him after while he cried. "Of course I will," I whispered. I felt a tear fall down my cheek. It upset me to think of him upset, it was heartbreaking to see this adorable boy in pain like that, but I did it because he needed me. I was the only one he ever really opened up to about his mom. He put on a tough act to everyone else that he was okay and unaffected, even to his dad.

"Thanks," he mumbled.

"You don't need to thank me. I'm here for you, you know that." I hugged him tighter and tried desperately not to cry as I heard him getting upset. His body trembled lightly as he cried silently in my arms. "Shh, it's okay," I cooed, not knowing what else to say.

Three years had passed since she died, but he still missed her like crazy. I'd always wished that I'd met her before she died. Judging by the way that Nick and his dad talked about her, she was a truly amazing woman. He fell asleep after a little while and I closed my eyes needing sleep too.

Chapter Eleven

In the morning I decided I needed to stop being upset over Will, after all we hadn't even dated for that long. I felt stupid being so upset over something so trivial after seeing Nick cry over his mother. That was real grief, that was something worth being upset over, not a relationship that barely even started. There was nothing I could do about Will now, sure I would love to see him again and have him kiss and hold me. I would be lying if I said I didn't want him to tell me he was wrong and that we could be together. Before all of this happened I was crazy about him, and could see myself falling harder and harder for him. If things had carried on going the way they were he would have been the love of my life, I could tell, but it was over now and I needed to stop being so hung up about it. It would be hard seeing him every day, but I needed to try and distance myself from him a little and start looking at him as just my teacher.

As Amy pulled her car into the parking lot on Monday morning I felt a lot more positive than I had done for the last week. The lunchtime detentions were over, so it was just his class I would have to deal with, but even then I decided to focus on the work instead of swooning over him. The anniversary of Nick's mom's death had kind of put a fresh reality on the situation for me and made my problems seem smaller somehow.

I followed Amy up the hallway and we stopped outside our lockers, grabbing books for the morning. Out of nowhere someone grabbed me from behind. My heart stuttered and I squealed from shock, jumping a mile into the air. I turned around to see Nick laughing.

"You're hilarious," I muttered, hitting him in the stomach with my notebook.

He grinned and threw his arm around my shoulder. "Sorry, couldn't resist."

I glanced at his feet to see he was wearing his new sneakers that we chose yesterday. "They fit okay?" I asked, nodding down at them.

It had been fun yesterday. Nick was so easy to be around, and even though I woke up lying all over him in the morning that still hadn't made

86

anything awkward between us. I silently wished I could just feel something more for him, but I just didn't. There was no spark there. I loved Nick dearly, but just not in the right way, not like a girlfriend should. I wasn't sure I ever did. I thought I loved him like that at the time, but after being with Will and knowing what it feels like to be in that kind of relationship, it made what Nick and I used to have seem immature and just a bit of fun.

He nodded. "Yep," he confirmed. "So I have a couple of practices after school this week, but I can fit in tutoring on Wednesday and Thursday." He cocked his head to the side.

"Sure awesome." I grinned.

The bell rang so he pulled away from me. "I'll see you guys at lunch," he called as he headed in the opposite direction to where mine and Amy's first class was.

As he ran off I looked up to see Will watching me. A frown lined his forehead. I grabbed my last book and walked with Amy towards gym. As we passed Will I smiled, trying to be polite. "Good morning, Mr Morris," I greeted, trying to sound confident even though my stomach had butterflies.

He shifted uncomfortably on his feet. "Good morning, girls. Did you have a good weekend?" He smiled, but it seemed forced to me, not like the easy smiles that usually graced his face.

Amy stopped next to him, which meant that I had to stop too. He looked incredibly handsome today in his jeans and pale blue sweater. His cologne filled my lungs making my heart rate increase. *Jeez, he smells good enough to eat! Wow, pretending I'm okay is harder than I thought.*

"It was okay, nothing special," Amy answered, shrugging.

Will turned his attention onto me. "And you, Miss Henderson? How was the date on Friday night with the ex's brother?" His questioning grey eyes bore into mine.

"It wasn't a date," I clarified. "But it was good thanks." I tried not to get angry again. The last time I'd seen him was in the parking lot Friday night and he'd been glaring and angry at Sam.

"How do you know it was her ex's brother?" Amy asked suddenly.

Will smirked at her. "If I remember correctly you said so. Something about getting over her ex by jumping his brother."

She laughed sheepishly. "Yeah that's not Chloe's style." She elbowed me playfully in the ribs. "Even if he was hot as hell," she added, winking at me.

I frowned and gripped Amy's hand, intending to pull her away. "Enough talking about my non-existent sex life. Let's get to class before we're late."

"Miss Henderson, do you think I could have a word at lunchtime? After you've eaten is fine," Will called as we walked away.

I sighed and nodded. "Sure thing." *Great, another lecture about not dating his brother. Just what I need.*

The morning passed quickly. I even managed to get through a whole gym class without injuring myself. When the lunch bell rang I headed to the cafeteria

87

grabbing a tuna sandwich and looking through the drinks trying to find a bottle of orange juice, but there wasn't any. I frowned and grabbed apple juice instead, pouting as I got to the cash register to pay.

After I'd paid I turned around, only to come face to face with Will. He looked down at my tray and frowned. "I thought you liked orange juice," he murmured.

I shrugged. "I do but they ran out."

He smiled and rolled his eyes. "Here, Cutie." He put his bottle of orange juice on my tray and took my apple instead. He smiled and turned to walk off without saying anything else leaving me watching him walk away in a state of shock.

Cutie? What the heck is that about? Why did he call me that? All week he's been adamantly calling me Miss Henderson! Darn, that guy is confusing as hell sometimes. Maybe I should ask him when I go to talk to him. I sighed as I plopped down at the table with my friends. I tried my hardest to listen to what they were talking about, but my stupid mind kept wandering back to Will even though I didn't want it to.

I hardly ate anything, just ripped my sandwich up and prodded it a little. I frowned. *I guess I can't put it off any longer. Time to get another lecture about Sam.* I sighed and put all of my ripped up sandwich onto my tray. "Guys, I better go see what Mr Morris wants."

Amy waggled her eyebrows at me. "Maybe he wants to lock you in his little office and take advantage of you," she teased.

I laughed incredulously. *The chances of that happening are pretty slim.* "You never know," I joked, rolling my eyes. I threw my food in the trash and headed to his classroom. I actually felt a little nervous. I didn't want to argue with him again, but I knew he was going to bring up Sam and what happened on Friday after school.

He was sitting at his desk, writing, when I got there. I knocked on the door and his head snapped up to look at me.

"Hey." He smiled, a nice smile too, one of the ones I used to get from him. *Why is he doing this to me? This morning I decide to make a real effort to let him go and then he starts smiling at me and calling me Cutie again? Life's just not fair.*

"Hey, you wanted to see me?" I looked around uncomfortably.

He nodded. "Yeah. Close the door." He frowned and sat back in his chair.

I sighed. *I knew this was going to be some sort of lecture!* I closed the door and walked cautiously over to his desk, waiting for him to shout at me or order me to stay away from Sam.

He frowned, seeming to look anywhere but me as he spoke, "I just wanted to apologise about what I did on Friday with Sam. I shouldn't have done that, and I'm really sorry."

Wait, he's apologising for it? That's sweet. "Why did you do it then?" I asked, confused. It had been bugging me all weekend. Will was a really nice guy so I couldn't fathom why he had started suddenly acting like a jerk all the time.

He sighed and shook his head. "No reason. I just kind of freaked out a little because I know what Sam's like. I don't think a girl like you should be mixing with someone like him."

I sat on the corner of his desk and looked at the ceiling. "A girl like me?"

"Yeah innocent, sweet, adorable. You're too good for the likes of Sam. He uses girls, and I don't want that to happen to you," he said quietly. His leg accidentally brushed against mine, and I felt excitement bubble up inside at how close he was.

"I'm not innocent." I smiled teasingly.

He laughed. "Oh I know that." He smirked at me knowingly. I smiled and blushed as thoughts of just how much he knew about that bombarded my brain. "Blushing again, that's too cute." He shook his head, his face soft and tender as he looked at me.

I didn't know what to say so I said nothing. I just sat there looking at him. His beautiful grey eyes burnt into mine; I wanted to kiss him so much that I could barely keep myself sitting still.

He sighed and looked away. "So how's the tutoring going?" he asked, obviously wanting to change the subject from our previous sexual habits.

I shrugged. "Yeah good actually, I think I should be okay. Nick's gonna tutor me twice a week."

"That's good. If you need any more help or anything then I can run through a few things, but we'll have to do it at the library at lunchtimes or something." He frowned looking a little annoyed about something.

"Why in the library?"

"Because I don't like being alone with you." He stood up, collecting all of his papers up roughly.

He doesn't like being alone with me? "Why not?" I questioned.

He sighed and looked at me like I was stupid. "You have to ask?" he snapped sarcastically.

The hair on the back of my neck bristled at his tone. "Obviously, otherwise I wouldn't have done!" I snapped back.

He sighed dramatically. "Forget it. Just go enjoy the rest of your free time before the bell rings. I've got to get this stuff written up on the board anyway." He shrugged and headed over to the electronic board behind his desk, grabbing a pen and starting to write out some sort of equation that looked slightly similar to something Nick and I had been working on.

I refused to leave it like that though. This was the first time we'd talked properly, and I wanted some answers. I deserved some answers. I was fed up with wondering what went on in the stupid guy's head. "Why don't you like being alone with me?" I inquired, gripping his arm and pulling gently, trying to get him to look at me again.

He span around so quickly that it made me jump. His arm wrapped around my waist as he moved me so that my back was pressed against the board. He pressed his body against mine; his face was so close to mine that I actually whimpered. His breath was blowing across my lips making my mouth water. I could barely breathe.

His hand came up to cup the side of my face as he slowly inched his face towards mine. *Oh my God, he's going to kiss me!* Excitement bubbled up making my stomach flutter.

"This is why," he mumbled. His mouth was so close that his lips brushed against mine as he spoke. I gasped and closed my eyes, so excited I actually thought it would kill me. Suddenly the pressure and warmth of his body was gone. I forced opened my eyes, confused as to what had happened. Will was a step away from me with his hands gripped in his hair. He had a pained, angry look on his face. "You need to go."

"Why?" I whispered a little hurt. I didn't want to go. He was so close, and I needed him.

"Because I need you to go. I have things to do." His tone was firm and final as he marched over to the classroom door and wrenched it open. He didn't even look at me as he silently waited for me to leave.

I felt my eyes stinging with tears again so I stomped out of his classroom. *Stupid asshole getting me all excited then disappointing me like that. I really need to let him go and just stop thinking about him like that. He isn't the hottest, most thoughtful guy I've ever met. Hmm, maybe if I keep telling myself that I'll actually start to believe it.*

Throughout the rest of my afternoon classes all I could think about was Will. 'This is why' he'd said. Did that mean because he wanted to kiss me, or because he knew how I felt about him and he didn't want to encourage me? I couldn't keep my mind off of how close he was and how his soft lips had brushed against mine ever so lightly. My mind wandered to kisses that we'd shared, and how he tasted. I sighed and shook my head, trying to concentrate on what the Spanish teacher was saying and the assignment I was supposed to be working on right now, but it was just pointless. My stupid traitorous brain refused to focus on anything other than Will.

When the bell rang signalling the end of class I groaned. I didn't want to see him again. Not with everybody around anyway, on our own I would love to talk to him and make him tell me what the hell he meant by grabbing me like that. Could he still want to be with me even though I was a student? Was that what he meant?

"Chloe, are you coming or not?" Amy laughed, knocking my elbow that was propping my head up. My head dropped down quickly. I just managed to catch myself before my chin collided with the desk. She laughed hysterically and shook her head. "Love sick Chloe is so funny."

I rolled my eyes in exasperation. "Come on then, let's go test and see if Nick's tutoring skills are worth me cooking for him." I linked my arm through hers, and we walked slowly to class.

"So nothing's going on between you two? Just friends?" she clarified, looking at me curiously.

"Just friends," I confirmed.

She sighed, looking at me sadly. "That's a shame because he was always so sweet to you."

"I know he was, but it just wasn't working out and I couldn't keep leading him on knowing that," I admitted. Amy and I had talked about it a lot before I broke it off with Nick. She didn't think I should have broken up with him and said that sometimes love grows. She thought that I should have just carried on dating him and that I would have fallen for him eventually. I wouldn't have been able to do that to him though. Nick was already crazy about me, and staying with him on the off chance of falling for him wouldn't have been fair on him at all. He deserved better than that.

"So what about you? Spoke to Ryan yet?" I asked, knowing that if I brought up her long-term crush she would go off on one talking about him and would completely change the subject from my love life.

She sighed dreamily. "No not yet. Did you see him this morning? Wow he looks so hot in blue. I think blue's his colour." She fanned her face, laughing.

I laughed and rolled my eyes. "I thought you said he suited black best."

She grinned. "He did, yesterday. I must admit the boy looks good in every colour. Whatever colour he's wearing is always my favourite for the day."

Amy had been crazy about Ryan Everett since first grade but had never even spoken to him once. To top it all off, whenever he was around she seemed to melt into a quivering puddle at his feet and made herself look like an idiot somehow.

"No one looks good in every colour, you're just bias," I said, rolling my eyes. *Well actually, come to think of it, I'm yet to see Will in a colour that doesn't suit him.*

I pulled her through the door of the classroom and scanned the room. We were a little later than normal but Will wasn't there yet. "Come on let's get a seat." I looked around and spotted two together, but they were at the front again. *Damn it, I don't want to sit at the front of his class every day! Why oh why does the Spanish block have to be on the other side of the school so all the good seats are taken by the time I get here?*

"There's two," Amy chirped, pulling us to the front row.

I sat down and pulled my books out, praying for this hour to pass without a hitch. I was really hoping that all of the time Nick and I spent studying on Saturday would pay off, and I at least would vaguely understand what was going on today.

Will strutted in a couple of minutes later. I felt my face immediately start to heat up as I remember how close he'd gotten to me at lunchtime. He put his laptop down on the table and looked up at the class. As his eyes met mine I saw him smirk. *Probably amused that I'm blushing yet again no doubt.*

"Right then, class, I want you all to partner up today with the person sitting next to you and we're going to be doing a project on pressure and how math can be used to accurately predict the outcomes of certain situations, even scientific ones. Math isn't just numbers, it can be used as the basis of a lot of things in life," he said, grinning happily. He obviously enjoyed this kind of thing.

I groaned quietly as he started talking about making a rocket from an empty soda bottle and balloons and stuff. He ran through how to work out the exact formula for the amount of pressure per square inch that would make the bottle soar into the air and land on the target. Each pair would be given certain variations of it, like a longer or shorter distance the bottle had to travel, so each formula would be different.

Apparently if we did well with this it would actually count as part of a science project too, so we wouldn't be getting homework from science for the week while we were doing this. I sat there in silence, feeling my heart sink. It didn't make sense at all, and I had a feeling I would be calling on Nick a lot over the next week.

I looked at Amy helplessly, but she shook her head signalling she didn't get it either. It would be no use us teaming up, because it would be like the blind leading the blind. I looked to my other side and cringed. *Erika freaking Dennison. Wow, could life suck any more than this exact moment?*

"You have a couple of lessons to work on it. At the end of the week I want you to present your findings to the class and how you came to that equation. We'll even do practical demonstrations outside," Will gushed, rubbing his hands together happily. I groaned out loud this time. *Well, my stupid ass question as to whether life could get any worse has just been answered, and the answer is heck yeah it freaking can.*

"You and me then, ice princess," Erika said, sneering at me hatefully as Amy paired up with Jessica on her other side. That was a nice pairing for her. Jessica was a bit of a geek, but genuinely nice with it, so they would at least have fun whilst trying to work this out.

"Awesome, can't wait," I lied forcing friendliness. *Hopefully if I try, really, really try to be nice to her, then she'll be nice back.*

"Just don't bother talking to me, I know you suck at this subject so I'll do the project and you can stand with me at the presentation and look pretty. Oh wait, I forgot you won't be able to do that, you'd have to actually be pretty for that job. Hmm, I guess I'll have to do that part too," she mocked, looking me over and turning her nose up.

My hand instinctively clenched into a fist. I was a split second from ramming it into her face when Will walked over. "Erika, I need you to help Martin." He nodded towards the back of the class where Martin was sitting on his own. *Wow, poor Martin!* Immediately, Erika stood up and grabbed her books before moving next to him. She looked more than a little relieved not to be working with me.

I looked around quickly for someone else, but everyone was already partnered up. "Wait, but then I won't have a partner," I noted, panicking because I had no clue as to where to start with this assignment at all.

"I'll help you, Miss Henderson." Will smiled kindly. *What the hell? What was all that, 'I don't like to be alone with you' crap about then? He's sending my partner away so I can partner with him?* "Tricia Marshall's off today so when she comes back you can have her as your partner; I'll just be helping you today," Will added, shrugging like it was no big deal.

I nodded breathlessly. I was grateful that I wouldn't have to work with Erika, but at the same time, I would probably rather work with her than with him. He made it so damn hard to be around him sometimes with his cocky good looks and his fun personality. *Wow this is going to be a fun hour... not!*

Chapter Twelve

"Let's go collect our things then, unless you'd rather look at the theorem first?" Will inquired, raising one eyebrow as he sat in Erika's seat.

"Can't you just tell me the equation?" I countered, pouting.

He laughed and shook his head. "I could, but then you wouldn't learn, so what's the point in that?"

"Well where's the point in learning what pressure makes a soda bottle fly up in the air anyway? I can hardly use this in real life; what the hell kind of occupation am I going to have that requires me to know this codswallop?" I ranted.

He laughed quietly. "You're way too funny when you're agitated, but at least you're not blushing." He raised one eyebrow and smirked at me - which of course immediately made me blush. "Oh there it is." He laughed before pushing himself out of the seat and heading to the front table to collect all of the equipment we would need to do the experiment.

The hour passed pretty quickly, and it was actually quite fun. Will was joking around and actually did a lot of it for me which I was grateful for. I watched him taping it together and adding the liquid, measuring it all out precisely, talking about the pressure inside the bottle and how the compressed air would build up. He looked like he was enjoying himself as he jotted down numbers and letters with a small smile on his face. *He looks so freaking hot right now!*

"Okay, come and do this bit." He motioned for me to take the bottle. I took it hesitantly not really wanting to do anything, I was happy just letting him do it all, but I guess I needed to have some sort of input. "Okay now I want you to pour this in slowly, then, when I say, you're going to get the lid on fast. The two substances will start to react together immediately so you need to be quick with the lid." He smirked at me as he stood behind me.

"React immediately what does that mean?" I asked as I started to pour the white powder which he said was bicarbonate of soda into the foul smelling yellowish-brown liquid already in the bottle. "What's in here anyway?" I asked, turning my nose up. It looked a little like urine.

"Vinegar," he answered. I nodded and poured the rest of the powder in all in one go instead of slow like he said. "Better get the lid on." Will laughed behind me as it started to fizz rapidly.

"Oh crud, what's it doing?" I asked as I grabbed for the lid… but I wasn't quick enough.

Will laughed and grabbed for the bottle putting his hand over the top just as the bottle looked like it exploded. It was spraying foul smelling yellowish foam all over the place. It looked a little like a champagne bottle when you shake it up. I screamed as it sprayed all over my shirt and jeans. People were yelping and hiding under their desks, laughing as the bottle continued to spray. It was going everywhere; it went in my mouth and wet my hair. I span around and buried my face in Will's chest as it spayed my back. I could hear him laughing his ass off, and I couldn't help but laugh too.

When it finally stopped I pulled away from the safety of his body. My was hair dripping and smelt foul. Will was soaked too. He smirked at me, rolling his eyes. "What part of 'pour this in slow' did you not understand, Miss Henderson?"

I looked back at the desk and winced. Everything was soaked, the notes I'd been taking as he worked, the floor, there was even foam on the ceiling. I looked down at myself and flicked the wet off of my hands as it dripped from my fingertips. I looked like I'd just stepped out of a vinegar foam party.

"Shit. I'm so sorry," I mumbled, looking back at him apologetically.

He ran a hand through his hair, ruffling it up and flicking drops of vinegar off of it. He laughed sheepishly. "I did that when I was learning this too, and watch your language." He smirked at me teasingly making me laugh.

The bell rang so he looked back at the class who were all laughing and grabbing their bags, preparing to leave. "Guys, make sure you put your names on your rockets and put them to one side. You'll be working on them again tomorrow. Maybe it's a good idea for people working near Miss Henderson to bring a change of clothes," Will joked, nudging me with his elbow before walking off to the little room off of his classroom.

I rolled my eyes at his insult. Amy came over then, brushing foam from her arm. "I'm so glad I moved over slightly so it only got on my arm because damn you smell!" She laughed, turning her nose up at me.

I put my hand to my nose and smelled it wincing as the acrid smell seemed to burn the inside of my nose. *Wow she's right. Gross.* "I guess I'm not getting a ride in your car," I mused, but looked at her hopefully.

She rolled her eyes. "I wouldn't be much of a best friend if I left you all wet and stranded, now would I?"

I smiled gratefully, but Will stepped forward and threw a cloth at me. "Miss Henderson, you can stay and help me clean up your mess. The school cleaners won't touch this." He waved his hand at the puddles and foam all over the place.

"Okay." I frowned and turned to Amy. "I'll walk, don't wait for me."

"I can drive you home if you want," Will offered as he wiped over the desk, sopping up the mess I'd made.

Amy grinned. "Awesome. I have to babysit again right after school so I don't have time to wait." I noticed with some measure of dissatisfaction that Amy was raking her eyes over Will's body. I frowned, glancing in his direction to see that his T-shirt was wet and was sticking to his chest a little, showing of his muscles. "I'll see you tomorrow then, Chloe. Goodbye, Mr Morris," Amy called, waving over her shoulder as she made a swift exit.

"See you tomorrow, Miss Clarke," he replied absentmindedly, still wiping the foam up.

I turned back to the table and looked at Will apologetically. "You really did this when you were doing this experiment?" I asked curiously.

He nodded. A mischievous smile stretched slowly across his face. "Yeah, but mine was done on purpose, and I aimed the bottle towards the schools cheerleaders."

I giggled. "Pervert." That was a typical Will comment. "Did you know that would happen to me?"

He grinned and nodded. "Hell yeah, I said pour it slow and get the lid ready. I knew you wouldn't have the patience to pour it slow. Why do you think I hid behind you?" he teased, raising one eyebrow at me.

I laughed and shook my head. "Jerk."

He made a little bow as if it was a compliment and laughed. "You got five bucks?" he asked suddenly, digging in his pocket.

I shook my head. I didn't have any money on me today. "No, why?"

"There's bound to be a freshman we could pay to do this," he joked.

I burst out laughing and went to the sink in his little room off of the classroom and rinsed my cloth out so I could carry on with the clean-up. It took about twenty minutes to get everything foam free, but even then the whole room smelt like vinegar.

We cleaned in silence; I stole little glances at his body as he wiped the table. I watched the way his bicep flexed and tensed, the way his T-shirt rode up a little, exposing his stomach as he stood on the desk and reached up to wipe the mess off of the ceiling. I felt my breath catch in my throat as I imagined running my tongue across his sculpted abs. I was so lost in my own world that I didn't even realise I was just standing there stock-still, staring at him like a complete moron.

"Chloe, you can't look at me like that," Will muttered, looking like he was in pain as he jumped off of the table landing, gracefully on the balls of his feet.

I blushed but didn't look away from him, I couldn't. I wanted him so much. "Why not?" I challenged, and then immediately felt stupid.

He frowned. "Because I'm your teacher and you're a minor. We need to forget what happened and just behave like teacher and student."

"What if the student has a crush on her teacher?" I countered, biting my lip as my hormones seemed to take over my mouth. *Whoops, why the heck did I say that?*

"Well then the student needs to keep it to herself." He shook his head and strutted into the little room off next to his classroom.

I sighed and sat on the edge of the desk as rejection washed over me again. *Why did I put myself in that situation, why did I just say that? Do I really like to feel rejected? Maybe I'm a masochist and I just like the pain of being humiliated.*

He came out a couple of minutes later in a clean and dry T-shirt. He threw me a sweater. I smiled gratefully. I chewed on my lip as I looked down at myself, I was soaked through, I couldn't just put it over the top because I'd ruin his sweater. I put it down on the desk and gripped the bottom of my shirt, pulling it off over my head so I was just in my bra. When I looked up at Will he was just standing there watching me. A look of longing was clear across his face that made my body tingle all over and my stomach get fluttery.

I smiled wickedly. "Will, you can't look at me like that," I teased, using his words that he'd said to me.

He nodded slowly, not taking his eyes off of my body. "I know."

I grinned and pulled the sweater down over my head, interrupting his ogling. I felt a little better knowing that it wasn't just me that felt this attraction. It didn't even matter that his attraction to me was just sexual, and not the connection that I felt to him. I liked that he liked my body, even if that was all he liked about me.

He sighed deeply and looked away. "Come on then I'll drive you home." He turned and walked to the door. I grabbed my bag and my ruined notes and followed behind him. As I got to his side he looked down at my notes and smiled. "You going to be able to read them?"

I shrugged. "I don't know, hopefully they'll dry okay, and I can just copy them out onto better smelling paper." I turned my nose up at the strong smell of vinegar following us both down the hallway.

He shrugged. "If you can't read them then I can help you write some more."

"In the library at lunchtime, right?" I teased, giggling.

"Yeah I think that's a good idea." He grinned sheepishly.

I followed him out to his car and looked in with a smile on my face. It was a mess again. *Looks like the keeping the car clean thing only lasted while we were dating, and he's now back to his old habits.* "Nice job with the car, slob."

He laughed. "You want to walk home, or are you done insulting my cleaning skills?" He smirked at me challengingly.

"I'm done with the insults; I don't want to walk home. Want me to take off my jeans so I don't ruin your seat?" I offered, looking down at my still damp jeans.

He shook his head quickly. "No, definitely leave the jeans on. It's fine, just get in."

He walked round to his side as I grabbed the couple of soda cans from my seat and put them on the floor along with the papers and candy wrappers. I threw my bag in the back and sat down looking at the mess on the floor, laughing in disbelief.

"Will, how on earth do you eat all of this junk and still stay in shape?" I asked, motioning to the floor. There was easily ten different empty candy wrappers casually discarded there.

He shrugged nonchalantly. "I have a lot of time on my hands so I work out a lot. I'm still running the classes at the ski slope so that's kind of a workout in itself too."

I smiled at that. "Start any snowball fights lately?" I asked. I grinned as I remembered our first proper date. *Still one of the best nights of my life.*

He laughed. "No, there are no rebel girls there that like getting hit with snow. Besides, I have to throw out people who start snow fights, it's against company rules."

"So if I came by there one night while you were working, and started a snow war, would I get thrown out?" I questioned, smirking at him.

He grinned. "No, but you may get your ass handed to you."

I laughed at the challenge in his voice. *If my memory serves me correctly, Will enjoyed that night almost as much as I did. Well, I thought at the time he did anyway.* "Maybe I will." I waggled my eyebrows at him.

We were almost at my house now, and I was a little disappointed. This was the first time he'd been like this with me since he broke it off. I didn't want it to end yet. I'd had a week without him, and I didn't want another one. Wasn't up to me though - he was the one that broke up with me, not the other way around, so I had no choice in the matter, much to my disappointment.

He pulled up outside my house and stopped the engine, turning to face me. He had that slightly pained face on again. *Does he not want this time to end either? Or is that just wishful thinking on my part?*

He leant through the gap in the seats, fumbling in the back for my bag. As he straightened himself up he was a lot closer to me because of how he was leaning. His eyes were locked onto mine making my whole body burn with excitement. It suddenly felt like someone had set a hundred butterflies loose in my stomach. His breath was blowing across my face making my lips tingle with the need for his to be pressed against mine.

He didn't move away, he just stayed there looking at me, as I was him. *Oh, Will, please kiss me.* It didn't matter to me that he was a teacher, or that I was a minor. When something is right you just feel it - and I definitely felt it, my whole body felt it. He was the one for me. The one that would drive me crazy and make me laugh even when I was sad. He was the one I wanted to hold me when I cried, the one I wanted to call when I had happy news. He was just the one.

I could barely breathe. I wanted to throw my arms around his neck and crush my lips against his. I wanted him to hold me and tell me that we'd work something out, that he'd figure it out because he wanted me as much as I wanted him.

He was looking at me softly, tenderly, just like he used to look at me. I could feel my heart crashing in my chest as his eyes flicked down to my lips for a split second before returning to mine. His mesmerising grey eyes trapped me in his intense gaze as he slowly started to inch his face closer to mine. I smiled and moved forward too.

Just as our lips were an inch apart my cell phone rang. Will jumped back quickly into his own seat, almost pressing against the door in a bid to be further away from me. I frowned as my heart sank down to my toes. *So near but yet so far.* His face hardened again and I knew the moment was over. I wouldn't get another chance because he didn't want me. That was just the sexual tension sparking up. That was all I was to him, something fun he could amuse himself with and get his jollies with.

"You should go inside and answer that." He turned back to the windshield and started the car before gripping the steering wheel so tightly his knuckles were white.

I sighed and nodded. I wouldn't let this upset me again. I needed to stick to the realisation I'd had over the weekend - worse things happen to people all the time and they cope with it. Our breakup wasn't a tragedy, it was just something unfortunate, but it was part of life. Heartbreak was something you got over in time. I just prayed that I could get over him quickly because this pain was almost unbearable.

"Thanks for the ride." I grabbed my bag and climbed out of the car not looking at his stupid handsome face again as I headed inside. I didn't bother to answer my cell, I'd call them back whoever it was. I didn't want to speak to the person who ruined my kiss with Will. Technically it wasn't their fault, but I couldn't help but be a little annoyed with whoever it was.

My parents weren't home so I went straight upstairs and headed into the shower to wash off the vinegar smell. As I stood under the spray I replayed the moment in the car. *Would he have kissed me if my cell phone hadn't rung? If he had kissed me would that mean that we could be together, or would he have just brushed it off as a mistake afterwards? Maybe he would have kissed me and realised that I was the one he wanted too, and he would have asked me for another shot.* I stood under the water for a good half an hour just playing out 'what might have been' in my head.

Chapter Thirteen

I hardly slept that night. All I could think of was how close his lips had gotten to mine and how his mouth had twisted into that sexy little smile that seemed like it was just for me. I'd never seen him smile like that at anyone else. That had to mean something, didn't it? Over the course of my sleepless night I had somehow convinced myself that it *had* to mean something. He felt more than just a sexual attraction to me, he had to.

I decided to stick to the decision I'd made over the weekend - worst things happened all over the world every minute of every day, and I shouldn't let this upset me anymore. But at the same time I decided I needed to try and work through it. If he felt anything for me then it was worth a shot. I needed to talk to him and see exactly what was going on in that sexy head of his. If he told me that it was just a sexual attraction then I would let it go and move on, if he wanted me for more than that then we'd have to work something out. I refused to be confused any longer. He either needed to admit it or leave it, that was final. I knew I wouldn't be able to stop caring about him overnight, but if he didn't want me then I would try my hardest to forget him.

The next morning after hardly sleeping and contemplating my options in my head; I felt and looked awful. No amount of make-up was going to cover up the dark circles I had under my eyes so I didn't even bother trying to disguise them. I pulled on the first clothes I saw in my closet, and went downstairs to wait for Amy to come and pick me up.

When I heard her horn, I walked as slow as possible to the car. I knew she'd give me the third degree about letting Will go and moving on, the same as she did every morning. I held my breath as I climbed in. I was right, the fifteen minute drive she was telling me over and over just to date someone else. She was going on and on about Oliver Hawk - apparently she'd heard that he liked me and wanted to take me out. She even suggested that I sleep with Nick again in a bid to help me get over my ass of an ex, those were her exact words. I just smiled and nodded along, not wanting anymore confrontations about it. I couldn't make any firm decisions until I'd spoken to Will.

When we got to school I made up the excuse of needing to go to the office, but instead made my way to his classroom. This was it; once and for all I was going to find out what he meant by that yesterday. He had one chance and one chance only. If he wanted me then he needed to admit it.

Though as I trudged in the direction of his classroom, I started to doubt myself. *What would a guy like Will see in a girl like me anyway? Will is awesome, funny, smart, caring, and when we were together he was the best boyfriend ever. What the hell would I have that would keep him interested in me? Nothing, that's the answer. I'm not good enough for him at all. I'm going to make myself look like a total moron doing this - just like a stupid schoolgirl crushing on her teacher. Wow, I suck!* I wanted to stop walking, but my stupid legs kept taking step after step of their own accord.

I stopped outside his classroom and took a deep breath, trying in vain to settle my nerves and pluck up the courage to go through with this moronic plan. *Be brave, Chloe!* Just as I was about to walk in I heard laughter. I stopped dead in my tracks and sneakily glanced in to see Miss Teller, the drama teacher, standing way too close to Will. She was giggling and flicking her hair over her shoulder as she smiled at him seductively. I couldn't see what he was doing because his back was to me, but no doubt he liked the attention.

Miss Teller was gorgeous and was pretty young for a teacher too; she was probably only about twenty-six or so. Most of the boys in school had a crush on her. Not that I blamed them. She was tall and athletic looking, with long blonde hair, big blue eyes, and a larger than average chest, which she had no problem showing off teasingly in her revealing shirts.

I felt jealously boil up inside as she put her hand on his forearm. "That was funny. You really have made this place interesting, Will," she purred, looking at him through her eyelashes.

"I'm sure this place was plenty interesting before I came along," Will responded, shrugging. I noticed that he didn't move his arm away from her hand. I had the strong urge to rush in there and rip her damn arm off for her.

"You want to meet up at lunchtime and get something to eat offsite today?" she asked, smiling seductively.

Oh God, please say no!

"I can't, I have a lot to do, sorry," he replied.

I breathed a sigh of relief, but deep down I recognised that he hadn't actually turned her down; he'd just said he had a lot of things to do. He hadn't said a flat out 'no thanks, not interested'.

"Oh, okay never mind. You still okay for after school?" she asked, looking at him hopefully.

"Yeah sure, I said so didn't I?"

Oh my gosh, he's seeing her after school? He turned her down for lunch but is going out with her after? Wow, that hurts so much. I felt my heart start to beat faster in my chest. He really was finished with us, and that little scene yesterday was just a mistake. *Damn it, the stupid jerk-face! Is he doing this on purpose to hurt me? Building my hopes up just to crush me again?*

"Great." She smiled.

"Just come meet me here after or something." He shrugged casually.

I suddenly realised that their conversation was probably coming to an end, and I was just standing in the doorway listening. Miss Teller's attention was firmly fixed on Will at the moment, but the minute she turned a bit to the right she'd see me and know I heard their little flirting session.

I moved back around the corner, trying not to listen to anything else. I couldn't hear any more flirting, it was too painful. My whole body hurt where I was so tense.

She walked out of the room and smiled to herself as she sauntered past in her black pencil skirt that showed off her pert behind. Suddenly I felt incredibly underdressed in my jeans and loose fit sweater. All of the guys in the hall smiled at her as she walked past and turned to get a look at her ass.

My hands were shaking a little with both jealousy and shock. *Why the hell am I so surprised about this? Miss Teller is beautiful and actually a really lovely lady too. Why wouldn't he want to date her?* Over the course of the night I had gotten my hopes up for us to be together again. It looked like there was no chance of that now. He'd already moved on to someone better and more suited to him.

The click of a door closing drew my attention. I looked up just as he walked out of his classroom. I didn't have time to get away before he saw me. I clenched my hands into fists, feeling both angry and betrayed. For some reason it felt like he'd cheated on me, even though he hadn't. I wanted to punch him and scream at him in front of everyone so they would know that he made me feel like a cheap piece of meat.

He looked at me shocked for a second before stepping closer to me, concern crossing his face. "You okay? What's happened?" he asked, bending to look at me. His eyes found mine as his warmth and smell surrounded me. My stomach started to ache.

"I'm perfect," I muttered, trying to appear unconcerned, pretending that his little plans with the hot drama teacher didn't bother me in the slightest.

I turned to walk off, but he caught my hand and pulled me to a stop. When he didn't let go of my fist I turned back to look at him curiously. I glanced down at our hands and tried my best to ignore the little thrill that was going through my bloodstream just because he was touching me.

"Are you allowed to grab a student, Mr Morris?" I hissed.

He frowned angrily and let go of my hand quickly. "What's wrong?" His tone was coloured with annoyance because of my comment.

"Why would anything be wrong?" I asked, shifting my heavy bag on my shoulder.

"You look upset, your hands are shaking, and your eyes are doing that little twitching thing they do before you cry," he stated, crossing his arms across his chest making the muscles in his forearms tense. I hated myself for suddenly wishing those arms were wrapped around me. *Focus, Chloe!*

"Twitching thing?" I was a little thrown by his comment; my eyes didn't twitch before I cried.

He nodded, shrugging. "Yeah it always happens right before you start to cry."

"How do you know that?" I asked, feeling stupid and willing my eyes not to twitch and give me away.

"Sad movies." *Wow, he really paid a lot of attention to me when we were going out if he noticed something small like that.* He smiled. I felt my anger melting away so I fought hard to hold onto it. I refused to forget this. He'd hurt me, and I wasn't going to pretend like him moving on so quickly wasn't ripping my heart out.

"Well I'm fine, nothing's wrong. Just tired," I muttered, gazing longingly up the hallway towards the gym, eager to make my escape to my first class.

"You didn't sleep very well?" He flicked his head to get his hair away from his eyes. *Jeez, I love it so much when he does that! Maybe I should ask him to cut his hair a little shorter so he'll stop doing that in front of me.*

I opened my mouth to answer, but the bell rang loudly from above my head. *Oh thank you, God!* "Got to go." I smiled and turned to leave. He didn't stop me this time, and I was grateful. His touch just had an effect on my body and I refused to let him have a hold over me any longer. *Stupid, arrogant, cocky, player teacher!*

The rest of the morning passed slowly. I tried really hard not to think about him. I threw myself into my classes, and every time I thought about him and Miss Teller, I mentally slapped myself and focused harder on what the teachers were saying. I even managed to make it through another gym class without hurting myself which I was amazed about. Maybe it was just mind over matter.

At lunchtime I sat with my group of friends listening to them arrange for us to all go and see a movie on Saturday night. I was definitely up for that. I hadn't really done anything much since Will and I broke up. Apart from the night out with Sam on Friday, I'd just sat around and wallowed.

Oliver plopped down next to me, smiling nervously. "Hey, Olly, good weekend?" I asked, finished the last of my juice.

"Yeah it was good. Yours?" he asked, offering me some of his chips.

I took a couple and shrugged. "Didn't really do much, studying and shopping. Nothing exciting."

"Right, that's good… I mean, not good that you didn't do anything exciting, just good that it was uneventful and…" he trailed off, frowning. He shook his head and looked back at me again. "I was wondering if you wanted to go and do something on Friday night?" he asked, looking really uncomfortable.

Oh no! He's asking me out again? Is this why he was staring at me for the whole of first period? Because he wanted to ask me out again? I gulped when I realised the whole table had gone quiet and were now listening to him ask me out. *Wow, talk about uncomfortable! How can I let him down gently?* I wracked my brain quickly for an excuse before I thought of one. "I can't, I have plans already, sorry." I relaxed. That wasn't a total lie, Sam had suggested we do something Friday, but we had no definite plans. I'd rejected Oliver twice now so he shouldn't ask me out again which would be a lot easier.

"Oh right, okay yeah. That's fine." He frowned, seeming to look anywhere but me.

Suddenly I felt awful. The whole table had just seen him crash and burn. "Maybe you could come to the movies with us on Saturday? We were just arranging something," I suggested, hoping that including him in our planned outing would make him feel a little better somehow.

His whole face lit up and he smiled broadly. "Yeah? I'd like that."

Oh crud, does he think this is a date or something? He does know that I meant it as friends, doesn't he? "There's like eight of us going I think," I added quickly so he would know I meant it in a friendly way.

He nodded still smiling. "Sounds good."

The bell rang so we all made our way to our respective classes; Amy looped her arm through mine and practically skipped along at my side. "Yay, you're going on a date with Olly!" she chirped.

I frowned. It wasn't a date. "Amy, we're all going, it's not a date."

She shrugged. "Seems like a date to me. Maybe you should get him to pick you up then if you have a good time you'll get to be alone with him at the end of the night." She waggled her eyebrows. I rolled my eyes but didn't bother to answer.

A couple of hours later, and it was time for Will's class again. *Please let Tricia be in today, please, please, please.* I repeated it over and over in my head as I made my way to his class, I even crossed my fingers and shoved my hands in my pockets so no one would see them. I didn't want to have to work with him again today, not after this morning; I certainly wouldn't be able to be civil with him today knowing that he had plans with Miss Teller.

"Hey, Chloe," Olly called as Amy and I walked into the classroom. I smiled and he waved us over to his bench where Jessica, Amy's partner, was already sitting. *Oh great, another uncomfortable hour!* Amy sat down next to Jess so I sat the other side of Olly and his partner, leaving an empty seat for Tricia if she had decided to grace us with her presence today.

"Hey, do you know if Tricia's in today?" I asked, looking at her empty seat longingly.

"Yeah I saw her this morning," Olly replied. I felt like a weight had been lifted off of my shoulders because I wouldn't have to work with Will today.

I smiled broadly as Tricia walked in and I resisted the urge to jump out of my chair and hug the life out of her. I waved her over to me excitedly. "Hey, you got stuck with me as a partner, sorry." I patted the empty desk next to me happily.

"I did, what for?" she asked, smiling, looking a little confused as she sat down next to me.

"Stupid calculus slash science project that has no bearing on our lives outside of these walls whatsoever," I replied, shrugging.

She laughed, still seeming bewildered. "Sounds awesome."

Will walked over and smiled at Tricia. "Hi, you're back. Miss Henderson should be able to fill you in on what you missed yesterday but if you two struggle or anything then let me know." He smiled kindly, and Tricia actually looked like she melted into a puddle at his feet as she stared at him dreamily. He put a few sheets of paper down in front of me. "You left your notes here last night, Miss Henderson." Without waiting for an answer, he turned and walked off.

Left my notes. What did that mean? I didn't leave my notes; they're in my bag, probably making all of my books smell like vinegar because I didn't bother to copy them onto fresh paper. I glanced down at the pages that he'd put on my desk to see they were in his writing. I frowned and flicked through them quickly. He'd rewritten everything we did yesterday for me. *Aww, that's so freaking adorable!* I sighed and pushed the notes towards Tricia, deciding that I needed to fill her in about the stupid rocket.

The class was uneventful. Our rocket was half made because of Will yesterday so we didn't need to do much, just work out the amounts of substance that would generate the pressure we needed. We worked on it all class and were pretty much done by the end, mostly thanks to Will's notes that he'd written for me. When he walked past to check on how we were all getting on I smiled at him gratefully. He winked at me and carried on walking past as if nothing had happened. My heart fluttered in my chest. Stupid traitorous heart.

There was about five minutes left until the end of class so Tricia and I were pretending to look busy. We'd done everything we were required to do, so for the rest of the week all we needed to do was work on the presentation which wouldn't be very hard because of Will's detailed notes he'd given me.

Someone knocked on the classroom door and walked in. I groaned internally when I spotted her blonde head. Not one hair was out of place and she looked impeccable and classy even though it was the end of the day. Miss Teller.

Every boy in the class stopped what they were doing to look at her with lustful expressions. She smiled at Will and headed over to him, swaying her hips as she walked. *Jeez, does she do that on purpose or does sexy just come naturally to her?* I felt my jealousy rise again as he smiled at her.

"Hey, you're early," he greeted, nodding at the clock on the wall.

"Yeah I had a free period; I just wanted to let you know that I have to speak to the textile teacher about costumes for the play. I won't be long, but I might be a couple of minutes late. Is that okay?" she asked, pouting, obviously going for vulnerable and needy. *Go away, stupid woman!* I felt my leg twitch, but I forced myself to stay in my seat. What I really wanted to do was go over to her and do the little vinegar explosion thing in her face. That would wipe the seductive smile off of her pretty face...

"Sure, I wouldn't leave without you, don't worry." He smirked at her making her giggle. *Oh my goodness, she actually just giggled! Does this woman have no shame? She's flirting with the teacher, right in front of his class.*

"Great, I'll meet you here then when I'm done." She turned and flicked her hair over her shoulder as she swayed out of the door, leaving all of the boys watching her with their mouths and eyes open wide.

The bell rang. I looked up at Will. He wasn't bothered at all that he'd just done that right in front of me. *It probably hasn't even entered his head that I would be upset over this. How can he go from so thoughtful and adorable one minute; to a complete jerk in the next?*

Olly smiled at me. I decided then that I could use him for a little payback. *Let's see how Will likes having it shoved in his face. It probably wouldn't bother him; he'd already told me that he didn't have feelings for me anyway. Jerk.*

I grabbed the rocket that Tricia and I had on our desk and followed Olly over to the side where we were storing them. Will was standing there moving them all around to make room for them all on the side.

I waited until I was close enough for him to hear before turning to Olly. "Hey, so I was wondering if you'd pick me up on Saturday for the movie?" I asked, smiling sweetly. I felt a little guilty flirting with Olly when he obviously liked me but to be honest he might be able to help me move on just like Amy suggested.

He grinned. "Yeah sure."

"Great. Maybe we could grab something to eat before we meet up with everyone else, what do you think?" I suggested, leaning in slightly as I spoke.

His smile got even broader. "I'd like that. Maybe we could go to that Mexican restaurant that just opened."

I laughed and shook my head. "Nah, a Mexican restaurant isn't a good first date." I shrugged, knowing that Will was listening from where he was. His shoulders were stiff, and he'd moved the same rocket four times already. He had his back to me and I kind of wished I could see his face to see what he thought about it.

"Maybe we could go there another time then," Olly replied, grinning boyishly.

I laughed and rolled my eyes. "And who said I'd want to go out with you again? Maybe your date will suck," I teased.

"I hope she does." He waggled his eyebrows suggestively.

I suppressed a groan. *Is he kidding me right now? Sexual flirting like that just doesn't work at all.*

I opened my mouth about to make some witty remark about him counting his chickens or something, but Will span around with a face like thunder and almost snatched the rocket from my hands. He glared at me angrily. "Maybe you could finish this little discussion outside of my classroom."

I faked shock. "Oh my gosh, I didn't even realise you were there, Mr Morris," I lied, looking at him with wide eyes.

His frown grew more pronounced. "Obviously, otherwise you would have left this little innuendo conversation in the hallway, right?" he retorted sarcastically, crossing his arms over his chest defensively.

106

Wow, pissed off definitely suits him. All that brooding and frowning makes him look super sexy. I desperately tried not to imagine pressing my body against his and running my tongue down the side of his neck, biting on the edge of his jaw just the way he liked so I could hear him moan my name. *Focus, Chloe! Oops, spaced out for a second there!* "Absolutely. I'm sorry, Mr Morris." I looked at him apologetically and tried not to smile at the way his body was tense and alert. He really didn't like to hear me flirting by the looks of it. *Oh well, he started it.* Olly was just smiling sheepishly so I slapped his arm playfully. "You got us in trouble," I scolded, smiling as I glanced towards the desk where Amy was standing there waiting for me with a grin on her face.

Olly grinned. "Sorry, my bad."

I rolled my eyes teasingly, throwing one last smirk in Will's direction as I walked off to pack up my bag. Olly grabbed his bag and headed out of the room with one of his friends, winking at me as he walked past my desk.

Amy giggled as soon as he was out of the room. "I hope my date sucks?" She laughed, shaking her head. "He is so bad at flirting."

I laughed and shoved my books in my bag. "I know, tell me about it. But that was super sexy. Really got to me and made me want to be with him," I joked, rolling my eyes.

She giggled. "I know, who says that to a girl? Epic fail on his part."

"Maybe he's never spoken to a girl before." I shouldered my bag and followed Amy towards the door.

"Miss Henderson, a word please," Will called just as I was about to make my escape.

I sighed and turned back to Will. He was still standing over by the rockets; his easy cocky attitude was totally gone now. He actually looked a little hurt, and I started to feel stupid for doing that and making him feel bad. I turned back to Amy. "I'll meet you by your car."

She nodded and carried on walking out of the room; I stopped and dropped my bag on the nearest desk before turning to Will. *Hmm, maybe I should apologise for that. That was way over the top. But was it though? He dumped me, not the other way around; I shouldn't have to be mindful of his feelings. He's the one that has already arranged a date with the hot teacher; I'm just following his lead and moving on like everyone suggested I should.*

"What the hell was that?" he snapped, frowning angrily.

I took a deep breath; I was just about to apologise when Miss Teller sauntered back into the room, smiling happily. "Hey, Chloe," she greeted as she spotted me.

"Hi. How are you today?" I asked, faking friendliness. I willed myself not to cry as she walked over to Will's side. He smiled at her, still looking tense and angry but obviously trying to hide it.

"I'm good. You're not taking drama this year?" she asked, perching sexily on one of the desks making her skirt rise a little.

"Not this year, unless I can trade for calculus," I suggested, shrugging. *Actually I would trade anything for calculus right now; I honestly never wanted to come to this class again.*

She laughed. "I don't think they do trades."

I didn't want to stand here and listen to them flirting; I looked longingly at the door. "Are we done now, Mr Morris? Can I be excused?" I asked hopefully, knowing he wouldn't want to talk about this with her sitting there.

He looked at me for a few seconds before he sighed and nodded. "Yeah, we're done, you can go."

I practically ran out of the room and down to my locker in a bid to be away from them both. Amy stood there waiting for me; she was watching me expectantly.

Why is she looking at me like that? "What?"

She made a scoffing noise and looked at me like I was stupid. "What did he want? Did you get into trouble or something?"

Eek, what do I say to that? I shook my head. "No he was just offering help in case Tricia and I needed it, because she was off yesterday," I lied. I winced, hating the fact that I was lying to my best friend - but I couldn't tell her the truth because I couldn't let anyone know about Will. I didn't want him in trouble for this.

"That's nice of him. You two seem to be getting on better now, not clashing as much as last week." She shrugged, closing her locker.

"Yeah I guess." I sighed and followed her to the car. *Another day down, only another ten and a half months to go, then I'll leave school and will never have to see Will's handsome face again.*

Chapter Fourteen

The rest of the school week passed without event. Will barely even looked at me except when he needed to in a teacher way, and even that wasn't very often. In a way I was grateful because I didn't want to talk to him. Especially after half of the school had witnessed him pull into the parking lot on Tuesday morning with Miss Teller in the passenger seat of his car.

After going out with him on Monday after school it was pretty obvious that she stayed at his place with him. It honestly made me feel sick but I tried my hardest not to let it affect me, well, I tried not to show that it affected me is more like the truth.

The rumour mill started immediately. Talk of the new hot teacher couple was all around school within minutes. Every time it was mentioned my stomach would start to ache but I worked hard on not showing it. Instead, I flirted with Olly and pretended I was looking forward to seeing him on Saturday.

After school was really busy all week, so that helped to keep my mind off of my calculus teacher. On Wednesday and Thursday I went home with Nick, and we studied. Though to be honest he didn't need to help me too much this week, Will's notes and his help on Monday had made everything pretty clear. It also helped that Tricia happened to like calculus, so she was leading the project during class. So after Nick and I studied for a little while, we watched a movie or something before eating.

Nick was fun to be around. He was totally avoiding the subject of his mom, we both were. The anniversary of her death was Sunday so we were going there early in the morning so he could pay his respects, and then we'd planned to hang out afterwards so I could cheer him up a little and take his mind off of it.

On Friday night I went out for dinner with Sam. It was good; as usual Sam didn't fail to make me laugh with tales of disastrous dates and his all-time best successes. He'd suggested we go out on Saturday next week instead of Friday. A friend of his, one that I had already met through Will, was throwing a party, and Sam wanted me to go with him. He said Amy could go too which I knew she would love to do. So, after making him promise me five times that Will wouldn't be there, I'd eventually agreed to it. It sounded like fun though so the party would probably be good.

Today was Saturday and I was sitting watching the clock tick round way too fast. For the hundredth time I looked at my cell phone, willing it to ring and for it to be Olly cancelling the date or something. *A nasty case of food poisoning would go down a treat right now. Maybe I could call him and tell him I have food poisoning...* When I heard a car pull up outside, I let out a long groan of frustration. He was right on time. Seven pm on the dot, I had to give the boy points for punctuality. I was really going to try on this date. Olly was a nice guy, and he was good-looking too, I was going to give moving on my best effort.

I headed downstairs slowly, letting my dad answer the door. *Maybe he'll scare Olly away for me then I won't even need to go!* I walked up behind my dad who was standing there, glaring. His posture wasn't very welcoming as he blocked the doorway, leaving Olly outside.

"I'm serious, I know you father and if I hear one thing about her being mistreated tonight then I'll be speaking to him before I come looking for you," Dad warned.

Wow, poor Olly, he hasn't even stepped through the door, and he's getting it already. I smiled apologetically as I tapped my dad's arm, letting him know I was there. He turned slightly to look at me, still frowning. He had always been protective of me; I was an only child so he went completely over the top. It was almost funny in an embarrassing as heck kind of way.

"I understand, and I wouldn't even dream of mistreating her, I promise," Olly vowed, looking like he wanted to run away from the door screaming. *Run, please run away.* He didn't run though. My heart sank as my dad waved him inside the house.

"Hey, Olly." I forced a smile and turned to my dad. "We'll be going, Dad, I won't be late," I promised as I grabbed my jacket from the coat rack and headed towards the door quickly before he could hassle Olly anymore.

"Okay, pumpkin, have fun." My dad smiled at me before turning to Olly and giving him one last warning look.

I gripped Olly's arm and almost pushed him out of the door, closing it behind me. He blew out a big breath before turning to me with wide eyes. "Damn, Chloe, your dad's scary!" he mumbled, shaking his head.

I laughed and rolled my eyes. "He's a pussycat, unless you hurt me in which case he'll hunt you down," I teased, smirking at him.

He laughed quietly, rubbing the back of his neck sheepishly. "You look great, by the way," he complimented, raking his eyes down my body slowly. I felt self-conscious even though I wasn't wearing anything revealing - just black pants and a green shirt; nothing special because I didn't want to give him the wrong impression. Though maybe flirting with him all week had kind of given him the wrong impression already. But I'd vowed to really try tonight. Maybe

110

he'd sweep my off of my feet, and I wouldn't have given him a false impression after all. I guess we'd see as the night progressed.

"Thanks, you do too." He did look good, his blond hair was styled nicely, he was wearing jeans and a nice blue button down shirt. *That shirt would look ten times better on Will. Oh for goodness sake, I need to stop thinking about my stupid teacher!*

"You ready to go?" he asked, looking towards his car. I nodded and followed him over to it, getting in and hating just how wrong this felt. Even his nice, clean car seemed wrong somehow. "So I was thinking we could go to Zac's?" he suggested, making it sound more like a question.

"Sure, I love Zac's." That was good because the place wasn't too romantic either, just a nice little place that did really great burgers. Olly smiled and started the car, pulling out of my drive. We rode in awkward silence for most of the journey, making small talk about school and the movie we were seeing tonight. I actually breathed a sigh of relief when we pulled into the parking lot of the restaurant because at least we would have something to distract from the awkwardness now.

I felt uncomfortable and weird the whole time we were in the restaurant. I honestly tried my hardest to like him. He was sweet and quite funny in a nervous kind of way, but we had nothing in common so a lot of the time was spent thinking of something else to talk about while we ate.

Deep down I knew that although I was trying to give him a chance, my heart just refused to even think about him that way. Throughout the date I kept comparing it to dates I had spent with Will, laughing easily and always having something to talk about. Maybe it was because Will was older or something, more experienced, so he knew how to make a girl feel comfortable. I really couldn't pin point exactly what it was, all I knew was that there was no spark between me and Olly.

After we had finished eating we decided to head to the movie theatre where we were meeting the rest of my friends. I silently hoped that once we were around other people that we would both relax, and maybe we'd be able to salvage the rest of the night.

Olly refused to let me pay for the food. As we walked out to the car I felt his hand brush against mine. Instinctively I jerked it away and pretended to look through my purse for my cell phone, just in case he was trying to hold my hand or something. I secretly wished I hadn't suggested this little private dinner in the first place. The only reason I did was to try and make Will jealous and get some payback, but even that didn't work out how I'd planned.

We talked about music on the way there, and luckily, by the time we pulled into the parking lot, there were only a few minutes until we were supposed to be meeting up with everyone. I felt myself relaxing because the alone part of the date was over with, well, until he drove me home anyway.

Amy smirked at me as we walked in the door. I resisted the urge to roll my eyes at her obviousness. I knew that she would immediately drag me to the bathrooms to get the gossip on the dinner. I wasn't wrong. As soon as we got

111

over to where her, Nick, and five of our other friends were, she grabbed my hand and nodded towards the restrooms.

"Let's go pee before the movie, Chloe," she chirped happily. I sighed dejectedly, knowing there was no point in arguing, and just allowed her to lead me to the ladies bathrooms. As soon as the door closed she rounded on me, looking at me expectantly. "So?"

I sighed and shrugged. "I don't know, he's a nice guy it's just…" I trailed off, not knowing what else to say.

"It's just that you're still hung up on the asshole," she finished, putting her hand on her hip with apparent disapproval.

"Amy, I'm trying, honestly I am, but I just keep thinking about Will all the time. This is too early for me to be out on a date with someone else. Olly's sweet, and funny, and hot, but I just couldn't stop thinking about Will all night." I pouted and sat on the counter next to the sink, waiting for her to scold me again for not moving on.

She didn't though; instead she sat next to me and wrapped her arm around my shoulder. "I know what it's like to have feelings for someone and not be able to do anything about it. Just look at me and Ryan, I've been crazy about him forever, and I've barely even spoken to him. It could be worse you know, you could have Will shoved in your face every day, because trust me, that's hard!" She looked at me knowingly.

I nodded and didn't say that I had Will in my face all the time; I wished I could just tell her and then she'd understand more about why I was upset and was struggling to move on.

"Give Olly a chance," she implored. "Hold his hand, kiss him, see if there's something there that you can build on. All you need to do is find him attractive. The other stuff might come along after. He's a nice guy. He'd make a great boyfriend I bet." She looked at me pleadingly as she squeezed my shoulder. "If you give him a shot and it doesn't work out, I promise to eat ice cream with you until it comes out of our ears." She crossed her heart and nodded.

I laughed at her solemn vow and nodded in acceptance. "Okay, you're right. Let's go watch the movie." I put on a fake smile and stood up. *I just need to try harder, that's all.* She smiled, and we walked out of the toilets, heading to where they were standing chatting in the foyer.

Olly smiled at me as we walked up so I smiled back and went to stand next to him. I gulped and let my hand brush against his on purpose. He looked down quickly, a smile pulling at the corners of his mouth as he traced one finger along the back of my hand. I held my breath and looked at him; his eyes were glimmering with hope, as if he was waiting for my permission or something. I smiled and turned my hand over so our palms were facing each other, silently giving him the go ahead; he grinned and took my hand holding it tightly.

Wrong. Feels wrong. I shouldn't be holding his hand! But I let it happen anyway.

"Want some popcorn or something?" he asked, grinning.

112

I shrugged. "Sure, if you do. I'll buy though because you paid for dinner." He rolled his eyes at me and pulled me towards the concessions stand, pulling out his wallet to pay even though I just said I would.

The rest of the night was better than the start of it. Olly draped his arm over the back of my seat but didn't make any other moves to touch me which I was grateful for. He kept stealing little glances at me through the movie, I saw him a couple of times from the corner of my eye.

When the movie ended I felt sick. A car ride home with him meant that he was going to kiss me; the date probably looked like it was going well from an outsider point of view. He probably expected to kiss me at the door at the very least. Amy nodded in encouragement as we said our goodbyes in the parking lot.

I chewed on my fingernails we walked to his car. He was still holding my other hand; his thumb drew little patterns against my palm as the silence seemed to overwhelm both of us. I smiled gratefully as he opened my door for me. *And he's gentleman too on top of being a sweetheart.*

We talked about the movie on the way home, telling each other our favourite parts. That seemed to fill the awkward silence that was lingering in the air. When we pulled up at my house I looked over at him nervously, only to see that he was already getting out of the car. He jogged around to my side and opened the door for me, while I just sat there wondering what on earth I was supposed to say.

Does he think I'm going to invite him in or something? Is that why he got out of the car? Wow, did he not get enough of my dad earlier that he wants to come in and see him again?

"Olly, I can't invite you in," I mumbled, looking between him and the door nervously.

He laughed and shook his head. "I was just going to walk you to the door." He took my hand and practically dragged me up the path to the front door. I felt sick. My heart was beating way too fast in my chest. At this rate I was likely to have a heart attack before he kissed me.

"I had a good time, thanks," I muttered, still a little lost for words.

He smiled and nodded. "Think I could take you out tomorrow?" he asked, looking at me hopefully.

For once I was grateful that I already had an excuse so I didn't have to think of one. "I can't tomorrow, I already have plans all day, sorry."

He looked a little disappointed, and I instantly felt guilty. I hated to upset people, which was usually why I ended up doing things that I didn't want to do all the time, because I had trouble saying no.

"Oh, that's okay... I guess I'll see you Monday at school. We could have lunch together or something?" he offered nervously.

Oh sugar lumps, another date. Well, kind of another date. I wanted to say no, I wanted to push him back to his car and tell him that I was totally crazy about my teacher. But all I could see was Amy's face when she said I needed to try and move on, and Miss Teller's face as she flirted with Will, and their little trips home and to school together everyday this week.

I took a deep breath and swallowed the immense doubt that I had in my mind as to whether I was ready for this. "Sure, lunch sounds nice," I agreed, trying to sound more confident than I felt inside.

He grinned. "Great!" he chirped. "Well, night then, and thanks for a great night." He stepped a little closer to me. I resisted the urge to slap his face as he started inching closer towards me.

Oh crap, just do it, Chloe, move on already and stop comparing him to Will. Will's moved on, so should you!

Olly's lips pressed against mine for a couple of seconds, and in that moment, I felt nothing. No heat, no sparks, no passion that seemed to run through every vein. Nothing. It was a nice kiss, soft and sweet, but it just didn't do anything for me. It obviously did something for him though because he pulled back and grinned like he'd won the lottery or something. I forced a smile in response.

He nodded back to his car. "I should get going then."

I smiled and laughed. "Yeah my dad's probably watching from the window so he'll be out here in a minute or two," I joked, laughing as he flinched and flicked his eyes to the window nervously. "I'm kidding. I'll see you Monday."

He laughed sheepishly and shook his head. "Yeah, see ya." He turned and walked back to his car as I headed inside. Once I was in I leant against the door and resisted the urge to cry. I actually felt like I'd just cheated on Will, but that was just stupid because he didn't want me. I sighed and pushed myself away from the door heading to bed.

The next morning I rolled over and my hand slapped against something hard. The hard thing grunted so I jumped a mile, a scream about to rip its way out of my throat, until I saw Nick lying there sound asleep. *What the hell is he doing in my bed?* I shook his shoulder roughly. He hadn't been there when I fell asleep last night.

"Nick, what are you doing here?" I croaked. I settled back down next to him, snuggling into his side and resting my head on his chest.

He yawned loudly. "Came to pick you up," he muttered.

I frowned and titled my head so I could see the alarm clock. It wasn't even eight in the morning. He wasn't supposed to be here until nine. "You came to pick me up an hour early and then just decided to take a nap in my bed?" I teased, laughing sleepily.

He smiled sadly. "I couldn't sleep so I thought I'd come over here early to see you. Your mom let me up here. You were still asleep so I decided to let you sleep instead of waking you up. I must have fallen asleep too," he mumbled, rubbing at his eyes roughly.

I groaned. *He couldn't sleep? I bet that's code for 'I was upset about my mom and laid awake upset all night'.* I hugged him tightly and pulled the sheets up around

114

us tighter. "Go back to sleep, we don't need to go yet," I cooed, setting my head back on his chest again and listening to his lazy heartbeat.

He sighed, seeming to relax again as his arm wrapped around me, stroking the back of my head. He was deep breathing within minutes while I just laid there awake, trying not to cry because he was so sad. Today was the day I needed to be the strong one. Today was the day where I needed to take care of him and make sure he was okay, instead of the other way around like usual. I closed my eyes and finally drifted off to sleep again too.

Two hours later and we pulled into the cemetery parking lot. I swallowed the lump that had formed in my throat on the drive over here. I hated it here just as much as he did, but I couldn't let him do this on his own. I held his hand tightly as we weaved up the path heading to the back left where she was buried. When we got there I stopped a few paces away and let him put the flowers down on her grave. White lilies; her favourites.

I stood there quietly, waiting to see what he wanted to do. Sometimes he wanted to stay for a while, but last time we came here, on her birthday, he couldn't stay more than a minute or so. He'd given her flowers, and we had to leave because he couldn't cope. Nick sighed deeply and sat down on the grass near her headstone. I moved and sat down at his side, pressing my body against his as I took his hand. His grip on my hand was tight as we just sat there in silence, looking at the grave, while he said whatever he wanted to say inside his head. After a little while I laid my head on his shoulder as his hold on my hand tightened, and his body began to tremble.

"I can't stay anymore," he mumbled after about ten minutes.

"Okay let's go," I whispered, not trusting my voice to speak. I wrapped my arm around his waist, clinging to him tightly as we walked in silence to his car. "Want to go get something to eat?" I offered, looking at his sad face.

He nodded and put on a fake smile. "I don't really want to eat anywhere out." He shrugged; his whole posture was sad and upset. It made my heart ache.

"Come to mine then," I suggested, knowing he wouldn't want to go home and see his dad while he was upset; they kind of avoided each other like the plague on sad days, with both of them coping on their own instead of with each other. Nick smiled gratefully so we headed to my house.

While we were eating, Amy burst through the door - without knocking as usual - and practically screamed my name as she skidded to a halt in front of me. I looked between her and Nick, shocked.

What on earth is this about? "Amy, what?" I cried as she practically bounced on the spot in front of me. She had her hands clasped together and the biggest smile on her face.

"So I was listening to the radio and guess what?" she screeched, gripping my arm so tightly it was actually painful.

"Ow! What?" I asked, trying unsuccessfully to pry her fingers from my arm.

"Daniel freaking Masters is coming to town!" she screamed making my ears ring.

"Holy mother of… no way!" I gasped.

She nodded, still jumping on the spot. "Oh yeah and he's doing a private concert for fifty people! It's in like a month, and you can win tickets on the radio. They're giving away two of them. All we have to do is wait for one of his songs to come on, ring the radio station, be the tenth caller and get the question right. They're practically ours already!" she screamed, clapping her hands and running over to the radio in the kitchen turning it on full blast.

I looked at Nick apologetically, but he was shaking his head in amusement. Maybe seeing Amy all gaga over a pop star was taking his mind off of his mom. That was certainly a good thing. "Daniel Masters isn't that good, his voice is kinda screechy," he joked, earning death glares from both of us girls. Daniel Masters was the hottest singer around. Amy and I both had a little obsession with him, in the best way of course, nothing stalkerish or anything.

All three of us sat there playing cards for over an hour before one of his songs came on. Instinctively Amy and I both dove for our cell phones, calling the radio station. And even though he couldn't stand Daniel Masters, Nick pulled out his cell phone and tried to get through for us too.

I shoved the phone to my ear excitedly, but it was just engaged so I hung up and tried again and again, but nothing. I glanced at Amy to see a desperate expression on her face as she pouted, doing the same as I was, just hitting redial over and over. When the song finished they brought someone on to the line who, of course, knew that Daniel's birthday was February 7th, so the silly girl won the tickets instead of us.

I growled in frustration and shoved my cell phone away from me, pouting.

Nick laughed and shook his head, looking at Amy and I as we both sat there sulking like little kids. "It's not the end of the world, it'll be on YouTube," he offered, shrugging.

Chapter Fifteen

My parents let Nick stay over that night. Of course we had to leave the door open all night so they could hear if anything went on, and Nick had to sleep on my bedroom floor, but they trusted us both to be in the same room which was nice. They knew we were just friends and that I was still hung up on Will so they let it pass because of his mom.

In the morning he drove us to school and I ignored the fact that we pulled into the parking lot at the same time as the new hot teacher couple. I held my breath as they walked up to the school chatting happily; it was obviously going well for them. Will's eyes flicked to me for a split second so I smiled and pretended I was fine with it. He smiled back and held the door open for his new little bed buddy to enter the school. As I walked up behind them, he stepped to the side, holding the door open for me too.

"After you, Miss Henderson." He smirked making my insides melt. *Stupid insides, just get over him already!* I wanted to slap myself and call myself names for still being under his spell when he had so obviously moved on to bigger and better than me - well maybe not bigger but undeniably older and sexier.

"Thanks," I mumbled uncomfortably.

"Think I could have a word with you before class?" he asked, cocking his head to the side looking cute as a button. I swallowed loudly and nodded wondering what this was about. "Great. Come to my room with me." He nodded up the hallway so I waved goodbye to Nick, promising to see him at lunchtime, and then followed Will up the hallway. I tried not to look at his butt as we walked, but I failed my task miserably.

When we got there he unlocked his door and immediately headed over to his desk, rummaging through his little bag thing that he'd brought with him. I just watched him curiously wondering if he was going to ask about how my date went on Saturday. I couldn't think of any other reason for him to want to speak to me. I'd done well all week with my project gaining an A grade for the first time in calculus for the presentation that Tricia did on Friday, so he couldn't want to lecture me about that.

He turned back and smiled. I tried desperately not to smile back, but it was so hard not to smile at the stupid guy. "Did you hear that Daniel Masters is doing a concert next month?" he asked, looking at me curiously as he perched on the edge of his desk.

I nodded. "Yeah I heard that on the radio on Sunday." I sighed sadly thinking about it again.

"You didn't get tickets?" He had a sly smile on his face as he asked.

I shook my head sadly and let my shoulders slump in defeat. "Nope, sold out. We tried to win some from the radio because it's an exclusive concert, but we couldn't get through."

He nodded, chewing on his bottom lip, looking amused about something. "What is it with that guy that you like? I mean, his music's terrible."

I rolled my eyes. "Yes, Will, I remember you don't like him. Is there a point to this little dragging me away from my friends thing or…" I trailed off, crossing my arms over my chest. I was already annoyed so he needed to stop winding me up.

He laughed and shook his head. "Here." He held an envelope out to me, his eyes shining with amusement.

"What's that?" I asked, frowning at it as I took it from his hand.

"It's a detention slip. Jeez, will you just open it and see, and stop with the attitude?" he said, laughing.

I swallowed my angry retort and opened the envelope, pulling out two tickets for the concert. *Oh my freaking God!* My mouth dropped open in shock as my heart started to beat way too fast. *Holy poop, I'm holding tickets to the concert in my hand! I'm going to see him live?* I squealed and jumped up and down on the spot, which just made Will laugh and shake his head at me. I looked up to him in disbelief. *He got these tickets for me, knowing I loved Daniel Masters? Damn it, he really is something else.*

"Are these yours?" I asked breathlessly. He smirked at me and shook his head slowly but didn't elaborate. "Who's are they?" I asked, praying he would say he was selling them to me.

"Yours," he replied, his voice all husky and sexy making my stomach get fluttery.

"You're going to sell them to me?" I asked hopefully, bouncing on the spot again.

"They're yours, I got them for you. I'm not selling them to you." He rolled his eyes as if I'd said something stupid.

"You got them for me?" I asked, swallowing the lump in my throat.

He shrugged like it was no big deal. "I heard that he was doing the show and thought you'd want to go. The manager of the club that I used to work at has some contacts. Apparently his brother is the guy who books the venues and stuff so I asked him to get me a couple of tickets. I know he's your favourite."

Why the heck did he do that? We're not going out anymore, so why did he go to the trouble to do that for me? "Why would you get them for me?" I asked, my voice breaking slightly as I spoke.

He looked at me intently, his grey eyes locked onto mine making my whole body feel like it was on fire. "I knew you wouldn't be able to get tickets, I thought you'd like to go," he explained simply.

"Thank you," I gushed. He nodded, his eyes still locked on mine. I wanted to throw myself at his feet and beg him to give me another chance, to beg for him to change his mind, to leave the hot teacher that was ten times better for him than me. "How much do I owe you?" I asked, breaking the silence before I did what my heart was screaming at me to do.

"Nothing, I didn't have to pay for them." He turned away from me, busying himself with moving his things around on his desk. "I pulled in a favour; they didn't cost me any money."

Did he really not have to pay for them? I stepped closer to him knowing the bell was about to ring and that his class would be here soon. I touched his arm, and he turned round to face me, his eyes tightening as his body tensed up.

Oh God, can I kiss him? Would he kiss me back if I did?

"Thank you," I whispered gratefully. That was probably one of the nicest things anyone had done for me, so thoughtful and adorable.

"You're welcome," he whispered back. He was so close I could feel his body heat seeping into mine. *Jeez, I need him so much. Why did this have to happen? Why did he have to turn out to be my stupid teacher?* "You should go, the bell's about to ring."

Before I could stop myself I stepped forward and pressed my lips against his cheek softly, letting my mouth linger on his skin for a couple of seconds while I enjoyed the feel of him under my lips again. He moaned in the back of his throat and turned his face towards mine slightly so my lips touched the corner of his mouth. I felt my heart skip a beat as hope started to build inside me. I wanted him to kiss me so much. If he just moved his face again our lips would connect. I pulled back ever so slightly so I wasn't kissing him anymore, but our faces we so close that I could feel his breath blowing across my cheek and down my neck.

"Please go, Chloe," he begged, closing his eyes as his hands clenched into tight fists.

"Thank you for the tickets. That was really sweet, Will."

"No problem, glad you liked them." He stepped back, folding his arms across his chest. "Not sure what you're going to tell Amy though, good luck with that." He smirked at me and laughed as I practically skipped out of the classroom. When I looked back at him, he winked, and my smile grew impossibly bigger.

I didn't tell Amy about the tickets. I was itching to though, especially when she was moaning and whining about not being able to go. They felt like they were burning a hole in my pocket and I couldn't wipe the excited grin off of my face all morning. When lunchtime came Olly plopped himself down next

119

to me, grinning happily. My heart sank. I'd forgotten we went on a semi date, and that I'd agreed to eat with him today.

"Hey, want to go eat outside or something?" he asked.

Crap, I guess I'd agreed to it so I can't exactly say no! "Sure."

I grabbed my sandwich and drink following him out of the building, ignoring Amy's proud smile. He walked over to the benches at the back of the school and sat down looking at me expectantly. I gulped and sat down next to him with a forced smile.

"So how was the rest of your weekend?" he asked, tucking into his sandwich.

I shrugged. "It was okay. I didn't do much really, I spent the day with Nick, and then Amy came over in the afternoon. What about you?" I asked, moving slightly further away from him as my arm kept brushing his as we moved to eat.

A frown lined his forehead. "You spent the day with Nick? So are you two back together then or…" he trailed off, looking away from me.

I smiled and rolled my eyes. People always assumed things about me and Nick. It drove me crazy. Couldn't two people just be friends? Why did something always have to be going on?

"Definitely *or*," I confirmed.

He smiled happily, turning in his seat to look at me. "Awesome, I thought you meant… never mind, I guess it doesn't matter what I thought."

"You thought I got back with my ex," I guessed.

He nodded. "Yeah sorry. It's weird you two being friends, you don't see that very often."

I shrugged. "Yeah but people forget that Nick and I were good friends before we even got together, so that makes it easier. I want to keep him in my life so we just need to work a little harder to make that happen. It was a little strained at first, but it's cool now."

He grinned happily and reached out to brush my bangs away from my eyes. "Well then that's great," he whispered. His eyes flicked down to my lips as he moved closer to me.

Oh no! I need to talk to him and explain a few things about Will before he starts to really crush on me and then he ends up getting hurt or something.

I reached up and took his hand that was tracing along my cheekbone. I pulled back, smiling apologetically. "Olly, I need to talk to you about something."

He looked at me curiously as he intertwined our fingers, leaving his hand in my lap. "Okay, what's up?"

I sighed. *How the heck do I say this without giving anything away and making myself sound like a moron who's obsessed with her ex-boyfriend?* "Well this summer I started dating someone." I frowned. The situation hurt to talk about so I would actually rather not do it at all.

He pulled away further, frowning as he let go of my hand. "Great, so you are seeing someone," he accused, frowning.

I shook my head quickly. "No I'm not, honestly I'm not. It's just I really liked him and then he broke up with me like two weeks ago and I still don't think I'm over it properly." *Wow that doesn't even cover a tenth of what I'm feeling.*

"The guy dumped you? What is he, stupid or something?" he asked, looking confused.

Aww, that's a sweet thing to say! I smiled. "I don't know. It just didn't work out and I don't want to rush into something if I'm not over him because that wouldn't be fair on either of us." I smiled apologetically.

"So you're still into this guy that dumped you. You think you two will get back together?" he asked, his expression was hopeful as he studied my face.

"No I don't." There was no chance that Will wanted me now that he was dating Miss Teller. He wouldn't want to down grade to a stupid school girl after being with her. Not to mention the fact that he thought I'd lied to him about my age, and he's my teacher. Everything just made it impossible for us to get back together so I could say with absolute certainty that what Will and I had was over - for him at least.

"So… maybe we could take it slow or something until you feel over it," Olly suggested, cocking his head to the side and giving me the puppy dog face.

Could I take it slow with him? What would that actually mean though? Going out on dates, kissing, and holding his hand. I guess I could do that, as long as both of us understood that it was nothing serious. I knew I didn't have strong feelings for him, but he was a sweet guy. Maybe, like Amy always says, my feelings would grow once I let myself get over Will. Maybe one day he would make me fall for him, and I would be passing up an opportunity that I should be grabbing with both hands. Will and I were over. I needed to accept that fact.

"What if I'm just on the rebound from this guy and we both end up getting hurt?" I quizzed, giving him the chance to walk away from me. I would hate it if I ended up hurting him.

He shrugged. "Who knows, but you'll never know if you don't try, and I want to try." His blue eyes were burning into mine, willing me to give him a shot. I could feel my resistance crumbling. *Why oh why can I never say no to people?*

"We'll have to take it really slow though, Olly," I whispered, not trusting my voice to speak. *I've just done it – taken the significant step and chose to move on. Now I just need to make my heart move on too.*

He grinned and took my hand again; I smiled and looked at our intertwined hands. It still felt wrong but it was nice to know that I was trying. "Then we'll take it really slow," he confirmed. The bell rang signalling the end of lunch, and I smiled at his disappointed face. "I guess we should get to class. I'll see you in calculus."

He stood up grabbing my empty lunch things throwing them in the trash for me. He smiled and held his hand out for me to take so I slipped my hand back into his as we walked down the hall towards my next class. He stopped outside the door to my Spanish class and smiled. "So I'll see you in a bit," he mumbled, tucking some of my loose hair behind my ear for me.

121

"Yeah. Thanks for walking me to class."

"No worries." He turned and practically ran down the hallway where he was late for his class because he walked me to mine. As I watched him run off, I spotted Will standing there. It was like he was frozen in place, staring at me, frowning angrily. Well, it was more like glaring actually.

What on earth is that look for? I sighed and headed into the classroom. *I give up trying to work out what goes on in that sexy head of his.*

Chapter Sixteen

I sat down next to Amy. She was grinning at me expectantly so I knew she'd just seen us in the hallway and now wanted the gossip on lunch. I smiled teasingly which made her almost bounce in her chair as she looked at me pleadingly.

I chuckled darkly. "It was nice," I stated, knowing she would want details, and it would kill her to wait.

"Annnnnnd?" she cried excitedly.

I shrugged noncommittally. "I don't know, it was nice. He was sweet. I told him about Will and that I wasn't ready for anything, and he said we could take it slow. Then he held my hand and walked me to class." That was it, no juicy details like she thought.

She sighed dramatically. "Well he's hot so you're lucky. I hope you give him a proper shot, Chloe, because he's a nice guy."

"I will give him a proper shot. Hopefully the taking it slow thing will help," I confirmed, turning to the front of the class as the teacher walked in. All through class I ignored Amy's stares and obvious frustration at not getting the gossip.

When the class was over she looped her arm through mine and skipped along at my side. "So did he kiss you again?" she asked with wide eyes.

I shook my head. "Nope."

"You think he will?" she asked, grinning.

I gulped. I didn't really want to be thinking about this yet. "Probably," I admitted reluctantly.

"Oh good grief he's hot," she gushed. "And you already know what his body is like because of all the swim meets. Oh my God, your boyfriend's on the swim team! You'll have to go to all of the races and stuff to support him. You get to perv on him in his trunks!" she squealed.

Wow, it's so wrong that Amy is more excited about this than me!

"Tone it down, Amy. He's not my boyfriend." I frowned as we stopped outside Will's room. This class would be awkward with both Will and Olly in the same room.

123

"He didn't officially ask you out?" she asked, pouting disappointedly.

"No," I answered. "Now come on let's get a seat before Mr Morris gives us detention for being late or something." I headed into the class to see Will was already sitting at his desk, watching as we walked in. I smiled but he didn't smile back.

What the heck is his problem now? This morning we had a great moment, and now he's looking all angry at me again.

Olly grinned as we walked in and nodded his head towards the empty seats next to his. Thankfully the seats weren't at the front this time. I smiled and walked up to him, plopping down next to him and Amy next to me.

"Hey, long time no see," he joked, grinning as he scooted his chair closer to mine. His side was practically pressed against mine, making me feel a little uncomfortable.

"Yeah I almost forgot what you looked like." I stuck my tongue out at him making him laugh as his arm slipped across the back of my chair, just resting there casually.

Will stood up. His body looking a little tense as he looked around the class. "So we only have half a lesson today as there's been an assembly called for seniors at two thirty in the hall. We don't really have time to start anything new, so how about we go over some of the rules of proportions ready for tomorrow." He shrugged, his eyes scanning the room. When they settled on me, he frowned and looked away quickly.

What on earth is his problem now? I honestly have no idea how his brain works anymore. I thought I knew him well, but all this just shows that I have no idea who he was in the first place.

I groaned and pulled out my textbook, flicking to the page he said. All sorts of equations and formulas jumped out at me on the page. My brain immediately started to switch off. I concentrated on what Will was saying at the front of the class, trying to understand what he was talking about, but I knew I needed more one to one help. I would never understand this stupid subject so I thanked my lucky stars for Nick.

Olly was playing with the back of my hair while we sat there, twisting it around his finger as I tried to concentrate, but failed miserably as I started daydreaming about Will again. He was walking around the classroom and I couldn't help but watch his pert little behind discretely as I bit my bottom lip. Thoughts of wrapping my arms around him, or trailing my fingers up his spine, bombarded my brain.

Suddenly he stopped in front of me, looking at me expectantly. *Oh God, what did I miss?* I looked around to Amy for help, but she was just looking at me with wide eyes.

"Er," I mumbled, not knowing what was expected of me.

He laughed humourlessly, his face hard. "Nice answer," he said sarcastically. He turned to Olly and narrowed his eyes. "Maybe you should let her concentrate instead of feeling her up in the middle of my class," he growled.

Olly's mouth dropped open as he whipped his arm off of the back of my chair. "I wasn't feeling her up," he replied innocently.

Will made a scoffing noise in his throat. "Mr Hawk, I know it's hard to keep your hands off of a pretty girl when you're seventeen, but try and restrain yourself, at least on school property. Otherwise it'll be lunchtime detentions for the next month," he snapped, walking back to his desk. I watched his back in stunned silence.

Amy was giggling quietly behind her hand. A quick glance over to Olly told me that he was grinning too, looking like he was trying not to laugh. *What the heck is funny about that? Will just made me look like a slut in the middle of his class and they both find it funny?* I ducked my head, blushing like crazy. *Please, please, please let this class finish soon!* I didn't look up for the rest of the time and at half past two Will announced that we were to head to the hall for the assembly with the Principal.

I packed my bag quickly not wanting to be in the classroom any longer than necessary. "I'll see you there, I need the bathroom," I muttered as I practically ran out of the room trying not to cry from embarrassment and anger. I headed to the nearest bathroom and locked myself in, slamming my hand against the side of the cubicle in frustration. *How dare Will do that to me in front of everyone!* After a couple of minutes I took a few calming breaths and unlocked the door. As I stepped out I almost screamed when I saw someone standing there leaning casually against the wall. Will's grey eyes were alight with concern, but I could also tell by the set of his jaw that he was angry too.

"What do you want? Don't you know these are the girls' toilets?" I snapped angrily as I headed over to the sinks to wash my hands.

"I need to talk to you," he muttered, passing me a paper towel to dry my hands on.

"Are you going to apologise for embarrassing me in front of everyone?" I hissed, glaring at him.

"Embarrassing you? What the hell is that about? *You* were the one letting him paw you in class," he retorted accusingly.

Paw me? Is he kidding me right now? "You really are an asshole sometimes, you know that?" I shouldered my bag preparing myself to storm off dramatically.

He snorted. "For what? Why am I an asshole? For telling that kid to get his damn hands off my girl?" he shouted, throwing his hands up in exasperation as he looked at me intently, his eyes boring into mine.

I looked at him in disbelief. *Did he just call me his girl? Oh my God, is he jealous of Olly? Was that what that little scene was about? No, no way, he can't be jealous. He's with Miss Teller. He's just saying this now because... because...* But I had no idea why he would say it, I couldn't think of a single reason for those words to come out of his mouth.

"I'm not your girl," I whispered, feeling my eyes fill with tears as I said the words.

He sighed and turned away from me, releasing me from his intense gaze. "I know that, I didn't mean it like that, I just meant…" He shook his head but didn't continue.

"What?" I asked, needing him to finish the sentence.

"It's just weird seeing it. I should go. I don't even know why I'm in here talking to you. I need to go," he mumbled as he grabbed the door handle ready to leave.

I gripped his arm stopping him from walking off; he turned his head back to look at me. "Why did you come here then, Will?" I asked quietly, not trusting my voice to speak properly.

He gulped and looked at me apologetically. "You looked upset. I wanted to make sure you were okay," he whispered. "I'm sorry I embarrassed you in class, I didn't mean to. I won't do it again." He frowned and pulled the door open, walking off quickly, leaving me standing there for the second time watching him shocked.

I stood there for a full minute wondering if he was jealous because he still wanted me, or if he was just annoyed because Olly had his hands on something that he'd had. I honestly didn't know the answer to that question, but I wasn't going to let myself start thinking about it again. He'd just had the perfect opportunity to tell me that he still wanted me, he'd had numerous opportunities before too, but he'd blown it every single time.

I turned on the cold tap and splashed some water on my face, trying to slow my breathing before I headed to the hall where the assembly was already underway. I hid at the side and listened to the end of what the Principal was saying. Something about voting with the social committee and then they would arrange the trip. I scanned the room for Amy. She was sitting next to Nick, both of them were grinning animatedly so whatever we were to vote for was obviously something good.

When everyone started filing out I waited off to one side for Amy. She skipped to my side happily. "This is going to be awesome, what are you going to vote for? I bet you like the sound of the horse sanctuary right?" She rolled her eyes jokingly.

Horse sanctuary? What exactly did I miss? "I didn't hear any of it, what horse sanctuary?" I asked confused.

She squealed and jumped up and down. "You didn't hear it? Oh my days, you're going to love this!" She grabbed my arm and started leading us down the hallway towards our lockers as she talked non-stop, giving me a word for word recount of everything that I'd missed.

Apparently because of the volunteer work that our year had done at the environment agency planting trees and picking up trash from the streets, we were being rewarded with a certain amount of money that was to be used towards a day out of our choice in a month's time. There were three choices that we had to all vote on. The one that had the most votes would be booked for one Saturday next month. The choices were: visit a horse sanctuary and ride and groom the horses, a day at a theme park, or paintballing.

I stated to get excited. I loved horses, but I knew there would be no chance that people would vote for that. My second choice would definitely be the theme park - even though I was a little scared of rides. The only thing I wouldn't want to do would be the paintballing. I wasn't into any sort of sports or activity that involved running, hiding, or getting dirty.

Nick grinned excitedly. "I am *so* voting for the paintballing."

A load of boys all cheered and started talking animatedly about who was going to shoot who, they started shoving each other around playfully. I rolled my eyes and headed to my locker silently praying that there was some way we could get out of it and do something fun that wouldn't involve me falling over, breaking my ankle, and making myself look like an idiot.

Chapter Seventeen

An arm slung around my shoulder. I smiled and rolled my eyes thinking it was Nick, but when I turned around it was Olly's smiling face that greeted me instead of Nick's. I resisted the urge to shrug his arm off. It was different when Nick did it because I knew it didn't mean anything, but with Olly I knew there was a motive behind it. That motive made me feel a little uncomfortable.

"Want a ride home?" he offered.

I flicked my eyes to Amy. I always rode home with her so maybe she desperately needed me to go with her or something, I couldn't help but hope. She smiled excitedly, and I mentally groaned. *I should have known she wouldn't help me!*

"Thanks, Olly, that'd be great," I lied, smiling back.

He waited patiently, talking to one of his friends from the swim team, while I grabbed my books from my locker. When I couldn't put it off any longer I turned towards him, plastering on a fake smile as he held his hand out to me again. I forced myself to slip my hand into his and he led us towards his car in an uncomfortable silence. Well, it was uncomfortable for me anyway; he didn't look like he felt that at all.

On the way home we made small talk about the day out. In typical boy fashion, he was going to vote for paintballing. I told him that I'd be voting for the horse sanctuary, and about how I used to go riding when I was a little girl but gave up a few years ago because it didn't fit in with my school schedule or going out.

I stole little glances at him on the way home. I had to admit, he was actually quite handsome. His blond hair was kind of messy and sticking up everywhere but looked nice like that. I'd never actually dated a guy with blond hair before; usually my type was brown hair. I guess there was a first time for everything.

When we pulled up outside my house I smiled gratefully, expecting that to be it. But much to my utter horror he turned the engine off and looked at me hopefully. "Think I could come in or something? Or we could go out and catch a movie?" he asked nervously.

I flicked my eyes to the house. My parents wouldn't be home yet; we had another hour and a half before they were due home from work. *I guess I can invite him in, that's the type of thing you do when you want to get to know someone, right?*

"Sure, come in we can watch a movie." I pushed the car door open and walked towards the house, feeling a little sick. *Is he going to kiss me? What do I do if he does?* As quickly as those thoughts formed, I dismissed them again. He'd said we could take it slow so he couldn't be expecting much today. I hoped not anyway.

He grinned sheepishly as he stepped over the threshold. "So, are your parents home or…" he trailed off, looking around nervously.

I chuckled. He was probably scared of my dad. "My dad's upstairs, he'll be down in a minute," I joked, nodding towards the stairs. His back straightened as he gulped, looking at the stairs with wide eyes. I burst out laughing and shook my head. *He is too easy to tease!* "I'm kidding, Olly, you're safe. They're both at work."

He laughed nervously and rubbed his hand on the back of his neck. "That was cruel," he scolded, but smiled at the same time.

An hour later and we were sitting watching a movie. I hadn't put on anything too romantic, not wanting to give him the wrong impression, so we settled for a comedy. The Hangover part 2. At the start of the movie Olly had sat himself close to my side and had his arm resting across the back of my seat. The whole time my heart was beating just that little bit too fast because I was just waiting to see what he would do next.

About half way through I turned to ask him if he wanted another drink or anything, only to see he was already looking at me. I smiled nervously and his arm moved to my shoulders, his hand playing with the back of my hair. He smiled, and I couldn't help but smile back. He had a really cute smile. It didn't make my stomach flutter like Will's smile, but it was cute nonetheless.

His eyes flicked down to my lips and my breath caught in my throat. "So, would it be moving too fast if I kissed you?" he whispered.

Oh crud. I guess I need to take the plunge sooner or later, so maybe it's best just to get it over with! I shook my head, not really trusting my voice to speak; he grinned and instantly started inching his mouth towards mine. I held my breath as his lips pressed against mine softly. I didn't hate it as much as I thought I would. I kissed him back, and after a couple of seconds, he pulled away, smiling at me tenderly before he pressed his lips to mine again.

When his tongue traced along my bottom lip wanting to deepen the kiss and take it further, I squeezed my eyes shut and opened my mouth, secretly wishing I hadn't said yes. Olly was actually a really good kisser but my head and heart were screaming at me that everything was wrong, that I needed to push him away and call Will to apologise.

Olly's arms wrapped around me pulling me closer to him, crushing my chest against his as he kissed me passionately. He moaned into my mouth as I looped my arms around his neck. He moved slightly forward, trying to make me lay back onto the sofa, but I kept my ground refusing to take it further than a kiss. When one of his hands trailed down my back towards my butt, my eyes snapped open in shock and I pulled back, breaking the kiss.

Groping me isn't exactly taking it slow, Olly! "I'm sorry; this is too fast for me."

He smiled his cute dimpled smile. "Okay, that's okay." He brushed the hair back from my face.

I smiled gratefully at how sweet he was. "Thanks."

"So was it the kissing or the hands?" he asked, grinning sheepishly.

I blushed and couldn't help but laugh uncomfortably. *Both actually.* "The hands," I admitted, biting my lip at how stupid and childish that made me sound.

"So if the kissing was all right, maybe I could sit on my hands?" he suggested, laughing.

I laughed nervously. "Maybe we should just watch the rest of the movie," I suggested.

He grinned and nodded, turning in his seat and taking my hand, watching the movie as if nothing had happened.

Ten minutes later the front door opened. Olly jumped away from me like a bomb went off, and I giggled at his concerned face. My mom and dad both walked into lounge talking about their days. My dad stopped walking and frowned at Olly menacingly as soon as he spotted him. Olly shrank back into the sofa a little more, seeming to squirm under my dad's accusing glare.

Hmm, I wonder if he'll pass the dad test. A couple of boys I'd brought home a year or so ago dumped me after meeting my dad, he liked to test them and behaved like this for a couple of meetings to see if they were serious about me. Luckily Nick had passed the test with flying colours so my dad now liked him. Olly just needed to get past this little glaring stage, and then he'd start treating him nicely.

I bit my lip nervously as I glanced at Olly who looked like he was trying to make himself breathe. "Dad, you remember Olly from the other night?" I asked, trying to keep the amused smile off of my face as my dad went for his bad cop routine.

Dad nodded slowly. "How could I forget? Nice to see you again, Olly. So what exactly are you doing here, unchaperoned, with my daughter?" he asked, raising one eyebrow.

"Er... We were just... er... watching a movie?" Olly stuttered, making it sound more like a question.

I rolled my eyes and stood up, taking Olly's hand and pulling him to his feet too. "Leave him alone, Dad, we were just hanging out."

"Yeah well two teenagers *'hanging out'* can lead to trouble," my dad replied, "and if you get my daughter in trouble, Olly, then you'll have me to deal with."

I blushed profusely because he was obviously talking about sex and pregnancy.

Olly shook his head fiercely. "No, sir, absolutely, I wouldn't ever get Chloe in trouble, I mean we're taking it slow and..." he trailed off, swallowing loudly. I sighed. My dad had just been pushing his buttons. Olly wasn't holding up well at all.

Before the situation could get any more embarrassing I walked out of the room, pulling Olly along behind me as I marched to the front door. I chuckled at his pale face. "He's trying to get to you. Just ignore it, he'll stop soon," I promised.

His eyes flicked over my shoulder as he nodded slowly. "Damn, he's scary. He's not like mafia or anything is he?" he asked, rubbing the back of his neck nervously.

I laughed. "No he's CIA, but he's not allowed to torture anyone under eighteen so you're safe until your birthday," I teased.

He laughed quietly. "Well that's a relief," he mused, rolling his eyes. "So I'd better get going. I'll see you at school tomorrow." He tugged on my hand making me step closer to him as he pressed his lips against mine softly again just for a split second. He smiled before turning for the door but stopped with his hand on the door knob. "I forgot, um, I was wondering... I wanted to ask you earlier during the movie but I chickened out... so, well... I know you said take it slow, and we can wait if you want to but... er..." he frowned uncomfortably.

I grinned at how adorable he looked when he was nervous. He'd had girlfriends before, most of the time serious ones too, because his last girlfriend he was with for a year and I hadn't heard about him seeing anyone since her.

I stepped closer to him, raising one eyebrow playfully. "Are you trying to ask me out, Oliver?" I teased.

He frowned and winced. "Yeah, sorry I'm not doing a very good job at it."

I laughed. "You're doing fine, just relax, and by the way, the answer's yes."

His nervousness faded instantly as a grin split his face. "Awesome!" he chirped. "Well I guess I should go before your dad comes out here and threatens me some more. I'll text you later, I do better by text, it covers up the nerves," he joked. I was grateful that he didn't try to kiss me again before he walked out of the door.

I breathed a sigh of relief and leant against the doorframe, mentally congratulating myself on getting through it. I waved as his car pulled out and sped off. I smiled sadly to myself and closed the door, leaning against the wood, thinking about Will. What would he think of me just agreeing to be

131

Olly's girlfriend, and more importantly, why did I still care what he would think?

The following morning Amy and I were gossiping by our lockers about the Daniel Masters concert. I'd told her on the phone last night that my parents had managed to get tickets as a surprise. She was so happy she'd actually cried with joy, she'd cried so much that I couldn't understand what she was saying so she had to call me back when she'd calmed down.

Suddenly an arm went around both of our shoulders. "So, girls, who are we talking about today?" Nick asked, looking around the hallway discreetly.

"Daniel Masters," Amy breathed dreamily.

"Oh, over-rated gay singers," Nick replied, nodding as if he wanted to join in. Amy gasped and elbowed him in the ribs making him laugh and move his arm from her shoulder. "Ow." He groaned, rubbing it roughly.

"Aw did the poor baby get hurt by a big bad girl?" she mocked.

From the corner of my eye I saw someone waking towards us. I forced a smile when I realised it was Olly. We'd text back and forth last night for about an hour, luckily my parents got me a contract with unlimited texts because otherwise he'd be costing me a fortune. He was right though, he definitely did do better by text.

He smiled back, but it didn't quite reach his eyes. His body seemed a little tense as he stopped in front of me and took my hand. I smiled weakly and interlaced our fingers. When he pulled me forwards gently making me move closer to him, Nick's arm dropped off of my shoulder.

"Hey you," Olly greeted, seeming a little more relaxed now that I was closer to him.

"Hey back." I squeezed his hand a little as he brushed his other hand across the side of my face softly.

"Want to do something after school today?" he asked, looking at me hopefully.

I winced. I was studying tonight with Nick. The best days for him were Tuesdays and Wednesdays so I couldn't exactly ask him to change his plans to another night just so he could help me out with my stupid class. I glanced at Nick to see if he was still up for the tutoring, but he was talking to Amy again.

"I can't, Olly, I'm supposed to be studying with Nick tonight. He helps me with my calculus," I said apologetically.

He frowned disappointedly, and I suddenly felt terrible about it. "I could help you study, I don't mind. It makes more sense for me to do it, I am your boyfriend after all," he countered, smirking at me cockily.

"I know you are but Nick already agreed to help me. We've been doing it for the last couple of weeks, and it's really starting to sink in. I think it's best if I don't mess around with something too much when it's working." I shrugged. Nick seemed to be able to explain it to me extremely well, and he was so patient with me. He didn't mind going over and over the same thing until I understood it. "Besides, it'd be embarrassing for my boyfriend to find out how much I suck at something," I added sheepishly.

He sighed but nodded in agreement. "Okay. Do you do it at the library or something? Maybe we could meet up after."

I shook my head. "No we do it at his place. It's part of the agreement; he tutors me and I have to cook dinner. I'll be at his place until late, sorry."

His frown became more pronounced. "So you study with your ex-boyfriend at his house, on your own, and then you cook him dinner after and stay there until late. That's what you're saying?" he asked, his voice slightly hard as he looked at me like I was crazy.

Holy poop, is he jealous of Nick now? What the heck is he thinking? "No. I study with a friend and cook him dinner as a thank you. *That's* what I'm saying," I corrected defensively.

He sighed and shook his head, forcing a tight smile. "Right yeah, sorry. Forget I said anything. We can hang out tomorrow night instead, if you're free that is."

I smiled and nodded. *Is he jealous? That was a really strange, surreal conversation, and not one I wanted to have with a guy I've been dating for less than twenty-four hours!*

The rest of the week passed slowly, news spread that Olly and I were dating which gained me a few glares from girls that had crushes on him. Olly continued to be really sweet - paying for food and the movie when we went out, driving me home, walking me to my classes, and texting me endlessly in the night.

The only thing I didn't like was his idea of taking it slow. It was a lot faster than my idea of it. He seemed to keep forgetting himself, and when we were kissing his hands were a little all over the place. A couple of times to the point where I had to push him off of me because he was trying to unclasp my bra or unbutton my pants. As soon as I said something about it, he stopped immediately and apologised, but I could see he was getting a little frustrated with me. I wasn't giving in though, it had been five days since he asked me out and that just wasn't long enough for those kind of things to be happening between us - well, not for me anyway. I had a feeling that he thought 'taking it slow' meant that we just wouldn't have sex for a while, I didn't think he realised I wasn't going to let him past first base.

Will was just the same all week, I felt a little awkward around him because of his little outburst in his classroom where he accused me of letting Olly 'paw me' as he called it. Things were just a little strained, a kind of forced friendliness between teacher and student. He didn't single me out but he didn't blank me, just kind of ignored everything that wasn't to do with his classes. A couple of times I'd seen him turn around and walk the other way when I was with Olly, his posture a little stiff. At those times I always wondered if he was jealous like I thought, but I honestly had no idea so I gave up trying to work him out.

After school on Friday Olly led me over to the benches outside so we could hang out for a while before he drove me home. I couldn't see him tonight because he was going to a family dinner at his uncle's house so he wanted to spend some time with me before he dropped me home. He seemed a little reluctant to come to my house after the uncomfortable scene with my dad on Monday. I sat on the bench, soaking up the sun with my eyes closed just looking forward to having the weekend away from this place and the stress that it brought with it.

"So what are we doing at the weekend?" Olly asked as he traced his hand up the side of my leg slowly. I put my hand on top of his, holding it still when it was about to snake round to my ass.

"Well I can see you tomorrow daytime, but in the evening, Amy and I are going to a party with a friend of mine," I replied, shrugging. Maybe we could go for lunch or something.

He pulled back looking at me curiously. "You're going to a party? Who's is it?"

"A friend of a friend, I don't know the guy really," I admitted. I actually didn't really want to go now but I couldn't pull out because Amy was so damned excited.

"Who's your friend?" His eyes were a little accusing, hard and annoyed.

I smiled uncomfortably. *Why is he looking at me like that?* "Actually it's my ex-boyfriend's brother."

His body tensed as he looked at me like I'd said something stupid. "You're going to a party with your ex-boyfriends brother? The same ex-boyfriend that you're still not over?" he asked, his voice hard and accusing.

"Yeah, we're friends." *Why on earth is he looking at me like that? I'm allowed to have friends.*

"Oh come on, Chloe, how many freaking male friends does one girl need?" he spat, pushing himself off of the bench and glaring at me.

Whoa! "Are you jealous?" I asked shocked.

"I have a right to be jealous, damn it! You're my girlfriend, but yet you're going to a party with another guy, and not just any old guy, but the brother of the guy who dumped you!" he growled, frowning angrily.

What the hell? There is no way I'm letting him tell me who I can and can't hang out with. I don't care if he feels jealous, there needs to be trust in a relationship. If he can't accept me having male friends then that's his bad luck.

"Olly, get a grip, he's a friend." I rolled my eyes. He'd been shooting little glares at Nick all week too. Every time Nick touched me or something Olly would kiss me or pull me away from him or something. I thought he was just being cute at the time, but was it something else? Was he being possessive?

"You can't go to a party with him, Chloe, that's out of order and you know it. How would you feel if I went to a party with my ex's sister?" he asked, throwing his hands up dramatically.

134

I thought about it. *How would I feel? I wouldn't mind because I trust him, and he should trust me too.* "Olly, I wouldn't mind. It's just a party with a friend, it's no big deal." I shrugged, picking up my bag so I could walk away from him.

He made a scoffing noise. "It's a big deal to me. All week I've had to bite my tongue when Nick's been draping his hands all over you, and now you expect me to let you go to a party on your own with a guy?" he growled.

"*Let me?* No I don't expect you to *let me;* I don't need your damn permission to go. Jeez, we've been going out for less than a week. I don't need to ask your permission to do stuff, that's stupid." I stood up and shouldered my bag.

"So you think I'm stupid?" he challenged, stepping closer to me, frowning.

"Right now, you're being childish. I'm not talking about this, call me Sunday if you want to." I shrugged and walked past him heading for the building. *Hopefully I'll be able to find Amy or Nick and grab a ride home; if not then I guess I'm walking.*

Olly's fingers wrapped around my wrist, pulling me to a stop. "Don't walk away. We can't just have a fight and then you walk off, that's not how a relationship works." His voice was softer than earlier.

I looked back at him. "People don't tell people what they can and can't do in a relationship either."

He sighed. "Okay I get it. I pissed you off, I'm sorry. It just drives me crazy these guys hanging around you all the time." He pulled me back to him and slipped his arm around my waist.

I smiled weakly and hugged him back. "It's okay, but there's no reason for you to be jealous. I'm not a cheater, I promise," I mumbled, pressing my face against his shoulder.

He stroked my back softly. "Yeah I know. Listen, how about we go out tomorrow night instead of you going to the party. We can go anywhere you want," he suggested.

I shook my head and pulled back. "I can't I promised Amy we could go to the party, it's been arranged for over a week."

He huffed dramatically and let his arms drop from my waist. "Nice, so you're choosing a party over a date with your boyfriend," he spat sarcastically.

I closed my eyes. I didn't want to be having this conversation with him; there was nothing to talk about. "Look, I understand that you feel jealous, I get it. But that doesn't mean you can get angry with me for doing something that was arranged before we even got together!" I cried.

"You know what? Just do what you want, I'll see you Monday." He snatched his bag from the table and turned on his heel, stalking off towards the parking lot.

I watched his back as he walked away. *So much for 'we can't just have a fight and then you walk off, that's not how a relationship works'. Fine, screw him. I'm not the one in the wrong here, I've done nothing wrong.* I could see why he was a little annoyed, but he needed to get over it and learn some trust if he wanted this to work.

Will never would've said anything like that to me, 'you expect me to let you go'. *I don't need his damn permission to go out!*

I stormed off towards the building, resisting the urge to kick things as I walked past them. I headed in to the building looking down the deserted hallways for someone I could get a ride from, but by the looks of it Olly and I had been talking for too long and everyone had already left. I sighed and turned back, deciding to make the forty-five minute walk home.

I pulled out my iPod and shoved in my headphones as I power walked down the road, letting out all my frustration. After a couple of minutes a car horn blasted from next to me making me jump a foot into the air and yelp with fright. I turned round to see Will's silver jeep creeping along the side of the road next to me. He waved me over so I headed to his open window.

"What's pissed you off?" he questioned, looking at me curiously.

How does he know I'm pissed off? "What does that mean?" I asked, flicking my eyes to the passenger seat of his car to see there was no Miss Teller with him today.

"You're marching, so you're obviously annoyed. For once it doesn't look like it's me that's upset you." He shrugged, smiling guiltily.

"No, it's… nothing. It's nothing." I shook my head, frowning, trying not to think of Olly again. *Stupid boy.*

"Want a ride home?" Will asked, flicking his head to move his hair from his eyes.

Actually I would love to not to have to walk home, but do I really want to be trapped in a car with him? I weighed my options. Just as I was about to decline the offer, a drop of rain fell on my head. I nodded quickly. "Yeah if it's all right." He smiled and reached over to the passenger side, flicking the lock for me. I ran round the car and jumped in as the drops started to fall harder. "Thanks, Will."

"No problem." He threw the car into drive and pulled away, heading slowly down the road as the rain continued to fall. "So what's rattled your cage then?" he asked, flicking his eyes to me for a second.

I sighed and rested my head back against the seat. "Olly. He actually had the nerve to tell me I couldn't go to the party tomorrow with Sam. He said I had enough male friends and that I was choosing to go to a party over going out with him. Stupid ass," I ranted angrily. The sound of Will's laughter made me open my eyes and cast them in his direction. He was grinning happily but stopped when he saw me looking. "What's funny about that?" I asked, frowning. *There's nothing remotely funny about that at all.*

He shrugged. "Nothing. So you two broke up now then or something?" he asked, glancing at me from the corner of his eye.

I shrugged, not knowing the answer to that question. "Doesn't look good. I mean, you just don't do that! He has no right to be annoyed with me about it; you know what he said to me?" I ranted. "He said; *you expect me to let you go to a party on your own with a guy?* I mean, let me go? What is he now, my keeper?" I threw my hands up in exasperation, and Will started laughing again.

I glared at him and he stopped laughing but looked like he was struggling a little.

"Sorry, it's not funny. I just can't imagine him telling you what to do. I tried to stop you going out with Sam once; it didn't go down too well then either." He shrugged.

"But he's being out of order, isn't he? I'm not in the wrong here, am I?" I asked curiously. *Am I just seeing this as an excuse to break up with him? Am I being extra stubborn because it would be easier without him? I don't think I am. No man should tell a woman what they can and can't do.*

He shook his head. "You're not in the wrong, Chloe. He shouldn't be telling you that you can't go to a party. I was wrong when I did it, and so is he." He pulled up outside my house and I turned to look at him, smiling gratefully.

"Thanks for the ride and the ear that I talked off."

He smiled his nice smile, the one I swear he only has for me. "Anytime. Have a nice time tomorrow night with Sam. Be careful okay?"

"I will, thanks. Have a great weekend." I pushed the door open and held my bag over my head as I ran inside with a smile on my face. I skipped to the kitchen to get something to eat thinking about the party tomorrow. I hadn't actually wanted to go before, but now that Olly had made a big deal out of me not going, I actually wanted to go. Sam was fun, and Amy was looking forward to it so I'd make myself have a good time there too.

Chapter Eighteen

A car pulled up outside my house, and a second later a horn blasted. I cast a quick glance out of the window to see Sam's car sitting there. We'd already agreed he shouldn't knock for me because I'd told him what my dad was like. After shouting a quick goodbye to my parents, I headed out of the front door with my overnight bag. I was staying at Amy's after the party tonight because her parents were a lot more lenient with curfews than mine were.

I skipped to the car excitedly. I hadn't been to a party for ages, the last one was actually another one of Will's friends that he took me to. Sam smirked at me as I got in the car, looking me over obviously.

"I pass the inspection or should I change?" I asked sarcastically. I hadn't dressed up too much tonight, but I was still pleased with the outcome. I had on black tight pants that were cropped just below the knee, a killer pair of black heels, and a gold sparkly top that hung off of the shoulders and had a matching tank top underneath. Amy had helped me pick it out today while we were shopping.

He smirked at me. "You definitely pass. What about me? I'm guessing I pass too, hell, I always pass."

I sighed and rolled my eyes. "You don't need my comments to build up your already overinflated ego so I'll just stay quiet." I stuck my tongue out at him. He laughed, heading in the direction on Amy's house as I told him where to turn.

"Will's definitely not going, right?" I asked worriedly as we pulled up to Amy's street.

"Definitely, I promise." He nodded, looking at me seriously; he knew I would be angry with him if he was lying so I didn't think he'd do that to me. I smiled gratefully and he pulled into Amy's drive honking the horn.

She walked out of the house wearing a jean skirt and black top, her hair all pulled up nicely. I smiled. She really was pretty and would have the guys fighting for her tonight. I'd always secretly wished I looked like her. Her hair was always straight, even when she woke up in the morning, and the colour of it was beautiful - unlike my dirty, straw coloured hair that seemed to have a mind of its own.

Sam whistled appreciatively as she walked to the car. I slapped him in the stomach, glaring at him. "If you make a move on my best friend tonight, Sam Morris, I swear I'll never speak to you again, and that's not me being melodramatic," I promised.

He pouted. "She's a big girl, she can take care of herself," he whined.

"I'm serious. Do it if you want but don't ever expect to see me again. I'll take the side of my friend, and as her best friend, I'll have to take part in the torture of the Sam voodoo doll," I warned, trying not to smile as he burst out laughing.

"Fine, I guess you're right. I won't make any attempts to hit that tonight," he confirmed somewhat grudgingly as he watched Amy's every move while she slid into the back seat of the car.

I smiled at him gratefully before turning back to Amy. She was practically bouncing in her seat with excitement and it actually made me more excited too.

I glanced nervously at Sam as we walked into the packed house. The party was crazy already even though it was only nine o'clock. People were drunk, staggering around, talking animatedly. I honestly didn't know where to look because it seemed that every wall had someone dry humping against it. Amy squealed and squeezed my hand tightly. "This is going to be awesome!" she squeaked.

Sam grinned and threw his arm around her shoulder. "I'll show you girls how to have a good time." He winked at her and guided her towards the kitchen as I lagged behind, praying that he would keep his promise and not hit on my best friend tonight. She didn't need a player like him hanging all over her - not to mention the fact that he was Will's brother.

As I walked into the kitchen I spotted a couple of guys that I'd met before, a couple of Will's friends. Jack smiled at me curiously as we walked in. His eyes flicked to Sam questionably before returning to me. "Hi, Chloe, what are you doing here?" he asked.

"She's with me," Sam chirped, grabbing three Smirnoff Ices and passing one each to me and Amy.

Jack raised one eyebrow. "Really?"

"Not with me, with me, just accompanying me tonight. She's Will's girl," Sam clarified, doing air quotes around the 'with me' part. He nodded to Amy. "This is Chloe's friend, Amy."

Will's girl? What the heck does that mean? I frowned at Sam as I drank half of my bottle of drink. I was planning on getting wasted tonight; hopefully I'd even throw up in his car on the way home for that little dig about Will.

"Where is Will tonight?" Amy asked.

Whoa. What on earth is she asking that for? Maybe she's hoping to meet him or something so she can kick his ass for hurting me. I looked at her confused as I downed some more of my drink. Hopefully this Will conversation would finish soon, and that would be the end of it. Best to get it all out in one go then we could enjoy the night.

Jack shrugged. "He's working at the club."

I snapped my eyes up to him, confused. "I thought he didn't work there anymore?" Why would he still be working there if he was a teacher now? I knew he still worked at the ski slope - surely he wasn't holding down three jobs.

Jack looked at me knowingly. "He's working there every weekend for the next month to pay for the concert tickets he got."

I choked on my drink and almost spat it everywhere; Amy rushed over and patted my back while I tried to catch my breath. *Will is working there to pay for the tickets for me? He said he didn't have to pay for them! Why on earth would he give up four weekends just to buy me some concert tickets? That's just stupid. Incredibly sweet, but stupid.*

Sam smiled at me, and I just looked at him curiously, trying to drag the truth from his eyes. There had to be some other concert tickets that Will had gotten. He wouldn't give up a whole month of weekends for me, would he? Sam shrugged and drank some of his drink, obviously not going to say anything about it now; I'd just have to catch him out later when he was drunk or something.

"Let's dance then, girls." Sam grinned, grabbing Amy's hand and pulling her into the lounge where there were already a lot of people dancing. I sighed and chugged the rest of my drink, and grabbing another one, before following them.

Two hours later I was already wasted. I leant against the wall heavily as I laughed uncontrollably at something Jack had said. Amy grinned and giggled too. Her arm was wrapped around Sam as they sang along to the song loudly. I'd already had way too much to drink, but that didn't stop me from grabbing another shot of vodka jelly from the side and choking it down. Sam was supposed to be driving tonight, but he'd decided he wanted to drink instead, so apparently we were getting a cab to Amy's now instead.

Jack pulled his cell phone out of his pocket as his arm wrapped around my waist, holding me up as I swayed on my feet. I pushed away from him, dancing with Amy. I could hear Jack talking into the phone, but I had no idea who he was talking to.

"Hey, it's me. Yeah, your girl's a little wasted. No. No Sam's trashed too, and she's going to need a ride home before she pukes all over my floor. Yeah I'll watch her. You coming now? Okay yeah, see ya." He eyed me curiously as he spoke.

I frowned, flicking my eyes around the packed room, looking for a drunken girl that he was worried about puking on his floor. But to be honest, drunken girls were everywhere so it could have been a lot of them.

140

Amy grabbed my hand pulling me off a little way to dance some more. I was having an awesome night and I was totally glad that I'd blown Olly off to come tonight.

After another couple of drinks Amy gripped my arm tightly. Her nails dug into my flesh making me laugh at the stinging pain that would probably hurt when I was sober. "What?" I giggled at her wide eyes.

"You will never freaking guess who just walked in!" she cried excitedly.

"Er, Brad Pitt?" I offered, laughing. She shook her head happily. "Channing Tatum?" I guessed again. *Oh my days, I would die if Channing walked in here!* I flicked my eyes to the door excitedly thinking it must be someone gorgeous... and it was. In the doorway stood Will looking incredible in black pants and his black club T-shirt with the little red logo on his chest.

My heart sank. He wasn't supposed to be here tonight. Sam had promised me that he wasn't coming which is the only reason I agreed to come. "For fuck sake! Are you freaking kidding me? What the hell is he doing here?" I cried angrily. I glared at Sam. "You promised me!" I accused, frowning.

He shrugged looking at me innocently as Will walked over to the group where we were standing. I turned my back not wanting to talk to him. I just wanted one night out without thinking about him, and he had to waltz in and ruin it.

"Hey," he greeted as he stopped next to me.

"William, how are you doing?" Jack asked, giving him the man hug thing. They were whispering something but I didn't even try and listen, I wasn't interested in anything he had to say tonight.

He pulled back and smiled at me and Amy worriedly. "Aren't you girls a little too young to be wasted at a party?" he joked.

Amy giggled and gripped my arm even tighter as she practically drooled over him. "We're not wasted," she protested, shaking her head and slopping some of her drink on her shirt. *Oh yeah way to prove a point, Amy. Spilling your drink - good going!*

"Not that it's any of your business anyway," I added under my breath. Well, I thought it was under my breath anyway, but I'm pretty sure he heard it because his jaw tightened a little and his shoulders hunched slightly.

He looked at me intently, his beautiful grey eyes boring into mine and trapping me in his intense gaze. I found myself struggling to remember how to breathe as I literally couldn't look away from him. *Get a grip on yourself, Chloe, and stop looking at him like that! But jeez he looks so damn hot tonight.* His T-shirt was fitted and just hinted at the perfection that I knew was underneath. I longed to run my tongue down his abs and bite the edge of his jaw so he'd moan my name. *Damn it, stop looking, Chloe!* I forced my eyes away from his and turned back to Amy who was staring at him like she wanted to eat him right now.

She stepped closer to me, leaning in close so she could whisper conspiratorially. "He looks even hotter outside of school," she hissed a little too loud in my ear.

"Really? I hadn't noticed." I shrugged casually, ignoring her disbelieving expression. *Yeah she doesn't believe that any more than I do! Wow, I suck at lying, I need to practice some more!*

"Oh you noticed," she teased, grinning at me knowingly.

Sam stepped forward and smiled. "So what are you doing here?" he asked Will, offering him his drink.

Will's eyes flicked to me for a second and I rolled my eyes in exasperation. *That's who Jack was talking to? He called Will to tell him I was wasted and he needed to come and look after me?* I shot Jack a dirty look and got a smirk in return which I wanted to smack right off of his face for him for interfering.

"Just finished early that's all. Thought I'd drop in." Will shrugged looking at his brother a little annoyed. "I thought you were driving tonight, Sam." He nodded to the bottle of beer in his hand.

Sam shrugged easily, obviously not catching the icy tone to Will's voice. "I was, but then I just decided we could share a cab. No big deal."

"It's a pretty big deal if you're supposed to be looking after two underage, drunken girls," Will replied, smiling a fake smile although his voice was hard and annoyed.

I couldn't listen to this anymore. He was ruining my night for me, I didn't need him to come here and start something with Sam, we were fine without him here. Jack had no right to call him.

"Will, just leave him alone for goodness sake. Go get a drink and chill out," I ordered, trying not sound stern but it lost some of its authority when I hiccupped in the middle of my sentence.

"I don't want a drink. Maybe I should get you two home." He nodded his head towards Amy but his eyes never left mine.

I crossed my arms over my chest and glared at him. He didn't even flinch, just glared back at me clearly annoyed. "I'm not ready to leave yet," I stated confidently.

He sighed and nodded. "Fine, I'll wait until you are. Maybe you should stop drinking now though."

He actually looked really tired, and I felt a little guilty. He probably just wanted to go home to bed or something. He worked Saturday afternoons at the ski slope and then he'd had to go into work at the club tonight too. My heart throbbed at the thought of him working at the club again to pay for the concert tickets. *That reminds me... I haven't asked Sam about it yet. Maybe I could ask Will about it. Would he tell me the truth though? What on earth reason would he come up with to explain why he was doing that for me? Giving up his time like that just so Amy and I could to go to a concert. Damn sweet boy.* But that damn sweet boy was now frowning at the drink I had in my hand as if it was poison or something. He clearly disapproved by the look on his face. He hadn't seemed to mind me drinking when he brought me to a party just like this one when we were dating, but then again at the time he thought I was old enough to drink.

I frowned and raised my glass in cheers as I downed the contents. Instantly I wished I hadn't done it. I was just trying to prove a point and win a small battle, but I wasn't a big drinker and I'd already had more than enough to make me sick in the morning. Will laughed and shook his head as I winced and screwed my face up probably looking like a moron or something. I frowned and swallowed a couple of times as he just looked at me with a big smile on his face. I suddenly found myself smiling too just because it was one of his warm smiles and not a smirk.

"Nice try going for the 'in your face' kind of thing, but the alcohol after burn kind of ruined the effect I think you were going for," Will teased, grinning at me.

I laughed and shook my head, slapping him on the shoulder playfully. "Yeah well it was worth a try," I joked, sticking out my tongue at him.

Amy gripped my hand and I turned in her direction to see her looking from me to Will and back again. She had a bewildered expression on her face.

"What's up?" I asked worriedly.

"What's up with you?" she countered looking at me like I was crazy. Suddenly I realised I just had a whole conversation with Will like I knew him and he was supposed to be nothing more than a teacher. *Oh no, I even called him Will right in front of her!*

"Er, nothing… um, want to dance some more?" I asked nervously.

She nodded, still looking from me to Will as if she was trying to work out one of his stupid math problems. I followed her to the middle of the room where people were dancing. She frowned, pulling me closer so she didn't have to shout over the music.

"What the heck was that? Were you two flirting? And how did you know his first name? I didn't know his first name!" She frowned, looking at me questionably.

I shrugged and tried desperately to keep my face neutral. "Jack called him William; I didn't know it until then. And no, I wasn't flirting. As if," I lied, waving my hand dismissively and praying she would believe me and let this go. I loved my best friend to death, but I didn't want her to know about Will. I didn't want to take any risks with him being in trouble for what we did, none of it was his fault, and although I was hurting over it now, at the time it was worth it. The time that I'd had with him was actually well worth any pain or heartache that I felt now that we weren't together. I wouldn't change a thing. Actually that was a lie; maybe I'd protect my heart from him a little more, but I'd never regret spending time with him.

Amy nodded, still looking thoughtful. "O.M.G, I love this song!" she cried suddenly, dancing to a song I'd never even heard before. It was some kind of dance beat that she loves but wasn't really my thing. At least it got us off the subject off of Will for a little while.

After another couple of songs I'd had enough. My feet were hurting in my shoes. If I hadn't had so much alcohol I would probably be crying with pain, but the drink was numbing it a little, thank goodness.

Out of nowhere a sleazy looking, greasy haired guy walked over to us and smiled. "Well hello there, girls, can I dance too?" he purred, raking his eyes over us both slowly.

"Actually I need the bathroom," Amy said apologetically. She looked at me and nodded towards the back of the house where the bathroom was. I opened my mouth to agree to go with her and tell the guy I couldn't dance with him, but Will appeared at my side.

"They're with me," he stated, looking at the guy warningly.

Whoa, what is that tone about? Will looked really annoyed as he stepped closer to me, well actually he stepped half in front of me to be exact.

The guy held his hands up innocently. "Easy there, buddy. I didn't realise. No harm done." He turned to walk off and I got more than a little angry about it. *What on earth is Will's problem being all possessive like that? I wasn't with him so I could do whatever the hell I wanted and he wasn't going to tell me what to do.*

I turned to glare at Will. "What on earth is your problem?" I asked angrily.

He rolled his eyes and looked at me a little bored. "He's too old for you and you shouldn't be dancing with guys that you don't know." He crossed his arms over his chest defensively.

Oh my days, he is so freaking annoying sometimes! "Will, seriously, have you forgotten the conversation we had yesterday in the car where you said that it was wrong for people to tell others what to do? Or does that only work when it suits you?" I asked sarcastically.

He laughed humourlessly. "This situation is a little different, Chloe, I'm doing that for your safety. You don't know that guy, I don't know that guy, he could be anyone. So I say again; he's too old for you. Besides, did you see the way he was looking at you?"

"For goodness sake, Will, just leave me alone. I'll dance with whoever the hell I want to okay?" I growled as I pushed my way through the crowd in the direction of where that guy went, ignoring Amy who was watching with her mouth open in shock. I decided to dance with that guy just to spite Will and show him he couldn't order me around. I could definitely shove that in his face better than downing that drink earlier!

I spotted the guy leaning against the wall scanning the room. I smiled and he grinned. "Got rid of your keeper?" he asked as I stopped at his side.

"He's not my keeper, he's my damn teacher," I muttered. Anger was still burning through my system at the cheek of him telling me what to do. The guy laughed and looked at me like I was joking, but I wasn't in the mood for playing around. I didn't want to dance with this guy, but I knew Will would be watching so I had a point to prove. "Are we dancing or what?" I asked.

He nodded and smirked at me. As he pulled me a little closer to him I instantly regretted doing this. I really didn't want to be anywhere near this guy. He was probably in his mid-twenties, and Will was right, he was looking at me like I was a piece of meat or something. *Oh well, it's too late now. One dance should show Will not to order me around again.* I purposefully stayed at a safe distance and didn't really let myself go and dance properly; this was only for Will's benefit after all. The song was almost over. I smiled gratefully. I needed to go sit down, take my shoes off and rub my feet. When the song finally finished I smiled a small satisfied smile knowing that I'd won for once. *Take that, Will!*

The guy moved away a little, smiling. "Want a drink?" he asked, picking up a cup from the side and passing it to me.

I shrugged and downed the cup of what I thought was juice, but it had an alcohol burn too so maybe there was some vodka in it too. "Thanks," I mumbled.

"So, your guy's still watching. Want to dance again?" he asked, running his hand down my arm. I flinched my arm away from him, not really liking him touching me. *Hmm, I can dance again I guess. I wonder how long I would have to dance with this guy before Will comes over and tells me we're leaving.* I probably had about another two dances I guessed before he would come over and put a stop to it and demand we leave for home.

"Okay sure." I nodded. As the song progressed, my head felt a little woozy. I had definitely drunk too much, and my eyes were a little heavy. The guy grinned and stepped closer to me, putting his hand on the small of my back.

After about five minutes I felt terrible. It was like the drink had caught up with me all of a sudden or something. My whole body felt heavy, and I was so damn tired all I wanted to do was sit down. My head slumped forward onto the guy's chest as I struggled to carry on dancing. My energy was fast running out. *I need some fresh air or something to clear my head.*

I pushed back away from him unsteadily. "I need to go sit outside or something. I don't feel well," I mumbled, but my voice barely worked and I wasn't even sure if I'd said it out loud.

"Okay, come with me, I know a back way out. We can sit outside for a little while until you feel better." He took my hand and instantly starting to pull me through the crowd, heading for the back of the house. I followed weakly behind him, and he pushed open a door, ushering me through it. I stopped and frowned. *This isn't outside! It's a bedroom. Huh?*

"What the?" My head spinning, making me feel slightly sick.

The guy smiled and tugged on my hand, making me move to the bed. "Why don't you just lie down for a little while. You'll feel better soon," he cooed. I sat on the bed and put my spinning head in my hands, willing myself not to throw up. There was pressure on my shoulder as he guided me to lie back. My whole body felt weak so I wouldn't have been able to fight him even if I wanted to. I laid down on my back. *Hopefully my head will stop spinning in a minute and then I could go find Will and ask him to drive me home or something. Wow, I hope I'm not sick in his car.*

I was snapped out of my thoughts of Will when I felt something on my neck. *What is that?* I forced my heavy eyelids open to see the guy hovering above me. The guy was kissing down my neck as his hands were lifting my

145

shirt. I groaned groggily and tried to push him off, but I could barely even lift my arms. They felt like they were ton weights or something.

Oh God, why aren't my hands working properly? What is he doing? "Stop it, I don't want to," I slurred, but my voice was barely above a whisper.

He pulled back and grinned at me wickedly. "Oh come on, you'll enjoy it." His eyes raked down my body slowly making my skin crawl.

I shook my head and tried to push myself up using my elbows, but I was so damn heavy that nothing really happened. As I moved my head I suddenly felt dizzy and lightheaded. The guy laughed and pushed me back down onto the bed, his hand trailing up my leg cupping my ass as he pressed his lips against mine.

Oh my God, am I about to be raped? Why the hell is he on top of me, and why don't I feel right? My whole body felt heavy, but yet weightless at the same time. My heart was beating so fast in my chest that it was banging in my ears. I was literally scared stiff.

I whimpered and tried to move my head away but I was so tired that my movements were barely even recognisable. Every time I blinked, my eyelids would get heavier and harder to open. I was fighting a losing battle. The blackness was taking over and I knew I needed to go to sleep; there was nothing I could do. I didn't even have the energy to scream or cry.

Chapter Nineteen

Just as I was about to give into the blackness, the guy's weight was gone from on top of me. I heard a crash and the sound of a scuffle. I forced my stinging eyes open; turning my head towards the sound just in time to see Will slam the guy against the wall. He pulled back his arm and punched the guy in his already bloodied face.

Will's here! My heart stuttered in my chest. The panic receded. I smiled weakly, trying desperately to keep my eyes open. I tried to roll over so I could push myself up on all fours, but I was so uncoordinated that I almost rolled off of the bed. Will threw the guy on the floor, screaming profanities as he kicked him in the stomach and chest. His face was the picture of rage. I actually felt a little scared for the guy on the floor who was covering his head with his arms and trying to curl into a ball.

Someone else ran into the room and grabbed Will, pulling him back from the guy on the floor. Will was still thrashing violently, trying to throw off the arms that restrained him. His face murderously angry. I squinted through the haze and realised it was Jack holding him. He was saying something in Will's ear, holding on to him tightly. Will's head snapped round in my direction, and his face softened instantly. He nodded and calmed himself down immediately. Jack let him go and Will ran to my side, gripping my shoulders pulling me up to sitting as he wrapped his arms around me.

"Shit, Chloe, are you okay? Did he..." he trailed off, looking at me horrified.

I buried my face in the side of his neck and breathed in his delicious smell as I gripped the front of his T-shirt. I couldn't stop the silent tears from falling down my face. *I was almost raped and he saved me. It was so close. If he was just a few minutes later it would have been too late.*

Will's arms tightened around me as he stroked my back, rocking me soothingly. I forced one of my heavy arms around his neck even though it took almost all of my strength to do it. I clung to him as tightly as I could while he pulled me into his lap, murmuring soothing words that he was there and that I was safe. I could hear him talking to Jack, but it was like he was a long way away or something instead of pressed against me.

"Do I need to take her to the hospital? What should I do?" Will asked, sounding almost desperate.

"No, I found an Ambien packet in his pocket. It's a sleeping sedative. If he's given her that then you just need to let her sleep it off. The hospital wouldn't do anything for that, and if she was going to have a reaction to it she would have had it already. Just put her to bed," Jack answered. I knew from previous conversations with him that Jack was a resident doctor at the hospital, so he knew what he was talking about. Will obviously trusted his opinions.

His arms tightened around me. "Chloe, I'm going to take you home okay? Can you hear me?" he asked as he shifted me in his arms.

I nodded but didn't bother to open my eyes. I tightened my arm on his neck as I was jostled. I cracked my eyes open, wincing against the light in the room, to see that he'd stood and was carrying me. He strutted effortlessly out of the room, heading through the lounge, weaving past people as he muttered "excuse me" here and there. The party still carrying on, oblivious to what had almost happened to me. Crying to my right caught my attention. I glanced over to see that Amy was stumbling along behind us, crying uncontrollably. I tried to smile reassuringly, but I was just too tired. Cool air blasted against my face making me moan and press against Will more as I got goosebumps.

"Get in the backseat, Amy; I'll lay her down with you so you can watch her. Shit, her parents are going to go crazy," Will mumbled. I winced at the thought of my parents. *I can't go home like this, I'll never be allowed out again until the day I die!*

"I don't want to go home, don't make me go home," I croaked against Will's neck, gripping my hand in his hair as he moved me and laid me down with my head on something soft. I didn't move my hand, not letting him pull back from me. "Please, Will, my parents will kill me," I begged him with my eyes.

He sighed and reached behind him, pulling my hand from his hair effortlessly. He frowned and looked like he was trying to decide something before he groaned and nodded. "How about I take you to mine?" he offered, looking from me to Amy. I turned my head looking up at Amy and realised I had my head in her lap.

"She's supposed to be staying at mine tonight though." Amy shook her head sadly, obviously knowing we were both in deep trouble for this.

Will straightened himself up and nodded. "You can both stay at mine. Text your parents and tell them you've decided to stay at Chloe's instead," Will ordered as he moved my legs slightly and then pulled back, slamming the car door closed.

Amy smiled weakly and pulled out her cell phone. I looked at her apologetically, but she just smiled and stroked my face softly. "It's okay now, Chloe. Don't worry, Will's got it," she cooed.

I smiled and closed my eyes. I knew she was right, Will had everything under control and just being here with him made everything okay. I didn't need to worry about anything when he was near me.

I was vaguely aware of being moved again, this time I didn't even have the strength to hold onto him as he carried me to goodness knows where. I felt him settle me on something soft and I gripped his shirt weakly, not letting him away from me.

"Where are we?" I mumbled, forcing my eyes open but it was fairly dark in the room so I couldn't make anything out.

"You're at my place. Everything's fine now. Amy's going to sleep in with you and I'm sleeping on the couch. Do you need anything?" he asked, brushing my hair from my face softly. His fingers left a burning trail along my cheek.

"I need you to stay with me." I pulled him closer to me as I snuggled into the bed more. I should have guessed where I was, his smell was all around me making me feel safe and content.

"I can't, Chloe," he whispered, shaking his head slowly as his eyes flicked behind me. I felt the bed dip as Amy got in the bed the other side of me.

I gripped his shirt tighter; I needed him near me tonight. I didn't want him to leave. "Please?" I begged, trying not to cry.

He sighed and nodded. "I'll stay until you fall asleep." He sat down on the floor next to the bed and took my hand, tracing circles in the back of it with his thumb. I smiled at him gratefully and he smiled back tenderly, his other hand stroking my hair softly. "Go to sleep," he whispered. I nodded and closed my eyes again, gripping his hand for dear life, afraid to let go because I knew he would get up and leave.

After a few minutes of silence I felt his hand leave mine. I tried to open my eyes but I couldn't. I needed to sleep now and I couldn't fight it anymore.

"You're Will aren't you? Chloe's Will," I heard Amy say behind me.

"Yeah I am," Will answered. Something soft pressed against the top of my head. *Was that his lips? Did he just kiss the top of my head?* I smiled, but no matter how hard I tried, I just couldn't open my eyes. "We'll talk about it in the morning. Get some sleep, Amy," he muttered. I heard the door open and close, but I couldn't remember anything else.

Chapter Twenty

I slowly started to come around in the morning. I fought desperately to hold onto the last moments of sleep though, because in my dream, I was surrounded by a beautiful smell. I didn't want to open my eyes and wake from this incredible dream. I felt so contented and happy that I never wanted it to end. I ignored the pounding in my head and just focused on the scent that could only be one man, the one I was crazy about, the one I needed in my life. Just Will plain and simple.

My mind started to wake even though I didn't want it to and I sighed deeply, squeezing my eyes shut, begging silently in my head for more sleep. After a couple of minutes I cracked my eyes open to see red numbers flashing on an alarm clock, instead of the usual green. *What on earth?* I pushed myself up a little and groaned as the room span making my stomach lurch. The pounding in my head got louder as I glanced around the familiar room, a room I never expected to wake up in again in my life.

Wait, am I still dreaming?

Something moved behind me in the bed. I gasped with excitement as I flicked my head around, expecting to see Will. *Maybe the last couple of weeks have been a horrible dream. Maybe he isn't my teacher, and this was all just some sick nightmare that he'll laugh at when I tell him about it.*

Though my thoughts were crushed when I saw the person there. Instead of Will lying behind me, spooning my back, it was Amy. I felt a rush of disappointment as I swallowed the lump in my throat. She was still sound asleep. Her make-up had smudged under her eyes making her look like a panda. I laugh quietly. I sat up slowly, gripping the edge of the mattress, wondering if I was going to be sick. I definitely needed to get out of the bed because lying down was making me feel worse.

Why on earth am I at Will's apartment with Amy? The last thing I remember is going to the party with Sam, then Will showed up and we had a little argument then that's about it. My memory was all a little hazy from then on. I swung my legs off of the bed and tentatively stood up. I needed to find Will and ask him what the heck we're going to say to Amy about how we both wound up in our teacher's apartment for the night.

I crept over to the door and rested my forehead against the cold wood for a couple of seconds, trying to soothe my throbbing head, but I knew nothing would touch the pain except pills. I headed out quietly, trying not to wake Amy; I needed to know the cover story before she quizzed me about it.

As I stepped into the lounge my eyes instantly found the sofa, but he wasn't there. It looked like he'd slept there though. The mess that was probably from his sofa, was piled on the floor instead, and there was a throw and pillow there all scrunched up. I headed over to the only other room in the apartment.

As I walked into the kitchen his eyes snapped up to mine as he jumped out of the chair looking at me worriedly. He grabbed my arm quickly. "Are you okay?" he asked, bending to look at me as he guided me over to one of the two kitchen stools.

I frowned. "Yeah, I have a headache, but I'm okay." I nodded, pulling my arm from his grasp. I didn't like him touching me, even a casual touch like that was making my stomach flutter. I didn't need anything else making me feel sick, the alcohol was doing a pretty decent job of that on its own.

"I'll get you some pills. Sit down." He headed over to the cupboard and I couldn't stop myself from watching his toned back as he reached up and grabbed the little first aid box he had. *Why on earth does he have to be shirtless? Is he trying to tease me to death; a little reminder of something that I couldn't have?*

He passed me a glass of water and two pills, sitting down opposite me, still looking concerned. I swallowed them gratefully, silently praying that I wouldn't throw them back up again in five minutes.

"Thanks Will. So er... why are we here?" I asked nervously as I looked around his kitchen. Everything still looked the same, and I'd missed it so much. I missed hanging out at his place with him. I missed him flicking water at me as we washed up the plates and stuff we'd used; I missed the smell of this place. I even missed the stack of newspapers that he still hadn't gotten around to taking to the recycling like he said he was going to. Just little things but I missed them all.

He looked at me quizzically. "You don't remember what happened last night?" he asked, recoiling.

Something happened last night? Oh no, please don't tell me I threw up all over Jack's place or broke something expensive! I shook my head, looking at him curiously, waiting for him to hit me with the bad news.

He sighed and ran a hand through his already messy bed hair making it stick up everywhere. "Chloe, someone put something in your drink last night. You don't remember almost being... attacked?" he asked, his hand making a tight fist on the table.

Attacked? What on earth is that about? I closed my eyes and thought about it, suddenly little pieces of it started to come back. It was like a dream; the more I tried to think about it, the further away it seemed to get, but there were some things coming back. Like how I'd danced with a guy and he led me into

151

the bedroom instead of outside, I couldn't quite remember his face, but I remember feeling scared and that I couldn't move properly. I remember Will punching the guy and shouting at him. *Oh God, was I almost raped last night?* I gasped and snapped my eyes to his face to see if I was remembering right, Based on the sombre, sympathetic look on his face I knew it was true. *Holy crap, I owe him a lot for that!*

"I got there in time, everything's fine. He didn't....." he trailed off, looking like he was in pain.

"Thank you," I whispered trying not to cry about it.

He smiled weakly and shook his head. "You don't need to thank me, Chloe. Just please don't ever take a drink from someone you don't know again, I can't even think about what could have happened. I just-" He groaned, squeezing his eyes shut and clenching his jaw tightly.

I pushed myself off of the stool and moved to his side, wrapping my arms around his neck tightly, hugging him as if my life depended on it. He really was a hero. I didn't know what to say or how to show him how grateful I was to him for saving me. His arms snaked around my waist and he pulled me onto his lap, holding me tightly. I tucked my head under his chin. I could hear his heart beating steadily in his chest. I smiled because of how close he was. His naked torso was pressed against me, he smelt so delicious and mouth-watering. He stroked my hair softly, and we just sat there like that, neither of us speaking or moving until I heard the bedroom door open again and I knew that Amy was now up.

Will's arms loosened around me but I noticed with some small measure of satisfaction that he didn't push me off of him or anything. I smiled to myself a little and forced myself out of his lap, looking towards the kitchen door, waiting for her to come in. Will's hands dropped down into his lap as he looked in the other direction, his shoulders hunched.

Amy stopped in the doorway tentatively, looking from me to Will. "Am I interrupting something?" she asked, blushing. I wanted to say; hell yeah you are, the best hug I've had in three weeks, but luckily I resisted the urge.

I frowned. *That's actually a really weird thing to ask. Why would she think she might be interrupting something?* I smiled and gave her a quizzical look. "No, why would you be?" I asked confused.

She frowned in disapproval and shook her head. "You can give up the act now, Chloe. Why didn't you tell me?" she asked, looking a little hurt as she sat down on the stool that I was sitting on earlier.

Okay this conversation is getting weirder and weirder by the second! "Tell you about what?" I questioned, trying to look innocent. *She can't know about Will, can she? She was just as drunk as I was last night so surely she wouldn't think anything of me knowing his name and talking to him...*

She rolled her eyes. "About you... and Will." She pointed to Will who was just sitting there tense and uncomfortable, and actually dreadfully sad looking.

I gasped as I screamed a list of profanities in my head. *How the hell did she guess that? What on earth do I say? Can I tell her about us? What does Will want me to do, deny everything or confirm?* I felt sick with worry. I could feel my hands starting to shake with stress as I questioned everything. What if Amy saw it as rape too and told someone, what if she went to the police and Will got into trouble for it? Best case scenario he could lose his job, worst case scenario he would go to prison.

I opened my mouth, but nothing came out. *Come on, stupid brain, think of something to say! Why couldn't I have been born a witch with the ability to turn back time?* If I could then I would have never gone to the stupid party with Sam last night, and then I wouldn't be sat in Will's kitchen, facing Amy who was just looking at me accusingly waiting for my reply.

I gulped and shook my head trying to look innocent. "Amy, what are you talking about? Are you still drunk?" I asked, my voice breaking slightly like it always did when I lied.

She raised one eyebrow and gave me the look that said one thing; 'I'm your best friend and I know you're lying'. I gulped again and looked at Will for help. He'd be able to lie to her; she didn't know all of his tell-tale signs like she did mine.

He sighed and leant forward, resting his elbows on the table as he looked at Amy. "I didn't know she was seventeen. We met at the club and when Chloe said she was in school I thought she meant college. She thought I knew, and I thought she was twenty-one. Another unfortunate thing that happened is I get assigned to the one school where you both go, I mean, talk about coincidence." He laughed humourlessly. "It shouldn't have happened, but it did. I don't know what else to say apart from that." He shrugged, looking at her sadly, as if he was waiting for her to shout at him or call the cops from the kitchen or something.

I just sat there staring at him in shock; did he really just say all that to my best friend and fellow student? I couldn't breathe. I literally couldn't breathe, and my lungs were starting to burn. It was like I'd forgotten how to suck in air or something. I started to panic. I couldn't take my eyes off of Will, I didn't want to look in Amy's direction and see the accusation there. I had definitely broken the best friend code by not telling her who Will was, but she'd forgive me, I knew that. Yes, I'd hurt her, but she'd forgive me anything, the same as she knew I would if this were the other way around.

Will looked up at me a little concerned as he suddenly gripped my upper arm and stood up, facing me. "Are you all right? You look really pale," he said desperately. I swallowed loudly and nodded, trying to calm my racing heart, but I just couldn't. He smiled reassuringly and brushed my hair back from my face softly, the back of one finger lingering on my flushed cheek. "It's okay. Amy has a right to know so we couldn't exactly lie about it. I'll take whatever punishment I get, it's fine, stop stressing about it."

I couldn't look away from his eyes. He did that trapping me there thing that I both loved and hated at the same time.

"Why would you get punished?" Amy asked suddenly.

Will sighed. "Chloe's a minor. I'm in a position of responsibility, as her teacher she's in my charge. It wasn't legal for us to… it's classed as statutory rape," he explained effortlessly, as if we were talking about the weather.

He looked like he'd been thinking about this for a long time, actually, come to think of it, he didn't look like he'd slept at all. There were dark circles under pink, tired looking eyes. Had he laid awake all night worrying about Amy knowing and had resigned himself to the fact that he was going to prison or something?

"It wasn't." I shook my head fiercely. I hated it when he said that word; it made what we had feel cheap and dirty. I refused to think of it that way.

He sighed and his hand dropped from my cheek, hanging loosely at his side. In that moment I would give anything for him to put it back on my arm or my face, just any sort of physical contact because I was seriously freaking out.

"I'll leave you two to talk, and I'll go in the shower." He smiled sadly again before turning and walking out of the kitchen, leaving me there with Amy who I still couldn't look at.

I heard the stool scrape against the floor tiles, and suddenly her arms wrapped around me. I just stood there shocked for a couple of seconds before hugging her back. I expected her to be mad at me for not telling her so I really wasn't expecting this at all.

"It all makes sense now. How you were so happy then just kind of freaked out in the middle of his class and ran out, then said he broke up with you. Oh Chloe, it must have been so hard for you having me keep talking about how hot he was all the time, when you were so heartbroken over him. I'm so sorry," she whispered, stroking my back.

I smiled against her shoulder and hugged her tighter. "I'm sorry I didn't tell you. I wanted to so badly, but I couldn't risk Will getting in trouble if someone found out. He would be in so much trouble if this came out. You're not going to say anything are you?" I pulled back and looked at her pleadingly, begging her with my eyes.

She smiled and shook her head. "Of course I won't." I smiled gratefully and felt the last of the tension leave my body. "I can't believe he's the teacher, I mean for goodness sake you find your Mr Perfect, and it turns out he's your damn teacher! How unlucky can you get?" she mused, shaking her head in disbelief.

I laughed humourlessly and pulled away, sitting on Will's stool. I rested my forehead on the table, closed my eyes and sighed with relief. I actually felt like a weight had been lifted off of my shoulders now that I had someone to talk to about it. Of course I had Sam, but it was hard talking to him because one, he is Will's brother so there was only so much bad mouthing I could do as he was after all his family. And two, he was a guy, so he had no idea what I was talking about when I mentioned heartbreak and feelings.

"So he just broke up with you when he found out that he was your teacher?" Amy asked softly.

"Mmm hmm," I mumbled, not lifting my head from the table.

"Well that sucks! Couldn't you at least carry on seeing each other or something and just keep it secret?"

I shrugged. "He doesn't want to date a minor. I think he's still pissed at me because I lied to him about how old I was. Well, technically, I didn't lie, but I didn't exactly tell him I was seventeen either. We both just kind of assumed things instead of talking about it," I said sadly, trying not to cry. It was hard to talk about it, I wasn't used to having someone know the truth, and it all seemed to burn my throat as finally I said the words out loud.

She laughed. "Chloe, he doesn't look at you like a minor. He still likes you," she observed confidently.

I raised my head and propped my chin up on my hand, looking at her like she was crazy. *What on earth is she talking about, 'he still likes you'. He doesn't still like me; he's dating the freaking drama teacher for goodness sake.*

I shook my head fiercely. "He's made it pretty obvious, Amy. I'm just another student to him, someone he's bedded, another one of the many notches on his headboard."

She looked at me knowingly. "Just another student? Do you see him touching my face like he did yours? Did you see him that concerned over me? Did you see him beat the crap out of that guy for me last night, and carry me through the house? Did you see how sad he was when he was telling me about you two?" She smirked at me knowingly, but I just wasn't in the mood for this at all, my head was pounding. I couldn't argue about this right now.

I sighed and pushed myself up from the stool. "Can we just not talk about it? How about I make some breakfast? He doesn't ever have much in the apartment to eat, but I think there's some cereal and stuff." I headed over to the cupboard, looking to see if there was any of the Lucky Charms left that he bought for me when I used to stay here. I smiled when I spotted the box exactly where I left it. He'd always just laughed at me when I ate this kind of stuff but to hell with it; if something tastes that great it has to be good for you.

I shook the box at Amy in offer. She smiled, nodding eagerly. After digging out the last two clean bowls from the cupboard, I found the milk from the fridge before shoving some bread in the toaster for Will. I left it up so he could push the button down when he came out of the shower. I turned back to Amy. She was just watching me with a small smile on her face. I gave her a quizzical look which made her smile grow more pronounced.

"You know your way around his kitchen, that's adorable," she said, digging into her type two diabetes in a bowl.

I shrugged but didn't answer. She was just trying to start the conversation about Will again and I just couldn't cope with that yet, at least not until my headache had dulled fractionally. After about a minute of silence she frowned and seemed to be losing the battle she was obviously having with

155

herself not to say anything about it again. I rolled my eyes and just looked at her expectantly waiting for her to get it off of her chest.

She let out a big breath and shook her head. "Okay I need to say it. Holy fudge, Chloe, you screwed a teacher? And a damn hot one too. Jeez, that chest. Swoon. Wow, just wow," she gushed.

I burst out laughing at her little outburst. "Are you done?" I giggled.

She nodded and fanned her face. "Yeah unless he comes back in shirtless again," she joked.

I smiled. *Trust Amy to lighten the mood.* I knew she was only doing it to cheer me up, and I loved her for it. I also knew this wasn't the end of it; she wouldn't let this go at all. Once we were out of here and on our own, she would quiz me for all of the details. She already knew a lot of the details, but I guessed she'd want all of the things that had happened since we broke up because I had told her I hadn't seen or heard from Will since he dumped me. There was lots of gossip and details that she would hound me for.

A few minutes later Will came back into the kitchen looking a little uncomfortable. I smiled reassuringly and nodded towards the toaster. "I put that there for you, or have you already eaten?" I asked, wanting to break the slightly uncomfortable silence.

He smiled gratefully. "No I didn't eat yet." He grinned and nodded at my empty bowl and the box of Lucky Charms on the table. "Glad you're eating that crap up, the sugar in it was tainting all of my health food," he joked.

I grinned and laughed. "You don't have health food in the apartment, Mr I like microwave food so I don't have to wash up too much," I teased, sticking out my tongue. He laughed and pushed the button down to make himself some toast while I just watched his back wondering if I could ask him about the tickets that he got for me.

He turned back and crossed his arms over his chest looking from me to Amy. "So I guess I have some explaining to do?" he asked nervously.

I flicked my eyes to Amy to see her shake her head. "Not really, Chloe's explained everything, and don't worry, I won't say anything to anyone. You two make a really cute couple," she said, smirking at us both before pushing herself up from the stool and heading out of the kitchen towards Will's bedroom.

I cringed and looked at Will worriedly, chewing on my lip. *Why did she have to say about us being a cute couple?* He smiled at me sadly. I picked up my bowl and Amy's and put them in the sink while he just watched me curiously. "Are you really all right, Chloe? Not freaking out about last night or anything? You know you can talk to me, don't you?" he asked, touching the small of my back softly.

I nodded. I was actually fine. If I could remember more of it then it would be worse, but at the moment, it was all just a little hazy, like I was watching someone else through frosted glass or something, everything was a little distorted.

156

"I'm fine honestly. Thank you so much, Will, I owe you a lot. And I'm sorry I didn't listen to you. I shouldn't have danced with that guy, I was just trying to prove a point and piss you off," I admitted, feeling stupid and immature.

He smiled and nodded. "I know why you did it. That doesn't make it your fault though, that guy probably would have found someone else to do that to if it wasn't you; he had the drugs with him so he obviously planned it. In a way I guess we were lucky that it was you because I was keeping an eye on you. I saw him lead you off down the hallway. If it had been someone else, some other girl that no one was watching, then it could have been a lot worse," he replied, smiling sadly and brushing some of my hair behind my ear.

I closed my eyes and turned my face towards his hand, pressing my cheek against it, loving the feel of his skin against mine again. I heard a small moan escape my lips and I wanted nothing more than to step forward, press myself against him and hold him tightly. He didn't move. His thumb just traced across my cheek lightly making my whole body tingle. I could hear his breathing and nothing had ever sounded more important to me.

I knew right then that I loved him. I already knew I was crazy about him, but it just all of a sudden hit me like a truck or something. I was totally and utterly in love with him, and no amount of trying to move on was going to help me get over him. Time I guess would be the only healer.

The toaster popped making me jump. I laughed at how lost in the moment I was. His hand dropped from the side of my face, and I dragged my eyes up to meet his just wishing things were different. Wishing I'd met him in a year, when I was eighteen and had finished school and was starting college or something. I had nine and a half months left at school to get through then I could move far away from his handsome face. Maybe the distance would help with the getting over him.

He smiled sadly and sighed. "I'll drive you and Amy home when you're ready," he muttered.

"Thanks." *Is now a good time to ask him about the tickets? Would I get another chance to ask him if I didn't do it now?* "Will?" I frowned. Was this just going to make things even more awkward between us?

"Mmm?" he mumbled, buttering his toast with his back to me.

I took a deep breath. "Why were you working at the club last night? I thought you would have stopped that now that you were working full time," I asked, going for the subtle approach.

He shoved the butter back into the fridge and shrugged. "I just had some hours to make up before I left."

"Really? Because Jack said you were paying for some concert tickets you got." I watched him, waiting for his reaction. His eyes tightened marginally but other than that he showed nothing else. *Damn he's a good actor… unless Jack was wrong and I've just made myself look like an idiot or something.*

"Jack's mistaken," he replied, munching on his toast.

"So you're not working at the club to pay for the Daniel Masters tickets you got for me?" I questioned. I honestly didn't know whether to believe him or not. Maybe Jack was just messing with me or something, trying to make me think he'd paid for them when he hadn't.

"Does it really matter?" he asked, looking a little uncomfortable.

Holy crud, he really is working there for me! I felt a little thrill go through me at the thought of him giving up his time for me. He'd agreed to work there for the next month for me, knowing that he wouldn't be able to see Miss Teller because of it, did that mean something?

"It matters to me," I mumbled breathlessly.

He sighed and frowned. "Then yeah I am. He wouldn't sell them to me. I got them in exchange for me working there for another month." He shrugged like it was nothing and I felt my heart skip a beat at how sweet he was.

"Thank you, Will, that's really..." I trailed off not knowing how to finish that sentence. A lot of words sprang to mind, but I wasn't sure which one suited him best: adorable, thoughtful, generous, incredible; the list went on and on.

"It's no big deal." He shrugged defensively.

Wow, no big deal, that is the understatement off the century. It's a huge deal to me. "Yeah I guess the extra money will come in handy." I shrugged, trying to make light of it. He was obviously a little uncomfortable talking about it.

He laughed and shook his head. "It would, but I'm not getting paid."

I gasped and looked at him shocked; he wasn't even getting paid for it? "Seriously?"

He nodded and put his plate in the sink with the other unwashed dishes. "That's the whole idea of payment, Chloe. Wouldn't be much of a deal for my boss if I was getting paid *and* getting the tickets on top would it." He laughed, flicking my nose playfully.

I smiled gratefully. *Jeez, this guy just gets better and better.* "Daniel Masters' tickets don't cost that much you know. I think maybe you were ripped off," I joked, grabbing his hand as he went to poke me in the ribs.

He laughed and wrapped his arm around me, pinning my arms to my sides, pressing me against the fridge and freeing his other hand as he tickled me making me giggle and squirm. "I was ripped off, really? They weren't worth my time? Shall I give them back?" he teased, laughing.

I shook my head, pressing my face against his chest as I squirmed and tried to get out of his hold, giggling like crazy. He laughed and pressed his face into the crook of my neck blowing a raspberry on me making me laugh hysterically.

"Stop, stop," I squeaked breathlessly.

He laughed and loosened his hold on me but didn't step back; I smiled and moved my head off of his chest looking up at his face. He was grinning happily and I felt my heart start to race at how close he was to me. His chest was pressed against mine; our legs were tangled together as he pressed me against the fridge.

158

The smile slowly faded from his face as he looked at me. His expression was torn, like he was trying to decide something. I could barely breathe. I could feel the sexual tension sparking up. If this had happened a month ago, before school started, he would have lifted me onto the counter by now and made love to me.

I gulped and ran my hand up his chest slowly until I got to his neck. I slipped my arm around his neck, tangling my fingers into his hair as my heart started crashing in my chest. He moaned lightly in the back of his throat as he pressed himself to me tighter, bending a little so our faces were at the same level as he just looked at me. He looked like he was trying to memorise every part of my face. He was looking at me so intently that it was making my legs a little weak.

His hot breath blew across my lips making my mouth water and my whole body tingle as a hundred butterflies seemed to take flight in my stomach. He gripped the back of my shirt tightly as he pressed his forehead to mine, his nose rubbing against mine teasingly making me arch my back so I could press against him harder. I was pretty sure that if he didn't kiss me soon I was going to pass out through lack of oxygen where I just couldn't seem to remember how to breathe.

Chapter Twenty-One

His eyes were boring into mine and a small smile pulled at the corners of his mouth. I tightened my hand in the back of his hair as his hand stroked down my back slowly making me shiver with desire. Just when I thought I couldn't take anymore teasing, he started inching his face closer to mine.

My insides were jumping for joy at the thought of him kissing me, if he kissed me then that meant he still wanted me and everything that he had done for me since we broke up really meant something. Was Amy right about him still wanting me? He couldn't look at me like I was a minor; because his mouth was now dangerously close to mine. Every inch of his hard, toned body was pressed against me, and I could barely stop myself squealing with excitement.

Just as his lips were about to touch mine, the bedroom door opened again and Amy's footsteps started coming in this direction. Will groaned as he pulled away from me. Disappointment washed over me. *Damn it, Amy, go away!* I looked at him pleadingly. He smiled sadly as he stepped back and let his arms drop from my waist. I felt my heart sink. He just kept doing that all the time, and it was killing me. One minute he'd look like he was going to kiss me and the next he was back to just being a teacher again. It was like he wanted to build my hopes up again, just so he could dash them for fun or something. I knew he wasn't doing that though. He probably just couldn't help himself, he was a player before we got together after all, so he was probably not used to being near a girl that wanted him and not doing anything about it. If he wanted a girl then he had her. I guess being near me was a little hard for him sometimes because of that. I just wished I was more than sex to him, that he wanted more than just my body, because he was hurting me so badly without even realising it.

I sighed and willed myself not to cry. "I'll go brush my hair and stuff then I'll be ready to leave," I mumbled as Amy walked in the kitchen. She looked a little sheepish; as if she thought she was going to be interrupting something. I resisted the urge to glare at her for ruining my moment with Will for the second time in the same morning. First she ruined my hug, and now she'd ruined a potential kiss and hot make out session. I loved my best friend, but sometimes I really could throttle her.

"You have your overnight bag in there. I got it out of Sam's car for you last night," Will muttered, rubbing the back of his neck and looking anywhere but me.

"Thanks, I'll just be a couple of minutes then." I grabbed Amy's hand and pulled her into the bedroom with me, not wanting to leave her on her own with Will. Things were awkward enough as it was without her adding any pressure or little comments about us being a 'cute couple' or anything.

She looked at me curiously as I grabbed my bag from by the door and stripped out of my party clothes that I'd slept in. "So are you going to tell me why you keep shooting me death glares?" she asked, laughing as she sat on the edge of the bed.

I sighed and closed my eyes. "Will was going to kiss me but you came out of the bedroom," I admitted reluctantly. She squealed and practically bounced on the bed. I shushed her and winced, hoping that Will didn't hear that and wonder what was going on.

"Sorry, oh God, I'm so sorry!" she whispered, giving me the puppy dog face.

I sighed and grabbed a pair of jeans, a tank top, and sweater from my bag, pulling them on. "Don't worry about it. It would have been a mistake anyway and would have just gotten my hopes up. It's best that you came out when you did because I can't keep letting him sucker me in all the time." I tried to make myself believe the words as I said them.

"Chloe, what are you going to do? You're still totally crazy about him," she said, looking at me sympathetically.

I shrugged. "There's nothing I can do. He doesn't want me so I'm letting it go and trying to move on, like you told me to."

She rolled her eyes. "I told you to move on because I thought there was no chance of you two getting back together. Hell, you *told* me there was no chance, but believe me; that guy still wants you. There's a chance there alright and I don't think you should be giving up. He made you so happy when you two were together."

I gasped in shock. She was the one that practically forced me to move on to someone else. She'd even made me go out on that date with Olly and give him a chance. *Holy crap, Olly!* I'd completely forgotten about him. I was so caught up in the moment with Will in the kitchen that I would have done anything with him, and Olly was only just now popping into my head. I was a terrible girlfriend.

"You're the one that told me to give it up, Amy. Move on you said." I threw my hands up in exasperation. "Besides, I don't have a chance with him. He doesn't like me like that anymore, I think he still wants my body, but he's with Miss Teller now anyway. I don't have a chance in hell competing against her, I mean, have you seen her? She's perfect," I whined, plopping down next to her on the bed trying not to pout like a three year old.

161

She shook her head. "You know what? I don't think he's dating her," Amy said thoughtfully. I looked at her like she was crazy. *Of course he's dating her; it's been all around the school for the last week.* She frowned and shook her head again. "I'm thinking he's not interested in her at all. No one has seen them kiss, or hug, or show any signs of being in a relationship. Everyone's just assuming they're together. Maybe it's innocent, maybe they're friends. He looks at you like he wants you, so why would he be with her if he wanted you?" she asked, biting her lip like she did when she was thinking really hard.

I sighed deeply. "Amy, he brings her to school every day and takes her home with him. It's pretty obvious that they're sleeping together. She's beautiful, and nice, and smart, *and* old enough for him. They make the perfect couple," I admitted grudgingly even though every word seemed to burn my throat on the way out.

She shook her head. "Maybe it's something else. I just don't quite buy it."

I'd had enough of talking about this, I didn't want to keep going over and over the same thing it was painful. I needed to get the heck out of Will's apartment because the more time I spent here the more I missed the old times I spent here.

"Let's just forget it," I said firmly, letting her know that this was the end of the conversation. She seemed to get the hint as she pushed herself up from the bed and nodded sadly before heading into his bathroom.

I grabbed my bag searching through for a hairbrush, but I must have forgotten to pack it. I sighed and went over to Will's chest of drawers where he kept a comb, so I could at least get the tangles from my bed hair. As I rummaged through the top drawer looking for the comb I noticed a picture frame on top of the drawers. It was right at the back, practically hidden by a pile of clothes. Curiosity got the better of me so I reached for it, wondering who it was of. I hadn't seen any photos when I stayed here, so this was a new one.

I gripped the frame and my breath caught in my throat as I looked at the couple in the picture. It was me and Will at his sister's wedding. Our first date. It was the professional photo that had been taken in the back of the church yard. We looked so cute all smiling at each other. I smiled at how tenderly he was looking at me in the picture.

Why on earth would he have bought this? Were we still together when he ordered it? But even if we were still together when he ordered it, we weren't together now, so why would he have it in a frame on his drawers? Surely if he wanted to keep this then he would have hidden it in a drawer or something so no one would see it. What if Miss Teller saw this when she stayed over or something? She would obviously know it was me and would ask him about it. Had he told her about us? Was he that into her that he'd risked telling her about him sleeping with a minor? It must be even more serious than I thought if he trusted her with the secret of it.

I rubbed my thumb over the picture lightly, looking at him in his suit. In a way I'd forgotten about that day a little, photos always had a way of reminding you of things that your mind forgot. I would actually really love to have a copy of this photo, I didn't have any photos of him at all, and I would just love to be able to stare at a picture of him before I went to sleep. *Wow, Chloe, lucky no one can hear your thoughts because you are seriously sounding like a deranged stalker right about now!*

Amy came out of the bathroom so I quickly put the picture back and searched the drawer again for the comb, dragging it through my hair, making myself look a little more presentable. I tried desperately to pretend that my heart wasn't trying to break out of my chest. I smiled at her when I was done and pretended I hadn't seen anything there, I didn't want her reading things into it again, I just couldn't cope with anymore today.

The ride home was uneventful; we were all sat in an uncomfortable silence on the way to Amy's. He stopped the car a couple of houses away from hers so that her parents didn't see her arrive in a strange guy's car when she was supposed to have been staying at mine.

I smiled at Amy as she grabbed her purse and opened her door. "Thanks for the ride, Mr Morris." She smirked at him making him groan quietly.

"No worries, Miss Clarke. See you at school tomorrow."

"I'll pick you up in the morning, Chloe," Amy told me as she climbed out of the car.

I nodded and smiled. "Yeah thanks, see you," I called as she shut the door and walked off up the street towards her house.

Will pulled out again, heading towards my house. I glanced at him from the corner of my eye. I had no idea what to say to him, so I just said nothing. I would actually rather he had dropped me off first so that I wasn't in the car with him on my own. That thing in the kitchen had made me feel a little awkward around him because I just couldn't stop thinking about it. Then again, I didn't really want Amy on her own with him either, just in case she said something to him about me and made everything worse.

He pulled up a couple of houses away from my house and cut the engine, turning in his seat to look at me curiously. "Do you think Amy will say anything to anyone? Because if you do then I'd rather we just go and say something first, it'll sound better coming from us, rather than me just being reported."

I shook my head fiercely. "She won't say anything, you don't need to worry."

He seemed to relax a little. "Okay, tell her thanks from me."

I nodded, chewing on my lip nervously. "Thanks for the ride, and for last night." I didn't really know how to show him how grateful I was to him for saving me and then letting us stay at his place so we didn't get into trouble for it.

"No worries, you don't need to keep thanking me."

"Would it be totally inappropriate if I hugged you again?" I asked, trying not to show him how much I needed it.

He smiled sadly and nodded. "Totally inappropriate," he confirmed.

I sighed and gripped my hand on the door handle, resigning myself to the fact that it truly was over, that he was back to being my teacher as of now and nothing more.

"Chloe?" He laughed and leant forward in his seat, slipping one arm around my shoulder, pulling me closer to him. I smiled gratefully and hugged him back, clinging to him, breathing in his smell. I really didn't want to get out of the car and back to normality. Being close to him, even for little things like this, just made my heart race. I would give anything for this to be normal, for this to be allowed and easy. But I guess not everything in life is easy because where would the fun be in that? I just couldn't see the fun in this situation at the moment.

I pulled out of the hug as I felt my eyes starting to prickle with tears; I needed to leave before I cried all over him. "Thanks, and I guess I'll see you at school tomorrow," I mumbled, forcing a smile.

He nodded and frowned. I swallowed the lump in my throat; did he not want me to leave either? He didn't say anything so I pushed the door open and walked off without looking back, fighting tears the whole way up the path.

The following morning Amy picked me up for school, quizzing me about Will the whole trip and what he'd said after she got out of the car. It seemed as though she wanted to know every single thing that had happened since we broke up. I'd refused to speak about it on the phone last night when she called; I just couldn't force the words out while it was still raw. After a good night sleep I felt much better about it. Yes, we'd had a couple of moments that might have turned into something else had it not been for Amy's interruption, but those moments were passed now so I just needed to get on with it.

When we pulled up at school I spotted Olly almost immediately, he was standing chatting to a group of his friends with a couple of girls standing there too obviously trying their luck with the swim team. I gulped and immediately felt awful. What was I supposed to say to him today? The last time I'd seen him we had a huge fight and he stormed off and left me to make my own way home from school.

I decided just to pretend like I didn't see him and head to my locker with Amy. I definitely didn't mind putting off a potential argument with him. I linked my arm through Amy's and smiled a big fake smile, which of course she saw through immediately.

"Olly's over there," she whispered as we walked through the parking lot.

"Mmm hmm," I mumbled, chewing on my lip, looking at the school, practically counting down the steps until we were safely inside so I could avoid a probable painful and embarrassing situation.

"Not gonna say hi? What are you going to do about him today?" she asked, guiding me around a group of girls who were squealing about the Justin Bieber concert they went to see this weekend.

I sighed and shook my head. "No idea. I'm still trying the whole moving on thing, but to be honest, he's probably still pissed at me for going to the party, and I'm still pissed at him for telling me I couldn't hang out with Sam. I'm not sure where we go from here," I admitted with a shrug.

Just as we got to the safety of the front doors I heard him shout my name. I groaned and immediately wondered how wrong it would be just to carry on walking and fake temporary deafness. I could pull that off, couldn't I? I could just spend the morning asking everyone; 'I'm sorry, what?' I flicked my eyes to Amy to see if she had the same idea as me, but she just looked at me sympathetically and I knew I couldn't be mean. Mean wasn't who I was, I was the person who did things for people all the time because I didn't like to hurt their feelings or tell people no.

"I'll meet you in class," I said to Amy as she unlinked her arm through mine and nodded, heading towards our lockers where Nick was already waiting for us with a big smile on his face. I took a deep breath and willed myself to be strong. I wasn't going to put up with Olly's possessive nonsense, so if he didn't apologise then that was it, I was breaking it off. Instantly I kind of wished he wouldn't apologise, just so I could have an easy passage out of it.

As I turned back in his direction I pretended I didn't realise he was there. He was walking quickly towards me looking a little sheepish but cute as usual. "Hey, I was waiting for you," he said as he got up to me.

I shifted my bag on my shoulder uncomfortably. "Yeah? Sorry I didn't see you."

He nodded, his eyes searching my face for something. "How was the party Saturday night?" he asked. One eyebrow was raised questionably, but no other emotions were on his face.

Okay how do I answer that question, do I go with the truth? "Actually, I was drugged and almost raped, but my ex-boyfriend, who by the way, is our teacher, burst into the room and beat the guy to a pulp before carrying me through the house, taking me to his and letting me sleep in his bed. Oh yeah and he almost kissed me this morning." Yeah I don't think the truth would go down to well here! Okay so I go with a lie.

"It was good actually; I got pretty wasted and spent most of yesterday in bed," I replied, trying not to give away any signs of lying to him. In fact it wasn't a total lie, if you took out all of the bad things that happened, that was actually my Saturday night to a tee!

He frowned, but his expression quickly cleared. "That's good. How was spending time with the ex's brother?" he asked. His tone was a little too controlled. That wasn't exactly what he was asking me, but I think it was his way of getting me to talk about Sam.

I shrugged. "Good, he's a great guy." I didn't bother to elaborate; he still hadn't apologised so I didn't owe him anything.

"Right, great guy, awesome," he muttered sarcastically under his breath.

165

"Well if there's nothing else then I think we're done talking. I need to speak to Amy before class starts…" I trailed off, gazing longingly up the hallway to where Amy and Nick were laughing together.

He didn't say anything so I turned to walk away; before I got more than two steps though he grabbed my hand making me stop. "Wait, we're not done talking," he insisted. I sighed and looked back at him, he looked uncomfortable and awkward, and I would imagine that I looked exactly the same. "Look, I'm sorry about telling you that you couldn't go to the party. As soon as I got to the car I knew I shouldn't have done it. I ran back to the school, but I couldn't find you. I shouldn't have tried to order you around like that, and I need to learn to trust you. It's just hard for me, I-" He frowned, looking a little pained.

I felt my heart sink. Olly the nice guy was back and he'd apologised, which I wasn't expecting, so did that mean that we could just start over? Could I start over with him after that almost kiss with Will? Did I need to admit that to him, or just forget it because technically nothing happened?

He smiled and looked at me sadly. "It's hard for me to trust a girl after Christina. She basically ruined everything and made me into that possessive guy from Friday. I'm really sorry." He squeezed my hand lightly as he looked into my eyes apologetically.

Christina? What did she do to make him like that? "Christina?" I asked a little confused. She was his last girlfriend that he'd broken up with about four or five months ago. She went to a different school, but apparently they were together for about a year.

He nodded and stepped closer to me. "She cheated on me," he admitted. "And since then I just find it hard getting close to a girl because I keep thinking about them doing the same thing to me." He was looking at me like I was the big bad wolf about to eat his grandma or something.

My stomach started to ache with guilt. Here he was, pouring his heart out about his ex and telling me why he had trust issues, and I'd had that little indiscretion with Will yesterday. I knew I definitely couldn't tell Olly now, I'd probably confirm everything bad that he thought about women. He would probably never trust a girl again!

"Oh, I didn't realise," I muttered, chewing on my lip and wishing the ground would just open up and swallow me to take me away from this painful conversation.

"Yeah I didn't tell anyone. I just wanted you to know why I was like that with you; it wasn't just that I was being an ass I promise." He stroked the side of my face with the back of one finger and I felt a smile tugging at the corner of my mouth. It kind of made sense and explained why he would freak out, but that still didn't excuse it and he still needed to know I wouldn't put up with it from him again.

"I get it, Olly; she hurt you so you think that every girl will do the same thing. But I'm not like that, I promise. I don't cheat." I said the words, but my mind flicked to Will's full lips inching closer to mine, and how the cold of the fridge had made me breakout goosebumps - or maybe the goosebumps were

166

caused by the anticipation of the kiss, I wasn't sure. I knew one thing for certain though; I sure as heck would have cheated yesterday if Amy hadn't walked in.

He nodded and cupped my cheek with his hand. "I know and I'm sorry. Forgive me?" he asked, giving me the puppy dog face. He looked so cute when he did that, all big blue eyes and sad mouth.

I swallowed loudly. "Yeah okay, but you won't do that again, right? I won't put up with it so you need to take that on board pretty quickly."

He smiled happily and nodded. "Absolutely, lesson learned I promise."

I rolled my eyes playfully and nodded. "So how was your family dinner?" I asked, wanting to change the subject because the guilt of the almost kiss was making me feel terrible.

He smiled and shook his head dismissively. "We can talk later," he whispered as he pressed his lips against mine. I whimpered, a little shocked that he was actually kissing me in the middle of the hallway with everyone standing around us. He didn't pull back either, it wasn't just a peck; it was a proper, full-on kiss. I kissed him back, but I could feel the heat flooding my face at the thought of the people watching this. I hated it when people made out in the hallway, Amy and I usually made jokes about it - and now here I was doing it.

He sucked on my bottom lip asking for entrance so I pushed him away, slightly breathless. There was no way I was full on making out in the hallway, not a chance in hell of that happening. He was grinning happily as his other arm snaked around my waist, pulling my body to his as he pressed his lips back to mine again softly. One of his hands trailed down my back towards my ass making me squirm and lean away so that the kiss broke. *Looks like we need to talk about the rules of 'taking it slow' again.*

Someone cleared their throat right next to us making me jump a mile. Olly pulled back a little reluctantly, and we both turned, expecting it to be Amy or someone playing around. It wasn't Amy though. Instead, Will stood there with a face like thunder. My heart seemed to stop beating as my blood ran cold. His jaw was tight, his eyes hard and furious as he looked at Olly. I silently thanked my lucky stars that I wasn't getting that death glare because he actually looked scary when he was angry. I blushed like crazy and stepped away from Olly quickly. I literally felt sick that the one teacher who had to walk round the corner was my ex. *I guess this is karma's payback for me lying to Olly about the party. Suck it up, Chloe, because karma can be a bitch!*

"I've spoken to you about this before, Mr Hawk. It's against school rules for this sort of thing to be happening on school property, and you know it. Therefore you'll both get detentions for the rest of the week. Lunchtime. My room," Will spat venomously.

My mouth dropped open in shock. *A week of detentions for a kiss? Is he crazy?* I couldn't help the glare that I shot him. I knew he was a hero and that I was supposed to be grateful, but I hated this part of his personality with a passion. "What for?" I challenged. *People do an awful lot more than that in the hallway and get away with nothing more than a telling off, and we get a whole week of detentions? What an asshole!* He looked at me as if I had said something stupid as he crossed his arms over his chest arrogantly. I could have slapped myself for noticing how his white button down shirt had three buttons undone so it exposed the very top of his chest. I shouldn't notice things like that when I was angry with him, actually, scratch that, I shouldn't notice things like that about him at all.

"Public display of affection, Miss Henderson," he replied smartly, smirking at me. *Is he enjoying this? Does he get off on making me angry or something?*

"It was a kiss!" I cried, throwing my hands up in exasperation.

"Which isn't allowed in the school hallway," he countered, looking just as angry with me as I was with him.

"This is stupid; no one else gives a week of detentions for a freaking kiss. Check with them, ask around, the most they would give would be one," I retorted, frowning. I could feel the anger boiling up inside me. I wanted to punch something just so I could let it out. *Hmm, maybe I should punch him in his handsome face and actually earn the detentions!*

"I don't care what the other teachers would do, it's not their decision, it's mine. A week, starting today." He turned to walk off, but Olly stepped forward quickly.

"I can't do this week, Mr Morris, I have swim meets all week ready for time trials, at lunchtimes *and* after school," he explained, looking at him pleadingly.

A smile twitched at the corner of Will's mouth. "Fine, next week then." He turned to look at me and I noticed that his smile turned into a stupid smirk which made my insides flutter a little. "Miss Henderson, you can still do yours this week." He turned and walked off, and I wanted to slap myself for watching his butt in his jeans.

Olly looked at me apologetically. "I'm sorry, that was totally my fault."

I closed my eyes and groaned in frustration. I didn't want to spend the week trapped in a classroom with Will. Why did this happen to me? What did I do to deserve this, this was more than karma, this was more like payback for something I'd done in a previous life or something, some kind of sick redemption.

"Don't worry about it, Olly." I sighed and shouldered my bag, trying not to be annoyed with him. "I'll see you later," I muttered as I headed up the hallway towards Amy who was grinning from ear to ear looking at me. I walked up to her, looking at her curiously. Maybe she missed the whole scene that Will had just made, or maybe she was grinning for some other reason entirely.

She grabbed my arm as soon as I got to her side. "Let's go to the bathroom before class!" she squealed excitedly.

I nodded and let her lead me along as I shouted a "hi" to Nick over my shoulder. As soon as we were in the toilet she clapped her hands and jumped up and down excitedly like a five year old that just got told they were going to Disneyland.

"What did I miss?" I asked confused.

"Oh my days, Chloe, did you not see how freaking jealous Will was just then?" she practically screamed.

Chapter Twenty-Two

*W*hat on earth is this girl on today? Jealous, he wasn't jealous he was just being an ass! I looked at her as if she was speaking a foreign language and she rolled her eyes at me, still jumping up and down excitedly.

"He's such a jerk." I frowned angrily. What had I seen in him anyway? Obviously his looks, but he was never this guy when we were together, he was sweet and funny, kind and caring. So what had changed to make him start acting like this towards me? Did he feel like he needed to make a strict name for himself at the school so he could be taken seriously or something, and he was using me to do it because he knew me? Was that what this was?

"Get a grip on yourself, Chloe, for goodness sake! He just gave you a week worth of detentions for kissing in the hallway! Did you see his face? He looked like he wanted to beat the crap out of Olly. I'm surprised he didn't just pee on you to mark you with his scent, it was that obvious!" she cried, grabbing my hand and squeezing it a little too hard.

Pee on me? She really has lost the plot here; he was doing his teacher duties and just went a little - okay, a lot - overboard with it. "Amy, you're reading things into it because that's what you want to see!" I protested, shaking my head fiercely as I pulled my hand from her ever tightening hold.

She growled in frustration and gripped my shoulders, even shaking me a little. "No I'm not! I'm the only one seeing things clearly here. You're missing things because you're hurt, he's getting angry because he's jealous of you with Olly, and I'm the only one that can see both sides!"

She can't be right. Why would he be jealous of Olly if he has someone already? Oh for goodness sake, my brain hurts! "Amy, I appreciate the effort you're putting into making me feel better, but seriously, this needs to stop. It hurts to keep talking about it. There's just over nine months left at school and then I never want to see him again. Just nine months, and then I can pretend like I never met him." I said the words more for myself than her. I wanted to try and believe that I could pretend I'd never met him, but I knew deep down that I could never forget him. He was my first love, and it would take me a long time to get over it, but I would get over it eventually. At least, I hoped I would.

Amy sighed and shook her head disappointedly. "All right, every time I see something that's not right, I'm going to point it out to you and then you can make your own mind up about it. Believe me if you want to, don't, whatever. But I'm telling you the truth, Will was jealous," she stated, looking at me knowingly.

I nodded and smiled, pretending that I believed her, but she saw through it immediately and laughed. I never could lie to my best friend. "Okay you do what you want, let's get to class though shall we?" I looked longingly at the door, needing to get this conversation finished. She nodded and linked her arm through mine as we made our way back to Nick who was waiting for us by the lockers.

"Hey, good weekend?" he asked, smiling as he slung his arm around my shoulder.

I opened my mouth to answer, but Amy cut me off. "Oh we had an awesome weekend, a lot of interesting things happened." She smirked at me so I tried not to show any reaction as Nick looked at her curiously, obviously wondering what that meant. He looked at me so I just shrugged and pretended to be confused too while Amy laughed to herself knowingly.

We headed to our respective classes. Amy and I went to the locker room and got changed into our shorts and T-shirts because we were running today apparently. I sighed as I pulled my hair up into a messy bun. *This has to be the worst class in the world. I just hope I can manage to run in a straight line and not fall on my face or something.* Olly was there too. He hung back with me and Amy, slowly jogging along instead of pushing it like some of the other people in the class.

I noticed that Olly shot a couple of guys little glares as they went past, his hand touching my back possessively when Spencer slowed down to talk to us – well, more like flirt with Amy, but that didn't stop Olly from taking my hand, purposefully putting himself in-between our bodies. I groaned quietly. I didn't want to be mean or anything, but if he was going to continue with the jealousy thing then I would end it. I understood that he'd been hurt before, but that didn't mean he couldn't at least try to trust me. I refused to put up with him being possessive all the time.

I frowned but didn't say anything in front of Amy and Spencer; I'd talk to Olly about it again when we were on our own. "I'll see you later," I mumbled at the end of class as he walked me to the girls locker rooms so I could shower and change.

"Yeah, not until the end of the day though, I have swim practice at lunchtime." He frowned.

I snorted. "Yeah and I have detention," I grumbled.

He smiled apologetically. "I'm sorry about that. Are you angry with me?" he asked, giving me the puppy dog face that he seemed so damn good at.

I shook my head in response. I was a little angry at him for kissing me, but most of my anger was directed firmly at Will. "No, it's fine. Just don't do that again okay? I don't really like PDA's or anything." I cringed and blushed again just at the thought of it.

He nodded and looked a little sad. "Well I'll see you at the end of the day. Hope detention goes okay."

"Yeah, hope your swim thing goes well too," I replied, then as an afterthought chanted, "Go team!" trying to be supportive and enthusiastic. He laughed and gave me a little push towards the locker rooms so I could change.

For the rest of the morning all I could think about was how Amy thought Will was jealous of Olly. Was he jealous? I'd once considered the same thing, but I knew that he'd moved on. He was the one that told me it was over, if he still had feelings for me then he wouldn't have done that. What possible reason could he have for breaking it off with me? Unless he was scared or something; maybe he was scared of getting into trouble if it continued. I could understand that of course, but did he have to do it in such a horrible way? To tell me that it was lucky it happened now, before we developed feelings for each other? That implied that he didn't have any feelings for me in the first place. So why would he be jealous?

"Oh for goodness sake," I muttered. *Why can't I stop thinking about him?*

"Chloe, you have something you want to share with the class?" Mrs Flats asked.

Oh crud, had I said that aloud? I shook my head quickly and looked at her apologetically. "No, sorry." I winced, hoping I didn't get into more trouble; I didn't need any more detentions on top of the ones from Will. The only good thing I could see to come out of the detentions was that I wouldn't see Olly for lunch for the next two weeks, that would give me time to stop feeling guilty about the 'almost kiss' with Will, and then we could put some space between us so he wouldn't be getting all possessive all the time.

"Get on with it then please!" Mrs Flats snapped, nodding at my textbook that was unopened on my desk. *Wow, how long had I been thinking about Will for?* I sighed and pulled open my book, trying my hardest to concentrate.

The morning passed slowly because all I could think about was Will and what he was going to say to me in detention. Maybe he wouldn't say anything to me; maybe he'd ignore me completely. I kind of hoped he did in a way; it would be easier than having a blazing argument with him or something.

I trudged behind Amy to the canteen, buying a sandwich and ignoring her sympathetic smiles. "Have fun," she joked, squeezing my shoulder in a supportive gesture.

"Thanks, I'm sure it'll be a laugh a minute," I mumbled.

I took a deep breath and headed to his classroom, feeling my heart sink with every step I took. When I got there he wasn't there yet so I let myself in, taking a seat near the window. Hopefully there would be other people that got detentions with him today so that it wouldn't be as awkward. I started munching on my sandwich absentmindedly.

He trudged in about five minutes later and smiled a little sadly at me. "Hi," he greeted sheepishly.

"Hi," I muttered, pulling out my English assignment so I could make a start on it.

172

I grabbed my iPod, but just as I was about to turn it on I saw him pull the chair out from the desk in front of mine and sit on it backwards so he was facing me. "Look, I'm sorry I keep being a jerk to you all the time, but you really need to stop talking to me like I'm more than a teacher to you. You can't answer me back and challenge my decisions in front of everyone. I know I went a little overboard with the weeklong detentions, but you wouldn't talk back to another teacher would you?" he asked, cocking his head to the side and looking adorable.

I shrugged. *I guess he's right I would never challenge another teacher like that, but he just makes me so mad all the time.* "I guess not, sorry."

"I get that I make you angry. I know that most of the time I'm behaving like a jerk to you, but I don't realise until after when I have time to think about it. I'm really sorry. I took this too far; you don't have to stay for the week. Just do today and we'll call it quits okay?" he offered, smiling. I couldn't help but smile in return. His smile was beautiful. Why did he have to be so good-looking, sweet and charming? I secretly wished he'd just stick to being the jerk so I could hate him easier.

"Really?" I asked hopefully.

He nodded. "Really," he confirmed. "And I'm sorry I'm an ass."

I bit the inside of my cheek and tried desperately not to smile when he smirked at me, but I just couldn't help myself. "You *are* an ass," I agreed. I felt a blush creeping onto my face, which seemed to make his smirk grow more pronounced.

"Yeah, but I'm an ass that apologises with Malteasers." He dropped a bag of Malteasers onto the desk, smiling wickedly.

I grinned. Those were my favourites, he knew that. "Well then you're forgiven," I chirped, grabbing the bag eagerly.

He chuckled. "So easily bought. A bag of those and you're putty in my hands," he teased, winking at me.

I laughed and ripped them open. His hand shot out grabbing one quickly. "Hey!" I protested, pretending to look annoyed as I slapped the back of his hand lightly. He just laughed and threw it up in the air trying to catch it in his mouth, but it missed and fell back onto the desk making me giggle. "Fail!" I chirped, laughing.

"Damn, let me try again." He grabbed another one from the bag and tried again, but it hit his cheek and fell to the floor. "Damn it, one more." He laughed getting another one from my bag. This one didn't even get near his mouth and I giggled hysterically at him.

"Lucky you're not a gym teacher because your throw sucks," I teased.

"Well you do better then, little miss cocky." He looked at me challengingly, crossing his arms over his chest. I grinned and grabbed one from the bag trying to throw it into my mouth, but it hit my teeth and bounced across the desk making him laugh. He picked it up and tried again to catch it, but it was apparent that both of us sucked at the game. "Ten points for the first to do it. I'll go buy more." He grinned and practically ran out of the room to go to the vending machine.

I laughed when he came back with three more bags, dropping them onto my desk, grinning wildly. When he was playing around like this it reminded me so much of the time we'd spent together that it made my heart race. This one was *my* Will, the Will that made me smile, and blush, and giggle.

By the time the bell rang, the floor was littered with little chocolate balls, and my sides hurt from so much laughing. It looked like giant bunnies had snuck in and made a mess everywhere. When the bell sounded Will frowned. "I didn't realise we were doing that for so long, I needed to grade some test papers for next class." He winced a little, looking back at his desk that was stacked with his work.

I smiled. "Well maybe you should have done it at the weekend instead of leaving it until lunchtime," I teased.

He shrugged. "Should have done, but I had other things on my mind." He smiled and pulled out another bag of Malteasers, handing them to me. "Here. I knew we wouldn't actually get to eat any so I bought you some to take away."

I smiled. *So freaking sweet!* "Thanks." I blushed again. *Wow, Chloe, stop blushing!* "Want me to help you clean these up?" I asked, looking around that the four packets of deliciousness that was scattered all over his floor. Out of the four packets we had played with, he had managed to catch about five, and I managed to get one - but even my one was only because he threw it into my mouth from close range to make me feel better.

"Nah, I got it. How about a rematch tomorrow?" he offered; his eyes were twinkling with amusement. My stomach started to flutter.

"I thought you were letting me off of the detentions," I replied. I was actually kind of hoping he would change his mind and force me to spend the week with him because this was so fun spending time with him; it was nice just to pretend like we were at his place fooling around, instead of a classroom.

"I did let you off for the week. But because of the mess you made of my classroom I kind of feel like you need to be punished for it," he joked, kicking the little balls over to one side of the room trying to get them into a pile.

I laughed and shoved my unopened books back into my bag. I hadn't done one single scrap of work this lunchtime, and I couldn't be happier because of it. "Punished, really? Most of these were your failed attempts!" I countered, smirking at him.

"Yeah but let's not forget who won overall. Your catching skills suck more than mine, Miss Henderson." He flicked my nose lightly making me giggle and blush like crazy. *I love it when he does that to me.*

"Okay, well then I guess I'll see you at the same time tomorrow." I shrugged and fought to keep the happy smile off of my face at the thought of spending another hour with him. I just prayed he was like this, instead of the jerk Will that I hated.

174

"Yep, and I'll see you in class in a bit." He turned and headed to his little store room, coming back with a broom so he could sweep up. I watched him for a few seconds; he looked so hot doing that for some reason. His T-shirt rode up slightly at the back, exposing a little skin as he bent over. I couldn't take my eyes off of that sliver of skin. *Wow, I'm seriously deranged if I'm getting hot for him while he's sweeping up. You really have lost the plot, Chloe!*

I swung my bag over my shoulder and headed towards the door. "See you class then," I said as I bit my lip. He nodded, smiling. I hesitated at the door. I didn't want to leave the room and go back to normality again. It seemed like every time I went away from him and saw him again, he changed. I didn't want that to happen again today.

I forced myself to walk out and headed straight for my Spanish class. Amy was waiting outside the door for me with Olly, he was looking at me apologetically, his hair still damp from his swim practice. He smiled as I got up to them. "So, how was it?" he asked, brushing his hand over my cheek lightly.

I shrugged and felt the blush creep up onto my face at the thought of what it was like. 'The most fun I'd had in ages' was what I wanted to say, but I couldn't exactly say that to him. "Okay, it was detention so…" I trailed off not really wanting to lie too much to him.

He smiled and wrapped his arm around my waist, pulling me closer to him. "I'm sorry. Can I make it up to you after school? Maybe take you out somewhere? I have swim practice until four, but I could come to yours after, or you could wait for me here until I'm done. You could watch if you want," he suggested, looking at me hopefully.

Watch him swim? Hmm, not quite what I'd call fun, but I guess that's what a girlfriend does! "Sure, I'll watch and then we'll go somewhere." I shrugged. He grinned and bent his head to kiss me so I turned my head to the side quickly, making him scowl at me. "Seriously? I've just done detention for that!" I snapped.

He laughed and kissed my cheek before pulling away quickly. "Couldn't help myself, sorry. Okay I need to go, I'm late for class. See you in calculus," he called as he ran off down the hallway at full speed.

Amy was leaning against the wall, watching me. "Well? How was it really?" she asked, raising one eyebrow. I knew I couldn't lie to her so I looped my arm through hers and dragged her into the class where we talked in hushed whispers at the back of the class. By the time I was done with my little lunchtime detention story she was practically vibrating with excitement.

"I told you!" she hissed, grinning like a mad woman.

I rolled my eyes. "Yeah, but that doesn't prove anything apart from he's a fun guy. It doesn't mean anything, Amy."

"Does blindness run in your family?" she teased. When the teacher walked past we both started the assignment we were supposed to be reading through and translating.

After class we walked quickly to calculus knowing that the seats would all be taken again. *Hmm, I wonder if Olly will save one for us again like last time, hopefully it won't be near the front because I'll probably blush if Will even looks in my direction.*

When we headed in Olly was sitting in the middle with a couple of his friends, two empty seats next to him. I headed over to sit next to him. "This seat taken?" I asked, smiling.

"It is now." He grinned and patted the chair for me to sit down.

Will walked in and I dropped my eyes quickly, pretending to look through my bag for something as I blushed like crazy. My heart stuttered in my chest. I heard him laugh so I looked up just as he bent down picking something up; he threw a Malteaser into the trash with a grin on his face. He'd obviously missed some when he cleaned up, there were a couple scattered around the floor. *Bless him he never was too good at tidying up!* I laughed too which made Olly look at me like I was crazy. I noticed that he was sitting quite far away from me today, his hands firmly on top of the desk. Will's little lecture about him pawing me in his class had obviously had the desired effect.

"Okay guys, so there's another assembly for seniors again today so we only have class until half past two. I was going to start something new today but because we won't have very long, how about a pop quiz instead?" Will offered, smiling.

"What the?" I cried shocked. *No way. I'm not prepared for a damn pop quiz! That's totally not fair!*

Will laughed. "What the... what, Miss Henderson?" he asked, smirking playfully at me.

"A pop quiz, seriously? Aren't we supposed to get notice before these so we can study?" I whined, trying the begging face that he used to say made me look cute.

He smiled and shrugged. "Well I guess this is an unannounced one. We'll see how hard you guys have been trying over the last couple of weeks."

I groaned and put my head on my arms, trying desperately to remember everything Nick had taught me in the last couple of weeks. I at least had to do better than the last little quiz he set where I got everything wrong and he'd suggested that I get a tutor. I heard Will laugh and a piece of paper being put on my desk so I raised my head to look at him. He smiled his little smile that somehow always made me feel like I was the only girl in the world. I sighed dreamily as I thought about him just holding me again, just a little hug or holding my hand, or something.

The test wasn't that bad actually. Nick did a really great job tutoring me on all of this stuff, and although I knew I didn't get everything right, I knew I hadn't failed completely which I was happy about. At two thirty we all made our way down to the hall for assembly. I sat on one of the seats at the end; I knew what this was about, the trip out with the money that we had been awarded. The voting had taken place on Friday so they were probably going to announce what we were doing.

I sat there nervously chewing my lip, listening as Principal Sherman was droning on and on about the options and how proud he was that we had done all of the volunteer work in the first place and how marvellously it reflected on the school. I crossed my fingers and prayed for anything other than paintballing, which wasn't my thing at all. If it got voted in then I'd just fake an illness or something. I would rather stay at home than run around getting shot.

"Okay, so with an overwhelming number of votes, the activity that eighty-three percent of you all voted for was…" he paused for dramatic effect, and I felt my heart sink with every passing second. "Paintballing!"

The whole hall erupted into cheers which drowned out my groan. A quick glance around the hall showed that it was only me and the group of cheerleaders that weren't pleased about it. They were all screeching in a high pitched voice about their manicures and how the paint wouldn't be good for their extensions. *Wow, I can't say I'm very happy about the company in my little 'I hate paintballing club'.*

"Bet you're pleased about that, huh?" Will whispered in my ear. I jumped because of how close he was to me.

I turned and groaned. "I don't want to go freaking paintballing!" I whined, pouting.

He laughed. "Aww, poor baby. You never know, maybe you'll like it. I know I'm going to enjoy it!" He grinned happily.

He's going? "Are you going too then?"

He nodded. "Chaperoning," he confirmed. "I got to vote too. I think it was my vote that swung it." He winked at me before smirking at walking off. I chuckled, watching him walk away.

Nick was practically jumping up and down with excitement. I laughed as he picked up Amy and spun her around making her scream and giggle. I smiled. It probably wouldn't be as bad as I imagined, but if it was I could always fake an injury or something if I totally hated it. At least my friends would enjoy it, and I could sit on the sidelines and watch. It wasn't for another two weeks anyway so at least I had a lot of time to prepare myself for it!

Chapter Twenty-Three

When the assembly was done everyone skipped off, talking excitedly about the trip. All I could hear were people talking about how 'awesome' it was going to be. Awesome my ass, this was going to be torture, but at least it pleased my friends. Amy and Nick were still fooling around like little kids, laughing. Nick looked so happy that it made my heart ache. I loved seeing him happy. Since his mom died I went to great lengths to make him smile that broadly, but it didn't happen terribly often, especially not around the anniversary of her passing.

An arm slung around my shoulder so I turned quickly to see Olly grinning from ear to ear. "Hey you. Are you ready to come watch me swim?" he asked.

Oh crap, I forgot about that. Wow, another hour of fun! I plastered on a fake smile. "Sure." I nodded. He smiled and started leading me off in the other direction from my friends. "Wait a sec I just need to tell Amy that I don't need a ride." I shrugged his arm off and went back to my group, with Olly following behind me like a little lost puppy.

Amy smiled as I got over to her. "You're so pissed about this, right?" She laughed wickedly.

"Well, I'm none too thrilled with the thought of running through the woods and hurting myself, then getting shot with paintballs that apparently bruise when they hit you," I admitted, frowning and pouting like a child.

Nick burst out laughing. "I forgot you'll probably break an ankle with all that running and we'll have to carry your butt to the hospital!" he teased as he grabbed my waist and lifted me over his shoulder.

I squealed, giggling breathlessly. "Put me down!" I cried, slapping his butt, laughing like crazy.

"Nick, take your fucking hands off of my girlfriend!" Olly growled.

Nick shifted my weight on his shoulder but didn't put me down. "Oh calm down, Olly, you'll burst a blood vessel," he teased, laughing.

I tried to look round at Olly, but I was facing the wrong way so all I could see was Nick's back, feet and the floor. *Is Olly being serious? He's actually jealous of Nick touching me again? Oh my God, this has got to stop. He's going to drive me crazy with all of this possessive nonsense!*

"Put her down, now!" Olly ordered.

I could feel the anger boiling up inside me. I was not being told what I could do and that went for my friends too. I had been dating him for exactly a week but even then we weren't even speaking this weekend so it was more like five days, and he thinks he can speak to my friends like that? Has he lost the plot?

"Put me down, Nick," I instructed, trying to push myself up. He immediately pulled me down into his arms and set me on my feet.

I looked at Olly warningly. I didn't want to have this argument in front of my friends and embarrass him so I'd just wait until we were on our own before I let him have it. I put my hand on his chest and pushed him back slightly, he was standing too close to Nick for my liking. The angry look on his face was a little scary and I didn't want them fighting or anything. He frowned and took my hand off of his chest, interlacing our fingers as he stepped back, pulling me to his side possessively.

I turned in Amy's direction, noticing that she was frowning at Olly. "I'm going to watch Olly swim tonight so I don't need a ride, Amy. I'll see you guys tomorrow, okay?" I smiled reassuringly at both Amy and Nick. Nick looked really annoyed and was glaring at Olly. I shook my head discreetly telling him not to say anything about it, I needed to take care of it, and I didn't want him involved.

He sighed and nodded, looking away, frowning. "Yeah, see you tomorrow," he muttered.

"Are you sure you wouldn't rather come home with me?" Amy asked, putting her hands on her hips as she frowned at Olly a little harder.

"I'm sure," I confirmed. "Olly and I have something to talk about." I raised my eyebrows in explanation. A smile pulled at the corners of her mouth, she obviously understood that I wanted to give him hell for that little stunt.

"Right, well I'll pick you up in the morning," she replied.

I nodded and smiled before turning back to Olly and motioning with my head that we were ready to go to his stupid swim meet. Once we were out of the hall and on our own, I pulled my hand out of his grasp angrily. "What the hell was that?" I cried, throwing my hands up in exasperation.

His eyebrows knitted together in confusion. "What? Oh come on he had his hands all over you! Am I just supposed to let that go?" he asked angrily.

"Heck yeah you're supposed to let it go! Nick and I are friends, nothing more. For goodness sake, Olly, this is pathetic, and you need to grow up! I won't have this kind of stuff keep happening all the time, you need to trust me or there's no point in starting anything!" I almost shouted.

His frown deepened but he didn't say anything for a few seconds as we just glared at each other, neither of us wanting to back down. I refused to be the one to break the silence. I hadn't done anything wrong. He needed to accept that Nick and I were friends long before we went out, and I wanted to keep it that way.

After about a minute he sighed heavily and looked away. The thrill of victory coursed through my veins. I always backed down in these types of situations; I never won an argument like that, so I was more than a little proud of myself.

"I'm sorry, I shouldn't have said anything about it," he admitted grudgingly.

I shook my head. I was still angry with him so I wasn't letting him off the hook that easily. "No you shouldn't. Nick and I are friends. You either accept that fact or don't, it's your choice." I shrugged, crossing my arms over my chest defensively.

He nodded and stepped forward, bending slightly so he could look into my eyes. He plastered on the little lost boy face again. "Sorry, Chloe. I'm such an ass; I shouldn't keep taking my insecurities out on you." He reached out and brushed my hair behind my ear lightly.

"You're damn right there, and it's not just me you need to apologise to," I said sternly. I wasn't just conceding because he was doing the face, if he wanted to try and be with me then he actually needed to try.

He frowned, his jaw tightening slightly but he quickly rearranged his expression and smiled. "Yeah, I'll speak to Nick tomorrow or something and say sorry." He gripped my waist and pulled me closer to him, pouting at me. "Don't stay mad at me. I'm really sorry. Forgive me?" he pleaded as he looked into my eyes.

I sighed in defeat and nodded. *Damn it, why can't I grow some balls and just say no to people once in a while?* He had one last chance, and that was it. As soon as he screwed up, that was it, we were over. No one could accuse me of not trying to get over Will; I was trying my hardest that's for sure.

"Olly, I won't put up with it again. You need to stop with the being possessive stuff, I mean it," I warned. He smiled and nodded, inching his mouth towards mine. I gasped when I realised he was about to kiss me on school grounds. *Is he freaking serious?* I put my hands on his chest and pushed him away from me. "Again? For goodness sake we're at school and got into trouble for that this morning!" I cried in disbelief.

He rolled his eyes. "We're in a deserted hallway, Chloe; no one would have seen it." He gripped my hand and pulled me towards the pool. I skulked behind like a spoilt child. He walked me to the poolside seats before going to get changed into his swim stuff.

The swim meet was boring. I vowed that the next time I had to subject myself to this I would make sure that I brought a book or something to read. I was so bored that I even contemplated reading ahead in my calculus book in preparation for my next class.

I let my mind wander to other places and was happily daydreaming about Alex Pettyfer when I felt the row of seats that I was sat on move. I glanced to the side to see that Will had sat down in the seat next to mine. He wasn't looking at me; he was watching the swimmers with a mock interested look on his face. I chuckled, wondering what he was doing here. A smile pulled at the corners of his lips as he finally turned to look at me.

"What are you doing here?" I asked.

He shrugged. "Same as you."

I laughed. "You're watching your boyfriend swim?" I teased. "Which one is he? Do I know him?"

He grinned and pointed to one of the guys who were just about to dive in. "That one, the one with the nice ass and lickable chest," he joked in a camp voice, making me giggle hysterically.

We sat there laughing for a couple of minutes which gained us glares from the swim coach, probably because we were disrupting his practice or something. I tried not to look at Will because every time I did I started laughing again.

He leant in closer to me. "You know, those speedos don't leave much to the imagination. Your boyfriend looks like he's a little cold," he joked, chuckling darkly. I burst out laughing again and quickly put my hand over my mouth to stifle the sound as I gained another glare from the coach. He grinned wickedly at me. "Maybe I should offer him a pair of my socks for next time you watch so you'll be more impressed," he whispered. I slapped his arm, biting my lip so I could stop laughing. I knew he was only teasing though, Olly hadn't gotten out of the water yet so neither of us had no idea if he looked 'cold' or not.

"Stop it; you're going to get us thrown out of here!" I hissed, still giggling to myself.

He grinned wickedly and shrugged. "Never mind, I'll just drive you home if we do, then you don't have to wait around being bored stiff."

Is it wrong to actually hope we got kicked out just so I could get in his car with him again? "I'm not bored stiff. I was actually just listing all of my music in alphabetical order inside my head," I countered, shrugging.

He raised one eyebrow playfully and I felt my insides do a little flip. "Maybe you could sort it into piles of good, okay, and downright awful, and then throw out all of your Daniel Masters crap while you're at it." He smirked at me.

I rolled my eyes at his comment. *What is it with guys and hating on poor Daniel?* "Oh you know you love him really."

He nodded, looking a little thoughtful. "Yeah his chest is pretty lickable too," he replied in a camp voice. I burst out laughing again but quickly turned it into a cough. Will patted me on the back, looking at me with mock concern as the coach glared at us. If Will wasn't a teacher we would have been thrown out by now for sure.

When I had calmed down, he smiled and stopped patting my back. "So what are you doing tonight?" he questioned, sitting back in his chair more and putting his feet on the back of the seat in front of him.

I shrugged; I had no idea what Olly wanted to do. I actually just wanted to go home, but I had agreed to give him one last chance so I guess I needed to stick to it. "I don't really know, maybe a movie or dinner, not sure yet. What about you?" I asked, biting my lip and hoping he wouldn't say he was seeing Miss Teller tonight. I would hate to hear those words come out of his mouth.

"Nothing much, I'm meeting Sam for a drink and then we're going to my parents for dinner. I haven't seen them in a while so my mom will probably want to feed me up or something." He shrugged, and I couldn't help but notice he looked a little sad for some reason. *Does he not want to go to his parents' house?*

"You don't want to go there?" I asked curiously.

He smiled sadly. "Yeah I do, it's just that I get ten thousand questions about you all night, which is sometimes kind of awkward." He shrugged.

"Yeah I guess it would be," I replied quietly. "Well tell them I said hi." As soon as I said it I frowned. *How the heck could he tell them that? I bet he's just told them we've broken up; he couldn't exactly say that he still saw me at school every day.*

"I will do." He nodded and smiled. He stood up and looked down at me. "I guess I should get going then. I'll see you tomorrow."

I nodded; I really didn't want him to leave. Talking with him was so easy, it was so nice to be around him again and just enjoy his company that I didn't want it to end. "Yeah, have a nice dinner tonight. I guess I'll see you in detention for that rematch."

He laughed and nodded. "Yeah, see ya." He actually looked a little reluctant to walk away, and I felt like grabbing his hand and pulling him back into the seat next to me just so I could hear him talk some more. Or maybe I should just tell Olly I felt sick or something and then ask Will to take me home so I could have another fifteen minutes of his time.

I didn't do either of those things though so he smiled and walked off, leaving me watching his back, my heart sinking with every step he took away from me.

Wait, why did he actually come in here in the first place? He was only here for a couple of minutes, and all he did was talk to me. Mind you I guess he could have actually been talking to someone or doing something before he spoke to me. I'd been too busy daydreaming that I probably wouldn't have noticed a herd of elephants if they were doing a little jig in front of me before he sat down. He could have been in here for hours for all I knew.

I turned my attention back poolside and tried my hardest to watch Olly swim, but I didn't even know which one he was. They were all wearing little blue swimming hats and goggles so they all looked the same. *Jeez, I suck as a girlfriend; I can't even pick my boyfriend out of a group of guys!* I laughed quietly to myself and waited patiently for the hour to be over.

When he was finally done and dressed we headed to this little restaurant that Olly said did the best scampi he'd ever eaten. I just smiled and went along with it, not really caring where we went. When we pulled into the parking lot I laughed to myself, it was a bar with a little restaurant on the side; I'd actually been here before with Will to eat. I smiled at the memory of us playing pool out the back and forced myself to get out of the car and follow Olly inside.

When we walked in we were told that there was a little wait for a table, they'd had a rush apparently, so we were told to wait off to one side. I was sipping my Coke while we talked about his swim trials and the race he was in next weekend against all of the surrounding schools. I tried my hardest to be interested in what he was saying, but sports and stuff just weren't my thing, so it kind of just went in one ear and out of the other.

Suddenly someone grabbed me from behind. I squealed and slopped half of my Coke over the floor as I jumped with fright. My heart took off in a sprint thinking I was being mugged or something. The person whose arms were now around my waist just laughed in my ear. Olly stepped forward looking over my shoulder, his face was murderously angry.

I squirmed and looked back quickly, only to see Sam grinning at me. I relaxed as soon as I realised I wasn't being attacked or something. I elbowed him in the ribs. Unfortunately it didn't really have much effect, just made him laugh harder and let go of me.

"What the hell, Sam? That wasn't funny!" I ranted as I slapped his chest, but laughed with relief at the same time. My heart was slowly starting to beat again and he just laughed his ass off.

"Hey, Foxy. Sorry couldn't resist. Maybe I'll have to buy you a new drink though huh?" he teased, nodding at the wet puddle on the carpet at my feet.

I rolled my eyes and looked at the glass I was holding, there was only about an inch left in the bottom. *Stupid idiot boy!* "Maybe I should throw the rest of this in your face for scaring me," I suggested teasingly as I smirked at him.

He shrugged. "It's not like that's never happened to me before, just try not to get it in my eyes would ya? Coke stings," he joked.

"We'll you deserve the sting, you jerk!" I laughed as I slapped his chest again. He grinned and I smiled back. I really liked Sam; he was a great guy so I couldn't really get mad at him.

Olly grabbed my wrist and pulled me away from Sam as he just continued to try and kill him with his eyes. *Oh my days, seriously? Again with the possessiveness?*

"Do you mind? You're interrupting," Olly growled.

Sam smiled and shrugged. "I don't mind at all," he stated confidently as he crossed his arms over his chest. I fought a smile at just how brash Sam was. That was actually one of my favourite things about him, and Will was just the same too.

Wait, holy crap is Will here too? He said he was meeting Sam for a drink, were they doing that here? I flicked my eyes around the bar and saw Will just walking out of the back, obviously coming from the bathrooms that were out there. His gaze met mine and a half smile crossed his face before he frowned and started walking over to us, weaving through the crowd. I couldn't help but notice how hot he looked. He looked no different than when I saw him an hour ago at school, but just being out of that place made him look different. Younger, cuter, and definitely more handsome.

I dragged my eyes away from Will and looked back at Olly as his grip tightened on my wrist. "Maybe we should go somewhere else to eat, Chloe. This place looks a little busy still," Olly suggested, his voice tight and controlled.

Sam grinned. "Nah, come on dude, they'll have a table cleared for you in a minute. Why don't I buy you a new drink, Foxy?" Sam smirked at me, his eyes twinkling with amusement. He turned to look at Olly. "Does your rebound guy want one?" he asked in a polite tone that didn't match the words he'd said.

Holy crap! "Sam!" I cried, frowning. *What on earth is he doing? Is he trying to upset Olly on purpose?*

He looked at me with wide eyes, giving me the 'I didn't do it' look. "What? I'm just being polite and offering to buy him a drink," he said innocently, but his eyes were playful and teasing.

Olly stepped forward, pulling me behind him roughly. "Why don't you just back the fuck off?" he spat.

Sam just laughed and rolled his eyes. "You don't own her, you know. I think I'll stay for a bit and talk to my friend." He shrugged.

"Just get lost before I make you!" Olly warned, stepping closer to Sam again.

I stared at his back in disbelief. *What the hell is his freaking problem?* I yanked my wrist out of his restraining hold and stepped away from him. *I know Sam is pushing his buttons, but he's freaking crazy if he thinks I'm going to let him keep me away from one of my friends just because it was a guy.*

"Olly, don't," I warned, frowning. I noticed Will walk to Sam's side, but I didn't take my eyes off of Olly who was scowling at me angrily, his whole body tense and annoyed.

"Let's just go somewhere else." He stepped closer to me and reached for my hand again. It actually looked like he purposefully stepped to the side to put his body between me and Sam - and that made me even angrier. Thankfully he hadn't noticed Will standing there. If he knew that Sam was Will's brother it might click into place that Will was the ex-boyfriend I'd told him about.

I shook my head in rejection. "No. Let's just eat here and we'll all play nice together," I suggested, wanting to see what he would do. *He needs to try and let this go. I am allowed male friends, and he needs to accept it.* This was his make or break, if he continued with this little jealous act then that would be it, his one chance would be blown.

"For goodness sake, Chloe. Is this a freaking joke? Yet another male friend that I'm supposed to put up with having his hands all over you?" he hissed, looking at me in disbelief.

I mentally groaned. He hadn't passed the test. "You know what, Olly? Just shove it up your ass," I retorted, turning and storming off towards the

184

door. I ignored Sam's laughter behind me, and Olly's sting of cuss words that he muttered under his breath. I had no idea how I was going to get home, but there was no way I was sitting in a car with Olly, so I'd just hope that there was a bus route or something along this road.

Just as I got about half way across the parking lot Olly grabbed my hand. "Shove it up my ass? What's that supposed to mean?" he asked, frowning as he yanked me to a stop.

I sighed and shook my head. *Could I have said it any clearer?* "It means you blew your last chance. I told you I wouldn't put up with you being all possessive and you've just done it again. You promised you wouldn't do it." I shrugged.

He looked hurt as he stepped closer to me, cupping my face in his hands. "Chloe, I'm sorry. I just don't like guys hanging all over you all the time. I'm your boyfriend, I'm allowed to get jealous!" he said fiercely.

I pulled my face out of his hands. "There's a big difference between being jealous and being a control freak, Olly. I told you that you have no reason to be like that, but you just carried on anyway. It's not right and I hate it. I'm sorry."

I flicked my eyes back towards the building and saw Will standing there, frowning angrily in my direction. Sam had one arm over Will's chest, looking as if he was holding him in place or something while he spoke to him, but I was too far away to hear what he was saying.

"So it's over? That's it?" Olly asked, throwing his hands up in exasperation.

"I'm sorry, but you can't do that. No girl likes being told what to do. You need to work out your issues, seriously, not all girls are like Christina but you've pushed my away because you can't trust me. There needs to be trust in a relationship otherwise there's no point in being together." I shrugged. A rather large part of me was jumping for joy that it was finally over, that I'd tried, but it didn't work out. Now I was free to wallow in self-pity about Will again.

He groaned and gripped his hands in his hair, looking at me desperately. I felt guilty that I was hurting someone, but to be honest, it wasn't my fault. We'd only been dating for a week, but yet he was acting as if we were breaking up from a marriage or something. It wasn't the end of the world so he needed to stop overreacting. This wasn't my fault.

"I really like you, Chloe," he said bending slightly, giving me the face that he was so damn good at.

I felt bad that I just didn't care this time. He'd gone way overboard today, first Nick and now Sam, that was too far, and he promised me he wouldn't do it. "I'm sorry, but this just isn't working," I replied, trying to keep my voice stronger than I felt.

He frowned angrily at me. "Fine. Whatever. Come on, I'll drive you home," he stated, his voice emotionless as he looked away from me, his face hard.

I didn't really want to get in the car with him again, I had a feeling he would be begging me for another chance all the way home and I really hated to say no to people and hurt them. I didn't want to go with him in case I caved in or something. But, on the other hand, I actually had no idea how to get home from here, and I probably didn't have enough money for a cab. I decided to call Amy and ask her to come and get me, she wouldn't mind.

"It's fine, I'll call Amy to come and get me." I shrugged.

He sighed and didn't say anything, just turned and skulked off towards his car, his shoulders stiff and his body ridged. *Well, Amy will be pleased now.* Since she'd found out about Will she had convinced herself that he still liked me still, so wanted me to try for him again. The girl changed her mind too freaking easy.

I felt an arm sling around my waist so I turned to see Sam smirking at me. "You can thank me later," he teased.

I groaned and put my head on his chest. This was going to make things a little awkward at school for a couple of days; we had two classes together so that would suck. At least we didn't really have the same friends so he would just go back to his group and I would hang out with my usual friends the same as before this little relationship mishap happened.

"You're such a jerk, Sam," I mumbled into his chest. He laughed and I could feel it rumble in my ears where I was pressed against him.

"Oh come on, I did you a favour. That guy wasn't right for you at all, you need someone older. And blonds just don't suit you at all," he teased.

I chuckled weakly. "Someone more like you, perhaps?" I joked, rolling my eyes and pulling back to look at him. *Stupid flirt.*

He looked me over with mock disgust. "No way, you've got Will cooties all over you, I told you that before. My brother, on the other hand, he suits you perfectly." He squeezed my waist lightly and started leading me over to where Will was standing. I laughed humourlessly about the little Will comment but didn't say anything. I didn't want to think about how perfectly he suited me.

Will was standing there looking a little awkward, but I noticed the small smile on his face that he was obviously trying to disguise. "Everything all right?" he asked as we got up to him.

I nodded and shrugged. I felt a little guilty that I didn't feel even the slightest bit upset about the breakup, but I couldn't force myself to feel something for someone after one week of dating, so I really had nothing to feel bad about.

Will grinned wickedly. "Well at least you know you're not missing out on anything, I mean you saw him in his speedos so it's no great loss."

I burst out laughing and shook my head. "Don't be mean," I scolded playfully.

He smiled happily and dug in his pocket for his keys. "Come on, I'll give you a ride home."

Aww, he is so freaking sweet! "Yeah? Thanks, that'd be great. I was just contemplating getting the bus." I smiled gratefully.

He turned to Sam. "I'll see you at Mom's."

Sam nodded and pulled me into a hug. "Now you two play nice, I don't want to hear anymore whining from him about how you made him act like a jerk to you," he whispered in my ear.

I pulled back and looked at him, confused. *Will told Sam that I made him act like a jerk? I didn't make him do anything; he's the one that just jumps on me all the time for nothing.* I sighed and rolled my eyes. Sam was probably just trying to push my buttons now.

"Whatever, Sam, call me and we can go out."

"Keep Friday open for me," he called to my back as Will and I walked to his jeep.

I waved over my shoulder signalling that I'd heard him. I smiled gratefully as Will opened my door for me. He always was a gentleman when we went out; I kind of forgot he liked to do things like that.

He kept stealing little glances at me as he drove; I smiled after about the tenth time I had caught him. "What is it, Will? Just spit out whatever's on your mind," I instructed, looking at him expectantly.

He frowned and opened his mouth to say something, but then just closed it again and looked back at the road. "I wasn't going to say anything." I rolled my eyes. *Does he think I don't know him at all?* I raised my eyebrows and just looked at him, waiting for him to man up and say what he was thinking about. After about a minute he sighed in defeat. "Fine, I was going to say that I'm glad you broke up with him. He wasn't good enough for you and you shouldn't let a guy dictate to you like that."

I nodded in agreement. "Yeah I know."

"And I loved the whole 'shove it up your ass' line. That was awesome." He laughed.

I laughed and blushed, embarrassed that I'd said that in front of him and Sam. In hindsight I really should have taken Olly to one side and broken it off instead of doing it in front of two other guys.

"Glad I impressed you," I replied, biting my lip and just thinking about how his smile lit his whole face and actually made him look beautiful to me. The drive to my house was way too short and when he pulled up outside I frowned in disappointment. "Well thanks for bringing me home."

He smiled. "Anytime."

I reluctantly opened the car door and forced myself to get out. "Have a nice dinner."

He groaned. "Yeah, I'm sure it'll be great," he said sarcastically. "I'll see you tomorrow."

I nodded and shut the car door, waving as I walked up the driveway to my house. As soon as I was inside I pulled out my cell phone and called Amy, explaining everything that had happened with Olly, down to the very last detail.

When Amy and I walked into the school the following day I felt so awkward that I just wanted to run away. Olly was talking with one of his friends in the parking lot. I didn't know what to do so I just blushed and dropped my eyes to the floor. *Oh man this is awful. At least when Nick and I broke up it was kind of on nice terms because we still vowed to be friends, but with Olly it'll just be downright awkward for a while because we'd broken up on an argument rather than a mutual parting.*

All through first period he seemed to avoid me. Whenever I looked in his direction he looked away or turned to talk to someone else so I wouldn't go up to him, not that I was planning to anyway, but I guess he was just playing it safe. Maybe it was easier for him just to cut me out and pretend like nothing had happened, but I would rather be friendly about it at least.

I was actually so excited about my lunchtime detention that I could barely think of anything else, that seemed to make the morning fly by. I grabbed a sandwich and headed to Will's classroom with a huge smiled on my face just because I would get to hang out with him for another hour. When I got to the door I mentally crossed my fingers that we would be the only ones there again. Suddenly a thought occurred to me; *what if he's given someone else detention and I actually have to sit there for an hour and do work? That'll suck big time.*

I hesitated with my hand raised about to knock. Technically he'd let me off of the detentions so if there was someone else in there I could just turn and walk away, I wouldn't actually have to stay and do work.

Just as I was lost in my thoughts, two hands fell on my shoulders making me jump and scream a little from the shock. I whipped around to see Will standing behind me laughing quietly. "You should have seen your face. Wow that was a picture," he teased. He nodded to the door that I still hadn't knocked on or opened. "Are you going to let us in, or will the rematch be in the hallway today?" he asked, grinning wickedly.

I bit my lip as my stomach started to flutter. The word 'rematch' had to mean we were on our own otherwise he wouldn't have said it. I grinned and pushed his door open; almost skipping in there because I was so happy.

I turned back to him, and he laughed. "I was thinking we could shoot basketballs instead of Malteasers this time, easier to clean up." He shrugged.

I laughed. "Not sure you'll get a basketball in your mouth, Will. Then again I guess you didn't get many Malteasers in your mouth either," I joked.

He grinned and pulled out a stack of scrap paper, rolling it into balls and sitting on the desk next to me. He nodded to a little hoop that was stuck on the wall, directly over the trashcan. "First person to ten wins." He smiled happily and proceeded to aim for a three pointer, and I just laughed. He was such a kid sometimes, but I actually loved that about him.

The next two weeks passed exactly the same, Olly continued to just look away with a little hurt expression every time I was near him - which of course earned me lots of glares from his little fan girls because precious Olly was upset. By the look of it though, he didn't waste much time in replacing me. He had a different girl hanging all over him all the time, begging for his attention. To be honest, he was probably glad that we'd broken up; at least he'd probably gotten past first base with a couple of them.

Will continued to be nice to me; it was weird just having a normal conversation with him about something random and unimportant. Every time he smiled at me my heart would race, and my palms would get a little sweaty. I was really enjoying just being able to talk to him occasionally. In his classes he was a teacher, but if I saw him in the hallway or something, then he was more like my old Will.

We only ended up doing two detentions, instead of the full week, because after that, he got roped into helping with the upcoming play by Miss Teller. He couldn't exactly refuse to help his girlfriend, so I quite often saw him lugging costumes around and painting the set for her at lunchtimes. I couldn't stop feeling jealous about it. Every time I saw her I just wanted to punch her in the face for being so freaking perfect. She was utterly flawless, but yet she was so nice with it too. It really wasn't fair.

The two weeks passed so fast that I barely knew what happened, and before I knew it, Saturday arrived, and so did the dreaded paintball game.

Chapter Twenty-Four

I followed Amy and Nick off of the coach, feeling slightly sick with nerves. *What if I fall over in the middle of the woods and hurt myself and no one even notices? What if I'm lying there for hours crying for help?* I knew I was being more than a little pathetic, but that was the kind of thing that would happen to me, a really typical Chloe moment.

As we climbed out we were directed towards a pile of jumpsuits. I grabbed one in my size and pulled it on feeling my heart sink with every second. This was not my idea of how to spend a Saturday afternoon.

Please, please, please let me get through this unscathed.

We were each handed a safety helmet, a gun and a spare packet of paintballs, and were herded to a little clearing where the instructor stood on a little platform ready to address us. He started to go through the rules; how to reload, where the flags were positioned, what to do if you got hurt, and all other kinds of things that I just wasn't interested in. I would actually rather be anywhere than here at this moment, especially when I looked up to see Will and Miss Teller standing directly in front of me, listening to the guy. They looked like the perfect couple, they looked so hot together, and that made me feel even worse.

I stood there discreetly watching as Miss Teller put her hand on his arm, smiling seductively. It felt like it was killing me inside. She laughed at something he'd said - well, giggled really. I immediately started to envision walking over there, grabbing her perfect natural blonde hair, and shoving her pretty face into the muddy puddle by her feet. I sighed. Why was I even here anyway? I should have just said no. I would end up getting hurt at some point today, so why did I even subject myself to this, knowing that the newest and hottest couple would be here, together. It was one thing hearing about it at school and knowing it went on, but seeing it was actually ripping my heart out.

Why couldn't I just get over him? What was so special about him anyway? Sure he was extremely hot, but I didn't care about that. He was smart and funny, sweet and thoughtful... but he was a teacher! I needed to just stop looking at him like that. I needed to just grab someone else and kiss the life out of them and hope that I felt the butterflies in my stomach like I did when I kissed Will. Maybe Olly just hadn't been the right person, maybe if I tried with someone else then I would feel something, anything, just to take the pain away and make me feel better.

Will and I had been getting on so well for the last couple of weeks that I'd kind of pushed the fact that he was dating someone else out of my head, but seeing it was like torture. It had been over six weeks since we broke up, and I still couldn't let go. I was probably bordering on obsessive. Maybe I should go get myself some therapy or something.

Miss Teller flicked her long, perfect locks over her shoulder and slapped Will's arm, laughing. He grinned and shook his head. I frowned. *What is he saying to her to make her laugh like that? He isn't that freaking funny!* They both turned and looked at the guy at the front of the group, I watched as she inched closer to him, making my fists tighten unconsciously. I really needed to punch something, something blonde.

"Earth to Chloe." Amy laughed, elbowing me in the ribs gently.

I jumped and looked at her. "What?" I asked, blushing. *Jeez, if people knew what I was thinking!*

"You're off in your own little world again. The instructor said we had to test our guns. Just squeeze the trigger and if it feels too tight for you to press then they can adjust it before the game starts," she explained, rolling her eyes pumping her trigger. *No doubt she knows I was daydreaming about Will again, she always knows, freaking psychic best friend.*

"Oh right," I mumbled. I raised my gun and squeezed the trigger. Instead of just clicking like Amy's did, my gun kind of jerked a little in my hand.

"OW! What the hell?" Will shouted from in front of me.

I looked up to see he had a large orange paint splatter on his shoulder. *Oh my God, did I do that?* I looked at it shocked.

"You should have put on the safety!" The instructor shouted angrily, glaring at me.

What? Put on the safety, where the heck is that? "No one told me to put the safety on! I just squeezed it!" I gasped, still in shock that I'd shot Will in the arm. I could hear everyone laughing quietly around me but obviously trying to hold it in. I looked at Will apologetically. Miss Teller was fussing over him with apparent concern, but he was looking at me with a small smile pulling at the corners of his mouth. "I'm sorry, it just went off. I didn't know I had to put the safety on," I apologised, blushing like crazy.

He shook his head and rolled his eyes. "Don't worry about it, Miss Henderson, accidents happen."

I turned back to the guy at the front who was finally done glaring at me like I was some sort of serial killer. He was giving us instructions on what to do once we grabbed the other team's flag and what to do once we were shot. We had three yellow bands on our arm, and when you were shot you took one off before resuming play.

Apparently we had already been split into two teams upon arrival which was why some of us had on black jumpsuits and some had green. I looked around to see who was on my team; lucky for me, I had Amy and Nick with me. I noticed that Will and Miss Teller were on the black team. I pouted. *Why couldn't the stupid guy have split them up?*

Once we were finally done, Nick and Amy went over to get their triggers tightened slightly, so I picked up my helmet, twirling it around in my hands as I walked off towards the starting position. As I was walking something hit me in the ass, hard. I yelped at the sudden pain and span around see what had hit me. I rubbed the spot, wincing. Wet slime slid through my fingers. I frowned and looked down at my behind to see that I had sky blue paint all over my butt and hand.

Soft chuckling caught my attention so I looked up to see Will smirking at me. "Sorry, it just went off." He laughed, shrugging.

Oh my freaking goodness, did he just shoot me on purpose? "You're such a freaking child!" I cried, laughing.

He walked closer to me and grinned that boyish grin that I loved to death. Everyone had already run off, hiding or getting to the starting positions already, so we were on our own. "Payback's a bitch huh?" he breathed in my ear making me shiver lightly.

"You are *so* in for it after that! I did mine by accident," I replied breathlessly. I could smell his aftershave and his shampoo. *My goodness he smells amazing today.* I'd forgotten how intoxicating he was when he was this close. My heart was crashing in my chest; it was beating so loud I was surprised he couldn't hear it.

"Oh you bring it, Cutie," he challenged, laughing as he pulled back and ran off into the woods leaving me on my own.

What the hell was that? He's with someone else, yet chooses today to call me Cutie again? He hasn't called me that for over a month and suddenly comes out with it like that? Damn, that boy's confusing!

I walked to the starting position finding half of my team there huddling and planning. "Where were you?" Nick asked. His eyes flicked down to my butt. "You got shot already? We haven't even started!" He laughed, shaking his head.

"I know, I know. I'm a dead weight on the team, so don't count on me for any help or anything," I said, rolling my eyes.

I listened to their plan. We were to split up into pairs and try to get as close to the flag as possible. If we got close enough, one of the two would draw fire and cover the other person, allowing them to run and capture the flag. It seemed remarkably easy while the boys were talking about it, but in reality, I knew it wouldn't be like that.

"Okay, Chloe, you're with me." Nick grinned.

Oh no! That means he's going to be making me run and play properly and get all into it and stuff! Why can't I be paired with another girl who doesn't really want to try that hard? "Why can't I be paired with Amy?" I whined as he gripped my jumpsuit and pulled me closer to him.

He grinned and nodded his head in Amy's direction. She was talking to Ryan, flirting her ass off, and by the looks of it, she was doing well too. He was definitely interested. "Because Amy's paired with Ryan, as per her request," Nick explained, waggling his eyebrows at me. "Is it that bad being paired with me?" He pouted teasingly.

I smiled and nodded. "Heck yeah, you're gonna make me run and stuff and you know what happens when I try to play games. I get hurt!" I winced and gave him my puppy dog face.

"Okay fine, we won't go crazy, and you can be the cover fire if we have to go for the flag, how's that?" he offered. I smiled gratefully and opened my mouth to say thanks when a shrill blast of an air horn filled the air, signalling the start of the game.

Nick grabbed my hand, and we jogged off through the woods, both slipping on our heavy helmets. It was actually quite fun hiding behind trees and jumping out trying to shoot people. I wasn't very good at it though. I'd used up two of my three lives within an hour. Nick hadn't even been shot once.

I winced and rubbed my stomach where the latest bullet had hit me less than ten minutes ago. Nick stopped suddenly, causing me to walk into him. "Ow, damn it," I mumbled as my nose collided with the inside of my helmet where I walked smack into his back.

"Shh, someone's coming. Hide," he hissed. He immediately ran off into the woods leaving me standing there on my own.

Crud, what the hell? I crouched down and looked longingly at the trees as a couple of guys walked past. *Oh man, I should have run after him instead of crouching. I totally suck at this game!*

"I swear I heard something," one of the two guys said, lifting his helmet and looking around cautiously.

"You didn't! Come on, they're nowhere near here," the other guy dismissed. I held my breath as they walked past. I didn't want to lose my last life because then I'd have to go back to the hut and wait for the other hour to be finished. That would be totally boring because I'd probably be the only one out already.

After a couple of minutes, I tentatively stood up again. Nothing shot me so I walked off in the direction that Nick ran in to find him and tell him we were safe. After a couple of minutes of searching, I hadn't found him.

"Nick!" I whisper yelled, looking around cautiously as I pulled of my helmet so I could see clearer.

I searched for him for a full ten minutes but didn't actually find anyone at all. *Damn it, stupid paintballing! Why couldn't people have voted for the other freaking option, either of the other two would be better than this. Heck, even pulling my nails off with rusty pliers would be better than this.*

I groaned and just decided to give up; I wouldn't be able to do anything on my own anyway. Out of nowhere someone grabbed me from behind and dragged me behind a huge tree. I screamed, but a hand clamped over my mouth. "Shh, Cutie," Will hissed in my ear.

My heart started to beat double time as I realised that my back was pressed against Will's hard chest, a chest that I had run my hands and mouth over many times. I heard a couple of voices heading in the other direction. After a minute of silence, he let me go, and I felt a blush creep up onto my face.

I turned around to look at him. He'd taken off his helmet too; it was hanging from his arm carelessly. His hair was a mess, all flattened and sweaty from wearing the protective headgear. He looked good though, as always. I immediately wondered what on earth my hair looked like where I'd been wearing mine. I cocked my head to the side, confused when he didn't make any moves to shoot me even though he'd blatantly caught me.

"What are you doing? Did you forget we're on different teams?" I asked, looking at him as if he'd gone crazy.

He smiled and shook his head. "No I didn't forget, but I saw you're on your last life. I didn't think you'd want to be out already." He shrugged.

I looked down at myself to see I had only one yellow band around my arm, signalling my one life. "Oh, well... thanks." I smiled gratefully.

"No problem. Where's your partner? Your team keep coming at us in pairs," he inquired, scanning the trees cautiously.

"No idea," I admitted. "Nick ran off about ten minutes ago, and I can't find him." I sat down on a fallen tree, setting my gun and helmet down onto the floor next to my feet. "So what's your teams plan? Lure your opponents into a false sense of security, then shoot them when they least expect it?" I asked, laughing.

He grinned sheepishly. "Nah, we were paired up too, but I ditched Caroline."

Who's Caroline? "Who's that?" I asked, frowning.

"Caroline... oh right yeah, Miss Teller to you," he clarified, rolling his eyes.

I felt the scowl line my forehead. *He got paired with her too? I bet he asked for that so he could protect her and stop her getting paint in her perfect hair. Stupid freaking woman.*

"What's with the face?" he asked, looking at me curiously.

Oh crud! "What face?" I asked, pretending not to know what he was talking about, even though it was probably blatantly obvious that I was sending hateful thoughts the drama teacher's way.

"That face," he waved his hand in front of my face, "the annoyed; I'm thinking about something really hard face."

I shrugged noncommittally. "No face. Why would you want to ditch her though? Shouldn't you two be working together?" I asked, trying to divert his attention away from my jealousy.

"She drives me crazy, flirting with me all the time." Will shrugged.

194

I laughed and shook my head. *He really is weird.* "I thought that was her place to flirt with you all the time, you never seemed to mind flirting when we were going out."

He smirked at me, his beautiful grey eyes boring into mine. "It was a little different between us, for one thing we were dating, so I wanted you to flirt with me," he replied. The way he was looked at me made my body tingle. The look was tender and intimate, and so much like the way he used to look at me that it hurt my insides.

"Well why is it different with her then? Shouldn't you want her to flirt with you too?" I asked, trying unsuccessfully to look away from his face.

He shook his head. "I don't like it because I'm not interested in her." His face looked a little pained; his eyes were a little tight.

He wasn't interested in her? Wow, he was using her for sex, nice. So he was back to his player ways, using the pretty blonde teacher. I'm sure that dating and using a colleague isn't going to blow up in his face!

"If you're not interested in her then why are you dating her?" I asked. Part of me was annoyed that he was using someone, but another part of me was secretly relieved that he wasn't into her. I knew he would settle down with someone eventually, but I secretly hoped he would wait until I was at college so it wasn't rubbed in my face.

"Dating her? I'm not dating her," he stated, looking at me as if I was stupid.

He's not dating her? What the heck? "Seriously? It's all round the school. You two are the newest hot couple and object of most of the gossip at the moment." I watched as his face turned from confusion to shock.

"I'm not dating Caroline, I'm not dating anyone," he insisted, frowning. "I'm not interested in anyone else," he added, looking at me intently, as if trying to tell me something.

"So you're just sleeping with her then?" I questioned. Each word felt like it burnt my throat on the way out. I didn't actually want him to answer that question but for some reason, I needed him to.

He frowned and looked at me like I had just suggested that we spend the day clubbing seals or something. "Seriously? Where the hell is this coming from? I'm not sleeping with her either."

"You two go home together and come in together every day," I muttered, a little confused as to what was going on. For the last month I had seen and heard all about their little affair, and now he was denying it... Could Amy be right, and everyone was reading something into something innocent? I didn't want to get my hopes up, but against my better judgment, I could already feel it happening.

"Chloe, Caroline lives down my street. I give her a ride to and from school because she doesn't have a car. I'm not interested in her!" He shook his head, seeming angry about it.

I smiled. Amy was right. I was being jealous and reading something that just wasn't there; he wasn't sleeping with the hot drama teacher after all. I felt myself relax. There was just another nine months then the school year would be over. I would go to college and leave him behind at the school. Hopefully he would stay 'not interested in anyone' until then, and I wouldn't have to see it at all.

His angry expression faded, and he smiled too. His hand stretched towards my face. My breath caught in my throat thinking he was going to touch me; instead he pulled a leaf from my hair, throwing it on the floor.

Suddenly something cracked amongst the trees off to our right. Will jumped up, grabbing me and spinning me around, one arm wrapped around me as he pulled me against his body. "Ow, shit," he hissed as I heard someone laugh.

"Mr Morris, why did you move her? I had a perfect shot!" someone whined. Will let me go so I moved back from his hard body, looking around, confused. Jimmy stood there looking a little disappointed.

"She's out already, no point in getting shot unnecessarily. I just took her last life," Will replied, shrugging.

"Oh okay, well we're gonna move for the strike. You coming?" Jimmy asked, already running off through the woods without waiting for an answer.

I looked at Will in confusion. "What happened?"

Will turned around and showed me his back, which was splattered with blue paint. "I took one for you. You owe me now, Cutie." He smirked at me.

He got shot for me? Jeez that's sweet! "Why did you do that?" I asked, shocked.

He shrugged. "I wanted to take your last life, that ass looks way too clean," he answered, raising one eyebrow at me.

"Are you looking at my ass, Mr Morris?" I teased, willing myself not to blush as I said it.

"You know I need to say no to that question, Miss Henderson." he said sighing. "Anyway, I'll give you a one minute head start, you'd better run." He waggled his eyebrows at me, nodding his head off to one side.

"Seriously?" *He can't really want to chase me through the woods so he can shoot me, can he?*

"Fifty four seconds."

"Are you kidding me? We're supposed to be getting the flags," I said nervously.

"Forty six seconds."

Holy crap, he is serious! I grabbed my gun and helmet, turning around and running through the woods, laughing like a crazy person.

"Time's up!" I heard him call.

I giggled and carried on running. A huge rock came into view up ahead so I sprinted to it, hiding behind it. I looked around wildly for him but couldn't see him anywhere. I realised the rock I was standing against had another one running along the side of it touching at one end in a kind of V shape. I slipped between the two of them, sliding in a little so I was hidden from view on all sides except the front. I could hear him running and crunching on the dry leaves. Putting my gun down carefully, I clamped my hands over my mouth so I didn't laugh.

"Come out, come out wherever you are," he sang, laughing. I giggled against my hand and pressed against the rock harder. He was close I could hear him breathing… maybe the other side of the rock. "Chloeeeee," he called teasingly. I bit my lip, trying desperately not to give myself away. I wanted to finish today with one life intact; Amy had bet me that I would be the first out, and I really wanted to win that bet.

I heard him run off in the opposite direction so I breathed a sigh of relief. I crept towards the edge of the crevice and peeked around, checking the coast was clear. As I tentatively stepped a little further out, he jumped around the corner. An involuntary scream left my lips from the shock.

"Found you! Turn around." He smirked, raising his gun, pointing it at my crotch, obviously wanting to shot me in the butt.

I laughed and stepped back into the crevice. "No way, you're gonna have to make me," I teased.

He laughed and stepped forward. As he stepped forward, I stepped back further into the crevice. I matched my step to his, watching the enjoyment on his face as I lured him in further, heading towards where I'd left my gun.

"I *am* gonna shoot you in the ass," he insisted, raising one eyebrow playfully.

My foot touched my helmet so I bent quickly and grabbed my gun from the floor, raising it at him. At the same time, he jumped forward, wrapping one arm around me and pressing me against the rock. His hand gripped my gun and moved it so it was pointing away from him. His hard body was pressing against mine securely. I was pinned against the wall, I couldn't move even if I wanted to.

His eyes locked onto mine, his face merely inches away, I could feel his breath blowing across my lips. He didn't move, just looked at me with a slightly pained expression. My heart was going crazy, I couldn't think about anything other than how close he was.

I raised my free hand, gripping the side of his jumpsuit and pulling him impossibly closer. His whole body was pressed against mine. "Chloe," he groaned, looking at me pleadingly. His eyes flicked down to my lips for a split second.

Oh please kiss me, Will, please. Please don't pull away like last time. There's no one to interrupt this time, please just kiss me before I spontaneously combust!

"Kiss me," I whispered pleadingly.

He squeezed his eyes closed, looking like I had just shoved a knife into his stomach. It was as if I was torturing him or something. He opened his eyes and gulped. "Close your eyes," he whispered.

I did as he asked immediately; barely able to breathe I was so excited. I felt his hand touch the side of my face and trace across my cheek, slowly moving along the edge of my jaw line. His thumb traced across my bottom lip, making me part my lips and moan breathlessly. My whole body was vibrating with excitement. It was erotic and sexy and almost too sweet to bear.

His hand moved down to one side of my neck, cupping it softly. His weight shifted against me, and then his soft lips pressed against my forehead. I tightened my grip on him, tilting my head up, waiting for his mouth to move down to mine.

He moved back ever so slightly, his hand dropped from my neck. I opened my eyes to see him looking at me with his jaw clenched tightly. His eyes were dancing with excitement, but his face was hardened. I inched my face closer to his, needing to feel his lips against mine.

He shook his head. "I can't," he whispered, looking at me apologetically.

You have got to be kidding me! He was still pressed against me making me hot and bothered. I ignored his protest and inched my mouth closer to his again.

"Please, Chloe, I can't do this. You're a minor, please don't make me do this," he begged.

My eyes started to fill with tears. "I'm not making you do anything." He was so close, closer than he had been for six weeks, but it still wasn't close enough.

"Chloe, you might not think you are but trust me, it's hard enough for me on a normal day, but this is like torture. I don't want feel like a paedophile all the time, but I just can't help it when I'm around you." His hand ran down my side slowly, making me shiver.

"You're not a paedophile, Will," I protested.

He bent his head forward and kissed the tears away as they fell down my cheeks. "Technically I am, because I shouldn't keep looking at you the way I do. I shouldn't want to kiss you and hold you. I shouldn't want to be near you, and to be the last thing you see before you fall asleep. I shouldn't, but I just can't stop. I've tried, honestly, I've tried so hard, but I just can't." He frowned and tightened his jaw.

He still looked at me like that? He still wanted me? Oh my goodness, is he serious? Had Amy been right and I was just too hurt to see he still liked me?

"Seriously… you… you still like me?" I asked. Hope bubbled up inside me.

He shook his head fiercely, and it felt as if he'd ripped my heart out all over again. "I don't like you, Cutie. I'm crazy in love with you," he replied quietly, looking almost ashamed to admit it.

Chapter Twenty-Five

*H*e loves me? He really loves me?

I didn't know what to say. I could barely breathe. Did he really just tell me he was in love with me? Hope and happiness was trying to consume me, but I didn't let it. He'd built up my hopes so many times before… what if this was just another one of those times? What if he suddenly changed his mind and took it back?

I wasn't good enough for him, he was incredible and so special that he deserved so much more than me, he deserved everything. He deserved someone like Miss Teller who was perfect, and classy, and wasn't a stupid little school girl that could barely even look at him without blushing.

He looked at me curiously. He looked a little scared actually, and I wanted to reassure him. I wanted to scream that I loved him too and that I wanted him so much, but nothing was coming out of my mouth.

His face fell even more at my silence. "I'm sorry, I shouldn't have said that. I'm so sorry," he said, looking at me hurt and sad. "I shouldn't have told you that, I'm your teacher I should be responsible and try harder. Maybe I'll quit my job or something so I can stay away from you," he mumbled, stumbling over his words because he spoke so fast.

He's thinking of quitting his job? I gripped the side of his jumpsuit as he went to pull away from me. "You really love me?" I whispered, not trusting my voice to speak properly.

He gulped and nodded. "Yeah, but I shouldn't have told you, I need to keep it to myself and deal with it like I have been doing for the last few weeks."

I smiled. I couldn't fight the feeling anymore, my whole body broke out in goosebumps. I felt my eyes filling with happy tears again as I realised that I couldn't not try to be with him if he wanted me. He'd probably rip my heart out again when he changed his mind, but I couldn't help but get my hopes up.

"I love you too, Will," I replied honestly.

His whole body seemed to tighten. His eyes widened in shock before a heartbreaking smile stretched across his face. "You do?" he whispered, pressing me against the rock tighter.

I bit my lip and nodded. *Surely it's obvious that I'm hopelessly in love with him; he had to know that before I said it. How on earth could he have missed it? It probably couldn't have been more obvious than if I'd written 'I love Will Morris' on my forehead.*

He sighed, his arm tightening on my waist. "I thought I'd blown my chance, I honestly thought I'd lost you, Chloe. It scared me to death. I've been miserable without you for the last few weeks." His grey eyes locked onto mine making me feel like I was weightless.

I couldn't talk to him anymore; I needed his lips against mine. My body was almost desperate for him. "Shh, it's time to stop talking now," I whispered, echoing the words I had said to him once before. I ran my hands up his chest, slipping them around his neck, tangling one hand in the back of his hair. He moaned in the back of his throat, and it felt like my body caught fire.

His mouth was inching towards mine so slowly that it felt like the anticipation would kill me, but the moment was so perfect, private, and romantic that I wanted it to last forever. Finally, his mouth reached mine, his lips pressed against mine softly, and I felt like I could breathe again.

Oh God, I'm kissing him again! I'd forgotten what it felt like when he kissed me, how incredible it was. My whole body was burning with passion, and I couldn't get him close enough, he seemed to feel that too as he pressed me harder against the rock, his hands tracing slowly down my back making the hair on the nape of my neck prickle.

His tongue traced along my lip so I opened my mouth, eager for more. His tongue slipped into my mouth, massaging mine softly. I moaned into his mouth as his incredible taste exploded on my taste buds. He kissed me deeply as I tightened my arms around his neck not letting him go anywhere, not that he was trying to but I just needed to be sure.

He pulled out of the kiss just as I was getting slightly dizzy. I thought he was pulling back, but he didn't, instead he kissed down my neck, nibbling on the skin lightly, actually making me go weak at the knees. I moaned breathlessly as he kissed back up my neck to my ear.

"I love you, Cutie," he whispered.

I grinned happily and tightened my hand in his hair. "I love you too," I mumbled, barely able to talk through the rush of feelings and sensations pulsing through my body.

He pulled back, grinning from ear to ear as he brushed my hair back from my face softly. "I'm so sorry I hurt you, but I promise I was trying to do what was best for both of us. It almost killed me to say that we couldn't be together. The look of hurt that was on your face, I swear it's been haunting me. I'm so sorry, Cutie; can you forgive me and give me another chance? I'll never hurt you again, I swear. Please?" he begged, resting his forehead to mine. His eyes burnt into mine showing his sorrow and regret.

I smiled and pressed my lips against his again for a couple of seconds. "Definitely," I confirmed, giggling and blushing. I was so happy I actually felt a little lightheaded.

He grinned and made what sounded like a victory growl as he wrapped his arms tight around my waist and lifted me clean off of the floor, spinning in a small circle making me giggle like crazy. He laughed and let me slide slowly down his body until my feet touched the floor again. He was grinning wildly and crashed his lips to mine again; kissing me so passionately that it was almost too sweet to bear. When he pulled away, I couldn't keep the happy smile off of my face. This amazing guy wanted me; he loved me and wanted to be with me.

"Will, please don't hurt me again," I begged against his lips.

He gasped and shook his head fiercely. "I won't, I promise. I honestly thought you'd get over me. I didn't think there would be any way you could feel for me like I felt for you. I thought you'd be able to move on and be happy. I hoped you would because you deserve to be happy. But then when you tried to move on, I couldn't stop the jealously I felt inside, and I was so horrible to you because of it. I'm so sorry, Cutie. I should be able to just turn this feeling off and ignore it, walk away from you, but I can't. I'm not even allowed to be talking to you like this, but yet I can't seem to stay away from you. You just deserve someone better than me."

I frowned. "There is no one better for me than you."

He smiled at me gratefully before pressing his lips against mine again, ending the conversation. I was getting really into the kiss, my whole body was vibrating with the need for more, but he didn't make any moves to touch me other than rubbing his hand slowly up and down my back. A loud, shrill sound cut through the air, making me squeal from shock. Will jumped away from me as if a bomb had gone off.

I looked around shocked, and he started to laugh. "Games over," he explained, shaking his head still amused.

Oh, was that the end of the paintball game? I'd forgotten that was what we were even here for. I was so into that kiss that an earthquake could have occurred, and I wouldn't have minded as long as Will's soft lips hadn't left mine.

I looked at him disappointed, I didn't want to go yet, we still had a lot to talk about. He held out a hand to me, smiling happily. I grinned and slipped my hand into his, sighing contentedly at how right it felt. He felt like home somehow. He picked up both of our guns and helmets with his other hand and gave me a little tug towards the opening of the rock. I pressed against his side as we walked and couldn't keep the happy smile off of my face. He let go of my hand, snaking his arm round my waist, pulling me closer to him as he kissed the side of my head tenderly.

"Want to do something with me tonight?" he asked.

I grinned and nodded. "Sure. What do you have in mind?" I asked, fighting the urge to skip along beside him.

He shrugged. "Anything you want, but I think we should talk some more. There are a lot of things we need to discuss." He frowned thoughtfully.

I nodded slowly. "Yeah I guess."

201

He pulled me to a stop. There was still no one around, but we had to be close to the clearing and paintball hut because the trees were getting a little sparser. "We need to act normal today, Cutie. We'll talk some more later and figure out what we're going to do, but for now we just pretend nothing happened back there, okay?" he instructed, looking at me hopefully.

I nodded in agreement. That kind of went without saying. He smiled happily and nodded towards the path again. I grinned and turned to walk off; as I turned something hit my ass making me yelp in pain. Will was laughing wickedly. I span around to see he was still pointing his gun at me.

I look at him in disbelief. He'd just shot me in the butt for the second time today. "What the hell?" I cried, making him laugh harder.

He stepped forward to me and gripped my upper arm. His eyes were burning into mine as he slipped my last yellow band off of my arm, pushing it into his pocket. "I told you I'd take your last life," he whispered sexily. He pressed his lips against mine again, making me forget the small stinging pain where he'd shot me at close range. I discreetly rubbed my finger in the fresh paint, getting a blob of it on my fingertip.

When he pulled out of the kiss, I quickly wiped it across his cheek, laughing. "Now that's sexy," I mused, giggling at his shocked expression.

He laughed and wrapped his arms around me tightly. "You're sexy," he countered, pecking me on the lips again softly. I blushed like crazy, and his smile became more pronounced as he traced his fingers across my burning cheek. "I love it when you blush for me, it's too cute."

I rolled my eyes and pushed him away from me. We needed to go and meet up with everyone else before they started to wonder where we were. "Come on, flirt, let's go. You can make me blush some more later," I suggested, grabbing my gun and helmet from his hand and nodding towards the path. I didn't trust him not to shoot me again if I was to walk in front of him.

"Oh I'll definitely be making you blush later." He grinned at me cockily making my cheeks burn again even though I was trying my hardest not to let them. He just had that effect on me though, I just couldn't help myself around him, and he damn well knew it.

He winked at me and walked up the path. I matched my step to his and couldn't help but steal little glances at him as we walked. He kept brushing the back of his hand against mine on purpose as we made our way to the clearing, his little finger hooking around mine subtly making my heart race.

We got to the clearing and I spotted Amy and Nick standing there with Ryan, all chatting happily. I smiled at how happy Amy looked; I was immensely pleased for her because she'd finally spoken to Ryan.

"I'll speak to you later, Cutie," Will whispered as he walked off in the other direction to me. I watched him walk away as I fought with my desire to do a happy dance in the middle of the clearing. He loved me, he genuinely loved me. Nothing else mattered other than those three words. The student and teacher thing, the minor thing, none of that mattered anymore, I knew we could work through it. It'd be hard, but we'd get through it together.

Chapter Twenty-Six

I reluctantly dragged my eyes off of him and headed towards my group of friends. I fought hard to keep the happy smile off of my face, but I probably didn't do a very good job at it. I had a feeling I would even be smiling in my sleep tonight. I ran my tongue over my still tingling lips, tasting him on the skin. My stomach fluttered, and I flicked my eyes to him again. He was leaning up against a tree just looking around at the students milling there.

"There she is, the disappearing woman!" Nick joked as I got up to them.

I laughed and shook my head. "I didn't disappear; you ran off and left me!" I scolded playfully, slapping his arm.

He rolled his eyes. "I didn't. I ran into the trees expecting you to follow me, but you just crouched down, which was downright stupid by the way. Then I watched you walk off in the wrong direction looking for me, but by then there were another couple of people around so I couldn't shout you or anything. I assumed you got caught and were out, you only had one life left," he explained, laughing to himself at my obvious lack of paintball skills. His eyes flicked to my upper arm. "And I was right by the look of it, you were out. Where have you been though? Amy and Ryan were both out too and said you didn't come back to the hut."

Oh no, what do I say to that? I shrugged. "Got lost?" I suggested, hoping he'd buy it. He did.

His eyes roamed my paint covered body, obviously checking out the damage. He burst out laughing as he turned me around to look at my back. "You got shot in the ass again? That's so funny. Only you, Chloe, only you!" he teased.

I laughed and pushed him back, pouting. "Obviously not 'only me' because Amy and Ryan were out too!"

I looked at Amy, she had her hand on Ryan's arm as she giggled at something he'd said, looking at him through her eyelashes. I was so proud of her I could burst; she'd been crazy about him forever. I personally couldn't see the attraction he held. He was cute, but not really my type. He was a complete jock, with big broad shoulders, and a thick muscled neck. Nothing like Will's toned, yet not too over the top, physique.

As soon as I'd thought about Will, my eyes flicked in his direction. Miss Teller was standing close to him, a seductive smile on her face as she pulled her natural blonde hair down from her hairband, shaking it out like one of those goddess women do on TV. *Oh my goodness, how can he be interested in me while she's doing that right in front of him? I've no chance in competing with that woman at all. If I was a guy I would totally be drooling over her too.*

I looked away as I started to get a little jealous. *What do I do if he cheats on me? He's never had a girlfriend before; does he even know what being faithful means? Is he going to get bored of me in a few weeks and go after someone more deserving of his attention? Wait, wait, am I over analysing everything again, like I was doing before?*

I looked over to Will again at exactly the same time as he looked at me. I smiled at him and got a heartbreaking smile in return before he looked away again to Miss Teller. I sighed and decided I just needed to play it cool. I needed to stop thinking about things too hard because most of the time I'd been jumping to entirely the wrong conclusions about him.

I could barely wait for tonight. Just to be close to him again, talk to him and just wrap my arms around him for a little while, it was going to be like heaven on earth. And his body... now that I was thinking about him, I couldn't help but want his body, knowing how hot and incredible making love to him was. I shivered with desire, and I felt something squeeze my arm.

"Chloe?" I looked up quickly, shaking my head to clear the thoughts away. Nick was snapping his fingers in front of my face, obviously trying to get my attention.

Oh no, was I daydreaming? "Sorry, what?" I smiled apologetically, making him laugh and roll his eyes. Ryan walked away, throwing one last smile in Amy's direction, which made her grin and bite her lip before she skipped to my side and grabbed my arm, digging her fingers into my skin as she looked at me with wide eyes.

"He asked me out! Oh man, he actually asked me out!" she hissed excitedly, almost shaking me where she was so excited.

I laughed and hugged her. "I'm so proud of you! I can't believe you managed to talk to him finally," I congratulated, grinning happily. *Looks like today was great for both of our love lives.* I sighed happily and risked another glance at Will; he was talking to Mr Young and then headed over to lean lazily against the door of the first coach.

"I know! Thank the lord for paintball," she gushed, sighing dreamily. I never thought I would agree, but I silently thanked the lord for paintball too because this was one of the best days I'd had in a long time.

"So when are you going out? What did he say? Give me all of the details," I instructed, linking my arm through hers and dragging her towards Mr Young so we could get checked onto a coach and I could gossip with her about Ryan. I was dying to tell her about Will, but I really needed to talk to him about it first to make sure he was all right with me telling her. The last thing I wanted to do was upset him or ruin anything when we'd only just gotten back together.

Amy sighed dreamily and began to tell me all about how she had arranged with Nick to get paired with Ryan for the game. We joined the line to get onto the coach, and I lost myself in her story about their time together. I listened with wide eyes and an enormous smile as she talked excitedly about them having a lot in common, how they'd flirted, and how she hadn't once make a fool out of herself in front of him for a change. I followed the line of the queue until I was at the door, ready to climb on board.

I raised my foot to step on, just as an arm shot out across the doorway blocking my entry. I looked up shocked to see Will leaning there casually, his arm stretched out so I couldn't enter the coach. A sexy little smirk was on his lips that I just wanted to run my tongue over. Amy was obviously lost in the story too because she crashed into my back not knowing that I'd stopped. I blushed like crazy, and Will's smirk became more pronounced.

"I think I'm going to get a bruise on my shoulder where you shot me, Miss Henderson. I may have to give you detention for it," he teased, chuckling quietly.

I laughed sheepishly. "You can't give me detention, Mr Morris; we're not on school property. Besides, it was an accident, and I've already apologised," I replied, playing along with the whole teacher theme.

He looked at me thoughtfully. "Hmm, I guess you're right. But one step out of line on school property and your ass is in detention."

I rolled my eyes at him; he obviously liked having this power over me. "I'll keep that in mind."

He grinned and moved his arm from the doorway, nodding for me to get on. I felt my insides tremble just because of the way he was looking at me, playfully, teasingly. *My* Will was back with full force. I loved it, I loved him.

I bit my lip so I didn't say anything inappropriate and climbed on the coach with Amy hot on my heels. She slumped down into the seat next to mine, but she was obviously still off in Ryan La La land because she'd totally missed the whole Will incident outside the door, and just continued her story from where she left off. I watched as Will walked in a few minutes later and sat up the front of the coach.

After half an hour of gossiping about Ryan and planning her date for tomorrow night, we finally started getting near the school. My cell phone beeped in my pocket so I pulled it out wondering who it would be from; when I read the name I immediately felt my face heat up. It was from Will.

'I have 2 drive Caroline home. Shall I pick U up from yours at 4?'

My heart jumped in my chest at the thought of seeing him. I was so excited I could barely sit still in my seat. *Wait, four o'clock?* He said he wanted to do something tonight, I was hoping to have time to shower and do my hair, make myself look a little worthier of his attention. But I couldn't really say no to him, if he picked me up and four then I got to spend extra time about which I certainly wasn't complaining about.

'You're eager, thought we were meeting tonight' I sent back to him.

Amy was looking at me curiously. I didn't know what to say. I wanted to tell her. I knew she would be crazy excited for me, but I just needed to check with Will if he minded. He'd said I was to pretend like nothing had happened and this really wasn't a conversation I could have with her with all of the other students around.

"It's my mom," I lied, shrugging and willing my flushed face not to give me away.

My cell beeped with his reply so I opened it excitedly. *'Definitely eager! Is 4 OK?'*

I sighed dreamily and looked at the time on my phone; it was only just after three so at least I would have a little time to change into something nicer than baggy jeans and T-shirt that I wore for paintballing. *'Sure, c u then'* I sent back to him, barely able to type with my shaky hands where I was so excited.

We pulled into the school, and Will got off first, standing off to the side watching everyone file out. Nick was waiting just outside the door for us with a euphoric I-got-to-shoot-people-with-paint smile on his face, just like the rest of the boys that went.

I skipped off with them excitedly towards Amy's car; I was literally counting down the minutes until four o'clock when I would see Will again. It felt like I was in some sort of dream, like I wasn't properly in control of myself or my actions, I was just moving around in some sort of trance, blissfully happy.

Amy pulled up outside my house and looked at me pleadingly. "So you'll come round tomorrow and help me pick my outfit, right?" she asked, chewing on her lip with either nerves or excitement, probably a mixture of both.

I nodded. "For definite, wouldn't miss the chance to tart you up for Ryan for the world!" I teased, hugging her as I got out of the car, waving as she drove up the road.

I turned and practically ran into the house. My parents gave me strange looks as I pelted past them at full speed, heading for my bedroom. "Hi, Mom. Hi, Dad!" I chirped as I blurred past them.

"Hey, pumpkin. Have fun?" my dad called to my back as I darted up the stairs.

"Lots!" I shouted from the top of the stairs, already stripping out of my clothes so I had a precious few extra seconds in the shower.

I showered as quick as humanly possible, being careful not to wet my hair, then headed to my bedroom, picking out tight jeans that I knew Will liked because the last time I wore them he'd barely been able to keep his hands off of my derrière. I grabbed a black tank top and a grey loose knitted sweater to go over the top. I ran a brush through my hair and put on fresh make-up, but to be honest I didn't really need much. My face was already alight with excitement, my eyes shining. I sighed happily and headed downstairs to tell my parents I was going out.

It was only just after twenty to four, I had managed to get ready in record time. I was actually a little proud of myself. I went into the kitchen; my dad was sitting there reading the newspaper, while my mom was starting dinner for tonight.

"Hey," I chirped, sitting on the spare stool next to my dad, hoping that they wouldn't ask me what I was so excited about.

"So you had fun at paintballing? I was expecting an irate call from Amy telling me I needed to come and collect you two from hospital or something," my dad teased, bumping my shoulder with his.

I laughed and shook my head. "Surprisingly, I managed to go the whole afternoon unscathed. Maybe my luck's turning around?" I suggested. My luck definitely seemed to feel as if it was turning around to me. I had my dream guy, who was in love with me, great friends, great parents, and next weekend I was off to see Daniel Masters in concert. What more could a seventeen year old girl ask for?

My mom smiled happily. "You'll always be a klutz, Chloe, you were born one and you'll die one," she replied, sticking out her tongue at me.

I laughed and nodded in agreement. I looked at her chopping up a mound of potatoes and suddenly realised she was probably cooking for me tonight, as well. "Mom, I'm going out for dinner tonight, is that okay?" I asked, praying she would say yes. My parents were pretty cool and easy going most of the time; hopefully this wouldn't be the only exception to the rule.

She shrugged. "Sure. Are you and Amy going somewhere nice?" she asked.

Okay, so I don't want to lie but I can't tell them the truth. Oh man, what do I say to that? "Er... I'm not sure." I winced, hoping that my answer was acceptable. Apparently it was because she smiled and nodded, continuing to chop up vegetables.

A couple of minutes later my phone started ringing in my purse. I grabbed it out excitedly, knowing it would be Will. I jumped out of my chair as I answered it, not wanting to be near my parents in case my face gave something away that I was having an illegal relationship with my teacher.

"Hi," I answered. I bit my lip when I realised how happy and excited my voice sounded. Was I going to scare him away by coming on too strong? Was he going to take one look at my flushed face and finally see me as an over excited school girl?

"Hi, Cutie. I'm outside, shall I come and knock for you or..." He trailed off and I felt my heart start to crash erratically at the sound of his voice. Suddenly I realised what he'd said. *He wants to knock on the door? Oh my days, my dad would literally kill him!*

"No don't, I'll be right out," I said quickly. My eyes were firmly fixed on the back of my dad's head in case he decided, at that exact moment, to go outside and saw Will sitting there in his car waiting for me. I disconnected the call and headed back over to the kitchen counter where I'd left my purse; I shoved my cell phone in and kissed my dad on the cheek. "I'll see you both later."

"Home before ten thirty, Chloe," my dad said sternly.

I gave him my best puppy dog face; I wanted as much time with Will as I could get tonight. I was actually considering the idea of telling them I was staying at Amy's for the night so I would get to stay with Will, but I couldn't exactly spring things like that on my parents. My parents liked a little notice and were less likely to kick up a fuss if I told them before I was just about to leave the house.

"Aww, can't it be later? Eleven thirty, please?" I begged, pouting at him. "It's not a school night," I added. He sighed and nodded and I kissed his cheek again, before skipping off towards the door. "You guys are the best, see you later!" I called over my shoulder.

As soon as I opened the front door I was overcome with happiness. Just seeing Will's silver jeep parked there made my skin feel like it had burst into flames and my whole body started to tingle with nervous excitement. He was watching me walk up the path, his eyes a little wide as he raked them over my body. I grinned smugly. *Someone definitely still liked the jeans!*

Sliding into the passenger seat of his car, I smiled. He was still raking his eyes down my body lustfully. My heart was beating so loud I'm surprised he couldn't hear it. He was still wearing the same clothes from earlier, but he always just seemed so much sexier outside of school grounds.

"Hi," I whispered, knowing my voice wouldn't come out if I tried to speak properly.

His eyes finally left my body and came back to meet mine. "Hi," he whispered back, grinning at me. His expression seemed to match mine, happiness, nervousness, and a little shock. He leant through into the back seat, and I frowned, wondering what he was doing - until he pulled his arm back into the front, holding out a bunch of red tulips. "Got you these."

So. Damn. Sweet! I forgot how adorable he was, how attentive he was as a boyfriend, how he always spoiled me and seemed to remember every single little thing I told him. "Oh, Will, these are beautiful. Thank you," I mumbled, fighting a wave of happy tears because this was real and he honestly wanted me and that the pain of the last six weeks was finally over. Hopefully for good.

"You're welcome, Cutie." He smiled happily, and my heart melted into a puddle when he called me Cutie.

He was moving closer to me, his luscious lips getting dangerously close to mine and I could barely breathe. *This is where I wake up with my alarm clock buzzing and realise I've slept in and am late for school...*

But I wasn't dreaming.

His lips pressed against mine, and I made a little squeak of excitement as my hands gripped into the back of his hair, not letting him pull away from me. I wanted him so much, no it wasn't want, it was need. I needed him. I drank him in greedily, kissing him as fiercely as he kissed me, feeling the little sparks of electricity that seemed to run through my body whenever he was close to me. I pulled myself closer to him, crushing my chest against his as I kissed him passionately, showing him all of my feelings for him.

Way too soon he pulled away. I struggled to catch my breath, but I still needed more. I pouted at him letting him know that I wasn't done. He smiled, pecking me on the lips again quickly before pulling all the way back and starting the car.

I sighed happily and sat back in my seat too, trying to calm my body down before I literally burned into flames - I didn't want to ruin his leather seats. I snapped on my seatbelt as he pulled away from my house.

"So what do you want to do? If you want to go for dinner or something then we'll need to go a little way out of town so no one sees us," he suggested, frowning.

I shrugged; I couldn't care less what we did as long as I got to spend a few hours with him. I would happily shovel manure as long as I was doing it with him. "Whatever you want," I murmured, tracing my fingers over the waxy petals of one of the tulips, marvelling over their beauty. *Trust Will to buy me my favourite flowers.*

"Well, we need to talk, so how about we go to my place and order takeout?"

Oh heck yeah I want to go to his place! I loved his place, and of course, a visit to his bed would pretty much make my night too. "Chinese?" I suggested, trying not to let my dirty thoughts show on my face.

"Sounds good." He held my hand as he drove to his place and I couldn't help but steal little glances at him every now and again. He was so handsome and made my heart beat a little too fast in my chest. The whole car journey my body was on edge, my palms were sweaty, and my stomach was fluttering excitedly.

I just held his hand tightly, afraid to let go in case he changed his mind or something and didn't want to be with me after all. That would crush me. When we broke up last time that was hard but this time it would be even harder because we'd exchanged the 'L' word. I smiled and laughed quietly to myself as I thought about him telling me he loved me; coming out of his mouth they were the most beautiful words I had ever heard.

"What?" he asked, glancing at me from the corner of his eye as he pulled into the spaces for his apartment building.

I shrugged. "Just thinking."

He smiled and kissed the back of my hand before letting go and climbing out of the car heading around to my side. I got out before he could open the door for me, knowing he wouldn't like that, he liked to behave like a gentleman and do little things like open doors for me when we were dating.

He sighed and looked at me knowingly as he snaked his arm around my waist, pulling me against him. "Must we have this conversation again about you letting me behave like a proper boyfriend?" he whispered, bending and planting a soft kiss on my forehead. My heart stopped and then took off in overdrive when he said the word boyfriend and I couldn't help the excited little squeal that came out of my mouth as I grabbed his T-shirt and pulled him impossibly closer.

"Is that what you are?" I teased.

He grinned. "Unless you'd rather me behave like your teacher," he offered, shrugging and stepping back, narrowing his eyes at me jokingly.

"You think you can teach me a few things upstairs in your apartment?" I flirted, biting my lip and trying to look sexy, but my blush probably ruined the effect.

"Sure, did you bring your textbook?" he answered, smirking but looking a little uncomfortable at the same time.

"Damn it, I forgot to bring it. Looks like it'll just have to be a practical lesson," I purred suggestively, watching as he gulped, his eyes getting a little wider before he crashed his lips to mine, ending my pitiful attempts at seduction.

Chapter Twenty-Seven

He kissed me hard, pushing me against the side of his car, pressing his body to mine. I instantly wrapped my arms around him tightly so he couldn't pull away from me. His kissing was almost desperate, like he was determined to make up for the whole six weeks of missing me, right now. Not that I minded. I was pretty up for making up for lost time too, my body was on a slow burn, and the only one that could help me out of my little frustrated state was him.

However, it probably wasn't a bright idea to have a full on make out session outside his building though. He'd told me that Miss Teller lived down his street. If she saw us it would be really bad for both of us.

As he sucked on my bottom lip asking for entrance I reluctantly pulled my mouth away from his. But he obviously wasn't happy about that though because as I moved my head back, he just moved his forward and kissed me again. I giggled against his lips and finally he sighed and pulled away, pouting at me jokingly.

"Lesson one; you do everything a teacher wants, that includes kissing on demand. None of this pulling away nonsense," he teased, smirking at me.

I giggled again and rolled my eyes. "I just thought maybe we should take this inside in case anyone sees," I explained, shrugging.

He pressed his forehead to mine. "I guess. And we really, really need to talk," he said breathlessly, pulling away from me, taking my hand.

I smiled and interlaced our fingers, letting him lead me towards his apartment. With each step I got more and more excited because I wanted to just lay in his arms forever.

He stopped outside his door and looked at me apologetically. It dawned on me what the apologetic look was probably for. "Your place is a mess, right?" I asked, trying not to laugh.

"In my defence, I didn't know you were coming over," he replied, wincing.

I stepped closer to him and brushed my nose against his lightly. "Will, I know you're a slob. I like it actually; it proves you're human and not some super hot pod person. Everyone has flaws, and enjoying living in a pig sty is obviously yours."

He smirked at me. "You think I'm super hot?"

I grinned. "Hottest teacher I've ever seen."

He laughed and opened the door, taking my hand and pulling me inside. The place was just how I remembered, messy, dirty, and cluttered. But I loved it. I smiled and stepped closer to him, wrapping my arms around his neck, looking right into his eyes as happiness swirled around my system.

"I love your apartment," I confessed.

He smiled. "And I love you being in my apartment."

I pulled his mouth down to mine, eager to pick up where we left off outside. He kissed me for a couple of seconds but then pulled away from me, smiling a little sheepishly. "Chloe, let's talk for a bit." He guided me over to the sofa and sat down. A concerned frown lined his forehead.

I smiled and nodded, sitting next to him and holding his hand tightly. He played with my fingers, looking a little uncomfortable. "Will, spit it out!" I laughed, rolling my eyes.

"Okay, so I want to be with you," he started.

I grinned as my heart leapt in my chest. "Well that's pretty good considering I want to be with you too."

He bent his head and kissed me lightly, his eyes locked on mine. "We could both be in so much trouble for this. There's a couple of options for us and how we go about this." He frowned, and I nodded for him to continue. "We can either be together and hide it, or wait until after you leave school."

I smiled and scooted closer to him on the sofa. "You'd wait for me?" I teased, playing with the collar of his T-shirt.

He wrapped his arm around my waist and smiled sadly. "I was planning on asking you out the day you graduated. I had this big idea of showering you in tulips and getting down on my knees, holding a bag of Mexican food, and begging you for another chance," he admitted, brushing his hand down the side of my face.

I chewed on my lip. That was actually an incredibly sweet plan. He didn't look as if he was joking either, so maybe he really would have done that. "Would there have been tortilla chips in the bag?" I asked, trying to keep a straight face.

He smiled. "Absolutely, and sour cream dip."

"Then I definitely would have given you another chance." I giggled as he smirked at me. My heart was beating so fast that I could barely keep still. I'd missed this, this easy routine, the flirting, and the smiling. Everything was always so easy with Will.

"So we'll wait until after you leave school then. Everything will be easier then, and the nine months will pass really quickly. Well, I hope it does," he said, laughing uneasily.

He wants to wait? I don't want that at all. Now that I'd kissed him again I didn't ever want time away from him. "Will, I don't want to wait. You seriously want to wait?" I asked, begging him with my eyes to say that he couldn't stay away from me for a single second either.

He frowned. "Of course I don't want to wait, Cutie. God, I don't want to wait at all. But you said-" he started but I cut him off by putting my hand over his mouth.

"No more crossed wires. I want to be with you now, Will. I'm totally crazy about you and these last six weeks have been awful. We'll be together but keep it quiet. That's what I want," I said sternly, taking the upper hand for once.

He laughed. "Where did this sudden burst of confidence come from? I like it," he teased, waggling his eyebrows at me. I blushed as usual and he traced his finger across my cheek looking extremely proud of himself. "Okay, great. We'll keep it quiet then. I'm thinking that you'll need to tell Amy, she'll figure it out anyway otherwise."

I nodded and bit my lip. Amy was going to go crazy when she found out. "Amy's been telling me that you still liked me, but I didn't believe her. She'll certainly say I told you so when I tell her."

"Smart girl. I thought I was doing a pretty decent job at hiding it. Well, I was doing well until that little shit Oliver kept touching you..." he trailed off, frowning.

I squirmed on my seat. "Will, I didn't want to be with Olly, you know that, right? I was upset about us breaking up, and then you started seeing Miss Teller so I just tried to move on. And, I admit, that it started because I was trying to get back at you for moving on so quickly with her."

He sighed. "I know you were upset, and it's fine. I wasn't seeing Miss Teller though, I promise. Nothing ever happened with her, or anyone else, and it never would because I'm in love with someone else." His eyes locked onto mine, making my skin heat up. *Is it getting hotter in here, or is that just me?*

I kissed him, not knowing what to say. I'd been wrong about him and Miss Teller all along, and because of that I'd gone out with Olly. Sure, it was only for ten days but I'd still done it, and I couldn't feel worse about it. He kissed me back, making a little moan in the back of his throat that definitely raised the temperature in the room another degree.

I slowly lay down on my back, pulling him down on top of me, kissing him deeply. I ran my hand down his chest, slipping it under his T-shirt marvelling over the hard muscles on his stomach. He pulled away quickly and put his hand on top of mine, stopping me from moving it any higher under his clothes.

"Chloe, you're making me crazy," he whispered, his eyes raking down my body slowly. He rolled to the side, moving off of me, lying at my side. I smiled. He always made me feel so beautiful all the time. I had no idea what someone like Will saw in someone like me, but he clearly saw something he liked, and that thought made my heart swell in my chest. I moved back to kiss him again, but he shook his head. "We need to set some boundaries, and we need to do it quick before I lose my restraint," he said quickly.

I looked at him confused. "Huh?"

He looked at me a little pained. "I'm all up for us being together and keeping it secret because I'd miss you like crazy if we waited. But… I'm an adult, and I'm your teacher, so there needs to be some lines that we just don't cross."

Lines we don't cross? Please tell me he's not saying what I think he's saying. Suddenly I became very aware that he had barely touched me at all, every time I'd touched him he'd pulled away. Every time things were getting a little heated he'd stopped it.

"Meaning?" I prompted, praying he just wouldn't say it.

He looked at me knowingly. "You know what I'm talking about, Cutie. I'm talking about your pervert ways," he teased, flicking my nose lightly.

I rolled my eyes. *Great, well that's just great, he's going to leave me frustrated for nine months. Perfect.* I sighed and looked at him questionably. Would he actually be able to wait for nine months until I left school? The glint in his eye when he was looking at me and the way he kissed me certainly didn't say that he wanted to wait for a physical relationship.

"So what kind of thing is acceptable to you then?" I asked, resisting the urge to pout and whine like a little girl. I didn't really understand why he wanted to wait, no one would know if we took it further.

He sighed and traced his hand down the side of my face. "Well, I can't not kiss you, so kissing is definitely acceptable," he murmured, pressing his lips to mine softly for a second. "I just don't want to be groping you or anything. If we maybe just stick to outside of clothes, no skin."

I gasped. "Are you kidding me?" *He's blowing this way out of proportion; we don't need to take it that far!*

He sighed. "Chloe, come on, this hard for me. I'm an adult and technically you're not. I shouldn't even be lying here with you, or kissing you. Touching is kind of a stretch," he explained, looking at me apologetically.

"Will, no one will know how far it goes. We're keeping it secret from everyone; I won't tell Amy anything that happens. The only ones that will know are you and me. There's no reason for us to be holding back and being frustrated for the next nine months." I looked at him pleadingly.

"Cutie, *I'll* know, and *you'll* know. I can't sleep with a minor again, it's different doing it when I didn't know, but I can't knowingly commit statutory rape on a student of mine. Please understand, I just don't want to." He looked at me apologetically as he continued, "The nine months will pass really fast, I promise…" he trailed off, his eyes boring into mine, begging me to understand.

I reluctantly nodded. I guess the time would pass quickly enough; I would still get to hang out with him and kiss him. Maybe the waiting would make it better in the long run; I could tell he felt uncomfortable with me being this close to him. "Okay yeah I guess, if that's what you want I can go along with it," I grudgingly agreed.

He smiled gratefully. "Thank you. I honestly do love you, Cutie. As soon as you're old enough and have left school I swear there is nothing in this world that will stop me from being with you over and over. I'll make it worth the wait I promise… that's if you still want me then of course," he teased, tracing his finger along my bottom lip, making my mouth water.

I didn't even bother to answer the 'if you still want me' comment, that didn't justify a response because it was so ludicrous. *Okay, so he said no touching of skin, does that mean I can touch him over clothes?* "Will?"

"Mmm?" he murmured, kissing the side of my neck lightly, making me tip my head back to give him better access.

"You said no skin, right? So over clothes is fine?" I whispered huskily.

He groaned against my neck. "I don't know, Cutie, I guess so."

I rolled him onto his back, moving on top of him, straddling him. I could feel how excited he was downstairs, and it was making my whole body ache. "I think over clothes is a nice compromise," I whispered, kissing him passionately.

He moaned in the back of his throat, and the sound made my heart start to race in my chest. His hands trailed down my back, but he stopped just before he got to my ass and I couldn't help but feel a little frustrated about it. He kissed me just as fiercely as I was kissing him. Unconsciously I ground my hips against him, making a little burst of pleasure shoot around my body. He moaned into my mouth and gripped my hips, holding them still when I tried to do it again.

I pushed his hands off of me, interlacing our fingers. "This is over clothes," I whispered, grinding on him again, loving how intimately we were rubbing together.

He groaned. "Chloe, dry humping isn't really something-" he started, but I ground against him harder making him stop talking and look at me lustfully. *Oh yeah, he definitely likes that!* "We… It's not… I…" he stuttered, looking torn.

"There are better things you could be doing with your mouth than talking, Will," I whispered, brushing my lips over his lightly.

His hands left mine, one tangled into the back of my hair, pulling my mouth down to his roughly. I smiled against his lips as he wrapped his other arm around me, rolling me onto my back, kissing me like it was the last thing he'd ever do. His kissing was amazing; every nerve ending was on fire as my whole body tingled. He made me feel so special just because of how much he wanted me too. This incredible boy wanted me, out of everyone he could choose, he chose me. I'd never take his love for granted, ever.

"I love you, Will," I mumbled breathlessly.

He pulled back and grinned. "I love you too," he whispered. His breathing was just as ragged as mine.

The make out session was getting hotter and hotter by the second, but he didn't once try to overstep the invisible line that he'd drawn. I did though. My hands seemed to have a mind of their own. When one hand pushed down the back of his jeans so I could squeeze his ass, he pulled it back out quickly, pressing his face into the side of my neck, rubbing his nose along the skin there. "That was naughty, Miss Henderson," he whispered, biting my neck lightly.

"So give me detention then, Mr Morris," I teased, giggling.

He laughed and pulled back slightly, hovering above me as he brushed the hair from my face softly. "Seriously, over clothes, please?" he begged. I took comfort in the fact that he looked like he hated this agreement as much as I did.

I nodded. "Over clothes," I agreed, raising my head and kissing his lips softly.

He nodded and kissed the tip of my nose before pushing himself up, taking my hands and pulling me up to sitting. "I'm going to order the food," he stated.

I smiled and nodded. "You go do that, and I'll choose a movie to watch."

He looked at me so softly, so tenderly that it made my heart race in my chest. "I'd rather just watch you."

I giggled under his intense gaze. "Then you can watch me, and I'll watch the movie," I teased, flicking his nose like he always did to me. He just stood there looking at me with a small satisfied smile on his face. "What are you waiting for? Shoo, go order the food!" I ordered, waving my hand towards the door jokingly.

"I love you, Cutie," he said casually, before turning and heading to the kitchen to get the menu.

My heart melted into a puddle. I seriously wasn't getting used to that phrase coming out of his mouth, every time he said I wanted to jump for joy. I sighed contentedly, slumping down on the sofa with a big goofy grin on my face. Nine months was going to feel like a long time, but I was pretty sure he'd cave on that at some point. Someone like Will wouldn't be able to wait that long for sex. At least, I hoped he wouldn't be able to wait anyway, because I sure as heck didn't want to.

Chapter Twenty-Eight

That night passed in a blur. Saturday was the happiest I had been in a long time. Just chilling in Will's apartment, holding his hand, and talking to him like we used to was incredible. We settled back into our old routine so easily that it was almost like magic. The only trouble was that the hours that I spent with him just didn't seem enough; the night had finished too soon. He dropped me home with a small kiss and one of his beautiful smiles. It took me hours to fall asleep that night, all I could hear was him telling me he loved me.

On Sunday, I had to go and meet Amy so we could go shopping for her date with Ryan. She was ridiculously eager about it, so happy that I didn't even get a word in for almost an hour as we marched around the mall, trying on every single cute dress they had there. I just smiled knowingly and let her ramble on about him; she'd liked him for so long that I didn't want to interrupt her with my happy news.

After answering my twelfth text from Will, Amy frowned and looked at my phone. "Who do you keep texting? Nick?" she asked, holding up a short blue skirt inspecting every inch of it before putting it back on the rack, shaking her head.

I smiled and took a deep breath. "Will," I corrected, watching her mouth drop open in shock.

She grabbed my arm and yanked me closer to her. "Will? As in, Mr Hottie teacher who you used to go out with?" she hissed with wide eyes.

I laughed. "You know any other Wills?"

Her nails dug into my forearm, making me wince. "Oh my God, you... he... what?"

I smiled and pried her death grip off of my arm. "We got back together. But you can't say anything to anyone!" I said sternly.

She opened and closed her mouth a couple of times, and I laughed at how silly she looked. I blushed and looked around the store quickly to make sure no one was in here that I knew because she was going to have a squealing fit in exactly five... four... three... two...

218

"OH MY GOD, CHLOE!" she shouted as she gripped my shoulders and shook me a little in excitement.

I giggled and shook my head, putting my finger to my lips. "Shhh!" I instructed. "You need to chill, Amy! We need to keep it quiet, so shush!" I winced as a lady next to us looked at us curiously before turning and walking out of the shop, muttering under her breath about us being 'up to no good'.

Amy clamped her hand over her mouth, still looking extremely excited as she nodded. "Tell me!" she mumbled, the words were barely discernible through her hand.

I sighed dreamily and checked to make sure no one was listening again before launching into everything. I told her about the paintballing and how he had chased me because he wanted to shoot me in the ass. I told her about what he said about trying to stay away from me; how he told me he loved me and then kissed me. I told her how I went to his place last night, and that we talked and watched a movie. I told her how we agreed to carry on seeing each other but how we were going to keep it quiet until after I graduated.

The whole time I was talking she just listened with wide eyes and her hand clamped tightly over her mouth, making little squeaking noises every now and again. When I was finally done telling her, I felt as if a weight had been lifted off of my shoulders. I didn't realise how good that would feel to say the words to someone else, to have someone else know that Will loved me made it seem a little more real.

Her hand slowly came off of her mouth, she looked so happy for me that her whole face was alight. "Oh, Chloe, I told you he still liked you! I freaking told you! Didn't I tell you?" she chirped excitedly.

I laughed and nodded. "Yeah go on, rub it in, and get all of your 'I told you so' comments out now!" I joked, laughing.

She laughed and pulled me into a hug. "I'm so happy for you, but man you need to be careful! If anyone finds out…" she trailed off, cringing. I winced thinking about how much trouble he would be in, even I would get expelled, not that I was bothered because it would be totally worth it, but I couldn't stand the thought of him being in trouble because of me.

"I know. Please don't say anything, okay?" I asked, giving her my begging face.

"Of course not, did you really need to ask?" she scoffed, waving her hand dismissively.

I laughed and linked my arm through hers. "Come on then, let's get you a knockout dress for your date, and then we'll both have our dream men."

For the rest of the afternoon we shopped, talking in hushed whispers about Will, how hot and sweet he was, and how adorable he was buying me flowers last night. She smirked at me when I told her there was nothing going on between Miss Teller and him, and when I mentioned that he was jealous of Olly, she shot me the 'I told you so' look again.

By the time we had found the perfect dress, it was almost five o'clock, so we headed over to her place to get her ready for her date. I skipped back to my house once she'd been picked up, and found Nick sitting on my sofa, chatting easily to my parents.

I plopped down next to him and smiled. "You do know you don't live here, right?" I teased, nudging his shoulder with mine.

"Yeah, but your mom is cooking for me tonight," he chirped, grinning happily. "I brought my calculus books, thought we could make a start ready for next week?"

I groaned loudly. The subject was getting easier, but the thought of doing it on a Sunday night wasn't a particularly appealing prospect to me. I already knew I wasn't seeing Will tonight; he was working at the club to pay for the tickets that he got for me.

I sighed and nodded. "Yeah I guess. Want to listen to some music for a while or something? We can study after dinner," I offered, nodding towards the stairs.

My dad cleared his throat. "You two are still broken up?" he questioned, looking at Nick sternly.

I laughed and nodded. "Yeah, Dad. We're just friends, you can like Nick still, don't worry," I answered, kissing the top of his head as I made my way past.

"Okay good. Let me know if I have to switch back into overprotective dad mode, pumpkin," he called, grinning and winking at me.

I rolled my eyes; I wanted desperately to tell him about Will. I would love to bring Will home to meet my parents, but it was probable that my dad would scare him away from me; he did get pretty intense when it came to new boyfriends. He liked to test them, to see how much they liked me and pushed them to their limits. If they passed the test, then he went easy on them – like Nick. If they didn't do so well on the test, then he would keep up the tough act until they ran – like Olly would have probably done eventually, if we hadn't already broken up.

I grabbed Nick's hand and pulled him towards the stairs, just wanting to have a normal conversation about anything that wasn't Will or dating. The more I thought about Will the more I missed him. I needed a distraction and Nick would fit that perfectly.

He flopped on my bed while I walked over to my collection of DVDs. "Want to watch a movie instead of listening to music?" I asked, thumbing through the titles, going for anything non-romantic so my mind wouldn't wander to Will again. I settled on Transformers, Nick liked that one. Well, he liked Megan Fox anyway, and I wasn't opposed to a little Shia LeBeouf so it was a perfect choice.

I settled on my bed next to him, putting my head on his chest, using him like a pillow as we started watching. About half way through my cell phone started ringing. I lazily pointed to it on the side next to Nick. "Answer that for me?" I asked. I was half asleep because of how long I had been thinking about Will last night before finally dozing off. "Tell them I'll call them back, whoever it is," I mumbled, waving dismissively.

220

Nick smiled and picked up my vibrating phone, answering it for me. "Hello? Er, can she call you back? She's a little busy right now… yeah okay, I'll tell her." Nick closed my phone and put it back on the side. I yawned and pulled the blanket up over my feet, just deciding to tap a nap before dinner, when Nick spoke again, "It was some dude called Will, he sounded pretty pissed about something. I said you'd call him back."

I jerked up. *Will? What is he doing calling me, he should be at work! Pissed? Why would he sound annoyed?* I grabbed my phone, making Nick laugh as I practically fell on top of him in my eagerness. My heart was beating out of my chest. Was something wrong? Was he not working and he wanted to see me or something? The last thought made a smile tug at the corners of my mouth as I dialled his number, ignoring Nick looking at me curiously. He obviously wanted to know who Will was, I didn't know any other Will's so he probably didn't either.

Will answered almost immediately. Nick was right, he did sound a little angry as he growled a "Hey."

"Hey you, what's up? I thought you were working tonight." I chewed on my lip.

"I am, I just thought I'd call and say hi. I haven't spoken to you all day, but you're obviously too busy to talk to me though, so it's cool," he answered a little too quickly.

"I'm not busy; Nick and I are just watching a movie before we study. I didn't really want to talk to anyone. I didn't realise it would be you though; otherwise I would have answered the call myself," I said, frowning a little. Was he jealous of Nick? I prayed with every bone in my body that he wasn't, I couldn't stand possessive or controlling guys, and I would hate it if he was like that.

"Oh. Okay, yeah good. I thought you just didn't want to talk to me," Will muttered. I could just imagine the face he would be pulling right now, the little lost boy look with the slightly pouty lip.

I smiled. "Of course I want to talk to you, silly boy. I just thought that it wouldn't be you. Are you not working?" I asked, settling back against the headboard.

"Yeah I am. I just missed you. I'm on my break so I wanted to say hi," he answered, sounding happier now. I breathed a sigh of relief that he wasn't jealous, just annoyed because he thought I didn't want to talk to him.

"Well then, hi," I replied, grinning happily now. He laughed. I sighed contentedly at the sound, closing my eyes as I talked quietly to him for about ten minutes, keeping him amused while he was on his break. Nick just sat there, watching the movie and texting on his cell until I was done.

When I hung up the phone, he looked at me curiously. "New boyfriend?"

I nodded and bit my lip. "Yeah. It's early days though so I don't want to talk about it and jinx anything," I lied, squirming a little uncomfortably. I didn't want to lie to Nick, but I also couldn't have another person knowing the truth.

He nodded, seeming satisfied with my answer; we settled back to watch the end of the movie until my mom called us both down to dinner.

The next few weeks went to fast I could barely keep up with them. Amy and I went to see Daniel Masters. We were both still gushing about it weeks later. I owed Will a serious thank you for that one; I was gradually paying it off with kisses though, like we'd agreed.

He was the most adorable boyfriend anyone ever had. So sweet at times that I'm surprised I had any teeth left. I saw him every Saturday and Sunday. He slipped back into the inventive date mode that we had before, but now we were just a little more careful with where we went. The best date we'd been on recently was what he called 'blind croquet', we played it in a field with a flashlight each. It was almost impossible to play the game in the dark, but it was the most I had laughed in a long time, especially when he slipped over, dragging me down with him and then we had a kind of rolling in the mud make out session. I saw him a couple of nights during the week too, but those were usually limited to a takeout and DVD at his place. Because of my parents imposed curfew, we didn't have time to drive to the next town to go to the movies or dinner and get back before eleven.

Everything was working out perfectly. During school hours he was no more than a teacher to me, not singling me out at all, maybe smiling at me a little more than necessary, but the damn boy didn't let me out of my homework or anything which was a bummer. I was at least hoping to get preferential treatment, but he had made it that clear that wasn't happening. Will and his damn morals!

Physically he wouldn't let us do anything other than kissing and the occasional fumble over clothes. I could see how much it pained him to stop me when I got a little carried away, so I tried really hard to stick to his boundaries, but it was hard. We were managing, but I felt a little happier at the end of each day, because with the passing of each day, meant one less day I had to wait to get my hands on his body.

Every day I felt my love for him grow a little more. The more time I spent with him, the more I wanted. I felt like I couldn't get enough of his time and attention - thankfully it seemed like he felt the same. I would often catch him just staring at me while I watched a movie, thinking I didn't know he was doing it. We would just lie there side by side sometimes, not speaking, with him just playing with a strand of my hair, a smile satisfied smile on his face. It was sweet, easy, and so darned romantic that it made my heart race in my chest.

I couldn't be happier that he was mine, sure it was hard being with him whilst keeping it quiet from everyone when all I wanted to do was shout it from the rooftops that I was in love, but the time was passing, slowly, but it was passing.

Chapter Twenty-Nine

On Thursday morning Will picked me up for school. He'd been doing it every day for the last five weeks; he'd made some excuse to Miss Teller that he needed to drive his mom to work so he couldn't give her a ride anymore. He still took her home, but the mornings were mine - at least for the fifteen minute journey anyway. Every day picked me up and then dropped me off at the end of the street from the school just so we could spend a few minutes together before the school day started.

As I climbed in his jeep, he groaned and looked at me pleadingly. "Cutie, please stop wearing skirts to school," he begged, his eyes raking down my legs, a pained expression on his face.

I giggled and rolled my eyes. I hardly ever wore skirts, but on the days where I knew I was seeing him after school, I went for one in the hopes that I might be able to seduce him a little more than normal. Not that it ever worked, but you never know, one day maybe the sight of a little skin would push him over the edge.

"Oh suck it up, Will. I'll wear whatever I want," I replied, smirking at him.

He sighed and started the car, his hands clenched a little too tight on the wheel to be comfortable. I tried my hardest not to blush as I caught him several times stealing little glances at my legs. I giggled; it wasn't even as if it was a slutty skirt. It was just a denim skirt that cut off a little above the knee; it was actually pretty respectable in my opinion.

"You still going out with Sam tomorrow night?" Will asked.

I nodded in confirmation. "Yep," I replied, popping the p. I almost heard his eyes rolling, but he kept his gaze firmly on the road.

"Where's he taking you this time?" he asked.

I giggled and put my hand on his leg, squeezing his knee lightly, making his hands tighten on the wheel even more. "Stop being such a baby about me going out with your little brother. We're friends, and as much as you don't believe me when I tell you, we *don't* spend the whole night gossiping about you!" I stated, fighting my smile.

Will hated the fact that I got on with his brother and still went out with him on a Friday night. It wasn't that he was jealous of Sam or anything, more that he thought his brother was telling me little secrets and stuff about his childhood, dropping him in things all the time. Of course, it didn't really help that Sam told him that's what went on, just to make him paranoid.

Will smirked at me cockily. "Oh, Cutie, I know you do because you just can't help yourself thinking and talking about me all the time."

I laughed and leant over the middle seat, straining against the seatbelt so I could plant a kiss on his cheek. "Actually, yeah we do, but I just didn't want you to be worrying about what he was telling me. You were a pretty funny kid, and that thing you did with your mom's houseplant…" I trailed off, laughing. His face snapped around to mine with a shocked look on his face, seeming to completely forget he was driving. "Watch the road!" I instructed, giggling uncontrollably.

That was one of a very few things Sam had told me, but we actually didn't talk much about Will at all. We mostly talked about school, his past conquests, or failures, or we just watched a movie. Nothing exciting ever happened.

Will frowned and looked back to the road. "Chloe, I don't think you should hang out with my brother anymore, he's a bad influence on you," he stated, sounding a little grumpy about it.

"Psht, whatever," I replied, waving my hand dismissively.

He groaned and looked at me defeated, but with a small smile pulling at the corners of his mouth. I think he liked it when I stood up to him and told him no, I'm not sure why he would, but he almost looked a little proud of me or something.

We pulled up at the end of the road from the school and parked at the back of the little corner store that was there so I could get out and walk the rest of the way. His eyes raked down my legs again as he turned the engine off.

"I'm really hating that skirt," he groaned, shaking his head a little.

I pouted. "Really? Should I take it off?" I asked, my hands going to the button at the front, pulling it open.

"Whoa shit! No!" he almost shouted as his hands dove for mine, pinning my hands to my stomach. "Chloe, please? You know how hard this is for me; it's been so long since we… and I… I just… man, this skirt, it just…" He trailed off and kissed the side of my neck, making my whole body tingle. I moaned at the feel of his lips on my skin and tipped my head to the side as he bit my neck gently. "I want to give you a hickey," he mumbled.

I grinned and nodded. *I'd love that! Like a little Will badge that I could wear for a few days.* No one knew I was seeing anyone so it would be nice to have some sort of reminder of him with me for a little while. "Okay," I giggled, wriggling my hands free and wrapping them around his neck. I turned in my seat, facing him.

He smirked at me as he pushed my seatbelt button, releasing me from the restraint. He had a wicked glint in his eyes that I didn't quite understand. "I can't really, people would see it and ask you about it," he whispered, pulling me closer to him as he shifted in his seat slightly.

I felt myself start to pout; he smiled and kissed my bottom lip, sucking it into his mouth, before nibbling on it, making me moan breathlessly.

"I don't care, I'll lie," I whispered, gripping my hand around the back of his head, guiding his mouth to my neck again.

He laughed against my skin, his hot breath making me break out in goosebumps. "How about I do one where no one will see it?" he offered. His mouth travelled a little lower, his nose brushing against my collarbone. I gasped as he crushed me against his chest before laying me down on the seats, settling himself on top of me. When I didn't answer, he squeezed my waist gently as a prompt.

I nodded. "Yeah, wherever you want," I choked out huskily.

He smiled wickedly at me. I gasped as I felt his hand sliding up my calf, heading higher until he got to the bottom of my skirt. When his hand didn't stop there, I dug my fingers into his back and bit my lip. His hand brushed over my ass, just once, the heat of it leaving a burning trail behind on my skin. The whole time he just stared into my eyes, his breathing shallow, his whole body tense.

Then he was gone from on top of me. I was just about to protest and reach for him to pull him back to me, when I felt him push my skirt right up to my hips. He gulped loudly, his eyes tightened, and his shoulders stiffened. I just watched him, unable to breathe, unable to move while he just stared at me. *What on earth has gotten into him?* I opened my mouth to ask the question but he moved my leg out to the side, bent forward and pressed his lips to the inside of my thigh.

I gasped, and half jerked up so I could see what he was doing, when I felt him sucking hard on the skin there. I burst into a fit of giggles, his hand tightened on my thigh as his eyes flicked up to meet mine as he sucked a little harder. After a few seconds he was done, so he pulled away and looked at it, nodding with satisfaction. He moved up so he was hovering above me again, a sexy little smirk on his lips that made me blush like crazy.

"Do the other leg too," I whispered, wrapping my arms around his neck.

He smiled and shook his head, kissing me softly. "I'll do the other leg tomorrow. On one condition," he bargained.

I wrapped my legs around his waist and pulled him closer to me. This was definitely the hottest thing that had happened to me in a long time yet I still wanted more. "What's your condition?" I inquired, squeezing my legs around him tighter.

He kissed me again for a minute before he answered. His hands still firmly gripping the top of my thighs, one finger stroking the line of the panties I was wearing. "Stop wearing these damn skirts to school," he whispered in my ear, biting my earlobe gently. I burst out laughing, and he pulled back to look at me.

"I kind of like wearing them. If I wasn't wearing it today, then clearly this wouldn't have happened." I shifted my legs slightly, rubbing my calf over his ass.

He shook his head at me, a grin on his face that showed me that he both hated and loved the skirt at the same time. *If I wasn't his student and I wasn't a minor, I'm betting he would ask me to live in this skirt!*

"Get out of my car, Miss Henderson," he growled, running his nose up my cheek.

I sighed dramatically. "Okay fine. I'll see you later, Mr Morris."

He sighed too and pushed himself back up to sitting, moving so I could unwrap my legs from his waist. He grabbed my bag from the back seat and held it out to me. I took it and smiled gratefully, pulling my skirt down as I climbed out of his car.

I smiled and shut the door, slinging my bag over my shoulder. I was just about to start walking when the passenger window opened. "I love you, Chloe. There's just over seven months left now," he called.

I smiled and bit my lip as I nodded. "I know. I love you too."

He grinned and started the car. "You'd better get going. If you're late you'll get detention." He winked at me and reversed out of the space, leaving me there laughing and rolling my eyes.

I headed to the school, immediately spotting Amy making out with Ryan against her locker. I smiled as I quietly opened mine and pulled out the books that I needed for the morning, trying not to disturb them. They had been getting on so great for the last five weeks. They were getting pretty serious too; he would meet her and walk her to classes, and carry her books. It was sweet. She was really happy about it, which made me happier to see her with her dream man too. The only one that was still single was Nick.

I glanced up the hall to see him standing with a group of guys and girls. He fitted in with everyone so easily, he was such a lovely guy, and I knew a lot of girls liked him. He just never seemed to be that bothered by any of them. I just needed to find him a nice girl that would look after him and appreciate him because Nick honestly was amazing.

I headed over to him and dug my finger into his ribs, making him jump. He laughed and slung his arm around my shoulder, pulling me more into the group and they resumed their conversation on the biology assignment, making me wish I'd stuck to being a gooseberry with Amy and Ryan instead. Finally, after what seemed like hours of listening to them talk about dissecting a sheep's brain, the bell rang, saving me from bringing up my breakfast.

Amy and Ryan walked up to me, hand in hand and I suddenly felt a little jealous of her. Sure I had Will and everything, but we could never just walk along holding hands like that, it was a little sad really. We wouldn't be able to have that for a long time, even after I left school things would still be a little strained because of it for a while.

I shook the jealously away by thinking about the hot little moment that happened between us in the car. I was seeing him tonight too. He always

226

dropped Miss Teller home, then came straight round to pick me up from my house. *Hmm, maybe I can convince him to give me a hickey on the other leg tonight, instead of having to wait until tomorrow.* Then I remembered that I wasn't even seeing him tomorrow, I was seeing Sam. That was probably why he said it; he was probably thinking I would be so eager for it that I would cancel on his brother. *Very sneaky, Will, very sneaky.* I smiled to myself and trailed along behind the loved up couple, fake gagging as they kissed goodbye at the gym changing room.

When Ryan ran off to his class, Amy turned to me with a dreamy expression on her face making me roll my eyes and grin as I looped my arm through hers, dragging her to change into our gym clothes.

By the time lunchtime came around, I was starving hungry. I'd skipped breakfast this morning because it had taken me a few extra minutes to get ready because of the 'choosing of the skirt' process that I went through this morning. I grabbed a tray and got in line.

As I was standing there choosing a sandwich, someone came and stood next to me, a little too close for comfort. I frowned and moved up slightly to get some extra space, but the person just moved along too, pressing their side against mine. I scowled and looked around, only to find Will's handsome face. I gulped and tried hard to swallow the ridiculous happiness I felt just because he was in the same room as me.

"Hello, Miss Henderson, how are you today?" he asked, smirking at me, probably because he knew exactly what he was doing to my insides.

I bit my lip and saw that Mr Young was in line behind him. "I'm fine thank you, Sir. How are you?" I reluctantly dragged my eyes away from him and tried to choose a sandwich, but I couldn't keep still on my feet with his side pressed against mine.

"I'm good today. I'm looking forward to tonight, I have some plans. You have anything planned for tonight?" he asked, cocking his head to the side, pretending to look interested as he grabbed a bottle of water.

I laughed a little uncomfortably. "That depends on how much homework I get today. Are you planning on piling it on in today's lesson, Mr Morris?" I countered. I chose a sandwich at random and moved up the line, grabbing a bag of potato chips without looking at them either.

He laughed and flicked his head to get his hair out of his eyes, and I tried not to show any reaction even though that little movement made my heartbeat pick up double time. "As long as you guys get finished with everything in class, then it shouldn't be too bad," he answered, grabbing his food.

I smiled. Mr Young started to talk to Will then, so I made my escape to the cash register to pay. I was grabbing a couple of napkins from the table at the end, when Will stopped next to me again. I groaned quietly. I actually wish he'd just leave me alone during school hours; it was like torture not being able to talk to him properly or just touch him in some small way.

"Cutie, why did you buy a ham salad sandwich?" he whispered, nodding down to my tray as he got himself some napkins too.

I frowned and looked down at my tray. *I didn't, did I?* I read the label and winced, instantly recoiling from it. I hated ham. This was his fault for distracting me and making me all uncomfortable while I was choosing. He laughed and put his cheese sandwich on my tray, taking my ham one instead. He winked at me and walked off before I could even open my mouth to ask him what he was doing. *Jeez, he's so sweet!* I sighed dreamily and watched as he waited for Mr Young to finish paying for his lunch, before the two of them walked out of the lunchroom.

I felt like I was walking on a cloud as I skipped over to my friends' lunch table. I tried to concentrate on what they were saying, someone was planning a party for a couple of weeks' time, but I couldn't think about anything other than Will. My mind drifted to our moment in the car and I squeezed my thighs together thinking about his mouth being on my skin. A dozen fantasies started to play out in my head; things that I wanted to do to him or have him do to me. *Just over seven months and then everything will be easier. Just seven, I can do that!*

The warning bell rang, and I jumped a mile. I'd only eaten half of my food because I'd been daydreaming, so I choked the rest down quickly, following my friends to our lockers to get books for the rest of the afternoon.

By the time Will's class came around, I was grinning like an idiot, the same as usual. I laughed as all of the girls did their hair, reapplied make-up and unbuttoned shirts, before heading into his classroom. There were still some rumours about him and Miss Teller, but another rumour that had been circulating recently was that Will was gay. Some of the cheerleaders had started that one when he hadn't even batted an eyelid when they were flirting with him in their cheer uniforms. I wasn't sure if Will knew of this rumour or not, I guessed no, because he hadn't said anything about it to me and there was no way I was dropping a bomb like that on him.

The rumours didn't stop the girls flirting with him though. Some of their attempts were pitiful. I almost felt sorry for them when he just shrugged it off or ignored it. I didn't feel jealous. I thought I would do, seeing them flirt with my boyfriend, but for some reason, I knew I didn't need to feel jealous of them. *I* was the one he wanted, he could have chosen any girl, but he chose me, so I had no need to worry about a slut trying to talk to him.

As I walked into his classroom, the lights were already down low, and there was a projector sitting at the front. I frowned and took my seat next to Amy. As I bent down to get something out of my bag, someone crashed into the back of my chair, making my chest hit on the edge of the desk, knocking the wind out of me.

I frowned round at the person, only to see Erika Dennison and a couple of her girls smirking as she bumped my chair again on purpose as she moved along the row behind me. *Ugh, what a freaking witch!*

"Oops, my bad," Erika purred sarcastically.

I didn't say anything about it, just looked away. I didn't need a problem with her again. Erika had taken an instant disliking to Amy when we first started school, and because we were friends she obviously disliked me too. She made the first year of our school lives a misery. As she got older, she got prettier and prettier, and as her looks improved so did her bitchiness. I hated her with a passion but she seemed to stay out of my way this year, mainly because Amy and I ignored her daily attempts to annoy us. There was no way I was going to let myself get on her radar again.

I caught Amy's eye and she mouthed the word "Bitch" to me, nodding her head discreetly in Erika's direction. I just nodded in agreement and rolled my eyes.

"Right then, guys and girls, today we're going to be looking at the development of the Infinite Series, and the history of the theory. We'll just have a brief overview with the projector because I've found these incredible slides hidden in the back of the math block and there's no point in them going to waste!" Will chirped happily as he rubbed his hands together excitedly.

I resisted the urge to cough and call him a geek under my breath; instead I just grinned and pulled out my notes. *How can such an incredible guy get so excited over numbers? It really isn't right. Maybe I should be a little worried that I'm in love with a math nerd.* I giggled a little under my breath, and he looked at me with one eyebrow raised.

"Everything okay, Miss Henderson?" he asked.

I nodded quickly. "Absolutely, just looking forward to learning about the infidel series," I answered.

He burst out laughing shaking his head. "Infinite series, not infidel."

I laughed too. "Oh. I'll just shut up now and let you get on with the lesson," I stated, grinning at him.

He nodded, smirking at me. "I think that would be for the best."

I giggled quietly and grabbed my notebook as he flicked on the projector, looking like a kid in a candy store. It didn't start off too bad, learning about some guy in India in the 14th century who first came up with the theory. But the more it went on the more lost I became. As soon as the figures and symbols started appearing on the screen my brain seemed like it just refused to understand. It was nothing to do with Will's teaching at all, it was all me and my inability to understand the subject of calculus. I just didn't have the right brain for this kind of thing, science was the same. I was more of an English and Art girl.

It didn't bother me that I didn't understand this stuff, as long as I graduated then that was all I needed and then I would never look at another equation again. *Well, unless Will is marking them or something for his classes while I'm with him.* As soon as I thought that, my brain drifted to us years down the line… him grading his student papers while I sat around watching him. I sighed dreamily and then realised that the projector was off, and he was talking again.

I gulped and tried to concentrate on his words instead of the way he moved his hands when he spoke, or how his behind looked in his jeans when he was writing on the board. *Hmm, maybe it is his fault I have such a problem with his class. I clearly can't concentrate with him near me.*

He set an assignment for us to start and then whatever we hadn't done we were to finish as homework. I frowned and pulled my textbook towards me, trying to read it over, but failing miserably. I was pretty sure I read the same paragraph four times and it still looked like it was written in a foreign language.

Will stopped next to me, putting his hand on the table next to mine, his fingertip touching mine as he leant over to see how I was doing. "Okay? I could explain it again," he offered quietly.

I shook my head. "I'm all good. I'll read it again later, and if I have a problem I'll let you know," I replied, blushing, not really wanting this extra attention in front of everyone else.

"Okay, well you know I'm always here for you, Miss Henderson." He smirked at me giving it a double meaning. I smiled and nodded, not daring to meet his eyes because I knew I'd blush. Lucky for me someone called him over to help them so I didn't make a fool out of myself for a change.

When the bell rang everybody jumped up, packing up their books. I stuffed mine in my bag, just about to follow Amy out of the door when Will called to me. "Miss Henderson, think I could have a quick word with you?"

Amy smiled at me. "I'll wait by the lockers," she suggested.

"Okay, thanks." I smiled at her gratefully. Will didn't usually stop me after class so he probably just wanted to talk about tonight. I suddenly started to worry that he was going to cancel on me or something. I hadn't seen him properly since Monday so I really hoped he wasn't going to cancel on me.

Amy left and pulled the door shut behind her so I turned to Will, who was shuffling papers. "What's up?" I asked, heading over to him, perching on the edge of his desk, crossing my ankles.

He sighed, stepping closer to me. "Damn, these legs have been running through my mind all day," he purred, running a hand down over my hip until he got to the bottom of my skirt, his fingers tickled across the skin just above my knee.

I gulped and gripped the side of his shirt, pulling him even closer to me. "Well thoughts of your mouth on my legs have been running through my mind all day," I replied, my voice barely above a whisper because I was so excited by his touch.

He smiled and pressed himself against me, his face inches from mine. "You are just too hot for words, Cutie," he moaned. His eyes flicked down to my lips for a split second making me draw in a ragged breath as my whole body broke out in goosebumps. He smiled and cupped the side of my face in one of his hands as he brushed his nose against mine.

What on earth has gotten into him today? First the car, and now he's doing this at school? He had kissed me a couple of times at school, but other than a few indiscretions, we tried extremely hard to keep our relationship outside of the school grounds.

"My mom called me at the end of lunch," he whispered as he pecked my lips lightly.

His mom? Great, he's definitely cancelling on me tonight judging by the start of this conversation! His mom has probably asked him to do something for her or something. I frowned and pressed my lips to his again, making his hand move to the back of my neck, his fingers tangling in the back of my hair.

He pulled back after a few seconds and put his forehead against mine and I just waited for him to continue, to blow me off for tonight and tell me that he'd just have to see me Saturday instead.

"She's planning a surprise dinner for my dad on Saturday night. It's their anniversary, and she wants the family to go out for dinner," he whispered, kissing me again.

I nodded, not breaking the kiss. *So he's blowing me off for Saturday instead of tonight.* I gripped the sides of his shirt, pressing my body against his. He pulled away again to let us breathe, I smiled. "Okay, but I still get to see you Sunday, right? You're not cancelling both days, are you?" I asked, trying not to pout because I was missing a day of his company. *Hmm, maybe I should cancel with Sam tomorrow so I can hang out with Will instead.*

He laughed quietly. "You didn't let me finish," he teased, kissing the tip of my nose. "My mom wants you to come too."

I gulped. Suddenly I became both excited and scared at the same time. He'd told his parents all about me being his student, they knew we were dating. Apparently he'd told them everything when we first broke up because they kept asking about me all the time. They didn't seem to mind about it in the slightest, according to Will; they just liked seeing him happy. I had only met them once, at his sister's wedding, and they'd seemed genuinely nice at the time. They had to be great people to have two awesome boys like Will and Sam. From what I'd heard about Kaitlin she was just as nice too, but I'd only spoken to her for a few minutes on her wedding day so I didn't really know her much at all.

I looked at Will a little unsure what to say. It seemed quite weird to be taken home to meet his family when he had no chance of doing that in return, at least for a few months anyway.

"Really?" I mumbled.

He smiled reassuringly. "She's booked a restaurant a little way out of town so no one will see us together. It will just be us, my parents, my sister and her husband, and Sam. You'll be fine. If you want me to, I'll hold your hand all night long for moral support," he offered, raising one eyebrow, looking so hot that he took my breath away.

"That'd be kind of awkward when I want to cut my food," I teased, making him laugh. "Will, do they really want me there?" I asked, looking at him sceptically.

231

He smiled and kissed me again softly. "Of course they do, Cutie. You're my girl. We come as a package now, me and you." His eyes were boring into mine, and I could see how much me going to a family dinner meant to him.

I pushed all of my nerves away and nodded, biting my lip. "Okay sure, I'd love to meet your family again," I told him; trying not to show him how scared that made me. It wasn't that it was scary meeting his family; it was just a little weird that they knew that I was a minor and his student, and yet they still wanted me to go out with them for an anniversary dinner.

Will grinned at me happily before kissing me again. I wrapped my arms around the back of his neck and didn't let him pull away this time. When his tongue grazed my bottom lip, I eagerly granted him access, submitting to his request and pressing my whole body against his tightly. He moaned in the back of his throat, and before I even knew what had happened, he slammed me against the wall, his hands running down my body as he kissed me almost desperately.

My whole body felt like I had died and gone to heaven as he pushed my skirt up slightly, his hands massaging my bare thighs. I gasped as he kissed down my neck, biting on the skin gently, before returning to my mouth. The kiss was so all-consuming that my knees felt weak. He pressed me against the wall tighter as he lifted me off of my feet, guiding my legs around his waist as he kissed me like he could devour my soul.

He hadn't kissed me like this for a long time. It seemed like he'd completely lost all of his restraint. This was the type of thing that he didn't let happen at all, no matter how much I begged. My heart was beating like crazy, and some small part of me knew that we should stop. He would regret this if I let it carry on… but I couldn't force the words out to stop him. I needed this, we both needed this otherwise we'd end up going crazy.

I gripped my hands into his hair and pulled his mouth away from mine so I could breathe, but his lips didn't leave my skin, they just travelled down my neck instead, leaving a burning trail in their wake. I moaned his name and he pushed us away from the wall, heading back over to his desk again. He laid me down on top of all of his papers he was sorting earlier; I clamped myself to him tightly as he pulled back slightly.

He opened his mouth to speak, and I felt my heart sink. *He's regained his composure again; he's going to tell me that we need to stop.* His eyes were so excited that it made my breath catch in my throat, I could feel his whole body pressed against mine, and I knew that, physically, he didn't want to stop either, I could feel the evidence of that.

"I love you, Chloe," he whispered, kissing me again. His hands roamed my body again, one slipping under my shirt the other gripping my ass as he pressed his crotch against mine.

Wait, he isn't stopping?

I felt happiness building up inside that his hands were finally on me after five long weeks of playing it cool. My fingers were trembling as I started on the buttons of his shirt, pushing it off of his shoulders as I kissed over his chest.

Suddenly I heard a gasp. "Oh my god!" a girls voice cried.

I gulped, and Will and I both turned to see Erika Dennison standing there in the doorway, her mouth hanging open in shock, staring at us attacking each other on the desk like a couple of animals.

Chapter Thirty

I felt the colour drain from my face as I looked at her. Why her? She categorically hated me. If we had to get caught by someone, why did it have to be her? My heart sank as a slow smile started to stretch across her lips. *Oh God, please let this be a dream! Please tell me that his class was so boring that I fell asleep and am just having a nightmare right now, please!*

"What the hell?" She shook her head, frowning, as if she was trying to work something out.

Will hadn't moved, he was still pressed against me, pinning me to the desk, his hands exactly where they were two seconds before she entered the room. What on earth do we do? Will was going to get into so much trouble, I was going to be expelled, our lives were going to be ruined, and it was entirely my fault! Why did I have to wear a stupid skirt and tease him? Why did I have to want his attention and be such a freaking tease in the middle of school? I'm so stupid, and everything about this situation was my fault!

I gulped again and opened my mouth to try and speak; I had no idea what I wanted to say so I was hoping something coherent was going to come out of my mouth. Instead, what came out was, "I'm... we... no... it's not... no way..." I wanted to punch myself. Will still hadn't moved, it was like he was frozen. I wasn't even sure he was breathing, but I knew one thing for certain, he needed to get the heck off of me and start thinking of excuses for why he was kissing me and why his shirt was almost off!

I shoved on his chest, making him stand up straight, but he was still between my legs, his mouth just hanging open. His eyes were wide and his body tense. *Jeez, snap out of it, Will!* I sat up quickly, tugging on my skirt and top, righting myself as I blushed like crazy.

"Miss Dennison, it's not what it looks like," Will defended, shaking his head as he snapped out of his frozen state and started to button his shirt.

She laughed quietly. "Oh this is priceless. I came back to get my book, and I see this. This is too good," Erika mused, smirking at me. "I really think you could have done better though, Mr Morris. I mean, look at her, it's Chloe for goodness sake!" She looked me over slowly, a disgusted look on her face

234

and I felt my eyes prickle with tears, but there was no way I was letting them fall in front of her.

An angry expression crossed Will's face. "Enough!" he snapped.

She smiled sweetly and turned to grab her book that was lying on the desk. I had no idea what to say or do; all I could think about was that this was entirely my fault. Will was going to jail because of me.

She grabbed her book and turned for the door. "Well, it was nice knowing you," she chirped, laughing quietly to herself.

I swallowed the lump that was rapidly forming in my throat. She was going to tell someone, she was going to go and cause a shed load of trouble for both of us! I briefly considered my options. I could let her go, and we could pretend that she was lying. I could grab her, beat her to a pulp, and then chop her up and hide her somewhere. I could beg her not to say anything. Or I could just admit the truth, and we'd just pretend that this was a spur of the moment, one time indiscretion.

Personally I didn't like the sound of any of those options. I was leaning towards the cutting her into little pieces plan, but I didn't think Will would go for that. So I decided to go for the begging and try and appeal to her compassionate side, if she even had one.

"Erika, please!" I cried desperately. She stopped and looked at me, raising one eyebrow as I continued. "Please don't say anything; this is my fault, all of it."

Will shook his head. "No, Chloe, I was the one-" he started, but I pretended he hadn't said anything and carried on speaking.

"I started it, I just kissed him. It was my fault," I lied, begging her with my eyes.

"Tell it to the Principal." Erika shrugged and wrenched the door open, storming off.

I turned to Will; my heart was in my throat, my eyes prickling with tears. He cupped my face in his hands. "Don't you dare try and take the blame for this; I swear to God, Chloe, if you do I'm going to be so mad at you. If anyone's getting in trouble, it's me!" he said sternly.

I gulped and pushed his hands off of me. I wasn't giving up yet; maybe I could convince her not to say anything. I shoved him away and ran out of the door, ignoring how he shouted my name as I ran. I knew he couldn't follow me immediately; he still had to button his shirt and couldn't go tearing down the halls with his shirt off like that.

I streaked out and spotted Erika sauntering confidently down the hallway. She wasn't rushing; she had her head held high as she walked in the direction of the Principal's office.

I ran up to her and grabbed her arm, pulling her to a stop as I looked at her desperately. "Please? Please don't get him into trouble! It was entirely my fault, I just threw myself at him, none of this is his fault. Please don't make him suffer for something I've done, please?" I begged. I felt sick, my hands were shaking, and my whole body was cold.

235

She smirked at me. "It's your fault?"

I nodded quickly, and swiped at the traitor tear that fell down my face. "Yes," I whispered.

She tapped her finger on her chin, her long blood red nail touching her lips as she pursed them, thinking about it. "What's it worth then?" she asked, cocking her head to the side.

What's it worth? Is she going to want money or something to keep quiet? I mentally counted up how much spare money I had, and how much was in my bank account. "I... I don't know. I guess I could scrape a couple of hundred?" I offered, shrugging awkwardly. I could always get the money from Will; he was bound to have more than that.

She burst out laughing. "I don't want your money, Ice Princess. What else do you have to offer?" she hissed, sneering at me.

I frowned and shook my head. *What else is there to offer?* "I... I don't know. What is it that you want?" I asked quietly. I flicked my eyes around. Thankfully the corridor was empty because people had already left to go home. Amy would be waiting for me around the corner. *Maybe I could shout for her, I bet she'll help me with the chopping Erika up into little pieces plan!*

She looked me over slowly. "Well I definitely don't want the rags that you call clothes," she mocked with a distasteful look on her face. "I'm not totally sure. How about I have a think about it?" she offered.

I did a mental happy dance that she wasn't going to turn us in straight away, at least that would give me more time to come up with some more cash or something if she wanted to think about it. "Please don't say anything to anyone, Erika. I'll do anything that you want, just don't get him into trouble, please?" I whispered, trying not to cry again.

She smiled sweetly, but her eyes were hard. "You'll do anything?" There was a wicked, nasty tone to her voice that made a tickle run down my spine. I gulped and nodded in agreement. Somehow I knew I'd live to regret that comment. "For starters, I'll take that cash you offered, bring it in tomorrow with you." She reached into her schoolbag, pulling out her history and English books; she shoved them into my chest. "Do my assignments, they're due tomorrow, and I don't want less than a B so don't be trying to be cocky about it and make me look bad in class!" she hissed, waving her hand dismissively.

Money and homework, okay I can do that.

"I won't say anything because I actually like Mr Morris, he's a good teacher. But just know this, Chloe; I really dislike you and your cocky little understated good looks that draw attention from the popular guys. One step out of line, one thing you refuse to do for me, and I'm heading straight to the Principal's office to report you."

I gulped and nodded. "Okay, just please don't tell anyone, even your friends, please?" I requested, looking at her hopefully.

She smiled at something behind my shoulder. I turned to see Will walking up the hallway, his face was hard, but he was obviously trying not to show any emotions. She leant in closer to me. "He's so hot. How did he kiss?

Maybe I'll give him a try," she whispered, with her eyes still firmly fixed on Will.

I felt my hands tighten on her book that I was holding. The mere thought of her anywhere near him made my blood boil. *What on earth do I do if she blackmails Will and makes him kiss her or something? She wouldn't though, would she?*

Will stopped next to me. "Can we all just talk about this?" he asked, looking at Erika hopefully.

She smiled and shrugged. "It's all sorted. Chloe and I have talked about it, and I've decided not to say anything about it... for now." The mischievous glint to her eyes showed that she was enjoying having the power over both of us.

Will looked between us, clearly shocked by her revelation. He actually looked like he'd already accepted his fate and that he was in big trouble. He was looking at her like she'd just suggested that a pig flew past our heads or something.

"Really?" he gulped.

She nodded. "Yep. Just so you know though, Mr Morris, from now on I ace your class and don't need to turn in assignments," she said, raising one eyebrow challengingly.

He frowned and looked at me accusingly, as if this was something I'd agreed; he clearly didn't like the idea of that at all. I nodded encouragingly, begging him with my eyes to go along with it. He sighed heavily and rubbed the back of his neck, looking extremely annoyed about it. "Fine," he grumbled eventually.

"Will?"

We all turned to see Miss Teller walking up the hallway, her perfect locks swaying as she sashayed her way over. Erika leant in close to my ear. "I think his girlfriend would be especially pissed if she found out what you two were doing on the desk, don't you?" she whispered.

I cringed away from her, glowering and trying to kill her with my eyes. One good thing about that statement though was that she believed me when I said that I'd just kissed him, she hadn't worked out everything. I was incredibly grateful for that.

"Er... hey," Will mumbled as Miss Teller stopped at our group, smiling sweetly.

"Hi girls, what are you two still doing here? Not sick of this place already?" Miss Teller asked, smiling.

I shrugged and opened my mouth to answer, but Erika spoke first, "We were just talking to Mr Morris about the extra tuition that he's been giving to Chloe after class. I was wondering if I could maybe get in on those, you know, boost my grades and all that," Erika said, twisting her hair around one finger, a knowing smile on her lips.

Will frowned in her direction; I smiled inside at how much he hated that suggestion. "I don't think you need extra tuition, Miss Dennison, you're already acing my class, as you well know," he chimed in uncomfortably.

237

Miss Teller smiled, turning to Will. "Are we about ready to go? I know you have somewhere important to be, you said that you needed to leave as quickly as possible."

I bit my lip. 'Somewhere important to be', that was me. Will looked between me and Erika hesitantly, silently asking what he should do. "I'm not sure if we're done talking. Maybe you should wait in the car, Caroline?" he suggested, digging in his pocket and passing her his keys.

Erika shifted on her feet. "We're done talking. I need to go anyway. See you tomorrow, Mr Morris, Miss Teller," she stated, gripping my arm and turning me around quickly. I smiled and nodded a goodbye to Will and allowed Erika to guide me up the hallway. "Keep Saturday free. I have chores that you can do. My car needs valeting, and I have some shoes that need cleaning." She shrugged and let go of my arm, looking at her hand distastefully, as if she'd just touched something dirty.

I almost choked on my disbelief. *Cleaning her car and doing her chores? Is that some kind of joke?* "Really?" I asked, praying she would just laugh it off and tell me she was kidding around. She didn't though.

"Absolutely."

What a witch! "Fine, but then that's it, right?" I asked.

She laughed. "Oh no, Ice Princess, your ass is mine now. You want me to keep your secret then you'll do what I say, when I say it. You're like my own personal bitch now."

My hand curled into a fist, and I could feel my temper rising. I wasn't a violent person usually. I grabbed her hair and smashed her face into the lockers as hard as I could, hearing the satisfying crack of her nose as she screamed and cupped it. Blood overflowed her hand and ruined her slutty top.

"Chloe?"

I blinked a couple of times and looked at Erika; she was staring at me as if waiting for me to answer something. *Huh, was I daydreaming?* She clicked her fingers in front of my face a couple of times, looking more pissed off with each passing second.

"I said, give me your cell phone number, I'll text you my breakfast order in the morning!" she growled, impatiently shaking her cell phone in my face. I took the phone she was offering and punched in my number. *I really should act on that daydream and smash her face.*

I handed the phone back to her. She immediately turned on her expensive stiletto heels and marched off, leaving me standing there watching her with a scowl on my face. I had never wished anyone harm in my life, but if she stepped out of the building and a herd of stray cattle stampeded her, I would laugh my ass off.

I sighed and shook my head. What on earth had I got myself into? She was going to make my life hell from now on, and I had another six months of school left too. I guess it didn't matter though; I would do anything to protect Will, even if I had to kiss her feet for a few months. Everything would be fine, things would settle down once she got bored of playing with me. Some small part of me knew that wasn't true though.

I shifted her books in my arms and headed round to where I knew Amy would be waiting for me. When I saw her leaning up against the lockers, picking her nails impatiently, I sighed. When I got to her side, I dropped all of Erika's books on the floor, not caring if the pages got messed up. I pulled my best friend into a hug, just needing her comfort.

It took her a couple of seconds to get over the shock and then she hugged me back. "What's happened?" she asked quickly.

I groaned and shook my head. "I'll tell you in the car." I couldn't exactly talk about this in school, from now on I would take no more risks.

She nodded, frowning and looking at me concerned as she bent to help me pick up the books from the floor. "Why do you have Erika's books?" she asked, frowning at the history textbook in her hand that had her name scrawled on the front cover.

"Amy, we'll talk about it in the car," I moaned, closing my eyes and just wishing I would wake up and this all be a horrible nightmare. She nodded and together we walked silently to her car. I was barely inside before she turned to me, obviously wanting an explanation.

I put my head in my hands. "Erika just walked in on while I was in the classroom with Will," I explained, hating myself all over again for wearing the stupid skirt and pushing his buttons. *Why didn't I just stop him? Why didn't one of us think to lock the door before doing that? Everything would have been fine if we had just cooled down and broke away long enough to lock the damn door!*

Amy looked at me with wide eyes. "What were you doing?" she asked, her voice barely above a whisper.

I groaned again. *Oh man, this is so bad!* Where was the giant hole that I could jump into when I needed one? "Full on making out," I admitted.

She gasped. "Holy shit, Chloe. What are you going to do? You'll both be in so much trouble!" she cried, looking at me horrified. "You'll be expelled, and he'll be fired... and, oh my God, what if they send him to jail?"

I shook my head; I would never let that happen. If it all came out then I would just say that I kissed him, and he responded, neither of us would admit to anything more than one kiss. The most he'd get was fired. I'd never let him go to jail for me, never.

"I've done something really stupid," I whined, shaking my head in disbelief at the open-ended agreement that I'd made with Erika.

"What?" Amy asked, taking my hand and squeezing gently.

"I've made a deal with the devil."

She drove us home at a snail's pace, but frankly I was glad she didn't drive too fast because she was barely even looking at the road. I told her everything. Will and I making out on the desk, that Erika had walked in when his shirt was almost off, I told her about the deals and agreements that I'd made with her. The whole time she just drove and watched me with her mouth hanging open in shock and disbelief.

When we pulled up at my house, she suddenly rounded on me. "I freaking hate Erika, freaking, Dennison! You know what we should do? We should go round to her house and kidnap her cat and send her little ransom notes!" she growled, slamming her hand down on the steering wheel.

I laughed at her half-assed plan. "Does she even have a cat?" I asked, shaking my head.

Amy frowned. "I don't know," she admitted. "Well we'll find something of hers to ransom. Maybe we could steal her cell phone and send out loads of bitchy texts to her friends?"

I rolled my eyes. How exactly would we get hold of her phone in the first place? "Amy, let's just play nice and see how it goes. I'm hoping she'll get bored of playing with me after a couple of weeks and move onto torturing someone else," I suggested, trying to convince myself at the same time.

She frowned, obviously not liking the idea of just taking her abuse. "I hate her," she grumbled.

I nodded and hugged her again. "Me too. Look I'd better go, I need to pee before Will comes to get me," I said quietly.

Would Will even come to collect me after what just happened? Would he totally blame me for wearing the skirt and now he wanted nothing more to do with me because we'd been caught? How would I cope with that if he broke it off with me? I didn't think I'd cope particularly well at all. He was probably really angry with me right now for encouraging that to happen. He probably hated me and wanted nothing to do with me ever again.

"Okay, well if you need help with her assignments then call me, all right?" she offered, nodding at the books on the seat in the back.

I groaned in frustration. How on earth was I going to do her English and History assignments tonight, and do my own work, and see Will? There just wasn't enough hours in the day for it all!

"Thanks, Amy, you really are the best friend a girl could ask for, you know that?" I gushed, looking at her gratefully.

She nodded, pushing a strand of her long hair out of her face. "I know. So you are."

I sighed and pushed myself out of her car, heading inside the house. As soon as I was in solitude of my bedroom I immediately changed out of the stupid skirt, throwing it in the trash angrily. I pulled on a pair of baggy sweats and sat on the edge of my bed playing with my cell phone. Will was due here any minute. Would he call and tell me that he wasn't coming, or would he just not show up?

I felt like crying. This had messed everything up, he was going to decide that a stupid high school girl wasn't worth risking his career over, and he'd break it off for sure. I looked at Erika's books, deciding to make a start on her English assignment.

I flopped down on my bed and pulled out my iPod, putting on the headphones and turning it up as high as I could stand as I read through what she had to do. It didn't look too bad, thankfully I'd covered all of this stuff in my last semester, and I was in AP English so her assignment should be a breeze. I grabbed my notebook and started breaking down the poem, writing out all of the hidden meanings and paying particular attention to the symbolism like she was supposed to.

Suddenly something pressed down hard against my back, squashing me onto the bed on my stomach. I jumped a mile and let out a scream as I tried to get up, but someone was pinning me down with their bodyweight. I could feel the vibrations of laughter, their chest rumbling against my back but I couldn't hear anything because of the music banging in my ears.

I thrashed trying to throw them off as I started to panic, but one of the earphones was pulled out of my ear and I could hear familiar laughter. I gulped and looked over my shoulder, my heart returning to the normal rate when I realised it was just Will. He was grinning from ear to ear, still laying on me, and pressing me down to the bed.

What on earth is he doing here? And why is he smiling at me? Shouldn't he be hating me for possibly ruining his life?

"What are you doing here? And how did you even get in my house?" I asked, frowning and trying not to let my emotions get the better of me.

He kissed my cheek softly, rolling off of me and laying against my side. One of his hands played with my hair as he looked at me. "I came to get you, of course," he replied as if it was obvious. "I called your cell, but it just kept ringing and going to voicemail. As for how I got in, I knew your parents wouldn't be home yet and you left your front door unlocked."

I turned to face him. He came to pick me up? After everything that just happened, he still wanted to see me tonight? "You came to get me? Why?" I asked, my voice breaking where I was so close to tears.

He frowned, looking a little confused. "Well, I thought we had a date tonight," he answered, looking slightly worried. I couldn't hold my emotions anymore. I burst into tears. He gasped and pulled me close to him, stroking his hand down my back soothingly. "Cutie, what's wrong?" he whispered.

I cried harder at the sound of his nickname for me. How was I going to cope when he left me for a second time? This was already so painful, and he hadn't even said the words that I knew would come out of his mouth any minute.

"Chloe?" He pushed me away from him slightly, cupping my face so he could look at me. "What are you crying for?"

I gulped, and he wiped the tears from my face with his thumbs. "I thought you wouldn't want to see me anymore. I thought you'd hate me because of what happened. It was all my fault. I'm so sorry, Will," I whispered, shaking my head and looking at him apologetically.

He frowned looking even more confused. "I could never hate you, Chloe. And that wasn't your fault, it was mine. I was the one that kissed you; I was the one that moved us over to the desk, I'm the adult; I should have known better, and had more restraint." He kissed a stray tear away as it fell down my cheek.

"It *was* my fault… the skirt… and now Erika!" I wailed, losing control again.

He sighed and pulled me to his chest again, rocking me gently. "Everything's fine. I'll just pass her like she said, and everything will be fine. As for the skirt being to blame… that was one sexy skirt, Cutie, but I was losing my will power long before you chose that to wear today. It would have happened sooner or later, I've been finding it harder and harder to keep my hands off of you every day," he said, looking at me apologetically.

I gulped. "You don't blame me?"

He shook his head fiercely. "I'm to blame, Cutie. Everything is my fault, and that's the story we go with if anything ever comes out about us. Okay?" he said sternly.

I frowned and opened my mouth to protest, but he must have known I was about to argue with him because he smiled and pressed his lips to mine, silencing me before I even spoke. He rolled me onto my back, half hovering above me and kissed me deeply while I clung to him for dear life. By the time he pulled away, I was a little breathless.

He smiled and kissed the tip of my nose. "Come on then, are you ready?" he asked, pushing himself up and holding down a hand to help me off of the bed.

I looked back at Erika's assignments on the bed and winced. I really needed to get them done, which meant that I wouldn't have time to go hang out at his place tonight. "I don't think I can. I need to do her assignments for tomorrow, and I have to do mine too…" I trailed off, pouting.

"Do who's assignments?" he asked, frowning at the papers on my bed.

I sighed sadly. I guess he didn't know about the whole 'You're my personal bitch' agreement I'd made with the devil. As far as he was concerned, she was going to keep quiet in exchange for a free pass in calculus.

I sat up and frowned. He sat down next to me, taking my hand. "She said I had to do her assignments for her, I also have to wash her car on Saturday and do some chores," I told him, shrugging.

"What the hell?" he roared, jumping off of the bed again, his face hard and angry.

I gulped. "I said I'd do anything and I will. I won't let her get you into trouble, she'll get bored in a couple of weeks, and then she'll leave us alone. I may have to borrow some money from you, I'll pay you back though," I said quietly.

"She's blackmailing you? That little bitch!" he hissed.

I burst out laughing. "Language, Mr Morris! You can't speak about a student like that!" I teased, trying to lighten the mood.

He raised one eyebrow. "I'm pretty sure I'm not allowed to fall in love with one either, so I think that I just suck at teaching," he countered, smirking at me.

My heart melted a little when he said he was in love with me. "You don't suck at teaching; you're just young and can't control your hormones." I patted the top of his head condescendingly, grinning. "Never mind, baby, you'll grow up soon."

He laughed and wrapped his arms around me; pushing me down on the bed and pinning me down, blowing raspberries on my neck, ticking my sides, making me scream and squeal under him.

After a couple of minutes he pulled back and put his forehead to mine. "I'm sorry about all of this, Cutie. I hope you think I'm worth it. Are you regretting having anything to do with me?" he asked quietly, looking a little unsure about himself.

I shook my head and wrapped my legs around his waist, pulling him closer to me, gripping my hands in the back of his hair. "Will, I love you. I'll never regret anything that involves you being in my life. This will all blow over soon, and life can go back to normal. We just need to agree not to do anything on school grounds, ever again." I looked at him sternly.

He nodded. "Definitely." He kissed me again, running his hand down my side, gripping the waistband of my sweats I was wearing. "Maybe you could stop with the skirts at school too, so I don't have to fight the urge to jump you every time I'm within a few feet of you?"

I giggled and blushed like crazy as I pressed my face into the side of his neck and nodded. "Yeah, I'll throw them out," I confirmed.

He pulled back and grinned, shaking his head. "Don't throw them out, I like them. Just don't wear them at school. Deal?"

I nodded and pulled his mouth to mine again, kissing him softly. "Deal," I mumbled against his lips.

He kissed me for a few more minutes then pulled back, sitting up next to me and pulling me up too. He looked down at the papers I had spread on my bed. "You're really doing her homework?" he asked, scowling angrily at it.

I sighed and nodded. "Yeah, so I don't think I'll have time to come to yours tonight. I have two of hers to do, and then I have my own homework too." I smiled at him apologetically.

He shook his head and grabbed all of the papers and books, piling them up. "You're coming to mine; I'm not letting her ruin anything for us. I'll help you do her work and yours, and then we might get time to hang out and get a takeout or something."

I looked at him gratefully. I couldn't help the little "Aww," that escaped my lips. *That's so adorable!*

He rolled his eyes as if he knew what I was thinking and grabbed my hand, pulling me to my feet. "Let's go before your parents come home," he suggested.

I nodded and looked down at myself in my baggy sweatpants. *Wow, I look a mess!* "I just need to change," I said, heading over to my closet.

He laughed and pulled on my hand making me stop. "Don't change, I like the sweats," he said, waggling his eyebrows at them as he looked me over slowly.

I slapped his arm. "You're such a weird boy, Will!" I scolded playfully.

243

"Yeah, but you love me," he countered, looking at me confidently.

I rolled my eyes. "Yeah, I do."

Chapter Thirty-One

"Remind me again, why we're getting her breakfast order?" Will moaned as we pulled up outside Starbucks on the other side of town.

I sighed. "So you don't lose your job, or worse. And so I don't get expelled," I replied, rolling my eyes. We'd been through this and through this. He wanted to speak to her and tell her to 'shove it up her ass', those were his exact words. Apparently he would like to hear them again because those were the words I said to Olly when we broke up.

Will was convinced that the Principal wouldn't believe her anyway. He suggested that we could say something like she was jealous of me and just lashing out because I'd hooked up with a guy Erika wanted or something. In the end we decided just to go with her plan for now, and hope that she got bored after a couple of weeks. I wasn't convinced she would, but I just didn't want to take the risk of the Principal believing her story.

I jumped out of his car and ran in to Starbucks, buying her 'tall, half-skinny, half-one percent, split quad shot latte, with whip,' and an energy bar.

Once I had her complicated order, I sighed, and climbed back into his car. Today was going a long day no doubt. She'd already text me her breakfast order and told me to make sure I didn't let it get cold. Then I was supposed to meet her at her locker at exactly 8:40 to give her the assignments that I did for her, and of course, the two hundred bucks that I had promised her. *Stupid devil woman.*

As we were driving down the road, my cell phone started to ring. I pulled it out of my pocket and smiled, it was Sam. I smirked in Will's direction; he was still whining that I was seeing his brother instead of him tonight.

"Hey, Sam," I chirped, grinning as Will groaned.

"Hey, Foxy. Still up for tonight?"

"Yep. Are you gonna carry on with that story about when Will was at school?" I joked, trying not to laugh as Will frowned in my direction.

Sam laughed. "Is he there with you right now?"

"Abso-freaking-lutely," I confirmed, laughing quietly to myself.

"Mention something about summer camp," he suggested.

I smiled wickedly. "Summer camp? No, what did he do at summer camp?" I asked, playing along.

Will gasped and reached out to grab my phone while shouting at Sam, "Stop telling her stuff about me! I swear, Sam, you're gonna get it when I see you next!"

I laughed and held the phone away, pushing his hand away from the phone. "Drive the car, Mr Morris!" I joked, smirking at him. I leant away and started talking to Sam again. "Are you coming to get me from school?"

"Yeah, saves me waiting around. I thought we could go grab some dinner then go bowling. You up for that?" he asked.

"Sure thing. Hey, you know, you could do me an awesome favour while you're at my school," I said, shifting the devil woman's drink in my hands.

"What's that, Foxy?"

"Seduce a student and make her fall in love with you so she'll leave me alone," I stated, only half joking.

"Seduce a student? Done!" He laughed. I smiled and closed my eyes, resting my head back on the chair as we neared the place where Will would drop me off. I silently wished it would be that easy and that Sam could sort this out for me, but nothing is ever that easy in life. Erika would be on my back for the rest of the school year, and there was nothing I could do about it. "Seriously though, is something wrong? Is someone picking on you or something?" he asked, sounding concerned.

I chewed on my lip and then proceeded to tell Sam the whole story about how Erika saw us kissing, and how she was now blackmailing me. The whole time I was speaking he remained silent; I noticed Will's hands were gripping the steering wheel so hard his knuckles were white. He really hated playing along with her, but I just couldn't take the risk of someone believing her if she said anything about it.

When I was done, Sam blew out a big breath. "Wow, that sucks for you two. I guess you'll just have to see how it plays out today. I'll have a think and see if there's anything I can do to help, all right? Maybe you could break into her house, steal her diary, and find some dirt to blackmail her with?" he suggested.

I laughed. "You sound like Amy; she wanted to ransom her cat."

"Does she have a cat? I'm up for a little catnapping. We could dress it in a load of stupid outfits and take pictures and threaten to post them all over town if she doesn't leave you alone." He chuckled darkly, probably already planning on surfing the net to see if he could find cat dress up outfits.

I rolled my eyes at his lameness and noticed that we'd stopped in the parking lot of the store as usual. I frowned. "I gotta go, Sam. See you after school." We said our goodbyes and I pushed my phone back into my pocket. I turned to look at Will; he was scowling out of the windshield. "So, I'll see you in class then I guess," I muttered, not really wanting to get out of the car.

246

He sighed and slipped his arm around my shoulder, his other hand stroking the side of my face. "If she takes this too far and you get pissed off, then we just tell her shove it, right?" he said, looking at me sternly.

I nodded. "Up her ass, I remember," I joked, making him laugh. He pressed his lips to mine softly. I closed my eyes and just enjoyed the closeness of him, the feel if his lips against mine, the way my stomach fluttered. Kissing Will was out of this world and I wasn't sure I would ever get used to the intimacy of a single peck on the lips.

He pulled away after a few seconds and put his forehead to mine. "I love you. Just remember that. No matter what happens, I love you. If this gets to the point where we need to do something drastic then I'll quit my job," he said, stroking my face lightly with his thumb.

I scoffed at that suggestion. That was something else we talked about last night, we had been through a number of different scenarios, none of which I particularly liked. The one that was the fall back plan that would happen as a last resort - Will would get another job at another school. I didn't want that to happen though, he was lucky to get his position at our school because of his age. The Principal must have been desperate for a teacher to have employed a graduate with no experience. I had no doubt in my mind that he would find it hard to find another teaching job anywhere near where we lived.

I pulled back and grabbed the handle, juggling everything in my hands as I swung my bag onto my back preparing for the short walk to school. "Chloe," Will called just as I was about to step out of the car. I turned back to look at him. He was holding out a stack of money to me. I sighed and closed my hand over it, smiling at him gratefully because he had insisted on paying her off.

"Thanks. I'll pay you back," I promised.

He shook his head and pressed his lips to mine again, kissing me softly before speaking against my lips, "No, you won't."

I smiled weakly and closed my eyes, just wishing that things could be easier and that falling in love wouldn't be so wrong. Why did everything have to be so difficult? When a person fell in love, it was supposed to be all smiles, flirting and giggling, not sneaking around and stealing little moments in a disused parking lot. I would give anything to just walk down the street and hold his hand, to take him home and introduce him to my parents as my boyfriend.

"Will?" I traced my nose up the side of his as he played with my hair.

"Mmm?" he mumbled, his lips vibrating against mine where they were still so teasingly close.

"After the meal with your parents on Saturday, do you think I could come and stay at yours?" I asked. His hand tightened in my hair, so I quickly continued, "Not to do anything. I just want to wake up with you holding me, nothing more. Please? I really need that, please?" I begged. My voice was barely above a whisper.

He sighed, his warm breath blowing across my face, making my mouth water and my skin break out in goosebumps. "I really need that too," he admitted, kissing me softly again.

I felt my heart start to fly in my chest at the mere thought of going to sleep with his arms wrapped around me. I could cope with the non-sex stuff, but I just needed a little more intimacy, a little more private time with him where we weren't stressed and having heavy conversations about hiding our relationship and what to do if things turned sour. I just needed one night of just Will and Chloe, together, and alone.

"I'd better take this coffee to her before it gets cold," I said somewhat reluctantly.

"I'll text you through the day." He smiled sadly and pulled back into his seat, watching as I climbed out of the car and waved weakly at him.

I pulled my jacket tighter around me and hunched my shoulders against the cold wind. A quick glance at my watch told me I had a couple of minutes left before I had to meet her, but I headed straight to her locker anyway, wanting to get this over and done with as quick as possible. She was leaning against her locker, a guy leaning in, obviously flirting with her as she laughed and slapped his shoulder, all the while shooting him a seductive look. *Tramp!*

I cleared my throat as I stopped by her side, not wanting this to take a second longer than necessary. She looked at me, a distasteful expression on her face before she rearranged it and smirked at me wickedly. "Kevin, I just need a minute. I'll see you in class, okay?" she said to him, but her eyes not leaving me.

The guy frowned at me as he walked off, obviously a little put out that she was sending him away. As soon as we were on our own I handed her the coffee and energy bar. She frowned as she took it. "You got my order right? If this is wrong then you're skipping first period to get me another," she warned, eyeing me sceptically.

I frowned and bit back my angry retort. "Yes, it's exactly like you asked for," I hissed, putting on a fake smile as someone walked past, looking at us curiously.

"My work?" she prompted, snapping her fingers impatiently, looking around as if bored or something. I sighed and handed her the printed sheets that I'd managed to complete for her last night before Will and I had a Chinese takeout. "If this is below a B, then it's bye bye hottie teacher." She smirked at me as she scanned over it. I was secretly glad that I didn't just go with Will's suggestion of adding a cuss word to every line because he didn't think she'd notice.

I grabbed the money from my back pocket and thrust it at her, shoving it against her chest. "Just stay away from me from now on," I snapped, trying to make my voice sound stronger than I felt.

She smiled evilly at me. "Tomorrow, you come to mine just after lunch; you can do my chores while my parents are out. You might want to wear something old, I have a couple of horses that need mucking out," she stated, laughing to herself.

Horses, what on earth? I felt my face flush with anger, and my hands itch to punch her in her smug face. "You aren't seriously expecting me to shovel shi-" I stopped talking abruptly as Mrs Halston walked past. *Wow, that was close, almost got myself a detention then I'm betting!*

Erika laughed and tossed her platinum blonde hair over her shoulder. "Definitely. Unless you'd rather just back out of this whole deal? If you're not going to keep up with your end, then I won't have to keep up with mine. I wonder if the Principal is free right now." She looked up the hallway towards his office with mock interest.

I couldn't stop the angry growl that escaped my lips. "Fine! You'll need to give me your address or something," I muttered, shaking my head in disbelief. *What a little witch!*

"Oh don't worry, we'll be speaking a lot over the course of the day," she mused. She waved her hand in a buzz off gesture. "Run along now, little doggie. Just remember to come when you're called." She sneered at me one last time before I turned on my heel and marched off to where I knew Amy would be at this time of the morning.

The day passed unbelievably slowly. Erika was right, I definitely saw her a lot over the course of the day. I had to buy her lunch, lend her my gym kit, and get her books for her so that she could spend precious extra minutes reapplying her already overdone make-up. I had to deliver messages to her friends, and at one point I even had to pick a piece of gum from the bottom of her shoe because she'd stepped in it. I thought I did quite well by not flicking it into her hair as payback, though quite how I refrained myself I had no idea. By the time calculus came, I was exhausted both physically and mentally. All I wanted to do was curl into a ball on Will's lap and sleep.

Amy tried to help when she could, coming with me to run her errands, making herself late for classes too. The whole time she was ranting out little plans of revenge and payback. Her favourite one by far wouldn't be easy to pull off, for one thing, where would you even find the Batmobile and midgets with horns anyway?

We headed for the back row in Will's class. I ignored Olly shooting me a small scowl as we walked past him, he still wasn't talking to me, but I just couldn't bring myself to feel bad about it, he was the one that forced the breakup by being a possessive jerk, not me.

Will smiled as the bell rang, signalling the beginning of class. His eyes scanned the room for a couple of seconds, looking a little confused and that got me curious. I looked around the students, trying to see what had him so confused, only to see that Erika wasn't here. I smiled weakly to myself. Maybe there is a God after all and she was going to leave Will alone, skip his class and still get the pass. One could only hope.

Everything was going smoothly. I tried my best to concentrate on what he was saying and not the way he was saying it. I took notes; I even understood some of what he was saying, which would please Nick immensely. Fifteen minutes into the class the door opened, and everyone turned to watch Erika saunter in with a smirk on her face.

I groaned. *Maybe it isn't going to be that easy for Will after all!*

"Miss Dennison, you're late! Do you have a late slip?" Will asked, frowning at her angrily. I winced. I'd have to tell him to ease up on the death glares otherwise people might get suspicious; he shouldn't really look at a student that way.

Erika smiled and waved her hand dismissively, ignoring his comment and just headed to a free desk, immediately pulling out her iPod, making a show of putting it on. My mouth dropped open in shock.

Will marched over to her desk and held out his hand. "That's now confiscated. You can pick it up from the office at the end of next week," he growled. *Wow, he really needs to ease up on the anger!*

She laughed, not turning it off, raising one eyebrow at him innocently. "I don't think so, do you, Mr Morris?" she purred, fluttering her eyelashes.

"Turn it off now!" Will ordered, shaking his hand for it again. The whole class was watching him, and I felt sick. Why was she doing this? He was giving her the pass, I was running around after her at her beck and call, and she still felt the need to push him in front of his students?

She smiled and slowly pulled the earphones from her ear, making a show of winding the wire up around it, knowing that all eyes were on her. "You can take it for the lesson, but I'll want it back for the weekend. I don't think it's right that you can confiscate something over a weekend. Maybe I should the matter up with the Principal?" she suggested, smiling sweetly at him.

His shoulders stiffened, and his eyes flicked to me. I nodded quickly, encouraging him to just agree and give it back at the end of his class so that she wouldn't cause more trouble. His frown deepened and his jaw clenched as his eyes moved back to her. "Fine, you can get it back at the end of the lesson. I suppose it's a little unfair for me to deprive you of it for the weekend," he forced out, speaking through his teeth.

I relaxed. Just another half an hour and the class would be over, and then I would be free of her and her ridiculous demands. Well, until I needed to go and muck out her horses anyway.

He turned and walked back to his desk, shoving her iPod in one of his drawers and slamming it shut forcefully. "Let's just get on with the lesson," he snapped angrily. Half of the class groaned because he was now in a sour mood, which probably meant more homework being piled on tonight.

The rest of the lesson passed without incident. Erika didn't push him or say anything wrong, but she just sat there filing her nails the whole time, not even pretending to listen. I could tell by Will's angry expression that he wouldn't be putting up with much of her crap, which didn't bode well for our situation at all.

When the bell rang I deliberately packed my books slowly, making sure Erika left the room before I did. I couldn't get her comment out of my head

250

about her 'giving him a try'. What if she decided she wanted to blackmail him into kissing her or something? I knew I was being more than a little pathetic though, that was one thing I knew Will wouldn't do. He would rather quit his job. I still lingered behind her though, making sure she stayed the hell away from my man.

She sauntered up to him, holding out a manicured hand for her iPod, a satisfied smile on her lips. He didn't say anything, just dropped it into her hand, his whole body tense and stressed. I longed to rub my hands over his shoulders and massage some of that tension away for him. I'd need to wait until Saturday night for that though.

As soon as she was out of the room, Amy and I walked out too, I dropped a little note onto Will's desk on the way past. I hadn't written anything on there, just drew a smiley face, hoping it would cheer him up a little. He smiled weakly at me, and I made a mental note to call him as soon as I was off of school grounds so he could get the anger out of his system. He obviously needed to rant about her or something.

I linked my arm through Amy's as we walked to the lockers. "So, you seeing Ryan this weekend?" I asked, wanting a little bit of normality for a change, today had been crazy.

She nodded, grinning happily. "Yeah, I'm bringing him over to meet my parents this weekend," she said excitedly.

I put on a fake smile to cover up the jealously I felt because I couldn't do that with my boyfriend. I didn't realise just how much I was going to miss the small things in a relationship. "That's great. He'll do great with your parents. Your mom will really like him," I said, nodding enthusiastically.

She sighed dreamily and nodded. "He does great with everything."

From the corner of my eye I saw him walking up the hallway towards us. "Speak of the devil and he shall appear," I quoted, nodding at him. She squealed and threw herself at him as soon as he was close enough. I laughed and rolled my eyes. "See you two lovebirds later. Call me and let me know how it went," I said, making a hasty retreat to the front doors before they started making out in front of me like lovesick puppies.

As I walked out of the building, I saw Sam's car parked in the drop off, no parking zone at the front of the school. He was leaning against the side of his car, his face tilted up towards the sky, his eyes closed, obviously enjoying the sunshine. It was times like this that I wished I had a glass of water or something else that I could throw at him.

I walked up and jabbed my finger into his ribs, making him jump and look at me shocked. "Oh, hey," he chirped, grinning happily.

"Hey, Sam-bo," I replied, laughing as he tried to grab me. He hated that new nickname. I laughed and dodged his hands, pushing them away from me, laughing. "Sorry! Sorry, just quit it!" I squealed.

He smiled and rolled his eyes. "Stop with the whole, Sam-bo thing, Chlo-blow," he said, smirking at me. I stuck my tongue out at him and he just laughed, pulling me into a hug. When he let go he looked around the quickly emptying parking lot. "So, where's the girl I need to seduce?" he asked, raising one eyebrow, obviously liking the challenge.

I smiled sadly. "I think she left already. It's okay, that wouldn't work anyway." I shrugged.

He pursed his lips and nodded. "It's okay, I have a better plan anyway," he informed me, waggling his eyebrows.

I felt the excitement build up inside that he had a plan. I silently prayed it wasn't along the lines of Amy's: Let's dig a hole, push her in and throw in a pack of wild dogs, plan that she suggested earlier. "Oh yeah?" I prompted, looking at him expectantly, waiting for him to continue and tell me his genius idea that was going to save the day.

He nodded. "We just need to wait until the right time, then I'll fix everything for you and my brother," he said confidently. His eyes were still raking over the parking lot and school grounds. I stood there silently at his side, just waiting for whatever he was looking for to show up, not really having a clue what was going on in his brain. Sam really was strange at times.

After a couple of minutes, his eyes lit up, and he stood straighter. "Who are they?" he asked, nodding in the direction of the school building.

I frowned and glanced in the direction he nodded. I got even more confused when I saw who it was that was walking towards us from the main building. "That's Mr Young and Mr Bentley. Why?"

He grinned at me wickedly, his eyes playful. "You can thank me later," he said quietly.

Thank him? What on earth...

He grabbed me, pulling me towards him and crushed my body against his. Before I even had time to decipher what he was doing, his lips crashed against mine, kissing me forcefully.

Chapter Thirty-Two

I whimpered against his lips and put my hands on his chest trying to push him off of me. He turned me quickly so his back was to the approaching teachers, his lips left mine, and I opened my mouth to shout at him, but he spoke first, "Shh, I'm saving your ass!" he whispered, kissing me again before I could respond.

He pulled me closer to him and I had no idea what on earth he was doing. Sam pinned me against his chest as he continued to kiss me forcefully. I shook my head slightly, and he pulled out of the kiss, his eyes still playful, a smirk on his lips.

"Oh so that's what he sees in you," he mused. I stomped on his foot, which just made him laugh. He finally let me go and just as I was about to shout at him and punch him in the arm, he turned to the two teachers who were now only a few feet in front of us. *Oh great, on top of everything now I'm going to get detention for PDA on school grounds!* Sam smiled at them and slipped his arm around my shoulder. "Oops, sorry. My bad. You're not going to give my girlfriend detention, are you?" he asked, pulling an adorable pouting face to the annoyed looking teachers.

Girlfriend? What the heck is going on in that pea brain of his?

Mr Young frowned. "You shouldn't be doing this on school grounds, Chloe. I suggest you leave that kind of thing for a less public place."

I gulped and nodded. I was so going to kill Sam for this, but that was nothing compared to how pissed off Will was going to be that his brother had just kissed me. I felt a little satisfied smirk creep onto my lips when I thought about that. *Serves him right, stupid jerk!*

"Yes, Sir. Sorry," I muttered weakly.

Sam smiled and stepped forward. "I take it that you're a teacher at my girlfriend's school?" he asked, smiling politely.

Mr Young nodded. "I am."

Sam's smile grew more pronounced, and I got even more confused. He looked so proud of himself for some reason, but I just didn't get it. "Okay great. I was just wondering if I could go in and speak to my brother. I know

253

I'm not a student at the school so I was wondering if I needed a visitors badge or something so I could go to his classroom? It's important," Sam said, giving him the 'little boy lost' look.

Mr Young frowned, looking just as confused as I was. "You're brother? Is he a student here? I'm sure he'll be out in a minute," he answered, shaking his head.

Sam shook his head. "No, my brother's a teacher here. Will Morris. I really need to speak to him about something real quick. Do you think I could have my girlfriend show me the way to his classroom? We could stop by the office and get a visitors pass if we need one..." he trailed off, looking thoughtful.

Mr Young's eyes flicked to me, and I worked hard to keep the confusion off of my face. Sam had just lied and told a teacher that I was dating Will's brother. How exactly would this help? Had Sam completely lost the plot?

Mr Young looked back to Sam. "You're Will's brother?" he asked, looking a little taken aback.

Sam nodded. "Yep, he got the brains, and I got the looks."

I snorted at that comment; Will unquestionably got both in my opinion.

Mr Young smiled at the comment. "I didn't realise that Will even had a brother. And you're dating one of his students? That must a little awkward," he mused.

Sam shrugged. "It's not my problem. They seem to cope with it okay though. You get on quite well with my brother, don't you, Chloe-blow? We've been seeing each other for a couple of months now, so I guess they've had time to get used to it. Right, Foxy?" Sam lied, smirking at me.

"Yep, Sam-bo," I replied, grinning as his arm tightened on my shoulders, crushing me against the side of his body. He really hated me calling him that.

Mr Young nodded, looking a little taken aback. "I can't see a problem with you going into the school. Visitors are supposed to sign in though, so if you could just pop to the office first and sign in. Tell them that Mr Young said it was all right for you to come in for a few minutes."

Sam was grinning proudly, but I still couldn't see how this would help. *Maybe I'm just being dumb?* "Great, and it's nice to meet you, Mr Young, Will's mentioned you before," he said nodding and turning on the charm. "I'm Sam by the way."

Mr Young smiled and nodded. "Nice to meet you too. Go on in then," he suggested, nodding at the front doors. Sam's arm tightened on my shoulder as he led me towards the building.

I elbowed him in the ribs as soon as we were out of earshot. "What the hell was that? You know your brothers gonna kick your ass for kissing me!" I hissed.

Sam laughed and shook his head. "He won't, I've just saved your asses. Now you have two teachers to witness that you're dating a teacher's brother.

Who the hell is gonna believe one stupid student over three teachers? No one." He smirked at me. "I'll take that thanks now."

I gulped. *He's right, if Erika goes to the Principal she'll have no evidence at all, and now Will and I have two respected teachers that have seen me kissing his brother! Oh my freaking goodness, this is awesome! How did I not figure this out straight away?*

"Sam, you're a freaking genius!" I practically screamed as I threw my arms around his neck, hugging the life out of him.

He patted my back. "Yeah I know. Just tell Will not to kick my ass or anything for doing that, okay? Back me up a little? Tell him I didn't even once try to slip you the tongue," he said, laughing.

I laughed and punched him in the arm lightly. *I can't believe this! Jeez, I love Sam so much!* "You're the best, you know that, right?" I asked, looking at him gratefully. Will had such a terrific family, he was so lucky.

Sam nodded, smirking cockily. "So tell me then, Foxy. Who's the better kisser?" he asked, slinging his arm back around my shoulder and motioning up the hallway for me to start walking.

I looked at him sarcastically. "You, obviously!" I rolled my eyes and ignored him shooting me a smug expression. I led him to the office and stopped. "Are you really gonna go in here too?" I asked, biting my lip a little nervously.

He nodded enthusiastically. "Yep, I'm gonna go write my name in that visitors' book so that everyone knows I was here today with you. Extra evidence," he explained, winking at me and taking my hand, interlacing our fingers.

I laughed as he pulled me into the office and up to the desk; he smiled sweetly at the receptionist who was sitting there. "Excuse me, I was just speaking to Mr Young, and he said that I needed to sign in as a visitor," he said to the receptionist.

She looked between him and me curiously. "What exactly can I do for you?" she asked, pushing her glasses up her nose.

Sam smiled. "I just really need to speak to my brother, he's a teacher here. Will Morris."

Her face brightened at the mention of Will's name. *Ooh, someone obviously has a soft spot for my boyfriend!* "Really, you're Will's brother?" she asked, grinning happily as she pulled over a visitors' book.

"Yeah, can you not see the family resemblance? I know I'm better looking than him," Sam joked, running a hand through his hair.

She laughed, well, more like giggled, and I smiled at how charming Sam could be. *No wonder he's a player, he isn't even trying, and he could have this middle aged woman if he wanted to.* "I suppose there is a slight family trait there," she admitted, nodding. "So, if you'll just sign in then. I'll call him and tell him that you're here," she instructed, passing him a pen.

Sam shook his head. "Don't bother. My girlfriend will show me the way, won't you, Foxy?" he asked, winking at me.

I grinned and nodded, dropping my eyes to the floor so I didn't have to lie right to her face. "Yeah, I'll show you to his classroom."

He finished signing the papers and passed the book back to her. She smiled flirtatiously. "If you could just come back and sign out when you leave. This is all just a formality in case there's a fire or something, we need to know who's in the building," she said, waving her hand at the book dismissively.

"Sure," Sam agreed. "Does Chloe need to sign the book too, to show that she's still here with me in case there's a fire?" he asked, cocking his head to the side, looking cute as a button. *Wow, Will has that look perfected too!*

The lady frowned. "I don't think so. You're a student aren't you, Chloe?" she asked, looking at me.

I nodded and opened my mouth to speak, but Sam cut me off, "I think there should be some record that Chloe's in the school too. Otherwise you might think she's gone home like the other students. If there actually was a fire there would be no record to say that she was still here with me," Sam mused, pursing his lips thoughtfully. He was a very accomplished liar; I'd give him ten points for being convincing.

The receptionist nodded, still looking unsure as she pushed the book towards me. "Maybe you should, there's no harm in being on the safe side."

Sam laughed. "It's best to cover all bases, and having Chloe's name down there just offers everyone some more protection," he agreed, looking at me slyly.

Holy crap, pure genius! Now, not only do I have two teachers and a receptionist know that I was his girlfriend; I'm also signing myself in as a visitor with him! We owed him big time for this.

When we were done, he held my hand, swinging it happily as we walked up the hallway towards Will's classroom. Just as we got to his door, it opened, and Will stepped out. He stopped, jumping a little because he obviously wasn't expecting people to be right outside his door.

"Whoa, you scared me. What are you two doing here?" he asked, smiling but looking confused.

Sam winced and raised our intertwined hands to show him, while I just blushed like crazy. Will's eyes flicked to me. I smiled apologetically, praying he wouldn't be mad at me for this. "Shall we go into your room?" I suggested weakly.

He frowned, his eyes flicking back to our hands. "Yeah?" he said, but it sounded more like a question as he stepped back into his room, holding the door open for us. I pulled my hand out of Sam's as soon as we were through the door and stepped to Will's side. Immediately his hand went to the small of my back. I would imagine it was some sort of subconscious possessive gesture.

"Don't get angry with your brother, he just fixed everything with Erika," I pleaded, pushing the door closed and flicking the lock on it this time. There was no way I was getting caught like that again.

His frown deepened as he shook his head. "Fixed everything? What are you talking about, and why were you two holding hands?" he asked, looking thoroughly confused and still really stressed from what happened in his lesson earlier.

I looked at Sam, waiting for him to explain. I moved closer to Will, loving how his arm snaked around my waist without him even seeming to think about it. "So, I just kissed your girlfriend in front of a couple of teachers," Sam stated, shrugging as if this were an everyday occurrence.

Okay, I wouldn't have started like that!

Will's jaw tightened. He raised one eyebrow at Sam, already looking seriously annoyed. "That had better be a joke," he warned.

I gulped, and Sam shook his head. "Nope, no joke. I just saved your ass and told a couple of teachers that Chloe and I are dating. That way when the girl goes to tell the Principal about you two kissing, you have other people to witness that she is, in fact, dating your brother." He smiled proudly, obviously pleased with his plan. I was certainly pleased with his plan. Will on the other hand...

"You fucking kissed my girlfriend? Sam, what the hell is wrong with you?" he growled, his arm tightening on my waist.

I put my hand on his chest. "I think it's an excellent plan. Seriously, think about it. Two teachers now believe I'm with Sam so that explains why you and I might appear a little closer than student and teacher. Sam just signed us both in to the building as visitors too. There's now documented evidence to say that Sam and I came in here together. It's a brilliant plan," I explained, looking at him pleadingly. I didn't want him angry with Sam; we really owed him big time for this.

Will swallowed loudly, a frown creasing his forehead. "I'm not supposed to get angry that my little brother just kissed my girl?"

Sam laughed. "I didn't even slip her the tongue. Did I, Foxy? Back me up," he chirped, grinning and sitting on one of the desks, looking the picture of ease.

Will's scowl deepened. "You really are one annoying little runt sometimes, Sam. You know that?" he scolded, looking at him with disapproval.

Sam waved his hand dismissively. "Relax, it's not like she admitted that I was a better kisser than you... oh wait, she did!" he joked, smirking at me.

I felt my face heat up as I shook my head fiercely. "I was joking; did you not hear the sarcasm in my voice?" I asked, rolling my eyes at him.

He pouted at me. "I didn't hear the sarcasm, Foxy, your voice was too breathless from the make out session," he replied, waggling his eyebrows at me. Will punched him on the arm, which made Sam wince but laugh at the same time. He held up his hands innocently. "I was kidding. Jeez, relax, big brother. I should be getting thanks right about now, not abuse!"

I took Will's hand and squeezed it gently to get his attention. "Stop and think about this. Sam just really helped us out. Now we can tell Erika to shove it," I said, grinning.

A small smile pulled at the corners of his mouth as he looked at me softly. "Shove it where?" He pulled me closer to him, crushing my body against his.

I laughed quietly and slipped my arms around his neck, knowing that the door was locked this time. "Shove it up her ass."

Will laughed. "Is it wrong for me to love the sound of that coming out of your mouth, Cutie?" he asked, tracing his fingertip across my bottom lip.

I nodded. "Yeah, it does make you sound a little strange, Mr Morris." He laughed and kissed me gently before putting his forehead to mine and looking into my eyes.

Sam cleared his throat. "Okay, so once and for all, Chloe, who's the better kisser?" he asked. Will moved so fast I barely saw it, he turned and grabbed a book from his desk and threw it at Sam. Sam just laughed and caught it, grinning happily as he started flicking through the pages. "You know, I don't know what you see in him, Foxy. I mean, he's a math nerd," he stated, looking at the pages distastefully.

I laughed and shrugged. "I get an easy A this way," I joked.

Will laughed. "I've got news for you, Miss Henderson, you're barely scraping a C in my class," he mocked, laughing as I punched his chest lightly.

"Then maybe I should try a little harder to impress the teacher," I flirted, gripping his shirt and pressing myself to him tighter.

Will nodded, looking thoughtful. "Just don't start wearing the skirts again." Will and I both laughed, and Sam just looked at us like we were crazy, obviously not in on the private joke.

The door handle turned which caused me and Will to jump away from each other. I looked at Sam worriedly but he just shrugged casually and stepped to my side. The person knocked on the door when they couldn't open it. Will looked from me to Sam. "I think that'll be Caroline," he muttered, straightening his shirt. He stepped to the door, unlocking it and pulling it open, a fake smile on his face. "Oh hey," he said to whoever it was.

"Everything okay? How come the door was locked?" A seductive female voice purred.

Will nodded and pulled the door open, gesturing for her to come in. Will was right, it was Miss Teller. Her eyes flicked to me and Sam, and I felt his body jerk next to mine. "Holy crap, she's fiiiiiine," Sam hissed in my ear. I chuckled as I nodded. *It seems that the only one who doesn't lust after Miss Teller is my boyfriend.*

"Hi, Chloe," she chirped, smiling and setting her purse down on the desk, her eyes flicking to Sam for a second.

"Hi," I replied, smiling uncomfortably at how close Will and I were seconds before she walked in.

She looked at Will curiously, obviously wondering who Sam was. Will stepped forward and smiled. "Oh sorry, this is my little brother, Sam. Sam, this is Caroline Teller, she's a teacher here at the school too," he introduced, shrugging.

I saw a smirk slip onto Sam's lips as he shook her hand. "Nice to meet you." His arm slipped around my shoulder, pulling me close to his side. He played with the side of my hair, and I saw Miss Teller raise one eyebrow at the movement.

"Nice to meet you too," she said slowly. "So are you and Chloe..." she trailed off, looking at me for confirmation.

I gulped and flicked my eyes to Will, who was frowning and looking a little tense. *I guess I need to play along so that we have another backup.* I nodded and opened my mouth to speak, but Sam got there first. "Oh hell yeah, I'm banging one of my brother's students. Awkward, right?" he said, laughing as I elbowed him in the ribs.

Will's scowl deepened; luckily he was standing slightly behind Miss Teller so she wouldn't notice his grave mood. "I don't think the word 'banging' is very appropriate, Sam," he growled. He was obviously trying to play along and keep his cool, but it wasn't working very well for him.

Sam grinned at him before turning to me. "Oh right, sorry, Foxy. Making love to," he corrected, shooting me a flirtatious wink.

Oh my God, Will is going to enjoy ripping Sam's head off for this!

I smiled weakly, trying not to cringe away from him as he pulled me closer to him. Miss Teller laughed. "That is kind of awkward," she admitted, before turning to Will and smiling. "I hope you're not giving your brother's girlfriend a hard time in class, that could make family get-togethers a little strained."

Will shook his head, looking at the floor as Sam, kissed the side of my neck. I took the opportunity to stamp on his foot while Miss Teller was looking in the other direction.

"Ouch! Shit, careful, Foxy," Sam gasped, wincing and shifting his weight onto the other foot.

"Sorry, Sam-bo." I smiled sweetly.

He looked at me warningly before grabbing my face and kissing me full on the mouth. Before I had time to react, he was gone; I looked up to see Will had grabbed the back of his shirt and pulled him off of me.

"No PDAs at school, little brother. And you," he pointed at me, "you get detention with me on Monday lunchtime for that."

I fought a smile. That wasn't exactly a punishment, spending time with him. I nodded trying to look appropriately abashed. "Whatever you say."

Miss Teller laughed. "It's after school you know; can't you cut them a little slack? He's your brother after all, and it was his fault, not Chloe's," she persuaded, winking at me, obviously thinking she was helping me out when in actual fact an hour with Will on Monday was awesome in my book.

A smile pulled at the corner of Will's mouth. "If I could give that little punk detention I would," he said, punching Sam in the arm a little harder than playfully.

Sam shrugged him off. "We're now going. So anyway, Mom said to make sure you're at the restaurant by eight tomorrow. That's what I came to tell you," he said.

"Yep, thanks." Will shrugged, looking at the door, nodding for us to leave.

Sam threw his arm around my shoulder again. "See you tomorrow then, Will. It was nice to meet you, Caroline." Sam smirked in her direction again, and I knew that he'd be talking about the hot teacher tonight when we went out. Just as we got to the door he stopped and looked back at Will. "You don't have any spare condoms, do you?"

Will's face hardened instantly. I gasped and elbowed Sam in the ribs again. *That one was totally unnecessary. He's just trying to wind Will up on purpose.* "I can tell you with absolute certainty that you won't be getting any tonight, Sam Morris," I growled. *Jerk.*

He laughed and kissed my cheek. "Whatever you say, Foxy." He waved over his shoulder and dragged me out of the room. "See you later, big brother," he called, laughing wickedly to himself.

Chapter Thirty-Three

When I woke up in the morning I couldn't stop the happy grin that stretched across my face. Sam had been hilarious last night, and I had laughed until it gave me stomach ache at some of the things he was doing. He really was a great friend, and I was lucky to have him in my life. We had barely made it to the bowling alley before Will had called Sam. I had just sat there, trying not to listen to him being shouted at down the phone, but Will was shouting so loud that I could almost hear every word. I couldn't help but giggle at him, especially when Sam pulled the phone away from his ear and just put it on the table, before proceeding to order our bowling shoes while Will ranted on the line, oblivious to the fact that his brother wasn't listening. He was seriously pissed that Sam kissed me, from what I could gather from the rant, he hated the condom joke too, but I think the whole someone else kissing his girlfriend while he was standing there thing had really gotten to him.

I had slept so well last night. Everything was going to work out. Sam's plan was genius, and although Will and I would now need to be even more careful around each other, if anyone got wind of anything suspicious as to why we were so friendly towards each other, then we had the excuse that I was in a serious relationship with his brother. Perfect.

I rolled over and looked at my alarm clock. It was after ten, and I was due at Erika's at twelve thirty to do her chores as blackmail. Today was going to be an enjoyable day, I could feel it. When I spoke to Will last night before bed, he wanted me not to bother showing up at Erika's, or send her a 'get stuffed' text. But Sam and I had come up with something better than that last night, so I was definitely going to do Erika's chores today... and I would enjoy doing them too.

I had a quick breakfast before heading upstairs and packing up my clothes and make-up for tonight's dinner and a change of clothes for tomorrow. I 'accidentally' forgot to pack pyjamas for tonight, I would much rather sleep in Will's T-shirt instead. I left my stuff in my room and slipped on my bulkiest jacket so I could hide my supplies in there without them being seen, and then I almost skipped to Erika's house. When I got to the address

261

she'd given me, I gasped and looked at the large white house in front of me. The drive way was so long that my legs ached by the time I got to the front door.

I was all out grinning with delight as I raised my hand and pressed the large gold doorbell. *Calm down, Chloe. Wow, my poker face sucks!* I giggled to myself and then bit my lip, trying to chill out and not give anything away. She opened the door with a scowl on her face as she looked me over distastefully the same as she always does.

"Well, I'm glad you came in old clothes, you'll be getting messy today," she said, smirking at me as she waved me into her house.

I nodded, still trying to keep the grin off of my face. "So, what is it that I'm to do exactly?" I asked, praying it would be the things that she already told me I was going to be doing today.

She smiled evilly. "Some of my shoes need polishing. My clothes need ironing, and my car is a mess, it needs cleaning inside and outside. After you've done all that, you can muck out the horses at the stable," she instructed, nodding towards the back of her house. Her house was beautiful inside. All high ceilings, expertly decorated walls, and real oak floors. I knew her parents had a lot of money, but I didn't realise that they had enough for horses in their back yard. *No wonder she acts like a spoilt brat all the time.*

I nodded, trying to look annoyed, when in actual fact I was hoping for two of those jobs. Everything was working out perfectly. *Jeez, I love Sam so much for being an evil genius!* He reminded me a little of Amy and her harebrained schemes. I was secretly glad that he was a man-whore and that she was in love with Ryan, because if those two ever got together, they would have dangerous kids.

She pointed to a pile of leather shoes and boots that she'd put at the bottom of the stairs, and a polishing set. "Get started then, Ice Princess," she ordered, grinning at me cockily.

I smiled sweetly and headed over there, sitting on the floor, polishing her shoes just like she'd asked me to. She only watched me for about five minutes before she got bored and went to make herself something to eat. I giggled as she walked out of the room and reached into my inside pocket, pulling out the little packet of itching powder that Sam and I had bought last night. I sprinkled it into all of the shoes, taking a photo on my phone as I did it and sending it to Sam, knowing he would laugh his ass off. I shook them to spread it in so it wasn't noticeable and then got back to polishing them all, with a huge smirk on my face. *Payback number one, complete.*

When they were all sparkling, I headed into the direction of where Erika went, nosing around her house as I did so. I felt a little like a stalker, but Sam had instructed me to keep my eyes open for anything incriminating. I didn't really know what he was expecting me to find, maybe a photo of her as a fat kid, or a letter that said she was actually born a guy. What he told me to search for was her diary. I had a feeling he would get a kick out of reading a girl's diary, a 'forbidden pleasure' he called it. I was pretty sure that Erika wasn't stupid enough to leave that lying around knowing that I was coming over though.

I found her sitting at the kitchen table, nibbling on a pile of green salad, plain salad too, no dressing, it looked so bland. "Erika, I'm done with the shoes," I said quietly.

She dragged her eyes away from reruns of The Hills and glared at me hatefully. I genuinely had no idea what I did to make this girl dislike me so much. She hated Amy too, but there was just no explanation other than the fact that she was just an evil witch. "I have some clothes that need ironing before the party that I'm going to tonight," she informed me, pushing her half eaten rabbit food away from her and stalking off. I assumed I was meant to follow her so I did.

She led me into a separate laundry room and pulled open a cupboard where an ironing board immediately came out and set itself up. *Whoa, my mom would love one of those cupboards.* I couldn't imagine having enough money just to dedicate a cupboard to a fold out ironing board. *Oh how the other half live.*

It wouldn't take too long to iron an outfit for the party, so this one wasn't going to take very long at all. Except, it turns out she wasn't sure what she wanted to wear. She pointed at a pile about three foot high with clothes on the side. "Don't put double creases on the sleeves, I hate that, it looks so cheap," she sneered, her eyes flicking to my arms as if to imply that I had a double crease in my clothes. "Why are you still wearing a jacket? Aren't you hot?" she questioned, looking at me as if I was stupid.

I shook my head, trying not to grin. "I'm fine."

She rolled her eyes and waved at another cupboard. "The stuff is in there, use the scented water." She disappeared out of the room, and I silently cursed myself for not saving some of the itching power so I could sprinkle it in her clothes too. But then again, I didn't want her to catch onto me too quickly; I wanted her to figure it out slowly that I wasn't playing her game anymore. The longer she got me to do stuff for her, the more I could mess it up.

If I could have, I would have gone with Sam's outrageous suggestion of buying her new clothes in smaller sizes, so that when she put them on she would think she gained weight. It had taken me a long time to explain to him that it really wasn't practical, because one, I didn't have the money, and two, how would I know what clothes she had in the first place? He had pouted about it for over half an hour.

When I was done with the ironing I was actually quite proud of the fact that I'd stopped myself from burning those little brown iron stains into the back of her clothes. I didn't actually want to damage anything of hers; I knew I would end up paying for it if I did, so I was extremely careful.

I carried the clothes back to the kitchen, finding her sitting there still watching 'The Hills'. *How can she not get annoyed with this show? I could barely stomach an episode or two, but she seems like she's on some kind of marathon!*

"Want me to hang these in your closet?" I offered, raising one eyebrow, trying to look innocent. In reality, I wanted to find her bathroom; I was hoping she had a private one that I could get a couple of minutes alone in.

She nodded and headed out, again without speaking to me. I followed her up the stairs, into an enormous bedroom that looked exactly like how I would expect it to look. It looked like a Disney Princess had vomited all over it: it was pink, fluffy, girly, and with a white sheer canopy thing that hung over the bedhead. *Wow, what is she, five?*

"Nice room," I muttered, grinning. I longed to take a picture of this room so I could show Sam. He would piss his pants laughing.

She smiled happily. "Yeah, I had the designer come in and do it a couple of months ago. Cost Daddy a lot of money, but I'm pleased with the result," she gushed, running her hand over her mountain of pink cushions at the head of her bed. She'd obviously missed the glaring sarcasm in my voice.

She flopped down onto her bed, pointing to her closet. "Put them in there. Use the wooden hangers, not the metal ones," she ordered, frowning distastefully.

I gave her a little bow and headed in there, spotting her private bathroom on the way past. *Jackpot!* I hung her clothes up quickly and then headed out. "Do you mind if I use your bathroom? I really need to pee," I lied, looking at her hopefully.

She frowned but nodded to it. I bit back the laugh that was trying to escape and headed in there. I went straight to her cupboard and pulled out her shampoo and conditioner, tipping some down the drain to leave a little space in the bottle. Then I pulled out the brown hair dye that I'd bought last night. I tipped some into each bottle and gave it a vigorous shake to mix it with her shampoo. I wasn't sure if it would work, but the plan was that each time she used it, that her natural platinum blonde hair that she was so proud of, would get just a fraction darker. She would hate that. I was the proud creator of this one. *Payback number two, complete. Now I just need to get my hands on her car!*

When I walked out of the bedroom she wasn't in there. I spotted her cell phone on the side, and gasped with excitement. *Oh hell yeah!* I whipped out my phone and dialled Sam, hoping he'd answer quickly.

"Hey, Foxy. How's the revenge going?" he asked, laughing.

"Great. Listen I just found Erika's phone so I need the number of a premium rate number, Busty beauties, Horney babes, whatever, just get me a number!" I giggled, excitement building up inside me. He immediately reeled off a number to me. I frowned and screwed my face up. "Should I be worried that you know that off by heart?" I asked, slightly concerned for him.

He laughed. "No, Foxy, it's all good; I'm not addicted to sex chat lines. That one just stuck in my mind because that's where your mom works," he joked.

I rolled my eyes at his lame 'your mom' joke. "Okay, I'd better go. Speak to you tonight." I disconnected the call and dialled the number on Erika's phone, then put it back where I found it. I briefly wondering how long it would be connected to the line for, hopefully long enough that she'd have to pay her parents the two hundred bucks of Will's money that she'd blackmailed out of us already.

Last on my hit list was her car. I could feel the package in my jacket pocket and I winced thinking about it in there, touching everything. I would have to make sure I put it in the wash as soon as I got home. "Erika?" I called as I walked out of her room. She walked out of another room, talking on her house phone, flirting unashamedly with whoever it was.

"Car next, you'll find everything you need in the garage. My car's unlocked already." She nodded towards the front door, signalling where her Mercedes would be parked. I saluted and headed out there, skipping to her garage and grabbing everything I needed.

I spent a lot of time on it; I wanted it to be perfect so she would have no reason to doubt that I was doing a great job. I washed and waxed it until I could see my reflection perfectly. I vacuumed everything, shampooed the seats, emptied the ashtray of the candy wrappers. It seemed that 'Little Miss rabbit food for lunch' had a weakness for chocolate.

When I was finally done cleaning the car to within an inch of its life, I pulled the pièce de résistance out of my pocket and laughed my ass off. I grabbed the duct tape I'd brought with me and broke off a couple of strips of it, and then proceeded to tape the large piece of raw steak to the underside of her dashboard. It would take a while to rot, but she would have no idea it was there, and would drive around for ages wondering what the putrid smell was. This was another one of Sam's genius creations.

And with that, payback three is completed!

I didn't mess with the horses. Sam wanted me to let them out so she'd have to catch them, but I didn't want to do that in case they got hurt or anything. I absolutely loved horses, so surprisingly I enjoyed the time I spent with them. I took my mucking out punishment like a man and just got on with it, dry heaving every couple of scoops. It took a lot longer than I thought it would, but this was the only time I was doing it so I made sure to do it properly so the horses would be comfortable.

When I was done with that and had scrubbed my hands for a solid five minutes, she finally dismissed me. She handed me her English, History and Biology assignments that were to be done by Monday morning, instructing on nothing below a B again. *B my butt, she is getting a detention for all three of these if Will has anything to do with it!* He had made me promise that he could help me with her work if she gave it to me. I had a feeling he was going to insist on a few additions that weren't on the syllabus.

I called him on the way home and arranged for him to come and get me in an hour so I would have time for a shower. I felt disgusting after all that cleaning. When I was clean and smelling like my old self again I headed downstairs to spend a few minutes with my parents before Will showed up.

"Are you sure I look all right?" I asked for the hundredth time. We'd just pulled up at the restaurant, and I could barely even stand because my knees felt like they were shaking with nerves.

Will smiled and shook his head, obviously amused by my antics. I'd been asking him the same thing for the last hour, but he never seemed to get annoyed with me for it. Instead of mocking me for it, or telling me to shut up, he'd calmly smiled and told me that I looked beautiful, perfect, incredible, amazing, or some other superlative he could think of.

He took my hand now, pushing my carefully curled hair over my shoulder, his fingers brushing against the skin there making me break out in goosebumps. "I'm going to have the most beautiful girl in the whole restaurant," he cooed, kissing me softly.

I smiled. "Well do you think you could drop me home before you get your freak on with her, you were my ride after all," I joked, trying to calm my nerves by straightening my black dress again.

He laughed and snaked his arm around my waist. "If you feel uncomfortable at any point and want to leave then we should have a kind of code word or something so that we can escape," he suggested, looking thoughtful.

"Like, hedgehog or tadpole?" I offered, laughing at how silly he was being.

"Tadpole, like it, we'll go with that," he agreed, obviously thinking I was serious. I laughed harder as he led us towards the door of the restaurant. My smile faded as I saw them all standing in the bar section, obviously waiting for us seeing as they were all together.

"Oh crud," I mumbled under my breath.

"Relax, Cutie, you'll be great, and they'll love you as much as I do by the end of the night. Hell, my mom already loves you." He gave me a little squeeze as we closed the distance to his family. I plastered on a smile and hoped that it covered the nervous face I was bound to be pulling unconsciously.

As soon as we got to the group Sam stepped forward and slapped Will around the back of the head, frowning at him. "How many times do I have you to tell you to keep your hands off of my girlfriend!" he scolded.

I looked at Sam and burst out laughing. Will, on the other hand, didn't laugh. I had a feeling he wasn't going to enjoy the night at all. He looked like he wanted to seriously maim his brother; clearly he still hadn't forgotten the condom joke from yesterday.

Will turned and looked me right in the eye. "Tadpole?" he asked, almost pleadingly.

I burst into a fit of giggles, probably making myself look like a complete and utter moron in front of his family. This was not exactly the impression I wanted to make on them. I was definitely acting like the little school girl that I was. Will laughed too and pressed his forehead against mine, his arm tightening on my waist.

266

I looked over to his parents, shooting them an apologetic smile, but they were all grinning at us, Angela, his mom, was gazing at us like we were the cutest thing ever. Will sighed and pulled away. "Guys, this is my girlfriend, Chloe. Chloe, this is my crazy family. You know their names, right?" he asked.

I nodded and smiled, holding out my hand politely. "Sure, it's nice to see you all again."

Angela made a little 'Aww' noise as she shook my hand, grinning at me happily. "I'm so happy you could come, Chloe. We've been badgering Will to bring you over to the house, but he's insistent in keeping you all to himself," she said, shooting him a fake glare.

Will laughed. "I don't like to share," he joked, brushing his hand down my back.

I shook hands with the rest of the family, making polite conversation with them for a few minutes until we were called through for our table. As we were walking to our table, Sam grabbed my hand and pulled me closer to him, leaning in to whisper in my ear.

"How did the things we discussed turn out today?" he asked, obviously wanting to know about Erika but was trying to ask subtly because of his family.

I grinned. "It was just as we planned," I told him, nodding happily. He held out a fist to me, obviously wanting to do one of those cheesy fist knocks that he does with his brother. I just looked down at it and raised one eyebrow. "Grow up, Sam. You Morris boys are so immature," I stated, shaking my head in mock disapproval.

He grinned and grabbed my hand, balling it into a fist and bumping it against his. "You love it," he teased, winking at me. "By the way, did she have a diary?" He looked at me with an extremely hopeful expression on his face.

"No, Sam-bo. I looked, but she doesn't have one," I confirmed, watching how he frowned. He really was a little weird to get so excited about a girls diary. "Why so interested anyway?"

He smiled longingly. "If I can finally understand the inner workings of a female brain then there will be no girl in the world that will be able to resist me," he stated, running a hand through his hair, trying to look serious but there was a smile twitching at the corners of his mouth.

I burst out laughing. We got to our table then and Will pulled my chair out for me, like the incredible boyfriend that he is. "Maybe I'll let you read my diary," I joked to Sam. I didn't have a diary, but I could make up some trash and let him read it as a joke.

He scrunched up his face and shook his head fiercely. "You think I want to read details about you and my brother getting your freak on? Man, I can't even think about you two getting naked and having se-" he started, but he was cut off by Angela.

"Sam Morris! That's enough," she scolded, looking at him shocked.

I clicked my tongue at him and shook my head theatrically. "Listen to your mother, Sam-bo, you're being rude," I chimed in, smirking at him.

He shot me a wink and grabbed his menu, looking at it with mock interest. I looked back to Will. He smiled and inched his face closer to mine, kissing me softly, holding his hand on the back of my head so I couldn't pull away. I blushed thinking about his parents seeing this, but it felt nice to be out in front of people as a couple. To have him acknowledge me in front of his family like this made me feel extremely special.

Sam cleared his throat. "You know, I'd pay to watch this if you weren't my brother, Will," he stated, making everyone laugh and causing me to blush harder.

Will pulled back slightly, leaving his hand on the back of my head as he stared into my eyes, a smile tugging at the corners of his mouth. "I love bringing you out and showing you off," he whispered.

I heard Angela make the little 'Aww' again, but I ignored it this time and just focused on Will and how he made me feel like I was the only girl in this restaurant. "Right back at ya, Mr Morris," I teased.

He smiled and kissed the tip of my nose before pulling back and letting go of me. "So, what's everyone having?" he asked loudly, changing the subject as he scanned his menu.

Sam elbowed me in the side gently. "Foxy and I are sharing the spaghetti so we can to the Lady and the Tramp thing," he stated.

I laughed and shook my head as Will sighed and shot him a dark look. This was going to be a fun night. It looked like Sam was intent on annoying Will as much as possible.

As it turns out I was right, the night was incredibly fun. Will's family seemed to welcome me with open arms. His parents were great, just like when I'd met them at Kaitlin's wedding. I was worried that they wouldn't like me because of my age and the whole their son could be sent to jail at any time thing, but they didn't once mention me being underage or his student. Talk was mostly what I liked to do, what were my family like, and general getting to know you stuff.

His mom seemed to just love the fact that Will was happy. She was incredibly cute. Her husband, William, was just like his boys, funny, witty and flirted with his wife endlessly. Apparently this was their twenty-eighth wedding anniversary, but yet they still looked at each other with that loved up look in their eye. Each time he would wrap his arm around her, or they would share a little smile or a laugh, I looked at Will and couldn't help but wonder if he would still look at me like that if we managed to make it that long.

Kaitlin, Will's sister, was adorable too. She was just like Angela, kind, sweet and very, very talkative. Her husband, Andrew, was the strong, silent type, but when he did add into the conversation he was incredibly witty. They balanced each other out perfectly; she liked to talk a lot, and he just seemed content to listen to whatever she had to say. They were obviously still in the 'honeymoon' stage of their relationship because he couldn't seem to keep his hands off of her - much to Sam and Will's obvious disgust and remarks about them getting a room.

All in all, I loved it, and I loved them already too. I really shouldn't have expected his family to be any less than what they were. With two incredible sons like Will and Sam, they were all bound to be great people. In a way, meeting them made me feel a little bad though. I longed to do this with Will and my family. I would love to take him home with me and have him shake my dad's hand and get his approval. I adored my dad, and his approval of the love of my life would mean a lot to me. There was just six more months and then I'd be able to do that. I couldn't wait until I could show him off proudly, just like he was doing with me right now.

As soon as we'd exchanged goodbye hugs with everyone, and promised to go round to his parents' house next Sunday for a family dinner, we finally left for his apartment. I couldn't wait to just have his arms around me; it felt like it had been so long.

"So, how did I do?" I asked, wincing nervously, waiting for his reaction.

He smiled and took my hand as he drove, pulling my hand into his lap, our fingers interlaced. "You did great, Cutie. They loved you," he assured me.

I bit my lip and sank lower in the seat, unable to keep the satisfied smile off of my face. "I can't believe they just wouldn't care about everything like that. How can they approve of me, knowing that I'm seventeen and your student?" I asked, shaking my head in awe of them.

He smiled and shrugged. "They just want me happy, and you," he brought my hand up to his mouth and kissed the back of it softly, "you make me very happy."

I sighed contentedly and closed my eyes. "You make me very happy too," I confirmed, grinning like an idiot.

When we got to his apartment he looked a little tense. I had a feeling he was worried that me staying over was pushing the boundaries a little. I squeezed his waist reassuringly and pressed my side against his tighter. He smiled down at me and pressed his lips to mine as he slipped his key in the lock, he pulled back and put his forehead to mine. "I love you," he whispered, rubbing his nose against mine in a little Eskimo kiss.

"I love you too," I responded immediately. He grinned and pulled back, taking my hand and tugging me into his apartment, shutting the door behind us. I watched as he locked the door, locking me into the apartment for a change. I loved the sound of the click. That sound signalled that I was here to stay for the night, the sound made my breath catch in my throat, and my knees to tremble a little with excitement.

"Want something to drink? We could put on a movie, it's only half past ten," he suggested, looking at his watch.

I shook my head and stepped closer to him, slipping my arms around his neck. "I just want to go to bed with you."

"Just to cuddle though, right?" he checked, bending to look into my eyes.

I nodded. I knew the rules, I respected the rules, I just didn't like them. "I just want you to hold me, that's all," I confirmed.

269

He smiled and traced his hands down my arms, when he got to my hands he interlaced our fingers and walked backwards towards his bedroom, pulling me along with him. I felt so contented, so happy, so fulfilled. I didn't need anything more than his arms to wrap around me, for his smell to fill my lungs, for me to drift to sleep knowing that I would wake up next to him. This was like heaven.

When we got to his bedroom, he picked up my overnight bag that I'd brought over with me earlier, he plopped it down onto the bed for me. I headed over to it and opened the top, knowing I didn't pack anything to wear to bed.

"Dang, I forgot to bring pyjamas!" I cried, frowning theatrically as I pretended to look through my bag for them.

He sighed. "On purpose no doubt." He looked at me knowingly and I laughed guiltily as I shrugged. He smiled. "Looks like you're sleeping naked tonight," he teased. His eyes raked down my body slowly, as if he was imagining it or something.

I felt the breath catch in my throat. *Is he serious? I'm going to be in his bed, naked? Oh hell yeah I like the sound of that!* "Really?" I asked, looking at him excitedly.

He laughed. "You really are a pervert. No, Cutie, I was kidding. The last time I checked you were still a minor," he teased, winking at me as he pulled his blue button down shirt off over his head, and threw it to me. "Sleep in that." I smiled gratefully, and I bit my lip as I looked him over. His body made my mouth water, and my knees tremble. I moved my hands to the back of my dress and was just about to unzip it so I could change, when he groaned. "You can change in the bathroom," he mumbled, nodding at the door.

I pouted as I headed into the bathroom. *Looks like I'm definitely not getting anything more than a hug tonight.* I wasn't really expecting to, I knew how serious he was about me being a minor; he really wanted to wait, so we'd wait. Tonight was more about being close to him, having him hold me like he used to, and spending time together without having to watch the clock to see if I was going to miss my curfew. Just relaxing as Will and Chloe, instead of teacher and student.

I pulled off my dress and bra, leaving my panties on as I pulled his shirt over my head. As it passed my face I breathed it in. His scent just amazed me. It sparked my senses, it was like some sort of drug, and it gave me an instant lift. Tonight I got to sleep with that scent all around me; I wished this night would last forever.

As I walked out of the bathroom, Will groaned. "I forgot how sexy you look in my clothes," he almost growled. I flicked my eyes to him quickly. He was lying in bed, with his chest bare. The sheets covered to just above his bellybutton. He made my stomach tingle because of how incredible he looked. I would probably never get used to the attraction that I felt for him, he literally looked like the most beautiful man in the world. Nothing and no one compared to Will.

I held my breath, trying to hide my desire for him as I walked over to the other side of the bed and climbed in slowly, just wondering if I would be able to stop myself begging for some physical attention. I could feel the words bursting to come out of my mouth; I wanted him so badly that it was almost painful.

He smiled, his eyes raking over my body as I did the same to his. "Come lay with me then, Cutie," he purred seductively. I gulped and scooted over to him as he rolled to his side and slipped one arm under my neck. I moved impossibly closer, putting my head on his shoulder, tilting my face so I could look into the eyes of the man I was in love with. I put one leg between his, tangling us together intimately.

His nose brushed up against mine slowly, his eyes looking right into mine. I could see the fight he was having with himself, it was clear across his face that he wanted me, but was trying not to let go of his control. His other hand slid down my back slowly, tracing across my ass, pulling me even closer to him.

"You don't know how much I've missed having you in my bed," he whispered, peppering little kisses from the edge of my mouth, across my cheek to my ear. He kissed the sensitive spot below my ear, and I felt myself shiver in his embrace, which made his fingers bite into my ass and back as he clutched me tighter. He let out a little groan; I wasn't sure if it was a good moan, like in appreciation, or if it was a groan of frustration. Either way it made a bolt of need shoot around my body.

Seeing as he was touching me a little, I assumed I was allowed to touch him. I bent my head and kissed the top of his chest as I trailed my fingers over his skin, following the lines of his muscles, worshipping the bumps with my fingertips. His hands were roaming my body too. I gasped when the one on my ass slipped under his shirt that I was wearing and tickled the skin on my stomach, his fingers finding my navel piercing.

He groaned again as he fingered it, his face coming back to mine as he kissed me softly, slowly, tenderly. The kiss was so soft that I could barely feel it, but yet at the same time it held so much passion that it made me want to cry. I needed more, I needed him, so therefore, I knew that I needed to stop him. He didn't want this and would be angry with himself if this happened; I didn't want him upset thinking he'd taken advantage. As much as it pained me to, I needed to get him to stop.

"Will, I thought there was an over clothes rule," I mumbled, hating myself for saying the words.

He sighed and pulled his face back, his eyes locked onto mine. "I can't do it, Cutie. I just… I just need to see you, to touch you," he whispered, looking at me as if he was asking for my permission. I felt like my world had stopped spinning, or maybe it had sped up, I wasn't sure which. The feelings that were coursing through my veins made me feel like I could fly.

"Oh God," I mumbled, not knowing what else to say. I pulled his mouth back to mine, and he moaned in the back of his throat. The sound kind of drove me crazy and I dug my fingernails into his back, but he didn't seem to mind in the slightest.

His arms tightened on me and he rolled onto his back pulling me on top of him, never once breaking the kiss. The feelings were taking over; I couldn't think about anything else, I was just a body made for feeling and nothing more. Every place his fingers touched me seemed like he lit me on fire, leaving me a quivering mess. When his hands started on the buttons of my shirt I suddenly became acutely aware that if he took it off, I would have nothing on but a pair of lacy panties. *Does he know that? Maybe he's assuming I was wearing a bra too....*

"Will, I have nothing on under that." I gasped as he kissed down the side of my throat.

"Good," he growled, tugging more forcefully on the buttons.

My heart was racing in my chest; I was so excited that I thought it would kill me. He pushed the shirt off of my shoulders slowly, his nails scraping down my arms as he pulled it off, making me bite my lip and moan quietly. His eyes didn't leave mine the whole time. His expression still looked torn, like he still thought this was wrong somehow but he just couldn't stop himself. I smiled encouragingly; his full lips pulled up into a breathtaking smile as he pulled it the rest of the way off and tossed it on the floor.

He rolled us back over so I was under him again, and then he pushed himself up to sitting, straddling my hips. I briefly started to panic that he'd changed his mind, that he was going to insist we stop or suggest that he sleep on the couch or something. He didn't though. Instead, his eyes roamed down my body slowly, from the top of my head, down my neck, lingering on my breasts before raking over my stomach, and then back up again, just as slowly, until his eyes met mine.

He lowered himself back down on top of me, his forearms either side of my head, supporting most of his weight. He looked me right in the eyes. I could almost see his love for me there, the depth of emotion that was there made me melt and my insides jump for joy.

"You are so beautiful, Cutie. Sometimes I just don't understand what you see in me, but I'm glad you see whatever it is," he whispered. His breath blew across my lips, making them part unconsciously. "New rules. Skin is allowed, panties and boxers stay on, hands and mouth have free rein. Deal?" he asked, looking at me hopefully.

Oh heck yeah I like the sound of that! I nodded eagerly. "Deal, definitely a deal!" I agreed maybe a little too quickly.

He laughed, his hand brushing my hair away from my face lightly. "You only love me for my body," he teased, shifting his weight on me, making us rub together in intimate places. It had been so long that I almost wondered if this was a dream, maybe I was having a dirty dream about him again – if I was, I didn't ever want to wake up.

I grinned and shook my head. "That's not true. I also love you because you buy me Lucky Charms for breakfast," I joked.

He burst out laughing and nodded, pressing his lips to mine, effectively ending the conversation.

Chapter Thirty-Four

As I slowly started to drift into consciousness, the first thing that I noticed was that I was hot, like seriously hot, sweating in fact. I blew out a big breath and tried to move but to no avail, the cover was all over me, wrapped around me, and it was making it hard to breathe. I groaned and tried to throw the cover off of me, but it didn't budge, so I began to get even hotter.

I need to get up and have a cold shower. What time was it anyway? It's probably time for school or something...

I cracked my eyes open to look at the time and came face to face with Will, who was still sleeping merely inches from me. I suddenly realised that it was his body wrapped all around me, instead of the cover like I first thought. I gasped from the shock of waking up next to someone, and then everything came flooding back to me at once, causing a blush to heat my face and a rush of longing to shoot down south as I remembered some of the more intimate details that went on until the early hours of the morning.

I grinned and literally pounced on him, causing him to grunt and his eyes to pop open. He sat up quickly, pinning me on his lap and looking around the room like he expected an axe wielding murderer to jump out at him at any second. I laughed harder and threw my arms around his neck, hugging him tightly.

"What the hell, Chloe? What was that?" he asked, shaking his head and still looking a little dazed.

I bit my lip, the sound of his husky voice first thing in the morning made my whole body vibrate with excitement. *How on earth did I manage to forget that I spent the night here last night?* Instead of answering I kissed him. He responded immediately, his arms dragging me closer to him so that I was trapped against his chest. His taste in the morning was out of this world. The incredibly boy woke up with breath as fresh as a toothpaste factory, while I would bet anything that mine was more like last night's steak.

I broke the kiss and put my forehead to his, smiling like an idiot. Last night had been incredible. The new rules were fabulous in my book.

274

Technically we still hadn't had sex, but the new rules allowed pretty much everything else. For the first time in over three months, I was physically satisfied, very physically satisfied in fact.

"Good morning," I chirped. I was so happy that my whole body was tingling.

He grinned. "It sure is," he answered, brushing my matted bed hair off of my face. We were still only in panties and boxers so my chest rubbed against his, causing a little moan to escape my lips. His hands brushed down my back to cup my ass; he shifted my weight on his lap, obviously getting more comfortable.

I smiled, but neither of us spoke, we didn't really need to. He just held me tightly on his lap, his hands stroking down my back as his grey eyes stayed locked on mine, a beautiful smile stretched across his face. Finally, after just enjoying his closeness, I couldn't take it anymore. I pressed my lips to his, capturing his bottom one between my teeth and nibbling on it gently, making his fingers dig into my back lightly.

The excitement and lust from the night before was building up again, he could obviously feel it too because he turned and laid us back down on the bed, side by side. He traced his hand down the side of my body, over my hip and down my thigh. When he got to my knee he pulled gently, hitching it over his hip.

He smiled. "I love you so much, Cutie. I love waking up to you in the morning, we should do this more often," he whispered, running his fingers through my hair, getting out the tangles and knots for me gently.

I nodded in agreement and snuggled closer to him, pressing my face into the side of his neck, just breathing him in as I ran my fingertips over his chest and stomach. The idea that this guy was mine to keep literally drove me crazy. I felt like the luckiest girl in the world that he loved me like he did, I couldn't ask for more than that.

"I love you too, Will." My voice rang clear and confident as I said the words. I kissed the side of his neck and dug my fingers into his shoulders. "New rules apply to daytime too, right?" I asked, pulling back and smiling at him seductively.

He grinned and nodded quickly. "Oh hell yeah," he muttered, flipping me onto my back and hovering above me.

I laughed at his eagerness. "You only love me for my body," I teased, using his words from last night.

He shook his head. "No, that's not true, I also love you because you make wicked grilled cheese," he joked.

I laughed and rolled my eyes, gripping the back of his head and pulling his mouth down to mine. We spent another couple of hours in his bed, just lost in each other's bodies, talking, laughing, and fooling around. It was the best morning of my life.

Later that afternoon, we were sat in his lounge doing Erika's assignments. I had three to do in total, one of them Will wanted to do on his own with no help from me. He kept laughing to himself as he wrote an original poem for her English class. I didn't ask what he was doing; he said he'd tell me when he was done, so I just focused on her history and biology ones instead. I made sure I got almost everything completely wrong. In her history assignment I linked everything to the wrong period and used examples from sources that I knew were unreliable and had been proven untrue. There was no way she would get a B for that one, she'd be lucky if she didn't fail altogether.

For her Biology assignment, I used Will's suggestion of adding a cuss word to it. Every couple of sentences I would throw in a random swear word then just carry on as if nothing had happened. I laughed to myself as I read it over; she was literally going to kill me for that.

When I was done, I sat back and watched Will chewing on his pen, still working furiously over the poem that she was supposed to write. Finally, after another ten minutes, he was done and looked extremely proud of himself. I smiled and raised one eyebrow curiously, wondering what he'd been up to.

He grinned and passed me the paper. At first I just didn't get it. He'd actually made a pretty decent job of it, the poem was great. I looked at him curiously, waiting for an explanation. He laughed wickedly. "Symbolism." Was all he said.

I read it again and noticed that he'd actually written a poem about a penis. Every line referred to it but never mentioned the word at all, if the teacher read into this properly like she was supposed to then Erika was going to get into some deep trouble for it. I laughed at his skills; he was obviously an evil genius like his brother.

"Maybe you missed your calling, you should be doing penis poetry," I joked.

He laughed. "It's acrostic too."

Acrostic? Doesn't that mean when the first letter of each line forms a word or phrase vertically as the poem goes on? He pointed out the first letters of each line, and I burst out laughing when I noticed that he'd spelled out 'I read erotica for fun' vertically down the page using the first letter of each sentence.

I shook my head at his inventiveness and wrapped my arms around him tightly. "You, Mr Morris, are a very gifted poet," I teased.

He smiled and nodded, laying me onto my back, settling himself on top of me. "And you, Miss Henderson, are the most beautiful girl I've ever seen," he countered, kissing me lightly.

By the time Monday morning came I was so excited I could barely keep still. Will had dropped me off at the corner store as usual. I was with Nick tonight, studying, so I wouldn't see Will again until tomorrow morning so we had a pretty heated make out session before I left the car.

As I walked into the school, I imagined a brown haired Erika driving to school in her rotten meat smelling car. I laughed quietly to myself, but in reality, I knew it probably wouldn't smell yet; it would take a few days before that would start to take effect.

When I actually got into the school and over to my locker, I was a little disappointed to see Erika was still her usual brilliant blonde. She was standing in her barely there skirt, and low cut top, flirting with another football player - Kevin was obviously last week's obsession, this week she'd moved onto the running back instead.

I watched her curiously. Had her hair darkened slightly or was that just wishful thinking? I didn't think the hair dye payback was working, I was pretty sure it wouldn't because the shampoo would probably just strip the dye from the hair straight away. *Oh well, it was worth a try anyway!* Erika was flirting furiously with the poor little running back, her hand on his arm as she laughed enthusiastically at something that he said. Suddenly she shifted from one foot to the other, one of her feet twitching slightly as if she was uncomfortable.

I felt the grin stretch across my face as my eyes widened. I flicked my eyes down to her shoes. They were one of the ones that I 'cleaned' on Saturday. I choked on my laughter and put a hand over my mouth to stifle the sound as she wriggled her foot again. *Oh God, Sam is just too funny! I really hope that she doesn't have another pair to change into and has to wear those all day. That would make my whole year!*

Nick and Amy came wandering over to me then. "Morning, guys!" I chirped happily.

Nick frowned and threw his arm around my shoulder, pulling me closer to him. "What's got you in such a good mood this morning?" he inquired.

Hmm, now let me see, it could either be that my boyfriend is incredible, or it could be that my sworn enemy is having trouble with itching powder that I put in her shoes! I couldn't tell him either of those things though, so I just shrugged. "Woke up on the right side of the bed?" I suggested. That wasn't strictly true, I'd woken in my bed this morning, the 'right' side of the bed would be waking up with Will, but I guess that couldn't happen two days in a row.

Nick looked at me curiously, obviously knowing something else was going on, but letting it go anyway. "Okay, whatever. You still coming over tonight? I'm in the mood for enchiladas," he said, giving me the puppy dog face.

"Stop with the face, you know I'll cook you whatever you want," I teased, poking him in the ribs with one finger, making him jump back laughing. Nick was very ticklish, something I'd discovered when we were dating.

He sighed. "You know, I'm gonna miss you girls so much when school finishes and we all go to college." He slipped an arm around both me and Amy and hugged us tightly, kissing the top of my head.

I frowned. I didn't even want to start thinking about college, even though there were only a few months left at school. I actually needed to start applying to colleges soon. Before Will, everything was so easy. Amy and I planned on going to the same school, it was always something that we dreamed of, moving to New York together, renting an apartment together. I guess that couldn't happen now. There was no way I was moving that far away from Will, not a chance in hell. I would just have to choose something more local so I could still see him every day.

I knew people would think I was stupid, giving up my dream for a guy, but I would still get to do the same course, I would still get to get the same qualification at the end, just from a different school to what I had planned for the last few years. I had no idea how I was going to break the news to Amy though, but that was something for another day, I didn't want to think about it yet. Maybe she'd be the one to pull out first, maybe she'd tell me that she didn't want to move to New York because of Ryan and then there would be no problem. One could only hope.

"We have months left yet," I told Nick, trying to appear unconcerned.

He sighed and nodded. Nick wanted to stay here and go to a local college; he didn't want to leave his dad on his own, so he planned on sticking around for him. He thought Amy and I were both leaving him, I guess he'd be happy when I told him about the change of plan.

"We have meetings with the school guidance counsellor in a couple of weeks, to talk about our options," Amy added, shrugging.

I opened my mouth to speak, but I was interrupted by someone clearing their throat loudly. I looked up to see Erika sneering at me. "Sorry to interrupt this little threesome, freak gathering," she stated, looking us over slowly.

"Oh go bleach some more brain cells, Erika," Nick scoffed, waving his hand dismissively.

I smiled and tightened my arm on his waist. I loved Nick; he always looked out for me and Amy. He was probably the only guy in the school to actually hate Erika Dennison. All other guys fell at her feet, but not Nick, he hated the way she was towards us.

Erika frowned, looking hurt for a split second before she rearranged her expression into the bitchy one. "Shut up, Nick!" she retorted.

He laughed. "Great come back, darlin'," he mocked, winking at her.

Her face flushed, and her eyes seemed to darken as her fist clenched - but instead of directing her anger at him for his comment, it seemed to be directed at me. "I want a word, Ice Princess," she hissed, nodding her head off to one side.

Nick's arm tightened on me, holding me in place. "Just go socialise with your own kind, Erika. The airheads are over there," he stated, pointing to the group of her friends who were giggling hysterically off to one side.

She made what sounded like a growling sound and flicked her hair over her shoulder. I could see the angry retort that was about to burst from her lips. I didn't want her to say anything about me and Will and our 'deal' so I quickly pushed Nick's arm off of me and shook my head, signalling that it was fine.

"It's okay; I need to speak to Erika about our History project anyway. We got partnered on Friday," I lied, smiling at Nick reassuringly. He frowned but nodded, letting his arm drop down to his side.

278

Erika turned and walked off without saying anything, so I grabbed my bag and followed her down the hallway. She stopped after a little while and turned to me, her eyes flicked over my shoulder and I knew that she was probably looking at Nick and Amy who no doubt were watching this exchange. "Why does he have such a problem with me?" she asked, frowning angrily.

I shrugged. "Probably because you're always such a bitch to me and Amy," I answered casually.

Her frown deepened as she looked back at me. "My assignments?" she requested coldly, holding out her hand for them, obviously deciding to ignore my comment about Nick.

I suddenly wondered why she was so bothered about little old Nick anyway. *She can't have a crush on Nick, can she?* I studied her face for a couple of seconds trying to see something there. *No, no way. Erika Dennison, daddy's girl, spoiled brat, and head cheerleader, could not have a crush on one of my best friends...*

Nick was very cute though, and a great guy, he undoubtedly had a lot of appeal, a lot of girls in the school thought so, but he wasn't one of the popular crowd because he didn't want to be. He really wasn't Erika's type either. For one thing, he wasn't a jock, sure he played basketball for the school, but he wasn't that into it and your typical jock stereotype that Erika usually went for. *Hmm, if she does like him though then that would explain why she hates me and Amy so much.* I decided not to entertain that crazy thought any longer. I was wrong; there was no chance of her liking Nick. And besides, even if she did like him, she had no chance with him whatsoever. He hated her with a passion the same as I did.

I handed her the assignments and prayed that she didn't look at them too much, she did a quick scan of them then shoved them in her bag, none the wiser to any of the 'additions' that I'd put on there. I bit back a laugh thinking about her handing them in. Hopefully she'd into trouble for them, I'd find out in a couple of days no doubt.

"So, you can buy me lunch today. I want a baked potato, plain, and some salad on the side." She picked at her nails as she laid out her orders for today. I smiled and nodded so she continued, "I'll meet you here at the end of the day and give you my assignments that I get today, don't be late."

I nodded and raked my eyes over her hair, trying to see a slight difference in the shade of it. It still looked the same so I assume that it either wasn't working, or that it needed a bit of time to build up and make a difference.

I spotted Will walking down the corridor, talking to a freshman about some math theorem that I just didn't even want to try and understand. He smiled discreetly at me, and I couldn't help but smile back, it was like an automated response, my body just responded to him without any conscious thought being involved.

"So anyway, I need you to come over to my place on Wednesday at six and drive me to my chiropractor's appointment, and then drive me home again," she stated. I came out of the daze I was in and shook my head, trying to

279

focus on what she was talking about rather than replaying memories of Will and I on Saturday night and Sunday daytime.

"Um… Erika, I can't drive you, I don't have a car," I admitted.

She looked at me like I was stupid. "You don't have a car? How can you not have a car? That's just stupid!"

I shrugged. My parents couldn't afford to buy me a car, but I wasn't that bothered anyway because Amy and I were usually together and she had a car, which meant I didn't need one.

She snorted and rolled her eyes. "Fine, I'll get someone else to drive me then."

She turned on her heel, flicking her hair over her shoulder, which actually whipped me in the face. *Did she do that on purpose? Stupid bitch!*

I watched her walk up the hallway and stop with her friends. She was shifting uncomfortably on her feet still. I giggled wickedly. I skipped back to Amy and Nick, slinging my arm around Nick's waist as he put his arm around my shoulder.

"You got partnered with her? That sucks!" he complained, looking at Erika distastefully. I loved how Nick saw past her obvious beauty that every other guy in the school was besotted with.

I shrugged. "I know, but at least it's almost done now, the project ends in a couple of days," I lied, hoping my voice wouldn't betray me. I was pretty sure that, in a couple of days, Erika would discover that I wasn't playing her game anymore. Once that happened I wouldn't have to have anything to do with her ever again.

He nodded, obviously accepting my story and started talking to Ryan who had come over to hang out with Amy before class. I relaxed. Just a couple more days of doing Erika's bidding and then I'd be able to stop being her 'personal bitch'. In the mean time I was just going to screw up everything that she gave me to do. Strangely, I was actually looking forward to it.

The next couple of days passed incredibly fast. True to my plans I messed up slightly on everything that she gave me. If I had to get her coffee order I asked for full fat milk, if I had to bring her lunch then I accidentally sprinkled some pepper or something over it. If I had to pass a message to her friends then I omitted a couple of details – which actually worked out pretty perfectly because she ended up leaving one of her friends at the school when she was supposed to be driving her home. The catty argument in the hallway the following day was entertaining to say the least.

Her hair was losing some of its blonde brilliance, only slightly though, but Amy and I could tell the difference. Over the two nights, I let Will make amendments and changes to her assignments. She obviously hadn't had any feedback about them yet though because she hadn't said anything. As far as she was concerned I was her perfect little slave. I did everything she asked of me, and never once complained.

But three days later was when the poop really hit the fan.

I heard her before I saw her. I was walking down the hallway, and I could hear a frustrated screaming sound coming from behind me. Amy and I turned, as did everyone in the hallway, only to see Erika screwing up a piece of paper, her face the picture of rage as she almost growled in frustration. People were milling around her, trying to soothe her but she wasn't having any of it.

She looked up and her eyes met mine. I actually flinched at the anger that I saw there. She sneered and stalked up to me, every step was taken with determination and confidence as she walked right up in front of me, glaring into my face.

"You little bitch!" she spat venomously.

I gulped. *Is she going to hit me? She looks like she wanted to rip my head off or something.* The way she was looking at me sent a cold shiver down my spine. I wondered what she had discovered, it had to have been the assignments that I'd been doing for her, there was nothing else I had done to get her this angry.

"What?" I asked, my voice a little weak. This was the part that I wasn't looking forward to; this was the part that I was dreading. It was fine doing all of those things and messing with her when she didn't know, but the way she was looking at me made me feel nauseous. I kind of wished I'd just stuck to the original plan and done her damn chores properly.

"What?" she repeated sarcastically. "What?" she sneered at me again. "Are you serious? That English assignment that you did for me on Monday just got me two days' worth of detentions! Now I can't practice with the squad and our cheer routine is going to be ruined for the game on Friday! You really have the audacity to ask me *what?*" she ranted.

I shrugged. "I'm assuming that you accept my resignation as your personal bitch?" I offered, raising one eyebrow, trying to appear more confident than I felt.

She stepped closer to me. "What the hell kind of game are you playing? You know I have you and Mr Morris by the balls. How is he going to feel when he loses his job because of a cheap little bitch like you?" she asked quietly, I was confident that no one else heard.

I looked at her in the eyes and pretended to be confused. "I'm not quite sure what you are going on about, Erika. What does Mr Morris have to do with me?" I asked, faking innocence.

She scowled. "You really want to go there?" she asked, her voice threatening and cold.

I shrugged. "I have no idea what you're talking about, Erika," I lied, going for unconcerned and aloof. I wasn't sure if I was pulling it off, Amy was glaring at Erika like she wanted to kill her in front of everyone.

Erika laughed, pushed her hair over her shoulder dramatically, and smiled sweetly at me. "Say bye bye to your education at this school, Chloe. You and Mr Hottie Teacher are out of here," she said softly, as if we were talking about the weather. She turned on her heel and marched off down the hallway. I flicked my eyes to Amy and willed myself not to cry. What if she said

281

something? She was bound to say something to someone, I knew what type of person she was, she would definitely do this.

Amy slung her arm around my shoulder, pulling me close to her as everyone started to whisper and talk about Erika's little outburst. "It's fine, Chloe. Everything's going to be fine, she has nothing on you, and Sam's plan is genius. Just chill," she whispered, rubbing her hand on my arm reassuringly.

We headed to the lunchroom, but I wasn't hungry. I felt sick. All I could think about was Will getting into trouble because of me. I needed to tell Will what had happened, but I didn't want to go anywhere near him right now in case someone saw and it added fuel to the fire. I looked up at Amy and forced a smile. People were looking at me worriedly, Nick was frowning at me.

"You feeling all right?" he asked, putting his hand on my forehead, checking my temperature.

I nodded and pushed his hand off. "Yeah, I'm fine," I lied. I looked at Amy. "I need to tell er..." I trailed off, hoping she would understand what I was getting at.

She nodded. "Want me to?" she asked, cocking one eyebrow.

I smiled gratefully. *I really have the best friend in the world.* I nodded quickly. "Do you mind?"

She shook her head and picked up the rest of her sandwich. "Of course not." She turned and kissed Ryan lightly. "I'll see you after school, okay? I just need to go speak to Mr Morris about my calculus assignment for today's lesson," she lied smoothly. He kissed her back, his hand trailing down her back to slap her behind gently as she walked away.

I sat there picking at my sandwich, trying to join in with the conversation going on around me, but I just couldn't concentrate. All I could think about was Will getting into trouble, him hating me and never wanting to see me again because of how much hassle I was to him. We were literally going to have to be ten times more careful from now on. That probably meant no going out in public at all until school finished, we probably couldn't even risk heading to the next town over just in case someone saw us.

I just prayed that Sam's genius idea held up if Erika decided to go to the Principal. *Maybe she won't even do it, maybe she'll decide that she's going to be the bigger person here for a change and let me off. Maybe she's going to turn over a new leaf and everything will be fine. Wow, that's a lot of maybes!*

The sound of my cell phone ringing brought me out of my worried thoughts. I pulled it out and glanced at the screen and saw Amy's number flashing there. I gulped and answered, not sure if I wanted to hear what she had to say. What if she told Will about Erika and he went crazy and hated me?

"Hey," I said into the phone, my voice barely above a whisper.

"Hey, Cutie." The sound of Will's voice on the line instead of Amy's made my heart race. I felt my eyes fill with tears, and I looked up that the ceiling quickly so they wouldn't fall.

"Hi. Did you hear what happened?" I asked, trying to keep my tone light and my words noncommittal to anything so that people wouldn't know what I was talking about.

He sighed down the phone. "Yeah, Amy just told me. It's okay, Cutie. We were expecting this, so it's no big shock. Just don't worry about anything; everything's going to be fine, I promise. You trust me, don't you?" he asked, his voice soft and comforting. I smiled and closed my eyes. *I really don't deserve this guy; everything about him is too good for me.* He was being so tender and caring even though he was facing jail, or at the very least, he was facing losing his career that he worked so hard for. Yet, he was still comforting me. He amazed me.

"Of course I do," I whispered.

"I'd better go. Just stick to the story; no one is going to believe her. It's fine, Cutie, I swear we'll be fine. Just don't worry, and try to relax," he instructed.

I nodded and took a couple of deep breaths. "All right."

"I love you, Chloe."

I smiled at the sound of those words, I still wasn't used to it, and I didn't think I ever would be. "You too," I answered.

The call disconnected so I slid the phone back into my pocket. He sounded so confident that it made me feel confident too. I did trust Will, and if he said everything was going to be fine, then I believed him. I just prayed his belief was justified.

The rest of the day I was on edge. Every time I passed Erika, she smirked at me knowingly. Amy was great; she didn't leave me for a second, supporting me and telling me how everything was going to work out.

When we got to calculus there was no Will. I took a seat and pulled out my textbook, ignoring the way Erika was whispering with her friends, shooting me little glances as they all laughed quietly. A couple of minutes later and Mrs French walked in; she stopped at the front of Will's desk and cleared her throat to get the class's attention. Everyone fell silent, and I felt my heart sink. *Where is Will?*

"Class, Mr Morris couldn't make class today. I'm substituting for him because he's been called away at the last minute. If you could all just pull up the next chapter in your textbooks and start reading in preparation for your next lesson with him. I'd like silence please. I have papers to grade so if you could just get on with it that would be fabulous," she requested, dumping her bag on his desk and pulling out his chair sitting and starting to grade her papers.

People started whispering. I flicked my eyes to Erika; she was grinning from ear to ear and winked at me. My whole body felt cold, the hair on the back of my neck stood up. She'd obviously not let it go. Was Will in trouble right now? Before I had a chance to think of too many questions and start to panic, there was a knock at the door. A student walked in and headed up to Mrs French, handing her a note. She read it and then looked up to the class.

"Chloe Henderson?" she called, her eyes scanning the room for me.

Oh my God!

I gulped and raised my hand, knowing my voice wouldn't work if I tried to speak. Amy gripped my free hand under the table, squeezing so tightly that it would have been painful if I could actually feel my body, but I couldn't feel it, I was numb.

"The Principal would like to see you in his office," Mrs French told me, waving at the door for me to leave.

I couldn't breathe. I didn't care about myself, but if Will got into trouble then it would hurt me more than anything. I gulped and forced myself to calm down. My knees felt a little wobbly as I stood up, not looking at anyone. People were whispering, all wondering what I had done wrong and why I was getting called to the Principal's office. I didn't say anything; I just packed my books into my bag, trying to do it as slow as possible so I could calm down.

When I couldn't stall anymore I walked through the classroom. As I passed Erika, she put her foot into the aisle, making me trip. Luckily I caught myself on the desk in front before I completely fell on my face, but people still laughed and called me a klutz. I felt my face heat up, but it wasn't from embarrassment, it was from anger. I wanted to smash her face in, rip her head off and chop her into little pieces and feed her to her horses. I wouldn't give her the satisfaction of letting her see that I was upset and worried sick. Instead, I pushed myself up from the desk I was leaning on heavily and smiled sweetly at her.

"You might want to be careful where you put your feet, Erika, that could have been a lot worse. I'm fine though, thanks for asking," I said keeping my voice friendly and light.

She grinned at me and nodded towards the door. "Better go see what the Principal wants, Ice Princess," she chirped.

I nodded and straightened my shirt, walking out of the classroom with my head held high. I needed to chill out and be confident. I was not going to let Will get into trouble for me, there was no way I was messing this up.

As I got to the reception I was waved through into the office. As I pushed open the door to the Principal's office, I saw Will sitting there, one leg folded over the other, his face serious. He didn't smile at me, but he didn't frown either. I looked away from him to the Principal who was sitting behind his desk with a grave expression on his face. I felt my heart rate speed up at the sight of his accusing stare; his beady brown eyes were boring into mine as if he was trying to ascertain the truth without even speaking.

Please don't let me screw this up!

Chapter Thirty-Five

"Chloe, have a seat," Principal Sherman instructed, nodding at the empty seat next to Will.

I put on a fake smile and nodded, sitting down. "Am I in some kind of trouble? Have I missed an assignment or something in calculus?" I asked, glancing at Will. *Oh man, hold it together, Chloe!*

"I just want to ask you a few questions," Principal Sherman said, smiling reassuringly but it didn't quite meet his eyes. I gulped and tried to keep my expression neutral as I nodded, pretending like I had no clue why I was brought here in the first place. "Okay, so I had someone come and report something to me earlier today that is very concerning, and it's my duty to investigate the accusation."

I frowned as my hand clenched in a tight fist on my leg. I seriously was going to punch Erika in the face next time I saw her. "Accusation? I don't understand," I replied, faking innocence.

Will and I had been over and over this; we knew this might happen once Erika cottoned on to the fact that we weren't playing her game. Deep down I was still hoping that there was a nice person inside of her somewhere though; I guess I was wrong to hope after all. We had rehearsed what I needed to say if this happened. I needed to stick to the plan that I was dating Will's brother and nothing more. This would all just be fine... if I could only stop my hands from sweating.

"Yes, a very serious accusation regarding you and Mr Morris." Principal Sherman pursed his lips and sat back in his chair, watching me intently.

"Me and Mr Morris? I don't get it," I lied, looking at Will as if asking for clarification.

Will smiled at me sadly and looked to the balding little man on the other side of the desk.

"Well, Chloe, another student is alleging that she witnessed you and Mr Morris in a compromising situation last Thursday at the end of school," Principal Sherman continued. "She claims that she saw you two kissing and touching, in Mr Morris' classroom."

I snorted and looked at Will with mock disgust. "As if! He's old!" I scoffed, turning my nose up at him.

Will burst out laughing and shook his head. "Thanks, Chloe, that makes me feel so good," he said, still chuckling.

I smiled. "Whatever." I waved my hand dismissively. I looked back to the Principal who looked like he was fighting a smile. "I'm dating someone else anyway. It's actually Mr Morris' brother, Sam. We've been seeing each other for about four months now, well, we did break up for a couple of weeks but then I made him jealous by dating Oliver Hawk so we got back together. But why would someone say I was kissing Will? That's just..." I trailed off, faking confusion and disgust, "gross," I finished.

Principal Sherman leant forward in his chair, resting his elbows on the desk, looking thoughtful. "I have a responsibility to my school and my students to thoroughly investigate any claim or accusation that comes into my office. I must admit I was a little shocked to have heard this earlier today, I've not heard even the slightest rumours about this before that meeting so I don't quite know what to feel about it," he said, nodding along as if he was thinking about it as he spoke.

I frowned. "What to feel about what? I don't get it. Am I in some sort of trouble for dating Will's brother?" I asked, playing along that I just didn't understand what was being accused.

The Principal shook his head. "No, Chloe. The allegation is that you are carrying on with an illegal relationship with your teacher," he said, looking at me as if I was stupid. That was exactly what I wanted him to think, I wanted him to think I was stupid and that I wasn't actually clever enough to have a secret relationship with Will, that I wasn't smart enough to pull off this plan with Sam. I wanted him to underestimate me.

I gasped and stood up, shaking my head. "That's stupid! Me and Will? I'm not being horrible but to be honest I wouldn't even talk to him if it wasn't for Sam, I kind of *have* to talk to him because of being with his brother. We don't exactly have anything in common, I mean, he's a math nerd for goodness sake!" I ranted, pointing at Will. I heard him snort in protest, but I didn't react to it, I'd apologise after. I'd already called him old so I figured I may as well go the whole hog and call him a nerd too.

"Sit down, Chloe. Like I said it's my job to look into these things. This is just an informal meeting to ascertain both sides of the story. Neither of you are in trouble for anything at this time. There is no evidence apart from one girl's statement, and from what Mr Morris has already told me about you and his brother, there doesn't seem to be a problem. I just don't understand why a student would come and make up a serious accusation like this if it was unfounded." Principal Sherman pointed at the chair again, signalling for me to sit.

I lowered myself into the chair and frowned. "Well this is just stupid! Who was it that said it anyway? Why would someone make up something like this? It's sick! Maybe they just want to get me in trouble or something," I suggested, acting hurt and upset. It was times like this that I wished I was an actress and could make myself cry on cue, that would be awesome if I could just burst into tears and throw myself on the floor wailing about how unfair it was that someone hated me enough to try and get me into trouble.

Principal Sherman shook his head slowly. "I'm not at liberty to disclose the person who made the accusation." He turned to Will and cocked his head to the side. "What is your relationship with Chloe, outside of school?"

Will shrugged nonchalantly. "She's dating my brother; I've seen her a few times outside of school, but only with Sam. I wasn't aware that was against the rules," he stated, frowning. It looked like his tactic was the pissed off approach, like he was annoyed to be being accused of doing something wrong.

"But you have never been alone with Chloe?" Principal Sherman clarified.

Will's frown deepened. "Well, I've been alone in the room with her if that's what you're getting at, but not for any great length of time. She's my little brother's girlfriend. If we're at my parents at the same time, or going to the same party then I've seen her out, but it's not like we hang out or anything. I don't really socialise with my brother that much," he lied, shrugging. I couldn't help but be impressed by him and his acting skills. He was doing seriously well with this, he was obviously coping a lot better under the pressure than I was. I discreetly wiped my sweaty palms on the leg of my jeans and tried to keep my heartbeat steady.

Principal Sherman looked away from Will to me. "Tell me about how you met Mr Morris' brother, Chloe."

I gulped. *Okay here's where it could get a little tricky.* We had all agreed to stick to the story as much as possible so that details wouldn't get confused or lost over time, so basically everything that had happened with Will I was pretending had happened with Sam instead. Which meant I was about to get berated for sneaking into a club underage.

"Well, it was near the start of the summer, I snuck into a club using a fake ID with-" I stopped and chose my words carefully not wanting to get any of my girls in trouble too. "Some friends. I met Sam there and we hit it off, and that was it. We dated for just over a month then he dumped me. I was hurt so I started seeing this guy from school trying to make Sam jealous. My plan worked, we got back together and have been together properly again for the last eight weeks," I rambled all of the words together, trying to sound like an immature seventeen year old girl, hopefully it would just make me look even dumber so that Principal Sherman would just dismiss me as being too stupid to carry on with a teacher.

The Principal raised one eyebrow. "You snuck into a club?" he questioned, not looking impressed.

I nodded. "Yeah, but it was in the summer and not on school time, so you can't give me a detention for that, can you?" I asked, trying to look scared.

He shook his head. "No I can't, but you shouldn't do that, Chloe. Dangerous things happen at places like that when you aren't properly supervised. There are rules there for a reason you know. I hope you won't be doing anything like that again," he chastised, looking at me sternly.

I shook my head quickly. "No, Sam doesn't like me going to places like that anyway," I lied.

He nodded, seeming satisfied with my response. "Okay good. So, carrying on from there then, when was the first time you met Mr Morris?"

I rolled my lip into my mouth and chewed on it, pretending to think. "I met him at a party that I went to with Sam a couple of weeks after we got together," I lied. Then I clicked my fingers and shook my head as if I just remembered something and turned to look at Will. "Wait, I met you before that too actually, at Kaitlin's wedding. That was the following day after I met Sam at the club. That was actually our first date; not a very good date to take a girl on, a family wedding, but I still had fun. Sam is hilarious." I sighed wistfully as I thought about the wedding and dancing with Will all night. Principal Sherman seemed to be writing down everything that was being said, scribbling quickly on a notepad.

I was feeling more and more confident by the second. Principal Sherman's shoulders seemed to be relaxing and his posture wasn't quite as stiff and accusing as it was before, he was buying the lie completely.

"When was it that you first discovered that Mr Morris was going to be your teacher?" he asked, rolling his neck on his shoulders, probably trying to relieve some of the tension from them.

I shrugged. "Not until I saw him in class. We didn't really speak much before that so I didn't realise that he was going to be teaching at my school. It was kind of awkward at first, but it's okay now though," I said, smiling at Will but just in a friendly way.

"Are there people that could witness your relationship with Sam?" Principal Sherman asked, looking at me hopefully.

I frowned. "Sure. Amy's met him. Um… he hasn't met my parents yet because my dad, well, he can get a little overprotective so I didn't want to scare him away from me or anything," I stated, wincing. This was where it got tricky, the proving it part, because none of my other friends had met Sam at all or have even heard about him. "He came to pick me up the other day from school, and spoke to Mr Young and Mr Bentley," I added, pretending that I didn't think it was a big deal.

Principal Sherman seemed to breathe a sigh of relief when I mentioned the teachers. My guess would be that just made everything easier to prove for him and made his job easier. He definitely looked a lot happier about it now. He smiled. "And what day was that?" he asked, scribbling on his pad again.

I shrugged. "I don't know. Er, it was last week sometime. What does it matter anyway?" I asked. *Oh my days, this is going freaking awesomely! I need to buy Sam something as a thank you for this!*

Principal Sherman smiled easily now. "It would just be handy to know so that I can cross check with the other teachers."

288

I frowned and nodded, pretending to think. "I can't remember what day it was. If you're that desperate for it why don't you just check the visitors' book, that'll have the date on, won't it?" I offered.

His mouth dropped open a little, another smile tugging at the corners of his mouth. "Visitors' book, he actually came into the school?"

I nodded. "Sure. We went to speak to Will about the anniversary dinner for Sam's parents on Saturday night, and then Miss Teller came in while we were talking and then we left to go bowling," I clarified, shrugging.

Principal Sherman looked at Will. "Miss Teller was a witness too?" he asked, looking like a ten ton weight had just been lifted off of his shoulders.

Will nodded. "Well yeah. I drive Caroline home every day after school. She spoke to Sam and Chloe when she came to meet me," he agreed casually.

I felt like doing a little happy dance in the middle of the office, everything was working out perfectly. He was totally falling for it and Will wasn't going to get into trouble, I wasn't going to get expelled, and Erika was going to get a punch in her pretty face next time I saw her. *All is right in the world!*

"I hope you two understand that I need to investigate this. It's my duty after all to ensure the welfare of all students within my school. I'll have to check out what you've said but if the stories match up then all I can do is apologise for dragging you both in here," Principal Sherman said, looking uncomfortable.

I didn't say anything, just tried to keep the smug happy grin off of my face. Will sat forward in his chair. "I understand, Richard, I know how it works. I just hope this won't be on my record that we've had this meeting. A false accusation of this magnitude could have a detrimental effect on my teaching career," Will said.

I felt my eyes widen in shock. I'd never heard Will speak like that before, he was always so young sounding when he spoke, but when he just made that speech with all of the long words, I was actually quite surprised by how much he'd sounded like a calculus teacher.

Principal Sherman shook his head fiercely. "This is just a friendly meeting to ascertain certain details, nothing is going on anyone's record you can rest assured of that. And if these accusations are proven to be false, then the person making the accusation will be punished accordingly for causing trouble," he said sternly.

I felt my heart jump into my throat; Erika was going to get into trouble for lying? I actually felt a little guilty about that, because technically although she was a mega-bitch, she wasn't just lying to get us into trouble.

Will nodded and smiled gratefully. "That's good."

Well, based on his smile, he obviously doesn't feel guilty for getting that blackmailing witch in trouble!

Principal Sherman cleared his throat. "I can't really say that I'm too happy about this whole situation though. A student dating a teacher's brother is always going to leave space for things to go wrong. For example," he picked up a file that had my name on it, and thumbed through it, "your grades have significantly improved in calculus this year, Chloe. One could argue that Mr Morris was going easy on you because of you dating his brother," he suggested, raising one eyebrow and looking between me and Will.

I frowned angrily. I was extremely offended by his comment. "No way. I worked hard to get that average up! Quite frankly I resent the accusation that he's giving me a free pass. I have a tutor; I study at least twice a week with him. I deserve that grade, and I think that it's mean for you to suggest that he's going easy on me because of Sam!" I cried, angrily.

Principal Sherman held up his hands innocently. "I'm not suggesting it, I'm merely proving what I just said about there being space for people to suggest certain things if you have a close relationship with a teacher. There is always going to be someone that suggests that there is favouritism going on. Just so I can prove that wrong before it is even suggested as an issue, who is your tutor?" he asked, looking at me, his pen poised over his notepad again ready to write it down.

I crossed my arms over my chest, still offended. *I worked damn hard on my calculus, and I'm not going to let some balding little man tell me that I'm getting off easy with it.* "Nick Golding," I growled.

Principal Sherman wrote that down. He now had almost a full page of quotes and things that we'd said. He nodded. "I think that's everything. The bell is about to ring in a few minutes. I'll investigate this quickly because I don't want anything hanging over our heads like this. As soon as I've finished speaking to the other teachers, I'll let you know. In the meantime, if you could just try and keep your distance from each other while this is ongoing, I know that will be difficult with the nature of the relationship, but hopefully I'll have this all sorted out by tomorrow," he requested, smiling almost apologetically as he stood up, signalling the end of the meeting.

Will stood and shook his hand and I grabbed my bag off of the floor. That was so much easier than I thought it would be. I'd actually been a pretty good liar; I was more than proud of both myself and Will. I stalked out of the door, not waiting for Will; I couldn't exactly wait around to talk to him after we'd just been instructed to stay away from each other.

Instead of heading back to his class, I went to my locker, grabbing my books that I would need for tonight's study session with Nick. *Hmm, should I tell Nick about Will, just so we would have someone else to back up our story? I can ask Nick to lie and pretend that he's met and heard of Sam too…. That's actually a great idea.* I loved Nick dearly and I knew that he would be annoyed about it at first but he would get over it and help me. He was adorable like that and I could always rely on him in a rough situation.

Once I had my books I headed out to the school grounds for the last five minutes. I sat on one of the benches and pulled out my phone, deciding to text Sam and tell him what had happened. We exchanged a few texts; he sent me a couple of flirtatious ones and instructed me to leave them on my phone as extra evidence of our relationship. While I thought about it, I quickly deleted everything that Will had ever sent me. It was a little painful deleting all of the 'I love you' messages and stuff that he'd sent me, but I was pretty sure I would get a ton more once all this was over with and I'd left school.

As soon as the bell rang Amy called me to see where I was. Less than a minute later she came streaking over to where I was, and engulfed me in a hug, talking so fast that I could barely understand what she said. "I've-been-so-worried-about-you! Tell-me-everything-what-happened-with-Principal-Sherman-did-you-get-into-trouble?" she said it all in one breath. I laughed at her as I pulled her down onto the benches and we spoke in hushed whispered about everything. She seemed to relax as I got half way through the story; she obviously thought we'd done well too.

"You know, now that you don't owe Erika anything, we should do something to her. Like TP her house, or spray paint on her car," she said, rubbing her hands together with a wicked glint in her eye.

I smiled at the thought of doing that. I would actually love to do that to her, but I had a feeling that she was going to be in enough trouble as it is. "Let's just see if she gets punished for lying first," I instructed, rolling my eyes at the evilness I could see flashing across her face. *Oh yeah, I definitely need to keep Sam and Amy apart. Two evil geniuses together could be a bad thing all round!*

My cell phone beeped so I pulled it out. 1 new message, from Will.
'You did so good in there. I'm so proud of you, Cutie. Call me when you get home from Nick's. Love you'

I smiled and hit reply: *'Thanks, you did great too. You should go through your phone and delete anything I've ever sent you, just to be on the safe side. Love you too, speak to you later x'*

My phone beeped again almost immediately: *'Good thinking, x'*

I sat with Amy for a little while longer before Nick came out looking for me. We headed to his car and I bit my lip, thinking everything through. *Should I tell Nick too and ask for his help? Jeez, I should have asked Amy what she thought, she would know if I should or not.*

Nick frowned and looked at me from the corner of his eye. "Everything okay, Chloe? You're a little quiet," he observed, sounding concerned. I smiled. He probably wouldn't know that I got dragged out of class to go see the Principal; he didn't have calculus with me.

"Yeah, er, everything's fine." I winced because my words just didn't sound believable, even to my own ears. He clearly didn't believe me either. He looked at me with one eyebrow raised, waiting for me to tell him the truth. Nick always was good at detecting my lies; I'd known him long enough.

"Oh really?" he said sarcastically.

I sighed and we pulled up outside his house. I shook my head and avoided looking at him, not really wanting to do this, but I just felt like I needed to, to get some extra backup. If I was supposed to be so loved up with Sam, then wouldn't I have bragged about it to more than one friend? If the Principal looked into this like he should, then he might find it a little weird that I hadn't spoken to anyone else about Sam.

291

"Actually I need to talk to you about something," I muttered, wishing the ground would open up and swallow me. He turned in his seat and looked at me curiously, waiting for me to continue. "Not here, let's go inside, yeah?" I nodded towards his house. He didn't say anything, just climbed out, grabbing both of our schoolbags from the backseat and walking towards his house, waiting for me at the door.

I took a deep breath and followed him into the house, praying I was doing the right thing. He dropped our bags by the door and looked at me expectantly. I headed into the lounge and sat on the sofa, putting my head in my hands. *Okay this is harder than I thought. Is he going to think Will did something wrong by being with me? What if he thinks he's a paedophile or something and refuses to help me? What if he demands that I break it off with Will or he would tell my parents? Jeez, do I really need his help this badly?*

He crouched in front of me and took my hands, looking at me with concern etched across his face. My worry started to ebb away as I looked at him. This was Nick, sweet, loving, dependable Nick. He was one of my very best friends yet I was freaking out about telling him about the love of my life. I was just being stupid right now.

"You know I've been seeing a guy?" I started, frowning and wondering how to word 'hey I've been sleeping with our teacher'. I couldn't exactly just blurt it out like that.

He nodded. "Yeah, Will, right?"

I winced. *Wow, it's lucky I am talking to him about this, because if I hadn't, and Principal Sherman had asked him my boyfriend's name, then Will and I would have been screwed right then!*

"Er... yeah." I sighed and closed my eyes, deciding just to go for it. "I'm in trouble."

He gasped, and his grip on my hands tightened to the point of pain. "What the hell? Are you pregnant? Did that asshole get you pregnant? Jesus, Chloe! What are you gonna do? He's sticking with you, right? He's not leaving you to do this on your own, is he? If he is I'm gonna..." he trailed off, muttering a string of expletives under his breath as he jumped to his feet, dragging me up with him where he didn't let go of my hands.

I felt my mouth drop open in shock at his little rant. *How on earth did he get that I was pregnant from that? Wow, this boy has some imagination.* "Nick, I'm-" I started but he cut me off, cupping my face in his hands, looking at me fiercely.

"You don't need to worry. You'll be okay, I'll make sure of it, I promise. Everything's fine. I'll look after you. I'll always be here for you, I won't run away like that asshole," he stated, pulling me into a bone crushing hug.

I felt my eyes fill with tears at how very sweet he was; I was such a lucky girl to have someone like him in my life. I couldn't help the little giggle that escaped my lips at the lunacy of this situation. I hadn't had sex for months yet here I was, pregnant, abandoned, and being comforted by my ex-boyfriend. This had to be one of the weirdest things that ever happened to me. I pushed him back and shook my head, grinning because I had one of the nicest guys in the world as my friend.

"I'm not pregnant, Nick," I told him, watching as he frowned and looked at me confused.

"But you said…"

I smiled and took his hand. "I said I was in trouble. I'm not pregnant," I confirmed.

He seemed to breathe a sigh of relief as he slumped down onto the sofa and closed his eyes. "Well thank God for that. I was envisioning us getting married and me changing diapers at two in the morning whilst working three jobs just to support us," he muttered, his face relaxing as he spoke.

I sat down next to him. *Why would he think that anyway?* "What? Why would you see yourself doing that?" I asked, giggling again at how crazy he was.

He shrugged. "I wouldn't let you do it on your own. We'd get married, and I'd take care of you and the baby," he stated as if it was no big deal.

I felt my insides tingle with emotion; I was overcome with a rush of love for him, not love like what I felt for Will, but more like a brotherly love. I loved Nick dearly and I always would, we'd been through so much, and every single thing only ever brought us closer. I hugged him tightly, digging my fingers into his shoulders as I tried not to cry.

"You have to be the sweetest, most adorable boy in the world, Nick Golding." I pulled back, and he smiled at me softly. "You would really do that for me?" I asked, biting my lip at how thoughtful and selfless he was.

He nodded. "Sure I would, you're my best friend and always will be." He wiped my tears away with the back of one finger and looked at me curiously. "Okay so if I'm not gonna be a stepdad, then tell me about this trouble that you're actually in."

I pulled back as reality set in. I still needed to say the words and get it out there. "Okay, so I met Will in the summer. We broke up for a few weeks when school started, but then we got back together two months ago. You know all that already."

He nodded. "Yeah?" he confirmed, his tone prompting me for more.

I gulped. I was less worried now though, Nick was willing to ruin his life to help me had I been pregnant; surely he would help me by telling a couple of little lies if the need arose.

"Will's a bit older than me. He's twenty-two actually, and when we met he didn't realise how old I was, and I didn't tell him because I thought he knew. And… and…"

"And?" he prompted.

"I'm so totally in love with him, Nick. He loves me too, this isn't just some fling or anything, we're both completely serious. I need you to know that before I say it." I looked at him, begging him with my eyes not to freak out.

He nodded, looking a little sad for some reason. "I know you love him, Chloe, I can tell. You never once looked at me the way you look when you talk about him; I've known for a while that you're in love with this guy."

He looked a little hurt and I was struck with a rush of regret that I couldn't love Nick the way he obviously wanted me to. I wished I did. I wished I could make him happy and give him what he wanted because goodness knows he deserved it. He smiled but it didn't quite reach his eyes. I think it was a forced smile so that I wouldn't know how much I was hurting him, but it was too late, I'd already seen it and he couldn't hide it from me now. I knew right then that Nick wasn't over me, which was probably why he wasn't seeing other girls. That thought broke my heart because I never wanted to hurt him, ever. I wanted him to be happy, but we just weren't right together, we never were. Deep down we both knew that, but I guess he still wished something different.

"Well?" I jumped as his voice cut through my mind ramblings. I shook my head to clear it a little and looked at him; he was obviously still waiting for my 'trouble' to be revealed.

"Will is, well, he's," I took a deep breath, "he's our calculus teacher," I stuttered weakly.

Nick sprang up from the sofa, looking at me like I was crazy, but the hard, accusing glint in his eye told me he believed what I had said. I gulped and waited for his reaction.

Chapter Thirty-Six

"He's what?" he cried, shaking his head in disbelief. "Mr Morris? Are you freaking kidding me? A teacher? Tell me this is a joke, Chloe, for God's sake, this is insane!"

I gulped, immediately regretting my decision to tell him. On top of the anger that I could see plain across his face, I could also see a lot of hurt. I hated the fact that I'd hurt him, Nick didn't ever deserve to be hurt.

"Nick, calm down," I pleaded, giving him my best persuasive face.

He frowned and shook his head again, his hands gripping into his hair. "You're serious? This is for real; you're dating the damn teacher?"

I nodded in confirmation. "Yeah, I love him," I whispered, looking at him apologetically.

He looked at me sceptically. "You love him? How can you love a guy that would date a minor? Not only are you a damn minor but he's in charge of protecting you and looking after your wellbeing. He's taking advantage of you!" he shouted, looking at me as if I was stupid.

I could feel the anger boiling up inside me as I stood up too. "He's not taking advantage of me! Will you get a grip of yourself and let me explain?" I cried, throwing my hands up in exasperation.

He laughed humourlessly. "Sure, go ahead, say something that's going to make me believe that this guy isn't a damn pervert that's abusing his position at the school to prey on underage girls," he growled sarcastically.

My hand was itching to slap his face because he was disrespecting Will, but I held back my anger. I knew Nick was only saying these things because he was worried about me. He was just defending me. He didn't know Will the way that I did. Most people would see our relationship through Nick's eyes too and I needed to keep in mind that he was just trying to look out for me.

"When I met him in the summer I didn't tell him how old I was. We started dating, and he thought I was older. When we found out he was my teacher and that I was only seventeen, he broke it off immediately; he said exactly the same things that you've just said. He's not a bad guy, Nick. Please just calm down and listen to me for a minute," I begged.

His face softened slightly. I knew that he wouldn't stay mad at me forever, I could always rely on Nick to have my back, he'd calm down once he got over the initial shock of it all.

"If he's not a bad guy then why the hell is he dating one of his students? He's sick, this whole situation is sick and illegal," he countered, crossing his arms over his chest defensively.

I felt my chin wobble as the tears started to build up in my eyes. I hated that people would think that about Will. I closed my eyes and shook my head. "You can't help who you fall in love with," I whispered sadly.

A tear fell down my face. He groaned. "Don't cry, you know I hate it when you cry," he moaned, wrapping his arm around me and hugging me. I pressed my face into the crook of his neck and took a couple of deep breaths, trying to calm down as he stroked my back. I could feel all of his muscles bunched up and tense, probably because of the situation and the direction the conversation we were in the middle of.

"Nick, please don't think badly of him. He's such a great guy, he makes me so happy. Age is just a number after all. In a few years the five year age gap will seem like nothing. Please just try to see this from my point of view, please?" I begged against his neck.

He sighed. "Chloe, I don't like this situation at all. If he's such a great guy then he should have waited until you left school, he should have waited until it was legal for you to get together. This is wrong," he whispered, his hold on me tightening as I went to pull back from him.

I shook my head. "He did want to wait. I didn't," I told him, digging my fingers into his back, willing him to understand. "Nick, please, you're one of my best friends and I need you to understand."

He sighed and pulled back, cupping my face in his hands. He was just looking at me, his eyes soft and caring like usual, but his jaw was tight and tense. He clearly didn't like it at all. The silence was deafening as he just stared at me, looking like he was choosing his words carefully. I decided to break the tension and say something first.

"Please? It's not just a fling, I love him. I really want you two to get along because you're important to me, your opinion matters to me, and I really want you to like him. Please?" I whispered, giving him my begging face. This face always worked with Nick, he was so soft he never could stay mad at me or refuse me anything.

He sighed and closed his eyes. "He's serious about you too?" he asked quietly.

I felt my strained body start to relax as I nodded confidently. "Yeah, he's serious about me too," I confirmed.

He nodded, his whole face sad. "You do know that because he's an old man already, that he'll be grey soon, right?" he joked, a smile pulling at the corners of his mouth.

I laughed with relief. The intense situation was over; Nick the sweetie-pie was back. I nodded. "Yeah, I'll make him dye it," I agreed, playing along.

He laughed and opened his eyes looking at me a little exasperated. "You do get yourself into some crappy situations, don't you? Just aren't satisfied with a boring life are you?" he teased, digging me in the ribs with one finger.

I laughed and squirmed away from him, sitting on the sofa and pulling him down with me. "You haven't even heard the worst of it yet, this is just scratching the surface," I told him.

He frowned, looking a little concerned as he waited for me to tell him what I was talking about. I told him everything: how Will and I got back together, Erika finding out, the blackmailing - which made him hiss a string of expletives again. I told him about Sam's plan, the payback chores I had done, and my meeting with the Principal. The whole time he just sat there listening, watching me intently. When I was done, he blew out a big breath and slumped back in his chair.

"Wow, you weren't kidding when you said you were in trouble. The whole plan seems fool proof though, this Sam guy is an evil genius like you said," he agreed, nodding.

I smiled at the thought of Sam. I still owed him a big thanks. "Yeah, but there's something that I'm a little lacking on." I winced wondering if he would help me. He seemed to be okay with me seeing Will, well, 'okay' wasn't exactly the right word, he had stopped sneering when I mentioned his name now anyway which I took as a good sign.

"What's that?" he asked.

I took a deep breath. "Witnesses."

He raised one eyebrow. "I don't get it, Chloe. Dumb it down for me," he instructed, laughing at his own joke.

I smiled weakly. "I was kind of hoping that you would back me up a little and tell the Principal that you've heard of Sam. You don't have to say you've met him or anything, just that you know we're going out and that he's Will's brother." I winced, waiting for his reaction.

He frowned. "Look, Chloe, I understand that you want to date this guy, that's your choice, but how can I help you two sneak around and have an illegal relationship if I don't approve of it?" he countered, looking at me apologetically.

My heart sank. I really thought he would help me. "Nick, less than ten minutes ago you were willing to marry me because you thought I was knocked up, but you can't even go along with a lie to help me and Will not get into trouble?" I asked, quietly.

He groaned and closed his eyes; he was quiet for a little while, obviously thinking about what I had said. Finally he spoke, "Yeah, you're right, it would be hypocritical of me not to help. I would have married you, I would have devoted my life to you and a baby that wasn't mine, so I guess that the least I can do is tell a little lie," he agreed.

Happiness burst inside me. I squealed and threw myself at him, hugging him tightly. "Thank you!" I squeaked excitedly. Everything was set now; if the

Principal asked my two best friends then both of them would say they knew about Sam.

Nick laughed, seeming a little shocked as he patted my back. "Chill out, Chloe. It's not like I'm giving the old dude my blessing to hit up my bestie. He needs to work for my approval," he said, laughing.

I grinned and pulled back to look at him. Will would win Nick's approval once he got to know him more; they'd probably even be friends because they were both awesome people. I kissed his cheek affectionately. "You know you're an awesome friend, don't you?" I gushed, smiling gratefully.

He nodded and rolled his eyes. "Yeah I know. How about you show me how grateful you are by making dinner, I'm starving!" he joked, pushing me off of him and nodding his head towards the kitchen.

"You're always starving, I think you have worms," I teased, winking at him as I stood up.

"Hey, I don't have worms!" he cried with fake horror. "They're snakes," he added, patting his stomach and grinning. I burst out laughing and grabbed his hand, pulling him into the kitchen to choose what he wanted for dinner. I really had some incredible people in my life; I was a seriously lucky girl.

I didn't sleep a wink that night. After studying with Nick, he'd driven me home and I'd immediately called Will, talking to him until well after midnight. I was tired, but I just couldn't relax enough to succumb to sleep. I just couldn't stop worrying, trying to think of any holes in the plan. I was pretty sure we had everything covered; there was no CCTV in the classrooms so no one would have seen us kiss. We never did anything in the hallway where there were cameras; no one else had seen, or suspected anything.

The thing I was worried about was the jobs that I did for Erika. What if she had some footage of me arriving at her house or something? She could show the Principal, and then he would ask why I was at Erika's house doing chores for her. I was pretty sure she wouldn't go down that route though; wouldn't she be in more trouble for blackmail if she admitted it? Anyway, if she did go down that route I was going to say that she paid me to do those things. It would be her word against mine, and she would already look bad in the eyes of the Principal because of all of the teachers that would hopefully back us up.

I turned off my alarm before it even beeped and just sat on the edge of my bed, cradling my aching head in my hands. I was exhausted, but at the same time extremely keyed up and excitable, like an adrenalin rush or something. It was like an oxymoron, the two feelings inside me were clashing against each other, part of me wanted to fall into bed and sleep forever, the other part of me wanted to run to school and see what was happening.

I dressed slowly, wanting to kill some time, and then pushed my food around my bowl not really wanting to eat anything in case it made me feel sick. My stomach was already full of butterflies; I couldn't possibly fit much else in there. My cell phone rang in my bag so I pulled it out expecting it to be Amy, it wasn't, it was Will. I smiled tiredly and answered it.

"Hey, Cutie. So I was missing you really badly, and I wondered if I could pick you up a little early today?" he asked.

I smiled happily. I would love a few extra minutes with him this morning. I needed him to wrap his arms around me and tell me that he loved me in person, rather than over the phone. "What time were you thinking?" I asked, looking at my watch. It was just before eight, he didn't usually pick me up until eight thirty.

"I just pulled up outside. Whenever you're ready, I'll wait," he replied.

I laughed. "You're eager," I teased, grinning like an idiot and throwing my untouched Lucky Charms down the waste disposal.

"Always," he confirmed, laughing.

I grabbed my bag and shouted to my mom that I was leaving early, and then headed out of the door quickly. I practically ran to his jeep, so excited to see him that my whole body was tingling and prickling. I climbed in his car and sighed contentedly as he smiled at me. His beautiful smile brightened my day and made me forget how tired I was. His smile made everything right in my world. I would do anything for that smile. All of this was just a blip on the horizon, something we would look back on and laugh at one day - at least, I hoped so anyway.

"Good morning," he whispered, his gaze raking over my face. "You look like you didn't sleep well."

I laughed and scooted closer to him on the seat, wrapping my arms around his neck. "Was that a polite way of telling me I look terrible this morning?" I asked, pretending to be offended.

He smiled and shook his head slowly, tracing his finger across my cheek lightly. "You never look terrible to me, ever. You just look like you need a few hours sleep; maybe you should sleep at mine tonight. You always seem to sleep well in my bed," he whispered, running his nose up the side of mine lightly.

My insides danced with happiness at the thought of spending the night with him. I bit my lip and nodded. "Your bed is a lot comfier than mine," I mumbled, playing along.

He nodded. "It's agreed then. I'll pick you up at about half past three," he suggested.

I smiled at the thought. "Will, just stop talking and kiss me already!" I ordered, trying to look stern.

He grinned. "Yes, Miss Henderson," he stated, crashing his lips to mine. I smiled against his lips and pressed my body to his, feeling everything fall into place. Everything that was going on at the moment, everything that was stressing me out and making me lose sleep, it was all so totally worth it. *He* was so totally worth it.

He pulled back and looked at me curiously. "Did you eat breakfast?" he asked. I shook my head, chewing on my lip. He smiled. "Great. Let's go to that coffee shop that does the pastries that you like," he suggested happily.

I nodded in agreement. "Okay, but I'll run out and get them and we eat in the car," I compromised. It was a little way out of town, and it was early so no one should be there, but it wasn't worth taking the risk, not when we were in so much trouble already.

He started the engine, putting the car into drive, and then took my hand. "Whatever you want, Cutie."

The morning was almost painful. Every second felt like an hour, every hour felt like a day. All I could think about was the Principal asking around and making his investigations. Erika was walking around smirking at me whenever she saw me, she made a couple of "nice knowing you" comments, but I just ignored them. Nick, bless his little heart, was by my side and made a couple of sarcastic remarks back to her which she seemed extremely offended by. I silently wondered if I was right, was Erika hot for Nick? Even if she was, it wasn't going to get her anywhere with him though. He really hated her, now more than ever.

In the middle of my Spanish class someone came in with a note and handed it to the teacher. She immediately walked over to the front of my desk and looked at me curiously. "The Principal would like to see you, Chloe," she said, nodding to the door.

Oh God, please let this be okay!

I nodded, swallowing my fear and shoved my books into my bag. Amy was whispering over and over that everything was fine, that it was all working out perfectly. The Principal had approached Amy early this morning, asking about Sam. She had confirmed everything, even dropping herself in trouble by telling him that she was one of the ones at the club with me, and that she met Sam that night too. She'd encouraged Principal Sherman to speak to Nick too, and from what he'd told me, that meeting went well too. Nick had just said that I talked about Sam nonstop and that I was completely in love with him, but that he hadn't met him yet.

When I was all packed up I headed to the office and took a couple of deep breaths, gathering my confidence. As I walked to the office door and raised my hand to knock, it opened before my hand could make contact with the wood. Will was heading out of the office, Principal Sherman behind him, obviously seeing him out politely. They were both smiling. I gulped. *Yes, they're smiling! That's a good sign. Please let this have been fixed.*

"Oh, Chloe, great timing. Come on in," Principal Sherman enthused.

I looked at Will curiously just as he turned back to look at the balding little man. "Thanks for getting this all sorted out so quickly, Richard. It's nice to know that there is such a supportive network here at the school, something like this could have been disastrous if it wasn't handled in the timely and professional manner that you handled it in," he stated.

Wow, there's the professional Will again, using the big words.

Principal Sherman smiled warmly, and Will turned to walk out, stepping to the side so I could get past him. "Kiss ass," I whispered so quietly that the retreating, ageing Principal wouldn't have been able to hear me.

I heard Will chuckle as he closed the door behind me, leaving me in the office to fend for myself with the head of the school. I wanted to beg him to come back and hold my hand, but instead I put on my big girl panties and marched over to the free chair, sitting myself down and looking at Principal Sherman expectantly.

He smiled. "Okay, Chloe, I expect you know why you're here. I told you I would investigate the complaint that was made to me, and I have. As I'm sure you were expecting, the accusation has been proven false," he said, smiling almost apologetically.

I felt my leg spasm. I pressed my feet together to stop myself from jumping on his desk and doing a happy dance. I tried my best to keep my cool calm exterior as I nodded confidently. "Of course it was, it was just plain stupid," I scoffed, rolling my eyes for dramatic effect.

He nodded. "I'm very sorry you were dragged into all of this. I'm not sure if it was just a harmless prank, or if the complaint was made with malicious intent, but rest assured the complainant will be dealt with properly. I do not take kindly to time wasters, especially those that make up lies about one of my most promising young teachers." He frowned angrily and I felt a wave of sorrow for Erika. She was in deep trouble by the look on his face.

"What does that mean?" I asked, wanting to know what her punishment would be, but at the same time not really wanting to know.

He sighed and picked up his pen, tapping it on the desk unconsciously. The sound of the rhythmic tapping started driving me crazy almost immediately. "She has already been suspended from school for a week. She'll be stripped of her head cheerleader role, but I have allowed her to stay on as part of the team because I don't want the squad to suffer. Mr Morris has agreed that the punishment is sufficient. He's been very understanding and gracious about the whole thing. You're lucky to have such a bright and gifted teacher," he said, smiling fondly.

Wow, Will's making a great impression at this school!

I smiled and shrugged. "I'm luckier that he has such an awesome brother," I countered, grinning at the thought of Sam. That statement held more meaning that the Principal knew.

He smiled and looked at me a little bemused, like I was that stupid school girl again that didn't understand that she'd just dodged a bullet. *Trust me, I understand all right.* "Right, well, thank you for your time and you should probably get to class. Do you need a note to explain why you'll be late?" he asked, pulling open his drawers one by one, obviously looking for paper.

I shook my head and smiled. "No, it's cool; I have Mr Morris right now. I think he'll understand why I'm late," I chuckled.

Principal Sherman laughed too. "You're probably right there." He stood up, signalling the end of the meeting so I grabbed my school bag and stood too. "Thanks again for being so cooperative, I know this investigation couldn't have been easy on you," he said, smiling kindly.

I shrugged. "It's fine. It was actually pretty funny. Sam was laughing for hours when I told him that people thought I was getting it on with his nerdy brother," I lied, faking disgust at the end. He laughed and gave me that 'you're a silly little girl' smile again. "Oh, wait! You said the person was stripped of head cheerleader. Does that mean it was Erika Dennison that tried to get me into trouble?" I asked, already knowing the answer.

He smiled sadly. "Yes, but I'd appreciate it if you could just leave it alone. She's been punished and spoken to. If you have any problems with her when she comes back after her suspension, then please come to me, don't try to settle anything or seek revenge. If there is trouble between the two of you then I'll have to treat it as a separate incident, and you'll both be in trouble, understand?" he asked, looking at me sternly.

I nodded. *There goes my punching her in the face fantasy.* "Okay," I agreed reluctantly. I slung my bag over my shoulder and practically skipped to calculus. I felt like a weight had been lifted off of my shoulders. Now that everything was sorted I felt like I could breathe properly again. I didn't realise how stressed it was making me.

Will smiled at me as I walked into his class. I caught Amy's eye and nodded. A smile stretched across her face too as she seemed to relax. I weaved through the rows of seats and chose an empty one, trying desperately not to grin like an idiot that had just won the lottery.

When the final bell rang I just packed up and left without saying anything to Will. I didn't need to; we'd already made our plans for tonight. He was picking me up from my house in half an hour. *I guess we'll be celebrating tonight!*

As I got to my locker my cell phone vibrated in my pocket. I plucked it out, expecting a call from Will so I didn't even bother looking at the caller ID as I answered it.

"Hey there, boyfriend," I chirped, grinning like a madwoman.

I heard laughter down the line. "Hey there, girlfriend," Sam answered.

I blushed and rolled my eyes. *I wasn't living that one down anytime soon I bet.* "Hi, Sam-bo."

"Foxy," he said, his tone warning. I laughed. He hated me calling him that. To be honest if he didn't hate it so much I probably wouldn't do it. His reaction to it was just too good to miss. "I'm outside, come meet me," he ordered lazily.

I frowned in confusion. *He's outside?* "Huh?" I shrugged at Amy who was looking at me curiously, I mouthed to her that Sam was outside. "Okay, let me just grab my books then. What are you doing here anyway?"

He laughed. "Just stop with the questions and get your pretty little behind out here. I'm bored of waiting already, and some of these high school girls are starting to undress me with their eyes, you know how self-conscious I get when people look at me," he joked.

I laughed and grabbed my books from my locker. Linking my arm through Amy's, I skipped out of the front doors and disconnected the line. Sam was standing there, leaning against the side of his car, looking hot as usual. He really wasn't lying when he said that some of the girls were looking at him, they really were. I couldn't exactly blame them; the Morris boys sure were easy on the eye.

I smiled as I walked up and he moved, pulling out a huge bunch of red tulips from behind his back, holding them out to me. I gasped and looked at them shocked. *Why would he buy me flowers? And, how did he know which were my favourite?* I frowned, a little bemused as I walked up to him. People were stopping to watch now. A hot guy parked in the no parking zone, holding out a bunch of flowers, wasn't something that happened every day at our school.

When I got up to him, he smiled and handed me the flowers. "From Will," he whispered, stepping closer to me.

I felt my heart speed up a little because Will had asked his brother to give these to me. *Aww, he's so freaking adorable.* I suddenly realised why Sam was here - more witnesses for our fake relationship. I just wished Will had told me that he'd arranged this so I wasn't so surprised.

"That's very sweet, thanks, Sam," I gushed, running my finger along the petals, just melting inside at how adorable my boyfriend was.

Suddenly Sam wrapped his arm around my waist and pulled me closer to him. I let out a little gasp of shock as I was yanked forward and crashed against his chest, barely managing to move my flowers out of the way in time. He smirked at me and crashed his lips to mine, kissing me for the fourth time.

I whimpered against his lips but didn't try to pull away. If this was Will's plan then I needed to go along with it. I trusted Will completely so if he asked Sam to kiss me in front of a load of students then I'd let him.

When he finally pulled back, I smiled awkwardly. "I'd rather Will give that gift to me in person," I joked quietly, knowing no one was close enough to hear our conversation.

Sam laughed. "No, that one was from me," he replied, shrugging.

What the heck? Will hadn't told him to kiss me? I slapped his arm and gasped. "Sam!" I cried, shaking my head shocked that he'd just kissed me again.

He laughed and grinned at me wickedly. "You know I love to piss off my brother! He goes that awesome shade of red, it's incredible," he stated, laughing as I slapped his arm again. "Relax, Foxy, it's not like I want to kiss you. I mean jeez, I need some mouthwash or something to kill all of the Will germs you just passed onto me." He faked a shudder for dramatic effect.

I closed my eyes and laughed quietly as he led me to his car. Sam really was too funny, and he just couldn't resist an opportunity to tease the life out of his brother.

Chapter Thirty-Seven

The following week was just a normal week. It actually felt so strange though because my life hadn't been normal for so long that I was just expecting something bad to happen, some jealous ex-girlfriend of Will's to pop out of the woodwork and tell him she was pregnant, or someone else to catch us and tell the Principal again. I was even waiting for Nick to beat the crud out of Will for 'abusing his position in authority to prey on young girls', but none of that happened.

Nick did speak to Will though, in private, Will had told me that night what he'd said. Apparently, Nick had told him how important I was to him and how he didn't want to see me hurt, how he didn't like the situation, but he liked how happy I was. I would imagine there were a few threats involved in that conversation too, but Will didn't go into details about those with me. All in all, Nick seemed a lot more comfortable around him; I was guessing it would only be a matter of time before they were friends. They were both great people and had awesome personalities, they would probably end up being drinking buddies or something – well, when Nick was old enough to drink anyway.

People were talking endlessly about Erika though. You couldn't walk down the hallway on the day following her suspension, without someone mentioning her name. Speculation started immediately about why she had been suspended and demoted from cheer captain. Will told me that night that Erika wasn't allowed to tell anyone the true reason because that would add fuel to a 'false rumour', so we were pretty much out of it at the moment. If she decided that she wanted to spread the news around school about me and Will, then there would be even more trouble for her, the Principal had apparently made that abundantly clear to her.

Because no one knew the truth about her suspension, the guesses were getting pretty wild. Some of them were actually outrageous. I heard one girl spreading that Erika had a nervous breakdown, that she'd ate a whole jar of mayonnaise and then stripped naked and done a dance on the Principal's desk. Another one was that she'd had a bad nose job and this was all just a conspiracy, that she hadn't really been suspended at all, she was just waiting for the swelling to go down.

The other gossip that was going around the school hallways: My hottie boyfriend. The same one that had picked me up from school with a bunch of tulips. Everyone wanted to know every single detail about Sam. When word got out that he was a teacher's brother – and not just any teacher, but the hottest one the school had ever had – people literally went crazy.

I was being hounded for information on Will; they wanted to know everything about him. Had I met his girlfriend, was he seeing Miss Teller, was he gay, has he come out to his parents yet, where did he live. The questions were endless and actually a little stalkerish. Will definitely had a lot of fan girls at school.

I had a great week, but it was only a matter of time before 'she' came back. I was dreading it. I had no idea what she would do or say. She was going to hate me even more now; I would definitely be back on her radar. I sensed a lot of things going wrong in my life again, just like it used to. Notes stuck on my back, my locker filled with mud, my books going missing. I had dealt with all of that from her before; I guessed I would have to deal with it again.

When that dreaded Monday morning came around, I stepped hesitantly into the school. Nick's arm was firmly around my shoulder for support. He'd picked me up this morning instead of Will because he didn't want me to walk into the school on my own on Erika's first day back. I chewed on my lip as I scanned the immediate area, but I couldn't see any commotion or anything. If she was here already then wouldn't people be surrounding her, asking for details and explanations?

I looked at Nick. "Think maybe her rich parents were so embarrassed by her behaviour, that they sent her to a private boarding school somewhere really far away, to finish her senior year?" I asked, smiling at him hopefully.

He laughed and shook his head. "Since when have you been that lucky?"

I sighed and closed my eyes, letting him lead me along towards my locker. I put in my combination and opened it hesitantly, stepping back, expecting piles of manure to fall on my shoes. But there was nothing in there, nothing unusual in the slightest. *Is she not coming in today? Maybe I've got the days mixed up, and she's due back tomorrow instead? Maybe she's sick?*

I breathed a sigh of relief, but obviously I did it too soon.

Whispers erupted from all around me, people stopped what they were doing and looked up the hallway as about ten people were all walking down the hallway, firing questions one after the other to the girl in the centre of the group. I gulped as her eyes met mine. There was a hard, icy edge to her look that sent shivers down my spine. *Wow, and she calls me the Ice Princess!*

Her jaw tightened, and my heart dropped into my stomach. Her long legs made her almost glide down the hallway towards me. It was like a scene from a movie where the bad guy makes their entrance and everyone parts for them as they keep their eyes locked on their poor victim. Yep, that poor victim

305

was me, and I was more than slightly intimidated by her entrance - maybe that was her intention, I wasn't sure.

Oh God, please don't let her accuse me of it in the middle of the hallway and start this all off again. Please don't let there be any more trouble for Will. I can cope with anything that she can throw at me, as long as she doesn't get him involved anymore.

She was ignoring everyone around her as they asked her where she'd been and if any of the rumours were true. I noticed with some satisfaction that her hair had definitely lost that beautiful shine that it used to have; it was now a dull blonde. I bit back a smile and wondered how much of the hair dye shampoo she had left before she would run out and her hair would return to its normal brilliance.

Nick stepped to my side and bent to whisper in my ear, I felt his breath tickle my cheek, but I didn't hear what he said. It was like everything else faded into the background except for me and her. I couldn't hear the commotion that was sure to be going on around me. All I could focus on was her evil face as she stared at me intently.

She stopped in front of me and I took the opportunity to speak before she did. "Hi there, Erika, where have you been? People were saying that you went on vacation," I chirped, faking confidence. I looked her up and down obviously. "You don't look very tanned; did it rain the whole time?"

She sneered at me and didn't bother answering my comment; she just flicked her hand in a dismissive gesture to the gaggle of girls hanging around begging for her attention. My mind dimly registered that they all left straight away. I knew they wouldn't go far though; they'd be waiting to speak to her as soon as she'd finished wiping the floor with my face. She turned her head and looked to my left, her jaw tightening, her eye making the smallest little twitch and started to soften slightly, before I felt an arm slip around my shoulder and Erika's eyes immediately blazed again.

"Just leave, Nick. I want to talk to her in private, we have unfinished business," Erika ordered, looking at Nick who was standing next to me protectively.

He laughed. "You think I'm gonna walk away because you do that nasty little hand flick thing? Yeah okay, whatever you say, sweetheart," he mocked, rolling his eyes. He turned to me. "Want to get out of here? There's a bad smell lingering in this area."

She made what sounded like a growl of frustration and gripped my arm. "I want to talk to you, now!" she hissed, her voice menacing and harsh.

I shook off her hold. My hand clenched into a fist as I desperately wanted to carry out that fantasy I'd once had where I smashed her face first into the lockers. I raised myself to my full height and pulled my shoulders back as I spoke, "You and I have nothing to say to each other."

She snorted and looked at me with disbelief clear across her face. Judging by the shock that was clear on her features, she was obviously expecting me to apologise or beg and grovel for her forgiveness for getting her

306

in trouble. She would be waiting a long time if that was what she was expecting from me.

She leant in closer to me; her lips pulling back in a menacing way, showing off her perfectly straight, pearly white teeth that I bet had cost her daddy a fortune. "Oh I think we have a lot to talk about. Now, shall we do this in private, or in the middle of the hallway?" she spat.

I gulped. The venom in her voice was truly scary, but if she laid one finger on me then I was giving as good as I got. I wracked my brain, trying to remember the lessons Nick had given me a couple of years ago, self-defence lessons and how to throw a decent punch. I didn't want to do a Bella Swan and break a bone while I broke Erika's face. Maybe I should have gotten Nick to give me a refresher course, ready for this moment.

I nodded back towards the bathrooms. If she was going to do this either way then I would rather it done in private. Maybe she didn't care if she got into more trouble, maybe she just wanted to get the truth out there. Even just a rumour could ruin Will's career, an accusation like that wouldn't be easily forgotten.

"Bathrooms?" I suggested.

She nodded and turned on her four inch heel, strutting in there, tossing her hair over her shoulder with a flick of her head. I winced and looked at Nick for support. I was probably lucky that Amy wasn't here because she would have probably thrown the first punch for sure; she had more of a fiery temper than mine.

Nick smiled reassuringly. "Want me to come?" he offered, looking like he actually wanted to.

I laughed. "You always did have a thing for the girls' bathrooms," I joked.

He laughed and nodded. "It's a magical place." He bent down and kissed my cheek, leaning in close to my ear. "Just tell her to go play with traffic and then ask her how much trouble she got in for lying," he whispered.

I smiled and pulled out of his arms. I couldn't help but wish Will was here with me. I needed a hug from him, a smile, a touch of his hand, anything. He always had a calming presence around him that I could really use right about now. I took a deep breath and followed Erika into the girls' bathroom.

When I got in there she immediately flicked the lock on the door so no one else could get in with us. I watched as she put her Gucci purse on the counter, moving it slightly until she was happy with it. She was probably worried about it getting damaged; it probably cost enough to refit the tired looking school restrooms.

"Well, have you got something to say to me?" she snapped, her eyes hard and accusing.

I raised one eyebrow. "Sure I have, but none of it is very tasteful," I offered, shrugging, smiling at her sweetly. There was no way I was causing trouble. *She's goading me, trying to get me to hit her or something so she can go and report me. Stupid witch!*

307

She frowned. "I can't believe that you've gotten away with this! You're the one doing something illegal, and I'm the one that gets suspended," she ranted, throwing her hands up in exasperation. I briefly felt sorry for her, she was right, all she was doing was telling the truth, yet she got into trouble for it. But the guilt faded as she sneered at me and carried on talking. "What does a guy like that see in a girl like you anyway? I mean, look at you," she hissed, raking her eyes down my body slowly, a distasteful scowl on her face. "You're nothing special, but yet he still kissed you."

I flinched under her scrutiny. *Do I really look that bad that she has to look at me with that much hatred and disgust? I know I'm not the prettiest girl around, but I'm not that bad, surely.* I was always happy with just being me, shouldn't that be good enough? Will certainly seemed to think so.

"Why do you hate me so much?" I asked her, shaking my head in confusion. I had no idea what I'd ever done to make her dislike me like she did; she always just had a problem with me and Amy.

"Because you have everything!" she shouted, glowering at me.

I took a step back from the venom in her voice, she actually sounded scary when she shouted like that. I looked at her curiously, trying to work out her comment. *I have everything? She's the one with the rich daddy that gives her everything she asks for, designer clothes, the latest technology, horses, shiny cars — even though that must now smell like rancid meat. What could I possibly have, that she doesn't have? She's Erika Freaking Dennison. She lives like a princess.*

"I... what?" I frowned; she must have lost the plot somehow.

She turned away from me, her shoulders slumping as she walked over to the sink and gripped the edge tightly. "You have everything, and you don't even see it. I've always been jealous of you, you and stupid Amy Clarke! Ugh, you were always together all through school, every year you just got closer and closer, and all I got were fake friends that want to use me for a bit of popularity and my parents status. Your parents come to the school plays, they take an interest in you, they care about you, yet my family would rather throw money at me than spend one minute in my presence," she muttered, so quietly that I had to strain to hear her.

Wait, she's jealous of me? Me and Amy?

She laughed, but it held no humour. She grabbed a paper towel from the side and ran it under the faucet, wetting it before dabbing it under her eyes, checking her make-up. She fiddled with her purse, moving it again, closer to me for some reason, probably scared to get water on the expensive little thing.

She turned back to me and shook her head. Her smile looked a little... sad? "You two found each other on the first day of school. I remember sitting there in fifth grade just watching you two laughing at some private joke, while I always struggled to make good friends that didn't stab me in the back or drop me at the sight of a cute boy." She sniffed loudly and I just stood there like an idiot, not knowing what on earth to say. "The boys all flocked to you two, because of your ability to laugh and joke around. Then as they got older, they liked your stupid honey coloured hair and brown eyes. I hated that I never had anything like what you have. Then along came… Nick," she said, her chin trembled when she said his name. I knew right then and there that I was right; she had a thing for him.

"You like Nick?" I asked weakly.

She snorted and shook her head a little too forcefully. "No way! As if! He's just, ugh, he's so frustrating and… no!" she stated, crossing her arms over her chest defensively.

I bit back a smile. To quote Queen Gertrude and Shakespeare: 'The lady doth protest too much, methinks'.

I nodded. "Just checking, I thought that was a little too out there. I mean, Nick's not good enough to be with you, right? He's just plain old Nick Golding, nothing special," I lied, watching her reaction to me putting him down.

Her face scrunched up and she looked a little angry for a second at what I'd said. I had the strong feeling that she was going to disagree with me, but then the look was gone to be replaced by the famous Erika scowl. Her eyes flicked to her purse again as she spoke. "Whatever, I'm not here to talk about him," she stated, waving her hand dismissively before tossing her hair over her shoulder. "I wanted to talk to you about how much freaking trouble I got in for telling the truth about your sordid little affair with Mr Hottie Teacher."

A sudden thought hit me. Was she trying to trick me into admitting it or something? It wouldn't surprise me if it turned out that the expensive purse that she keeps shifting around on the side, has a tape recorder in there or something.

The sneaky little…

I cocked my head to the side and smiled. *Okay, two can play at that game!* "Seriously? Why are you trying to get me and him in trouble? I don't get what I've ever done to you to make you want to lie to the Principal and get Will in trouble too," I replied, raising one eyebrow at her.

She frowned. "I wasn't lying and we both know it!"

I shook my head and sighed. "Look, I'd love nothing more than to break that expensive looking nose job for you for making up these ridiculous lies about me and a teacher. Erika, this is sick," I said, playing along.

I hope she does have a damn tape recorder in there to catch all of this stuff, if she's thinking I'm going to slip up then she has another thing coming. There was no way I was letting the love of my life get into trouble because some snooty little rich girl was jealous that I had great friends while she just had minions. If she weren't such a bitch in the first place then she would have normal friends. Heck, if she had wanted to sit with us in fifth grade, then Amy and I would have let her, all she had to do was show a little interest. I think we'd once asked her to come to lunch with us, and she told us that she'd rather pick fleas off of the class rabbit than be seen dead with two losers like us.

"Sick? SICK? You're freaking sick for dating a teacher!" she shouted.

I laughed at her. She was getting frustrated that this little plan wasn't working I could see it in her eyes. "I'm not dating a freaking teacher. I'm dating his little brother! Haven't you heard that this week? Oh wait, of course you wouldn't have heard that, you were suspended for making up vicious lies!" I countered, smirking at her.

She stepped towards me, her face like thunder. "Bitch," she spat. Her eyes were wild, like a crazed animal or something and actually a little scary.

I stood my ground though, there was no way I was letting her intimidate me, if she wanted to hit me then I was giving back as good as I got, that was for sure. "If you touch me then I'm ripping out that dull blonde hair of yours," I stated. Her eyes flashed as a hand instantly flew to her hair, smoothing it down. "By the way, did you dye it while you were away? If so, then I'm not too sure the colour works for you," I teased, trying not to laugh.

She stepped closer to me, her face inches from mine. "You'll get yours, Ice Princess. You'd better watch your back because I'll get even with you for getting me suspended, I swear," she growled.

She turned and stalked back to her purse that she'd left on the side. I pulled out my cell phone from my pocket, praying that my bluff would work. "Erika, I hope you know that I just recoded that whole conversation. If one thing happens to me, my friends, or even my boyfriend's brother, then I'm taking that threat that you just made, to the Principal. I don't think he'd be too happy to hear that you're continuing your malicious campaign against me," I lied. "He's already told me that if you give me any problems when you come back then I was to go to him straight away."

Oh crud, please don't ask me to play the recording, please don't ask me to play the recording! Poker face, Chloe. You can do it, don't back down!

Her mouth dropped open in shock as she looked at the phone in my hand. I gulped, praying that she would believe me. She looked to be weighing her options, thinking it though, I could see frustration and anger clear across her face, she looked like she wanted to rip my head off and flush it down the toilet or something.

"You little-" she started, but I cut her off with a wave of my hand.

"Now, now, watch your language. Don't want to get you cussing on tape too, do we?" I teased as I pushed the phone back into my pocket. I smiled at her smugly. *This is awesome; she's totally fallen for it.* I stepped closer to her. "I'm serious. If you start trying to get me in trouble again, start picking on me like you used to, or even start hounding Will or my friends, then I'm taking that threat to the Principal. Then you can say bye-bye to your education at this school," I stated, using her words that she'd once said to me.

Her mouth snapped shut, her shoulders stiffened as she glowered at me. "I hate you," she growled.

I nodded. "I know, but you should try not to play the victim all the time, Erika, it's not good for you. You know, if you tried a little harder to be nice to people, your life would change. If you go through life hating people, then they're going to hate you back. Try sharing a little compassion once in a while, you'd be surprised how far it gets you." I meant it; I wasn't teasing her or anything. She made her life into what it was; she was the one that forced all of the nice people out of her life by picking on them and being a spiteful jealous bitch. If she was nicer to people then she could have nice friends, instead of the users that followed her around at the moment.

She grabbed her purse and marched to the door, slamming her shoulder against mine as she passed me, almost knocking me over. "Just stay the hell away from me!" she ordered, obviously choosing to ignore my advice.

I shrugged. "My pleasure," I agreed.

Without another word she unlocked the door and stormed out. Within seconds the door opened again and both Amy and Nick came in with worried faces. I smiled weakly and shrugged. "It's fine," I reassured them. Amy smiled and pulled me into a hug. I looked over her shoulder at Nick; he was standing there with a smile on his face, his eyes flicking around the bathroom. I laughed and rolled my eyes. "As good as you remembered?" I asked him.

He laughed and rubbed the back of his neck awkwardly. "Last time I was in here it was definitely pretty magical," he stated, winking at me teasingly. I blushed and shook my head, knowing that the last time he was in here with me we'd had a pretty intense make out session. That was not too long before we broke up. He grinned and nodded back towards the door. "Come on then let's get out of here before I get the snot beaten out of me by Will and Ryan for being in the bathrooms with their bitches," he joked, winking at us teasingly.

We all burst out laughing at his comment, Nick always did know how to lighten the mood and cheer me up. Amy slapped him on the back of the head as we all walked out of the door; I ignored people looking at me curiously. I bit my lip worriedly. *Did Erika said anything when she came out? Oh please don't let her have said anything!*

I turned to Donna, the nearest girl who was looking at me. "What's up with everyone?" I asked, praying it would be anything other than me and Will.

She shrugged. "Did she tell you why she was suspended? What did she want?" she asked, raising an eyebrow at me curiously.

I breathed a sigh of relief and smiled. She hadn't said anything, we were safe. "We were just talking about our History project. She wanted to know how we got on with it because she missed last week so she didn't know where we were or anything. And no, she didn't say what she got suspended for," I lied, crossing my fingers that I sounded convincing.

Donna seemed to buy it; she frowned, looking a little disappointed as she nodded. "Oh well, I guess we'll find out sooner or later," she said easily as she turned and headed over to her friends who were also eagerly awaiting the Erika gossip.

I gulped, silently hoping that no one ever found out. With the threats of the Principal hanging over her head, she wasn't allowed to say anything to anyone, so as long as Will and I didn't slip up and admit anything, then we were practically home free. Just a few more months and then my school career would be over and we could put this whole mess behind us. All I would need to worry about then would be telling Amy that I couldn't go to college in New York with her as planned.

Chapter Thirty-Eight

"Cutie, just apply for your dream school!" Will ordered, looking at me sternly, using the teacher voice that he had.

I sighed and put my head in my hands. We were currently lying on his bed, my college applications scattered all over the place. We were right in the middle of having the painful conversation of which school I would choose. It wasn't an easy conversation at all. Will was seriously pissed off with me.

I shook my head, not looking at him and buried my face in his sheets. "No," I muttered.

He groaned in frustration. "Chloe, for pity sake, don't do this! You've had your heart set on that school forever, you said so yourself, so just apply to it! What harm will it do?" he asked, wrapping his arm around my waist and pulling me closer to him.

I sighed dramatically; he just wasn't listening to me at all. What was the point in me applying to go there if I had no intention of accepting even if I did get a place? There was no way in hell I was leaving him to go study in New York, it was hours away, and I just couldn't be away from him for that long. I'd hardly ever get to see him; weekends just weren't enough for me.

"What's the point? I don't want to go there anymore; I want to stay here so I'll be closer to you!" I moaned, burying my face in his chest. I didn't want to look at him, I knew the face he would be pulling right now, the cute puppy dog face with the begging eyes, and I couldn't see it because I needed to stay strong. Sure, that school had been important to me before, but now that I had him, everything just seemed less important. Why would I go there and make myself unhappy? But he just wasn't getting my point.

"Chloe, just apply to go there, if it's something that you want then-" he started, but I interrupted before he could finish.

"It's not," I stated confidently.

He stroked the back of my head softly, his body tight with stress. He obviously didn't like this conversation either. "Cutie, will you look at me?" he asked, quietly.

"No."

He laughed. "And why's that?"

I sighed. "Because you'll do that thing with your eyes and convince me to do something that I don't want to do," I whined, my voice still muffled because my face was pressed against his T-shirt.

"Cutie, just look at me! I don't want to have this conversation with the top of your head!" he cried, pulling on my arms to get me to move.

I groaned in frustration and sat up next to him, reluctantly dragging my eyes to his face, seeing the expression that I knew would be there. "See, there's the face. I knew it!" I stated, waving my hand at his face in example.

He smiled at me and we both burst into laughter. "You're silly sometimes, Miss Henderson," he teased, gripping my waist and pulling me down so I was now lying on top of him.

I rested my forearms either side of his head and smiled. He was so incredible, and I loved him so much - a little sacrifice over the destination of my schooling was nothing when you considered I would get him in exchange. I'd been thinking about it for the last two months, and I was totally sure this was what I wanted. I would go to a local school, but still do the same course. Sure, I'd miss Amy like crazy, but I'd still get to see Nick all the time so I'd still have a great friend nearby. And of course I would get to see the man of my dreams every day, which was the deciding factor here.

Everything had been perfect for the last two months. Erika had backed off completely; she didn't even speak to me. Sure, she still hated me, that much was obvious by the way she looked at me, but she hadn't said anything to anyone. Sam and I had kept up the act of dating. He picked me up a couple of times a week and drove me to Will's place, then he would either hang out with us, or leave us so we could have private time. Sam was incredible, still a slutty whore, but that made him all the more special to me.

Will was just being Will: sweet, thoughtful, generous, loving, he was just being the incredible boyfriend that he always was. We hadn't been out much, not even to the next town, because we didn't want to risk anything. The only places we hung out were his place, his parents' house, or if we went to one of his friends' parties, but then only if Sam was going too so if we saw anyone we knew then I could pretend to be with him instead. But just spending time with Will made my heart soar in my chest. It didn't matter what we did or where we went, I loved every single second of being with my boyfriend. We avoided each other like the plague in school, not even speaking unless it was about his class, and other people were around. We were leaving nothing to chance, and it was paying off. Two months had passed since the Erika incident and the Principal hadn't even looked twice at us since then.

We were on easy street; this was the home stretch now. Just three more months left of school and then it wouldn't even be illegal anymore for us to date. I was even turning eighteen in a couple of weeks so he wouldn't have to feel guilty about me being a minor. He was looking forward to that apparently.

314

The latest hurdle to be overcome: finish this stupid conversation about long distance relationships.

For the last half an hour he'd been listing ways that we would make it work, how there was always Skype, texting, phone calls, emails, and everything else that he'd thrown at me to try and convince me. None of that was enough for me though; I wanted to be able to touch him whenever I felt like it. I wanted to be able to fall asleep in his arms and hug him tight after a hard day. I wanted to look into the eyes of the man that I loved when we spoke, not into a stupid webcam.

"Can we please stop talking about this now?" I begged, pouting at him.

He frowned and shook his head. "Look, just apply for the school. Do it for me. If you get accepted then we'll talk about it some more then. Let's just not make the decision right now, okay? If you apply then that just gives you another option in a couple of months. You might decide you've had enough of me by then, and you might have thrown your dream school away for nothing," he stated, looking right into my eyes, his hands cupping my face so I couldn't look away.

I felt my heart rate increase. Was he getting me to apply there because he wanted me to leave? Was he hoping I'd leave so we'd have time apart? Maybe he wanted to break it off with me and just thought it would be easier to let us simply drift apart because of the distance.

"Will, is that really it? You don't just want me to go, do you? Because… you know," I shrugged, not wanting to know the answer.

He looked at me curiously. "You know, *what?*"

I sighed. "That you just want me to go so we won't be together all the time. Am I crowding you or something? Is this a subtle way of telling me tha-" He cut me off by kissing me. I kissed him back, pressing my body to his, loving the feel of his lips on mine.

He broke the kiss and frowned at me, shaking his head. "Are you actually crazy, Cutie? Should I be worried that you've lost your mind?" he teased playfully. I looked at him curiously, not knowing what he was talking about. He laughed and brushed his hand down the side of my face. "Stop that thought right now, okay? If you left I'd miss you more than anything, I'm not even sure how I'd cope. I'd definitely need to start working at the club again so I could pay the phone bill I'd run up from calling you all the time. I just want you to go to your dream school; I don't want to take that away from you. If you hadn't met me then you'd go there and do what you always planned to do with your best friend."

I felt my body relax. He was just being the sweet and concerned Will again; this wasn't about him wanting to get rid of me at all. I traced my nose up the side of his. "If I hadn't met you then I'd still be looking for my Mr Perfect," I whispered, kissing him again.

I felt him smile against my lips so I pulled back and sat up, straddling him, sitting on his stomach. "You think I'm perfect?" he asked, looking at me

315

cockily, trailing one finger up my leg slowly, making my hormones start to spike.

I laughed and shook my head. "No actually. You're a messy math nerd," I replied, grinning at his put out face. "You snore, you leave the toilet seat up, and you can't cook. Nope, Mr Morris, you aren't perfect at all," I teased, sticking my tongue out at him.

He smirked at me and grabbed my waist, pushing me down on the bed and rolling on top of me, crushing all of my college applications under us as he pinned me down. "Well you're way to clean. You always leave the toilet seat down so I have to put it up again. You eat disgusting cereal for breakfast, and you suck at math," he replied, pressing himself to me tighter. "But all of those things make you perfect in my eyes, Cutie," he finished.

"Aww, Will, that's so sweet," I moaned.

He smiled. "I love all of those things. I love every single thing about you, even the bad things," he cooed. "Wait, actually, there is one thing that I don't love about you," he said, frowning at me thoughtfully. I winced and waited for him to tell me I was too whiney or immature or something. His eyes were locked on mine as he spoke again, "You always wear too many damn clothes."

I burst out laughing as he frowned at the shirt I was wearing. "You're such a pervert! Maybe we should have one day a week where we just don't wear clothes at all. Just walk around all day butt naked. We could call it naked Saturday or something," I suggested, wrapping my arms around his neck tightly.

"Naked weekends are better," he chirped, grinning excitedly.

I smiled and nodded. "Naked weekends are definitely better. I'll check my diary and see if I can pencil you in for next week," I teased, gripping my hand into the back of his hair.

"Great," he whispered, kissing me softly. I sighed contentedly and closed my eyes, just taking in the luxury of being in this man's arms. I still wasn't used to it, I didn't think I'd ever be used it, I hoped I never took it for granted. He pulled out of the kiss and put his forehead to mine. "Apply to your dream school," he begged, his nose brushing against mine. "Just apply, that's all. Then, if you get accepted and still don't want to go there, then don't. Just don't throw away the option. Please?"

I reluctantly agreed. I had no doubt in my mind though that if I did get accepted, that I would reject the place. I wasn't moving to New York, and that was final. I didn't care how much he gave me the puppy dog face. But if it ended this conversation, I'd apply. It couldn't do any harm. If filling in a couple of forms and writing a couple of essays, stopped us talking about it, then I was all up for that.

He physically relaxed on top of me, his shoulders loosened, a beautiful smile stretched across his face. "Thank you, Cutie," he whispered, kissing me again. I wrapped my legs around his waist tightly, crushing his body against mine. My excitement peaked as his weight pressed my down into the soft mattress.

My hands roamed his body, slipping under his T-shirt, my fingers tracing across his back as he continued to kiss me as if he could devour my soul. Every kiss from Will literally made my toes curl up in ecstasy. It was beautiful. His kissing was almost poetic. I was a seriously lucky girl.

"So, about this naked weekend..." he trailed off, cupping my face and kissing the tip of my nose.

I smiled. *Was he serious about that? I was joking when I suggested it! I bet the damn pervert makes me do that now too! What have I gotten myself into?* "What about it?" I asked, my voice barely working as my mind wandered to his body, his perfection just on show for forty-eight blissful hours. *Actually, I hoped he does make us go through with it.*

He sighed. "It'll have to start from Saturday night I'm afraid. I have something I need to do during the day so I can't see you," he said, shrugging as he pushed himself up off of me, sitting next to me on the bed.

I frowned at his comment. Will and I always spent Saturday daytime together. What was he doing that meant I couldn't see him? "Oh really? What are you up to?" I asked, trying not to sound like an obsessive whiney girlfriend because he was blowing me off for the day.

He smiled and shrugged. "I have some shopping to do. A girl I know has a birthday coming up so I need to get her a present."

Wait, he's blowing me off so he can buy me a birthday present? Well that sucks! I pouted and pushed myself up too, moving so I could sit up on his lap, facing him. "What if this girl you know, doesn't want anything for her birthday?" I countered, wrapping my arms around his neck.

He laughed and flicked my nose, rolling his eyes playfully. "Tough luck for her I guess."

I sighed dramatically. "Will, don't buy me anything. I don't want you to spend your money on me," I insisted, pouting at him again. I really didn't want a present from him, his time and company were more than I could wish for.

He ran his hand down my back, stopping when he got to my ass, one of his hands pushed down the back of my jeans, his finger stroking across the material of my panties, making my whole body ache with need. "I'm getting you a present, Cutie. It's not every day that your girlfriend turns eighteen. It's a special birthday, one you should remember forever. I want to get you something that you can keep and remember too," he explained, shrugging. "Is there anything you actually want for your birthday? I mean, I have something I want to get you, but if there's something you want me to get then I'll get that too." He looked at me curiously.

His whole speech about my birthday being special and how I would remember it forever, made me want just one thing. If there was one thing that would make my birthday special, it was him. All of him.

I traced my finger across the line of his jaw as I wondered how to phrase it without me sounding like some sort of nymphomaniac or something. "There is actually one thing that I want. And you're the only one that can give it to me," I flirted, kissing the base of his throat.

"And what's that?" he croaked huskily. I moved up and nibbled on the edge of his jaw. His grip on me tightened. "Chloe, shit, I love it when you do that," he moaned breathlessly. I smiled proudly and kissed across to his ear, nipping his earlobe gently before I spoke.

"I want to spend my birthday with you. I want one night where we forget everyone else; I want one night where we put everything to one side and just be Will and Chloe. I want one night where we have no rules and no boundaries. That's the only thing I want for my birthday," I whispered.

He groaned and I pulled back to look at him curiously, praying he would go for it. If there was one thing that would make my eighteenth birthday as special as could be, it would be to have every single part of Will, body, mind and spirit.

"That's-" he started, frowning, looking like he was choosing his words carefully.

Disappointment settled in the pit of my stomach because he was about to say no. I didn't blame him really, that wasn't what we agreed on. We'd already stretched the rules a lot further than he wanted to, and yet here was me pushing a little further. I was being selfish by asking. I should think about what I was asking of him. He didn't want to compromise himself again like that, so I really shouldn't have asked, I knew that.

I shook my head guiltily. "Sorry, forget it. I shouldn't have asked," I muttered, flushing with embarrassment that I'd just thrown myself again him like that.

He sighed and put his finger under my chin, lifting my head so I had to look at him. His grey eyes searched mine and neither of us spoke for a couple of minutes. I just lost myself in the beautiful colour of them, they were mesmerizing. "Okay," he finally whispered, nodding slowly.

I gasped, looking at him with wide eyes. *What the hell? Did I hear him right? Did he just agree to make love to me? Wow, it's seriously wrong that I had to coerce my boyfriend into sleeping with me.* This whole situation was slightly wrong. Stereotypically it was usually the other way around, a guy begging the girlfriend to take things further. *I guess we're special… or maybe I'm a pervert like he always says.* I laughed at the ludicrous situation we were in, and then chewed on my lip trying to stop; I was probably making myself look like a crazy person. I still hadn't said anything back, and Will was looking a little confused now.

I shook my head and felt my face flame with heat. "It's fine. I'm sorry, I shouldn't have asked. We'll wait until after graduation," I said sheepishly.

He smiled, his eyes raking over my face slowly, as if he was trying to memorise every part of it or something. "You think I don't want you too? Chloe, of course I do. Being with you drives me crazy; sometimes I want to make love to you so much that it's actually painful. You're just too beautiful for my sanity," he cooed, stroking the side of my face with his thumbs. "I want to make your birthday special; if that's what you want, then that's what we'll do."

He stroked the side of my face again before pressing his lips against mine so lightly that I could barely feel them.

Happiness was trying to consume me as thoughts of making love to him started to run through my mind. *But my freaking birthday is still three weeks away! Wow, that feels like a long time now that I know what I'm getting.* "Really?" I asked, just needing the confirmation again, just to make sure I hadn't slipped off into another of my Will fantasies.

He nodded. "Yeah, Cutie. I want to give you everything for your birthday, if it's me that you want then that's what you'll get," he whispered, his eyes shining with love and adoration and made my heart crash in my chest.

I kissed him gratefully. "That's all I want. Just you," I confirmed.

He smirked at me. "I'm still busy next Saturday daytime," he stated, laying us down on the bed again, side by side as he wrapped his arms around me tightly. "And I have a stipulation," he added. "If we're having one night, then I want the daytime too. I want to spend the whole day with you too. Your birthday is on a Saturday, so stay with me on the Friday night so I can wake up with you."

Oh crud, that can't happen, my parents won't let me stay out and not see me on my birthday. "Will, I can't. My parents, I'll have to spend time with them too."

His eyebrows knitted together. "Ten o'clock then. You can have breakfast with them, and then spend the day with me."

I groaned and shook my head. "Will, usually my mom does a lunch thing, she makes a load of cakes and desserts, and we just eat junk food for lunch. It's like tradition," I explained, looking at him apologetically. I couldn't really break tradition, my parents would be both angry and upset, I couldn't do that to them. If I could I would have invited Will over to the lunch, but his stupid job made that impossible yet again.

He sighed and pressed his forehead to mine. "All right fine, I'll pick you up after lunch, but no later," he countered, shooting me his most serious face so I knew there was no compromising. I nodded and shrugged. I'd be able to convince my parents to let me out for the afternoon and night easily, as long as I didn't break the lunch tradition then I was certain they wouldn't mind. I'd just tell them that Amy was taking me shopping and then we were going out in the evening so I'd stay at hers. Will smiled. "Great. But just so you know, this is the last birthday that I'm not waking up with you. Agreed?"

Jeez, I love the sound of that agreement! "Heck yeah," I breathed. I snuggled further into his chest and sighed contentedly. "I love you."

He kissed the top of my head, the college applications still underneath us scattered on his bed, but neither of us seemed to care. "Love you too, Chloe. More than anything."

Chapter Thirty-Nine

"So then, girls, you think you'll buy much today?" my mom asked, spooning more chocolate cake into my bowl, looking from me to Amy curiously.

I groaned and shook my head, rubbing my bloated stomach. "Mom, I can't eat anymore!" I whined, giving her the begging eyes. I'd already had two slices of chocolate cake, a bowl of sherry trifle, a merengue creamy mess with berries in it, and a homemade double chocolate brownie. I had seriously had enough to send my body into a sugar coma.

Amy grinned and pulled my bowl towards her. She loved my birthday tradition and never missed a lunch at the Hendersons' when a birthday came around. "Waste not, want not," she chirped, tucking into it.

I rolled my eyes and sat back in my chair, nursing my swollen tummy. *I hope I don't feel bloated all day when I'm with Will.* As soon as my thoughts turned to Will I felt the smile stretch across my face and my palms start to get slightly sweaty. Today was my birthday, I was legally an adult, and I was really, really looking forward to collecting on the birthday present that he'd promised me. My night with him, no boundaries, no rules, just pure unadulterated bliss. It was going to be incredible.

I shrugged and smiled up at my mom. As far as she was concerned, Amy and I were heading off after lunch, and I wasn't due home until late tomorrow night. Everything had been set up in preparation. We had told my parents that Amy and I were going shopping today in the city, then seeing a show and then I was staying at her place. Nick had turned up early this morning too, so he could partake in the 'who can eat the most dessert without throwing up' tradition we had.

"I might buy some stuff if we see anything," I lied, knowing that I wasn't going shopping at all.

"Are you taking your birthday money? Maybe you'll see some things you want to buy ready for college?" Mom suggested, smiling a little sadly when she said college. She'd already admitted that she wasn't looking forward to me leaving home.

I nodded, but knew I wouldn't be spending any of the $150 I got for my birthday from various relatives. "Sure, I'll take it, you never know." I shrugged, hoping my blush wouldn't give me away.

My dad groaned and pushed his bowl away, putting his forehead on the table but gripping Nick's shoulder at the same time, squeezing gently. "You win, Nick. You win," he grumbled, his voice muffled from the table.

We all burst out laughing as Nick stood up and did a little bow, smiling proudly. I think the boy had been starving himself for the last day just to make sure that this year he beat my dad and ate the most. "I knew I'd win at least one year!" Nick chirped, grinning like an idiot.

My dad raised his head from the table and looked at him. "Next year I'm taking my record back. No two years a row record for you," he stated, but his voice wasn't very confident due to the fact that it was barely above a whisper.

I grinned and rolled my eyes, eyeing the clock on the wall. The sooner we were done with this little lunch thing, the sooner I could go and meet my gorgeous boyfriend. I'd told him I would call him when we were done, but he'd insisted that he would just wait in his car in the parking lot of the store where we usually parked in the mornings. Amy was driving me there so it would look like I was with her instead of Will.

It was already almost an hour after he said he would meet me. I knew he was getting there at twelve thirty, it was now one fifteen. I looked at Amy helplessly as she was still working on her cake, a sickly expression on her face as if she was two mouthfuls away from hurling.

"Think we'd better go hit the shops now, Amy?" I asked, almost begging her with my eyes.

She frowned and glanced longingly down at her cake, shovelling in the last three mouthfuls in one go; she could barely close her mouth as she nodded. "Smumm um rbebby," she mumbled, almost choking on her cake as she spoke with her mouth full.

My mom clicked her tongue. "Amy Clarke, where are your manners?" she scolded, but laughed at the same time.

Amy grinned sheepishly, still chewing. I pushed myself away from the table and started to collect everyone's bowls. A hand on top of mine stopped me; I looked up to see my mom smile. "Go on, I'll sort that out. Go have a great day," she said softly.

I smiled gratefully and hugged her tightly. "Thanks, Mom. Love you."

"You too. Now, go. Behave tonight, no parties just because it's your birthday," she warned. But then she smiled and winked at me. "At least just don't let your dad know, and make sure you're careful."

I laughed and blushed as I nodded; kissing my dad on the cheek and grabbing my overnight bag that I'd packed. Nick walked us out to Amy's car, hugging me tightly. "See you Monday," he chirped.

I nodded and smiled happily. I was literally on top of the world right now and it probably showed on my face. "See ya, Nick. Thanks for the CD, and congrats on finally kicking my dad's butt at eating cake," I joked.

He laughed and reached into his pockets, producing a slice of cake from each pocket. "I kinda cheated." I burst out laughing, and he shrugged as if it was no big deal. "Hey I had to win this year, there won't be another one what with you up and leaving me for the big apple next year," he said, crumbling the cake into the gutter next to the car.

I bit my lip. I wanted to tell him that I wasn't going, he looked so sad, but he was obviously trying to hide it. But I just needed to keep it quiet for a little while longer; I needed to break the news to Amy before I could tell Nick.

"Don't worry, I won't tell him," I promised, pulling him in for a hug.

He hugged me back tightly before stepping back and opening the passenger side door for me. "Romeo's waiting for you," he teased, rolling his eyes playfully.

I went up on tiptoes and kissed his cheek before climbing into the car, almost dancing with excitement. I could barely keep still as Amy drove us to the meeting place we'd agreed on. I kept my eyes on the clock. *What if he's decided that he's waited long enough, and went home again. Would he really wait an hour for me?*

The drive seemed to be taking forever. I tried to distract myself by chatting to Amy about her plans for the weekend, but I couldn't concentrate on her words, my mind kept flicking back to Will.

Will. Will. Will. It was like he was the only important thing in the world right now.

As we rounded the corner to the parking lot I spotted him immediately. He was sitting in his car, his head back against the headrest, his feet up on the dashboard. He'd obviously been waiting here for me the whole time. I chewed on my lip as he looked and up saw the car. A slow smile stretched across his face that made my heart crash in my chest.

I hadn't spoken to him all morning. I told him not to call in case people were around me or something because my family liked to crowd around when you have a birthday. Of course hadn't been able to resist sending me a happy birthday text though, which was sitting on my phone as soon as I woke up.

He climbed out of the car and started walking over to me, pulling the car door open before Amy even had a chance to put the parking brake on. I clicked my seatbelt just in time for him to pull me out of the car, press me against it, and kiss me passionately.

I laughed into his mouth. *Someone was a little lonely this morning! Or maybe he's just as excited for tonight as I am.* When he broke the kiss he put his forehead to mine, his eyes sparkling with happiness. "Happy birthday, Cutie," he whispered.

I sighed and wrapped my arms around his neck, pulling him closer to me. "Thanks. You been waiting long?" I asked, smiling apologetically. "Sorry. The whole lunch thing went on longer than normal. I told you I should have just called you when we were leaving my house."

He smiled and shook his head. "But then you would have gotten here before I did because your place is closer than mine. Can't have a girl waiting around on her birthday, can we? Besides, I haven't been here that long," he stated, flicking the tip of my nose playfully like he always did.

"An hour is 'not that long'?" I mused, rolling my eyes.

"Not when I know I'm waiting for you. You're worth waiting for," he answered, his eyes locked on mine, making my legs go a little weak.

Amy made a loud fake gagging noise in the car, so Will stepped back and leant down, peering into the car. "Hey, Amy, everything okay? I could get you a sick bag if you ate too much cake," he teased.

She laughed. "It's just the soppy conversation that's making me a little queasy." I could practically hear her smirk in her voice.

I laughed and pulled Will back to me. "Ignore her, she's just jealous," I joked, waving my hand dismissively. "Are we ready to go now?" I chewed on my lip excitedly.

He nodded and opened the back door, grabbing my overnight bag. He laughed when he pulled it out, looking up at me with one eyebrow raised. "You plan on moving in or what?" he asked as he pretended my bag was heavy.

Hmm, I guess I did go a little overboard when I was packing. He refused to tell me where we were going tonight, he said we were going out for dinner somewhere, so I brought three choices of outfit. Outfit one was very fancy – i.e., a black dress with sequins around the bust that fell to just above my knee. That would be for if we were going somewhere posh and respectable. Outfit two was another dress, but it was a little more fitting and cut off at mid-thigh. Amy said I'd need that one in case we were going somewhere a little more 'slutty' – her word, not mine. Then outfit three was a nice black skirt and blue top combo for if we were doing something more casual. On top of all that I had my brand new sexy lingerie, make-up, and clothes for tomorrow.

I shrugged. "You wouldn't tell me where we were going so I had to pack options," I countered.

Amy clicked her tongue in mock disapproval. "Men just don't understand the importance of dressing for the occasion. You should have just told her what to wear, Will," she scolded playfully.

He laughed and wrapped his other arm around me, pulling me close to his side. "Aww, and there was me getting all excited that my girlfriend wanted to move in with me, now I'm kinda disappointed," he joked, winking at me as I elbowed him in the ribs.

I smiled at Amy. "Thanks for the ride. See you Monday, and if my parents call then just tell them I'm in the bathroom and I'll call them back," I instructed. I didn't need to go over the plan, my parents thought I stayed at either Amy's or Nick's every weekend, when in reality I was with my sexy teacher at his place. We all knew the drill and how to avoid trouble.

"Have a great day, and night, and morning!" she called, smirking at me knowingly. She'd kind of guessed this was somewhat of a big occasion by how nervous I'd been, and how I had painstakingly chosen my underwear for the date, and preened myself to within an inch of my life.

"I will, and thanks for the sweater." I smiled gratefully and moved back waving as she pulled out. I turned back to Will who was smiling a little nervously for some reason. *Hmm, I wonder if he's nervous about us sleeping together, it has been a long time since we've actually done the deed.* "You ready?"

He sighed and stepped closer to me, taking my hand in his, making the familiar warmth spread throughout my body. "I can't believe you're finally eighteen. Thank heavens for small mercies," he said, laughing. "So, I wanted to give you my present later, if that's okay?"

I smiled and raised one eyebrow at him suggestively. "I wasn't expecting you to give it to me right in the middle of the parking lot, Will," I purred, running my free hand up his chest. He closed his eyes and made a little moan sound that made my whole body tingle with excitement. He didn't answer, just blew out a big breath and then turned and walked towards his car, tugging me along with him. I smiled and pushed my free hand into the back pocket of his jeans. I sighed contentedly.

When we got to his car he opened the door for me and smiled. "So, I'm supposed to take you to my parents' house for a little while, they want to see you on your birthday. That okay with you?" he asked, looking at me apologetically.

I nodded and shrugged, getting comfortable in my seat. "Sure. I don't care what we do today. As long as I'm with you I'll have the best birthday ever," I confirmed.

He laughed and pressed his lips against mine. "My, aren't we soppy at the age of eighteen," he teased, smirking at me.

I rolled my eyes and gripped the front of his shirt, pulling him towards me roughly. "Just shut up and kiss me," I ordered, narrowing my eyes at him, trying to look masterful. I probably didn't pull it off though, Will was definitely the strong one in our relationship, we both knew it, but I appreciated him always playing along with me.

"Anything for the birthday girl," he whispered, kissing me fiercely.

We spent almost three hours at his parents' house. I could see the pained look on Will's face. He desperately wanted to leave but I was actually enjoying myself the same as I always did when we visited them. Sam was hilarious as usual, making me laugh and teasing the life out of Will whenever he got the chance. I witnessed more than one play fight between the Morris brothers, all of them ended with them both being scolded by their mother like three year olds whilst I just sat there giggling.

Angela was lovely. I got on really well with both of his parents, but she was like a second mom to me. I felt like I knew her and was so comfortable around her that I could just be myself instead of having to put on an act or anything. I felt just as comfortable lounging around on their sofa with Will, as I would do if I was in my own lounge. I was just one of the family.

When we finally left the house, it was almost five in the evening. I had my arms full of presents, ranging from notebooks for college, to earrings, to a digital camera. Sam being Sam, bought me a diary and asked that I fill it with all things 'non Will related' and then let him read it.

I sighed contentedly as we drove away from the house. Today had to be the best birthday ever. We hadn't done anything much, but just being with Will was incredible. The only thing that could make what had already happened better was if Will had been there for the lunch tradition. I'm betting he could have kicked my dad's butt at the eating contest and wouldn't have had to cheat. Next year we'd see if I was right.

As we were driving down the road Will suddenly pulled over and shut off the engine. I looked around curiously wondering what he was doing, but I had no clue where we were. It was just a random street as far as I could make out.

"What are we doing here?" I questioned.

He smiled. "I want to take you somewhere, but I want it to be a surprise so you need to wear this." He reached into the back of the car before turning back to me and producing a grey knitted winter scarf.

I laughed, a little shocked. "Really? I thought we were going for dinner tonight," I inquired, a little lost as to what was going on in his very fine head.

He laughed. "We are."

I frowned and looked at the time on his dashboard clock. 17:42. "Well where are we going now then? I mean, what time are we going out to eat and stuff tonight, because I want to get changed first. I can't go to dinner like this," I countered, waving my hand down at the jeans and plain black V-neck top that I was wearing.

He laughed. "Cutie, don't stress. There's plenty of time for everything. Not sure why you would need to change though, those are my favourite jeans," he commented. He leant over and trailed little kisses up the side of my neck, as his hand traced my leg from my knee to the top of my thigh, making my body tremble and my eyes to close involuntarily.

I silently wished time would pass faster. I didn't even want to go to dinner; all I wanted was what was happening after, when we would go back to his place. I wanted the intimacy and the closeness; I wanted to renew the bond that we'd been missing for the last six months.

"You like all of my skinny jeans," I muttered breathlessly as he nibbled on my collarbone.

He laughed, his breath blowing across my skin making it prickle with sensation. "Very true," he confirmed. He kissed my neck one more time before pulling back and stretching the scarf between his hands, smiling at me reassuringly. "Turn your head and let's get going. Don't worry, Cutie, we'll have plenty of time to eat and stuff tonight."

I sighed and chewed on my lip before turning in my seat, letting him place the makeshift blindfold over my eyes. He tied it tightly at the back of my head. I smiled and touched the soft fabric with my fingertips, pushing it off of my nose so I could breathe properly. Will gripped my shoulders and turned me back to face him, adjusting the scarf until he was happy with it. "Perfect," he stated, before capturing my lips in a soft kiss.

I smiled and sat back, playing with my fingers, wracking my brain trying to think of somewhere he would want take me as a surprise. It had to be somewhere remote because we literally took no risks at all with people seeing us out. So I knew it wasn't going to be to the mall, or a ball game or anything populated like that. The only place I could think of was the field that he once took me too for a date, one of the best nights of my life where we had danced in the dark with only the car headlights shining. I actually hoped it was there, I hoped we were going to lie on the hood of his car and listen to some cheesy love songs while he held me tightly.

By the time the car stopped I was so apprehensive that I felt a little sick. We'd been driving for a good forty minutes since he insisted that I be blindfolded. *Where on earth is he taking me? This can't be our field, could it? It was only ten minutes' drive, tops. Unless he's driven around a few times so I had no idea where I was, maybe he's trying to trick me or something.*

I chewed on my lip as I heard his door open, and him fumbling with something at the back of the car, maybe getting something out of the trunk, or putting something in there.

When my door opened a minute later I jumped out of my skin, and he laughed quietly. "Here, take my hand, Cutie." His hand closed around mine. I frowned behind the blindfold. He wasn't going to let me see still? Where the heck were we?

"Why can't I just look now?" I whined, pouting.

Something brushed against my lips lightly, I barely had time to realise that he'd kissed me before he pulled away again. "Because I want to see the full effect of the surprise. This is supposed to be romantic," he answered, giving my hand a little tug, signalling he wanted me to get out of the car.

I stepped out and let him blindly lead me to wherever it was that he deemed 'romantic'. The wind whipped my hair around my face, making me hunch my shoulders against the slight chill. *Hmm, I really should have brought a jacket.* Will stopped walking and let go of my hand. I smiled, thinking we had reached the desired destination, but instead of taking off the blindfold, he draped something around my shoulders. I clutched at the soft material and pulled it tighter around me, smelling the familiar beautiful yet manly smell that was solely my boyfriend. He'd obviously given me his hoodie. I grinned and pulled it to my face, breathing in his scent.

He laughed and took my hand again. "Stalker," he teased, making me walk again by tugging me along gently.

We walked for a few more minutes. The ground was a little uneven under my feet, I had sneakers on so I had no idea if we were on grass or dirt, but it was bumpy so I knew we were definitely off road. He stopped again, almost making me walk into his back.

He let go of my hand and grasped my shoulders. "Stay right there. Don't move," he instructed, his voice stern.

"Did you just use your teacher voice on me?" I joked, sticking out my tongue like a five year old.

He laughed and pressed his lips to mine, kissing me passionately before he pulled away from me, leaving me alone and clutching his hoodie around me tightly against the slight wind. I could hear him fumbling around near me. I stood there patiently, waiting for him to tell me it was all right for me to move. In total honesty I kind of wished this moment would last forever, my birthday was incredible so far, and I wanted it to last forever, so he could take all the time he wanted.

Something cold brushed against my lips making them part as the smell of fresh strawberries hit my nose. I felt my mouth fill with water, and I heard a little moan then realised it came out of me.

"Open," he whispered, kissing my cheek lightly.

I opened my mouth and the chilled strawberry was popped between my teeth. Instinctively I bit down, the sweet juice hitting my taste buds. His lips closed over mine as soon as I had swallowed the berry, the taste was almost heady with his lips pressed against mine. He licked the corner of my mouth where there was probably a little of the juice. My senses seemed to be heightened with the blindfold. Experts always said that, that if you took away one sense then it made the others stronger. It definitely made the taste stronger; I had never tasted anything more delicious in my life.

As he kissed me I felt him fumbling with the knot at the back of my head, untying the scarf. I kissed him fiercely, clutching at the belt loops of his jeans so he couldn't pull back from me. I felt the soft material being pulled away from my eyes, but instead of pulling back and opening my eyes I pressed myself to him tighter, savouring the last few seconds before the kiss broke. I treasured every single one of Will's kisses; I treated each one like it was the last in case he never graced me with another one.

He pulled back and kissed the tip of my nose. "You can open your eyes now, Cutie," he whispered.

I smiled as I cracked my eyes open, wincing slightly at the sudden brightness after being in the dark for so long. The first thing I saw was his face, inches from mine, a beautiful smile on his lips. His grey eyes were burning into mine and held such a passion that it almost knocked me sideways. I reluctantly dragged my eyes from him, to my surroundings.

Emotion swelled over me, my heart was literally aching as my stomach trembled. My eyes filled with tears as I looked at what he'd done. Romantic wasn't the word to describe this scene, it was more like perfection. It was the epitome of all things romantic and spectacular.

We were at the top of break point, the highest point in town. We were at the edge of the cliff, he'd laid out a blanket with a few cushions scattered around too. A bunch of red tulips sat at the edge of the blanket, already in their own water. A picnic hamper rested in the middle with the lid off, I could see the box of strawberries on the top. I could also see most of my other favourite foods in there too; I chewed on my lip as a tear fell down my face because this special guy had gone to so much effort, just for me.

"Want to sit down?" he asked, stepping away from me and onto the blanket, nodding for me to sit down first. If there had been a chair, he would have pulled it out for me, Will was a little old-fashioned like that, but his dad was exactly the same from what I'd witnessed. The saying was certainly right in their family, 'like father, like son'.

I sat down at one end of the blanket and looked out at the spectacular view of the town. It was beautiful, I'd actually never been up here before and that made it all the more special for me because I was doing it with Will. I watched as he pulled out carton after carton of food, glasses, plates, and cutlery. He'd thought of everything.

When he pulled out a bottle of champagne I raised one eyebrow at him. "You do realise I'm not old enough to drink that yet," I teased.

He laughed. "Yeah, one birthday at a time. I just thought we could have a glass to watch the sunset with. You don't have to if you don't want one. I brought alternatives…" He tipped the hamper so I could see what was left inside and I burst out laughing when I saw a bottle of banana milkshake, my favourite kind of course, and a bottle of Dr Pepper.

"I'll have the alternative for now. Maybe I'll have the champagne later then, if we're staying here to watch the sunset," I mused, shrugging. *How did I get so lucky to get a guy like Will? I really, really don't deserve him.*

He smiled and poured me a glass of milkshake and grabbed a Pepsi for himself. I helped him open all of the cartons of food, marvelling how he seemed to have made every single one of my favourites. "You make this all yourself?" I asked curiously, eyeing the pasta salad warily. Will wasn't exactly the best cook.

He laughed and dug a fork into the pasta, spearing a couple of pieces, and then held them up to my mouth. As I opened my mouth I silently prayed he wouldn't give me food poisoning. I was pleasantly surprised by the flavour of it, it was delicious. "I cheated and had my mom make most of it. I thought it was better to play it safe rather than us be sorry later when we're both throwing up," he admitted, laughing sheepishly.

I got up to my knees and moved so I could kiss him, smiling at him gratefully. "Thank you." Was all I said, it was all that needed to be said, at least I hoped that he knew how grateful I was, because I couldn't find the words to express myself better than that. I was literally rendered speechless by him and his thoughtfulness.

We ate and laughed, talked and flirted. Everything was perfect. As the wind picked up, he pulled out another blanket, wrapping it around my shoulders. When I couldn't eat another bite he packed everything away into the hamper, before turning back to me with a huge smile on his face.

I looked at him curiously, wondering what caused that expression. He held out one hand to me, opening his fist to reveal a little black box the size of his palm. There was a red ribbon stuck on top.

I closed my eyes and smiled as I shook my head at him. "You really shouldn't have bought me anything."

He rolled his eyes. "I wanted to, so just shush," he stated, moving his hand closer to me, silently telling me to take the gift and open it.

I took it from his hand, revelling in the soft, velvety feel of the box on my fingertips. I bit my lip excitedly, knowing that it was a jewellery box and that he had already said he wanted to get me something I could keep. I was so excited that I could barely remember how to breathe. *I'll get to wear this, whatever it is, everyday and think of Will.*

"You're not getting any younger," he teased, laughing and scooting closer to me so that his legs were either side of mine. He hooked his hands under my calves and moved my legs so that they were draped over his, and were practically wrapped around his waist. His face studied every inch of mine as his hands rested on the tops of my thighs, squeezing gently as a prompt.

I smiled and opened the little box. My breath caught in my throat. Inside the box was a little gold charm bracelet. The links were delicate and intricate, there was one little charm hanging off of one side of it. I reached out a shaky hand and rubbed my fingertip across it, turning it over so I could see it better. Suddenly I realised what the little charm was. It was the sign for Pi, the maths symbol. I bit my lip and looked up at him in awe. I guess the charm was personal to him, something that kind of symbolised something that he loved, so it would be like I was wearing his sign in a small way. It was beautiful.

"This is incredible, thank you so much," I croaked. Tears pooled in my eyes but I tried not to let them fall.

He smiled and cocked his head to the side. "You like it?"

I leant forward and pressed my lips to his, kissing him gratefully, tasting a salty tear so I must have lost the fight with myself not to cry. "I love it," I whispered against his lips. I gripped the little box tightly in my hand so that I didn't drop it. I was already in love with this little bracelet, and once it was on my body I was never taking it off.

He smiled at me happily. "Good. I wanted to get you something you could keep. I'm really glad you like it." He brushed his hand against my face, wiping my tears away softly before kissing my forehead. "I love you, Cutie."

I closed my eyes and gripped the front of his shirt, pressing myself to him, tightening my legs around his waist, just marvelling over this guy actually being mine. *He's just too incredible for me, surely.* "I love you too. Thank you so much, Will. This is just beautiful," I breathed, kissing the side of his neck. I pulled back and held it out to him. "Put it on for me?" I requested, wanting to get the incredible thing on my arm as quickly as possible.

He grinned and plucked the bracelet from the box, unclasping it and wrapping it around my offered wrist. I smiled at the feel of the cool gold against my skin. The little Pi symbol hung against my wrist, shining in the last rays of the sun.

He kissed me again until I was literally feeling like my insides were turning into mush. I was like a quivering mess, and the only thing that was keeping me upright was his arms that were wrapped tight around my waist.

He broke the kiss and smiled. He took hold of my wrist and brought it up, examining my bracelet, playing with the little charm on it, fingering it a little nervously. "This charm looks a little lonely," he mused, kissing the inside of my wrist, on my pulse point. My skin prickled with pleasure at that one tiny little show of affection.

I smiled and brushed my free hand across his forehead, sweeping the hair away from his eyes so I could see them better. "I like just having that one charm on there. It's perfect. A math symbol, from my math nerd boyfriend," I teased, laughing as he bit my wrist.

He put my hand in his lap and straightened up, looking at me softly. "I actually bought you another charm to go on there too," he whispered, trailing his fingers over my wrist lightly, making my stomach start to flutter.

He's bought me something else? "You did? Will, you shouldn't have got me anything at all, this was already too much," I protested, shaking my head. I didn't need him to spend his money on me at all. Not that I didn't love the bracelet, because I did, but I just didn't need expensive things from him.

He sighed and pulled back, fumbling in his jeans pocket. He pulled something out, looking at it a little anxiously. I looked at the little black velvet pouch that he had in his hand, he was playing with the rope like string that held it closed at the top. I heard him gulp, and I started to get nervous. *Will is never like this, he's always so confident, why is he so flustered all of a sudden?*

I was just about to ask him what was wrong, when he took my hand and turned it over, palm facing upwards. He untied the string, tipping the bag up into my hand.

Out fell a miniature gold diamond ring, a charm for my bracelet, but it was a ring one.

My mouth dropped open. It was beautiful. "Will, that's…" I trailed off, my eyes filling with tears again.

He seemed to take a deep breath as he picked up the little charm, fiddling with the little clasp that was attached to it. "I wanted to get you this because… well, it's kind of like a promise ring, and I was wondering if you would wear it?" he asked, his voice a little husky and croaky. He was looking at the charm, seeming to be avoiding my gaze.

A promise ring? What's that supposed to mean? "A what?" I chewed on my lip and bent my head slightly so I could see his face better. When I saw his expression I felt even more confused. He looked terrified, genuinely scared for some reason. *What am I missing here?*

He gulped again, lifting his gaze to meet mine again. "A promise ring. Like, I promise one day to replace that ring, with a real one. It's like a commitment, but without the title," he explained. "I love you, Cutie, I'll always love you, and if things were different, if you were older and not my student and things were easier, then that wouldn't be a promise ring, it'd be the real thing." His beautiful eyes were searching mine, looking for some sort of response.

Wait, is he talking about an engagement ring? If things were different, he would be giving me an engagement ring? Oh my gosh, what the heck do I say to that? That is so freaking romantic!

"Really?" I muttered, looking from him to the little diamond ring charm that he put back into the middle of my palm.

He nodded. "Really," he confirmed. "Will you wear my ring, Cutie? I just need you to know how serious I am about you. I want to spend my life with you, Chloe, and one day, when you're least expecting it, I'll replace this little charm, with a ring that goes on your finger. All I want from you tonight is for you to tell me that if I asked you at some point in our future, that you'd consider making me the luckiest guy in the world."

Holy cow, he's seriously thinking about us getting married at some point in the future! He said 'our future'; I love those two words together. Not my future, or his future, but ours. My head was spinning a little, my heart crashing against my ribs. My whole body was alight with excitement as I nodded, grinning like an idiot. "I'd love to wear your promise ring," I accepted, trying not to let the ridiculous happiness that I felt inside, burst from me.

Before I knew what happened he'd jumped up to his feet and pumped the air above his head with both hands. "Yessssssssssssssss! Score! Come on, get in!" he shouted happily as if this was some sort of football celebration. I was almost expecting him to pull his shirt over his head and run around singing 'We are the champions'.

I burst into a fit of giggles at the sight of my supposedly mature teacher, almost dancing on the spot as he grinned like an idiot. He didn't even look embarrassed to have been caught doing it.

"You're a dork," I teased around my giggles.

He grinned and nodded, plopping himself back down in front of me, his eyes still dancing with excitement. "Yeah, but this dorky math nerd just got the girl of his dreams," he replied, smirking at me.

I literally threw myself at him, wrapping my arms tight around his neck as I pressed my forehead to his. I didn't know what to say. What words could I use to describe this feeling? I didn't know enough superlatives to describe it. So I settled for three little words, hoping they would convey my feelings.

"I love you."

He kissed me softly, his hands cupping my face. "I love you too," he whispered against my lips. I shivered, but it wasn't from the cool air or the wind that whipped my hair around our faces.

I pulled back and opened my hand, holding the little charm out to him. "You gonna put it on for me then?" I asked quietly.

His smile got even bigger as he clipped it onto the opposite side of the bracelet to the little Pi symbol. "You're mine now," he bragged, smirking at me.

I laughed, deciding to steal a line from a movie. "Will, you had me at hello. I've always been yours."

He sighed happily. "And you always will be."

We sat on the cliff top for a while, just talking and sipping champagne. Listening to the little music player that he'd brought up here. As the sun started to go down over the town. I watched in awe as the colours danced in the sky, making everything look beautiful. I kind of wished I'd brought my new camera from the car so I could take a few photos of it.

Will was still facing me, his back to the sunset. "Why don't you sit over here next to me, you're missing the view," I suggested, patting the blanket next to me.

He smiled. "I'm looking at the most beautiful thing here. The view can't get any better than this," he replied, his eyes raking over my face slowly.

Oh my days, that was amazing! "Cheesy," I breathed. My heart was beating way too fast to be healthy.

"Truthful," he countered, moving closer to me slowly. He moved so close that I had to lie down onto my back. He hovered above me but didn't touch me.

I swallowed loudly. His proximity was making me lose all coherent thoughts. "Corny."

A smile twitched at the corner of his mouth that I longed to trace with my fingertip. "Romantic."

He was so close now that I could feel the heat of his body coming off of him in waves, my brain was a little fuzzy, I couldn't think of anything to say at all. I wrapped my arms around his neck as he inched his mouth closer to mine. He was so close that I could almost taste the champagne on his breath as it blew across my lips. He hovered above me, just looking into my eyes as if we were the only two people in the world.

"You win," I whispered, guiding his mouth closer to mine.

He laughed quietly. "Always, because I have you. Therefore I'll always be the winner."

Jeez, can this guy blow my mind anymore? I knew the answer to that question though, and the answer was heck yes he can. I tightened my arms around his neck. "Will, make love to me now." My voice was breathy and husky because of the emotions and feelings that were crashing through my body.

He smiled and traced his fingertips across my cheek softly. I knew he would be tracing the line of my blush; he always seemed to take pride in the fact that he caused that reaction in me. "Now that would be my pleasure," he teased.

He smiled before he bent his head and captured my lips in the most beautiful kiss I had ever felt in my life. That one kiss conveyed so much feeling, so much love, and so many unspoken words that I could hardly even cope with it. The feel of that kiss almost brought me to tears again. But he didn't stop there, that one kiss was followed by another, and another as he made love to me. Neither of us paid any attention to what was sure to be a beautiful sunset that was happening behind us.

Chapter Forty

As soon as the doorbell rang Amy jumped up, grinning like a fool. She was ridiculously eager for tonight. She was wearing a sexy, yet classy, blood red dress that fitted her perfectly and showed off her long legs to perfection. Her face was alight with excitement, her eyes shining with glee. I smiled too, not because I was looking forward to tonight, but because she looked so happy. Tonight was going to be a long night for me. Tonight was Prom night. It should have been a night for celebration, I should have been bursting with excitement just like Amy, but instead I dreaded it. The reason? Because I couldn't go with the one I wanted to go with. There was no possible way that I could go to the dance with Will. So instead I was going with his brother. I hadn't wanted to go at all because I couldn't go with him, but both Will and Amy had insisted that it was part of the 'rite of passage into womanhood' or something, so they were literally forcing me to go.

Will had volunteered to chaperone the prom. Apparently he said that he wanted to be there for me, even if he couldn't actually 'be there for me'. He said he wanted to be part of it in some way even if he just had to stand on the sidelines. Plus he said he couldn't pass up the opportunity to see me in my prom dress.

I forced a smile and stood too, smoothing down the skirt of my knee length, strapless electric blue dress. The black netting that sat over the top of it was soft under my fingertips. I silently wondered what Will would think of my dress, and if he would like it. He would probably like the little black lacy belt that tied just under my cleavage. It did draw the eye to that area.

"That'll be Ryan and Nick," Amy chirped, clapping her hands excitedly.

I nodded, and we both headed out of the lounge and to the door. Of course, my dad was already there, talking to both boys in hushed whispers. I winced at Amy, praying that my dad wouldn't scare Ryan away from her by threatening him with disembowelment if he hurt her. Nick was of course used to this kind of thing so he was just smiling at my dad patiently.

I discreetly waved over my dad's shoulder, looking at Nick in his tux. He looked incredibly handsome tonight. His date was a lucky girl. He didn't actually want to come tonight at all, but Amy and I had practically forced him into it - if I had to subject myself to a school dance, then so did he. We'd set him up with Jasmine, a cute little brunette that was a junior instead of a senior. She was adorable, the quiet artsy type.

Technically, my date was Sam tonight, but we had all agreed that because we didn't want Sam to meet my parents, that Nick would pick me up instead and pretend he was my date. Will approved of the plan because apparently he didn't want Sam meeting his 'future in-laws' before he did and 'tainting the Morris name' for him. Sam's brilliant response to that was that the Morris name would already be tainted when they found out that I'd been 'banging my teacher for a couple of months'. I smiled as I remembered the conversation; it was actually pretty funny day and took place in front of his parents who found the whole thing rather amusing.

When my dad stepped back and waved the boys into the hallway, Nick grinned. "Hey, wow, you both look great," he gushed. I smiled, and before I could answer he held out a large bunch of red tulips to me. I gasped, looking at him with wide eyes. *Are they from him? What on earth…*

"Er, thanks," I muttered, taking them out of his hand and casting an uneasy glance at Amy. She was too busy shooting Ryan the doe eyes to notice my unease though. He stepped closer to me, smiling happily as he held out a box that contained a little white bracelet corsage. My dad had disappeared off to get the camera or something so I took my opportunity to quiz Nick. "Are these from you?"

He shook his head quickly. "Nope. Will asked me to give them to you. And I'm also supposed to tell you that you look beautiful and that he hopes you have a nice time," he replied.

My heart throbbed in my chest. *So thoughtful!* I sighed dreamily, but before I could respond my dad was back, my mom hot on his heels as she gushed and praised how lovely everyone looked. We had a few photos done and then we finally escaped into the chill night air.

It was a little early to be picked up, it was only just after seven, but we were going to dinner first apparently. As we stepped out of the door, I looked with wide eyes towards the road. Parked there, all shiny and long, was a black limousine. I looked back at Nick, shocked. I was told Ryan was driving tonight, I wasn't expecting a limo. "Seriously? A limo?" I gasped. Amy squealed as she saw it too.

Nick smiled and leant in close to my ear. "Will ordered it," he whispered.

Gosh damn, he's incredible! My eyes prickled with tears because of how much thought had gone into tonight - but yet he wasn't even the one that was taking me. Amy grabbed my hand, and we both ran across the grass to the waiting limo. A man in a black uniform opened the door for us, smiling happily. As I climbed in, the first thing I spotted was Sam. He was stretched out on the back seat, looking the picture of ease as he sipped orange juice from

335

a champagne flute. He grinned over at me, his eyes raking down my body as I clambered awkwardly into the car and plopped down next to him.

"Well dang, Foxy by name, Foxy by nature," he whistled. "Don't you scrub up nice."

I laughed and stole his drink, taking a sip and settling against his side. "You don't look too bad yourself," I replied, looking down at him in his black tux.

Amy and Ryan fell in the door behind me, laughing to themselves. Ryan shook his head and punched Sam in the arm. "No freaking wonder you sent Nick in to collect her, her dad's a fucking psycho!" he ranted, before turning to me and smiling apologetically. "No offense."

I smiled and waved my hand dismissively. "Sam's too scared to meet him yet," I lied. Ryan of course didn't know about Will, so obviously they'd told him that Sam was too scared to come to the door and had sent Nick to fetch me instead.

"Not surprised. Jeez," Ryan muttered, blowing out a big breath before he turned to smile at Amy sweetly. "I guess I got off lucky with your parents, huh?" She grinned at him and nodded, moving up and kissing him gently, ending the conversation.

Nick climbed in too, and then we headed off to Jasmine's house so he could pick her up too.

An hour and a half later we'd eaten and were about to leave the restaurant to go to prom. We were already fashionably late, but Sam still insisted that he needed to go and 'perfect' his look in the bathroom before we could leave. I took the opportunity to go and check my make-up before we went to the school gym where they were holding the dance tonight. I wanted to look my best for when Will saw me. The other guys all said they would wait in the limo, so I followed Sam towards the bathrooms, frowning when I saw the out of order sign on the ladies restrooms.

Sam smiled and grabbed my hand. "Come in the guys', no one will know," he insisted, dragging me in there behind him before I could protest. I squealed and squeezed my eyes shut, thinking I was going to see a load of guys all standing at the urinals or something. Sam chuckled wickedly. "It's empty, you're safe."

I cracked my eyes open, risking a glance around only to see he was right, it was empty. I slapped him with my little blue clutch purse and frowned before stalking over to the only mirror in the room. "You could have at least checked it was empty first!" I whined, shaking my head in disbelief.

He made a scoffing noise. "Like you've never seen a guy's thing before," he commented. I closed my eyes and shook my head, deciding not to answer, which just made Sam chuckle wickedly behind me. When I heard the sound of a zipper being unfastened, I cringed and whistled a little tune to try and block out the sound of Sam taking a leak behind me. *Gross boy!* When he was done, he walked to my side. "You know, Will's jealous he couldn't bring you to your prom," Sam he said casually as he washed his hands.

I frowned and looked at his reflection in the mirror. "He's jealous? Like proper jealous?" I winced. *Maybe I shouldn't go. Maybe I should just stay home and pretend I'm sick if he doesn't want me to go.*

Sam shook his head quickly. "Not like that kind of jealous, just that he wants to be the one to take you. He didn't say in so many words, but I think he feels a little left out. Make sure you make it up to him another night," he suggested, waggling his eyebrows at me.

I slapped his arm for being crude. "Shut up," I muttered, applying another coat of lipstick before blotting it.

"Okay, want to know something that'll make you go aww?" He bumped me with his hip to get me out of the way of the mirror as he started messing with his hair. I nodded, waiting for him to say it. "I told him I'd make sure you have the night of your life, and you know what he said to me?" Sam asked, still fussing with his hair.

"Stop playing with your hair, you girl?" I guessed, smirking at him.

He rolled his eyes and blew out a dramatic breath. "You're not even half as funny as you think you are," he commented. "No, anyway, he said, 'I don't want you to give her the night of her life, that's my job'. Thought you'd appreciate knowing that."

My heart melted, and all I wanted to do was call up Will and tell him that he always gave me the night of my life. "Aww," I mused.

Sam grinned cockily. "Told ya you'd say that."

I sighed dreamily, just wishing I could see him right now, throw my arms around him and just breathe in his smell that was like nothing else in the world.

By the time we got to the school I was ridiculously eager to see Will. I'd seen him dressed up once before, at his sister's wedding, and I couldn't wait to see him all suited and booted again. My guess is that he'd look amazing. I let Sam lead me towards the gym. The thump of music was already reverberating form the walls as the live band covered a Maroon 5 song. People were chatting animatedly as we waited in a messy line in the hallway so that we could enter the gym. Girls everywhere looked elegant and beautiful in their prom dresses of various colours, hair done, make-up applied. The scent of various perfumes all mixed into something that was almost heady as we stood there in line waiting to have our photo taken as we arrived. The guys all essentially looked the same, black tux, white shirt, but they all had different coloured ties on.

The line moved fairly quickly, and before long Sam and I were at the front. His arm snaked around my waist, pulling me to him as the photographer snapped a couple of pictures before waving us off so he could take the next couple's portrait. Nick and Jasmine were laughing and talking off to one side so Sam led me over to them, his arm still around my waist. I cast an excited glance around the room, noticing all the gold and silver balloons and banners that decorated the place. Little round tables with white and silver table cloths had been set up around the gym. The lights had been dulled, and a little candle sat at each table along with a pretty flower arrangement. It looked lovely - but it couldn't hold my attention. My eyes raked over the sea of people, seeking out one face in particular.

When my gaze finally found him, I felt myself mentally swoon. He was leaning against the wall opposite me, one leg crossed casually over the other, looking the picture of ease. His hair was styled but messy the same as usual, and the suit... 'wow' was all I could think. He was watching me; a little smile graced his full lips as his eyes raked over me slowly as if he didn't want to miss an inch.

Before I knew what I was doing, I'd left my friends and was making my way across the room to him. My feet had a mind of their own as I wove past people dancing, drinking, and eating. I needed to get to him and say hi.

As I walked to him his eyes seemed to darken, his posture changed as he stood up straighter. The look was like he was marvelling over me. I knew then and there that he approved of my choice of dress. Miss Teller was standing and talking to a student not too far away from Will so I knew we needed to be careful.

As I stopped in front of him, he smiled his heartbreaking smile. My breath caught in my throat as his hand twitched and raised, heading towards my face. Heat filled my cheeks because of how intimately he was gazing at me. I could practically see his love for me shining from his eyes. He seemed to catch himself quickly; dropping is hand back down to his side. I couldn't help but be disappointed because all I wanted to do was crush myself to him and spend the night dancing in his arms. The way he was looking at me made my heart soar in my chest. I loved the way he looked at me, the look that he gave me showed me that my feelings for him were reciprocated, that everything I felt, he felt too. At least I hoped that was what that look was otherwise I was in some serious trouble.

"Good evening, Miss Henderson. You look beautiful tonight. My brother sure is a lucky guy to be able to dance with you all night," he complimented.

I smiled at his sweet words. Obviously he knew to be careful too. "Thank you, Mr Morris. Did you see the flowers that Sam bought for me? They're beautiful, I was really grateful," I replied, discreetly thanking him for my tulips.

He nodded in acknowledgement, a smile tugging at the corner of his lips. "I saw them. Glad you liked them," he confirmed, playing along.

A heavy arm slung around my shoulder and I quickly looked to see it belonged to Sam. "Well, let's not stand here all night talking to the teachers, Foxy. Let's get some punch. I'm not sure if it's been spiked or not already so I brought some vodka just in case," he bragged, patting his pocket.

I chuckled as Will groaned, shaking his head in disapproval. "Seriously? I'm chaperoning, Sam. I can't let you do that, give me the bottle," Will ordered, holding out his hand for it.

Sam gasped and frowned. "What? No way!" he complained.

Will shook his hand impatiently. "There are a few juniors here too. Come on, no alcohol," he said sternly.

Sam groaned and pulled out a bottle of vodka, slapping it into Will's outstretched hand with a growl of frustration. His other arm tightened on me as he turned and pulled me away. I giggled at his hurt and annoyed expression on his face. Flicking my eyes back to Will I cast him a little wave. *I hope I get to speak to him some more later.*

"Aww man, he sucks ass!" Sam whined. "He was totally wasted on his prom night but yet he won't allow other people to have a nice time?" He sighed dramatically. "Well, if we can't spike the punch then let's dance, Foxy, and then we can check out the buffet," Sam suggested, leading us over to the packed dance floor.

The night passed quickly. Despite not being able to speak to Will at all during the night, I still had a nice time. Sam, as usual, was on top form and was entertaining everyone. I danced, I ate, I laughed and just generally enjoyed myself. Throughout the night my eyes kept seeking out my boyfriend. He was doing his job perfectly; wandering around the gym, making sure everything was in order, talking to people. A few times he caught my eye and in those few seconds, when our gazes would meet, it was like we were alone, like we were the only two in the room because I just didn't see anyone else.

At about ten thirty I looked around the crowded gym, trying to see his brown hair, but I couldn't see him anywhere. I hadn't seen him for ages now, not since I'd heard him tell Principal Sherman he was going to check the hallways and make sure everything was all in order. *Where's he gotten to?* I silently wished this night were over with already so I could talk to him on the phone or something. I hated being so close to him and yet so far away. Sam pulled me tighter against his chest as we continued to dance to the slow song. The night was winding up now; the band had just announced that there were only two dances left. I sighed sadly. I still hadn't gotten to speak to Will in private and thank him properly for the limo and the flowers. He'd gone to so much effort tonight and I hadn't even been able to tell him how handsome he looked in his tux.

I ground my teeth in frustration. *I can't wait for graduation. Everything will be fine once that's over with.* Once I was graduated I would be able to walk up to him and talk to him whenever I wanted without people being suspicious. I would be able to link my fingers through his as we walked down the street. I would be able to take him home to my parents and introduce him to them as the love of my life. I just couldn't wait for those things. Just a couple more weeks to go.

"Sam, where did Will go? I haven't seen him for ages," I whispered, scanning the room discreetly for him.

He shrugged in response. "No idea. Want to get another drink?" he offered, nodding off to the side table where the refreshments were.

I sighed and nodded in agreement, allowing him to lead me over there. I spotted Nick dancing with Jasmine; he had an enormous smile on his face as they spoke and laughed at the same time as twirling around the dance floor. I felt the grin slip onto my face that he looked so happy. He hadn't wanted to come to prom at all, but judging by the look on his face now though, he was probably glad that he did. He looked like he was having a nice time and they actually made a really cute couple.

When we got to the drinks table, I noticed that Sam kept glancing at his watch, and looking over his shoulder a lot. "What's up, Sam-bo? You spiked it or something? Why so jumpy?" I asked, taking the cup he was offering to me.

He sighed and shook his head. "I'm just waiting for something," he answered, still glancing around.

I laughed. *He is so freaking weird sometimes!* What you waiting for?" I inquired, taking a bite of a cheese sandwich and chewing distastefully because they'd gone slightly stale where they'd been left open all night.

His cell phone rang and he pulled it out of his pocket with a smile. He looked at the caller ID but didn't answer it, just rejected the call and put it back in his pocket, still grinning. "I need the bathroom. Come on, you can show me where it is," he stated, taking my cup back off of me and putting it on the table before I even got to take a sip.

"Sam, what on earth? You know where the bathrooms are, you've already been!" I protested, laughing as he dragged me to the door and into the hallway.

He nodded. "Yeah but those ones are always full. Show me the way to some other ones," he suggested, nodding down the hallway.

"Sam, what?" I moaned as he took my hand and started walking off, tugging gently.

"Come on, Foxy, I'm desperate," he whined, pouting at me. I rolled my eyes and followed him up the hallway, leading him to the next set of bathrooms on this side of the building. He smiled and cocked his head to the side. "Isn't that Will's classroom up there?" he asked, motioning up the hallway with his chin.

I nodded in confirmation. "Yep."

He smiled. "Go wait in there for me while I just take a leak."

I frowned. "I'll just wait here. You're not gonna be long, are you?" I asked sarcastically.

He made a disgusted face. "I can't go if I know you're waiting outside for me, it'll put me off."

"You didn't seem to have a problem with it when you peed when I was in the actual room with you earlier!" I scolded, shaking my head at the memory.

He chuckled wickedly. "Hmm, you're right, maybe you should come in with me again. I quite liked that in a kinky, peeing in front of your brother's girlfriend kind of way," he admitted, raising one eyebrow conspiratorially.

I laughed and rolled my eyes. *What a weird boy.* "Never, ever again. I'm still mentally scarred from it. I'll just wait in the gym for you. I'll go find Amy and Ryan," I suggested, turning to head back to the party.

He gripped my hand and shook his head. "I don't want to walk back in on my own, I might not be able to find you, and then we'll miss the last dance. Can't have a girl missing the last dance of her prom, can we?" he teased.

"Fine then, I'll wait here."

He sighed and shook his head adamantly. "Just go sit in Will's classroom for me. If you stay here then you'll get distracted with your ditsy little goldfish brain and end up wandering off somewhere."

"Goldfish brain?" I gasped, slapping his arm but laughing at the same time.

He grinned cheekily. "Go!" he insisted, giving me an encouraging little push towards Will's classroom. "I'll be right out and then we can dance."

I sighed dramatically and stormed over there, not really having the energy to argue with him about it. All I wanted to do was go home now; I'd had enough of tonight. This should have been the most special night of my life, dancing with the man of my dreams; instead I get to spend the night with his brother and look for him all night. Not how I would have expected my prom night to turn out before this whole Will situation happened.

I gripped the handle and pushed the door open, only to see someone sitting on the desk in front of me. I let out a little scream before I realised it was Will. I felt the goofy smile stretch onto my face as he pushed himself up off of the desk and headed over to me, taking my hand and pulling me into the room. He closed the door and pushed me against it, kissing me fiercely. I moaned into his mouth at his taste, his smell was all around me making my insides tingle with happiness. He pulled out of the kiss and put his forehead to mine, a beautiful smile stretched across his face.

"Hi," he whispered.

I wrapped my arms around his neck, tilting my head and kissing him again for a second. "Hi." I closed my eyes and pulled him closer to me, loving the weight of his body as it pressed against mine and trapped me against the door. "What are you hiding in here for?" I murmured with my eyes still closed, just breathing him in and savouring the moment.

He laughed quietly. "I couldn't let the night go past without dancing with my girl. I was wondering if I could get your last dance," he cooed, his nose tracing up the side of mine.

My last dance? How would that work? "Huh?" was my brilliant response as I opened my eyes to look at him quizzically.

He laughed and pulled back, taking my hand and stepping away from me. As he did that I realised that the light wasn't turned on in the room. Instead, there were little candles littering the desks and spotted at various points around the room, casting little shadows all around. On the desk nearest me there was a single tulip and two cups of punch. I looked back at Will in awe. *He is so freaking romantic sometimes. I really don't deserve this guy to be so thoughtful all the time. He'd planned this so we could have the last dance? Is that why Sam was so jumpy and insisted that we head to these bathrooms instead? They had this planned from the start?* My heart melted into a puddle, and I looked back at Will who was watching me intently.

"You are just too sweet sometimes," I breathed, stepping closer to him.

He smiled. "And you are just so beautiful in this dress that I'm not even sure how I'm managing to speak coherently," he mumbled, running his hands down my sides, his fingers tracing the lines of my dress. "I've never seen anything more angelic in my life, you're incredible." His breath blew across my face and neck making my skin prickle with sensations.

"Damn it, Will, stop making me fall more in love with you!" I whined playfully.

He grinned and did a little bow, holding out his hand. "Would the lady care to spend her last dance with me?" he asked, putting on a fake British accent.

I grinned and curtsied in my dress. "I would be honoured," I accepted, taking his hand. He grinned and pulled me to his chest, wrapping his arms around me tightly. The music from the gym was drifting down the hallway to his classroom; it wasn't loud, but just loud enough for it to be perfect. I wrapped my arms tight around his neck, clamping my body to his as we swayed to the beat of the song. The candles flickered, casting romantic shadows across the walls and ceiling. In the candle light he looked so handsome, the way the hue caught his features made him look incredibly beautiful. And impossibly, I actually did find myself falling even more in love with him.

When the song finished, he pulled back and kissed me. His lips claimed mine in a kiss that was so tender and soft that it was almost hypnotic. He pressed his forehead to mine again, his eyes locked onto mine making me feel weightless and like we were dancing on a cloud. "I love you so much, Cutie," he mumbled, his lips brushing mine as he spoke. I just sighed dreamily in response, which made him laugh quietly. "Thank you for the dance," he whispered.

"No. Thank you," I replied, looking at him in awe.

He smiled and pulled back even more, letting his arms drop from my side as he shoved one hand into his pants pocket. "So, I couldn't let a special occasion go by without marking it with something," he mused, pulling his hand out and holding out a little velvet pouch, the same type of one that held the little ring charm that he gave me on my birthday. I gulped and made an excited little aww sound when I realised he'd bought me another charm from my bracelet.

"You didn't need to," I whispered, taking the little bag from his hand and pulling on the string.

342

"I know, but I wanted to. I want to get you a charm for everything significant in our lives, then maybe when we die you can pass it down to our kids, or if we're really, really old then we'll have great-great-grandchildren by then, and you can pass it to one of them, it'll be an heirloom by then," he teased.

I laughed. "You plan on living a long time," I joked, feeling my eyes fill with tears at the sweetness that was dripping out of his mouth like honey. He smiled and watched as I tipped a little gold tulip charm out of the bag onto the palm of my hand. It was beautiful and had little red petals. "Will," I breathed, not quite knowing what to say. *How does he manage to make me feel so special all the time? He just seems to know the perfect thing to buy, something so thoughtful that it makes my heart ache.*

"Here, I'll put it on for you and then you'd better go and find Sam. The prom's finished now and I need to help with the clearing up," he suggested, stepping closer and taking it out of my hand. I smiled and held out my wrist to him. He clipped it onto my bracelet that I had yet to take off in the last two months, and then kissed the inside of my wrist on my pulse point. I sucked in a breath through my teeth when he did that, I loved that one little move, and I was pretty sure he knew that too because he always seemed to keep doing it to put me in the mood. *The damn boy knows that drives me crazy.*

I closed my eyes and gripped the lapels of his jacket, pulling him closer to me, crushing my chest against his. "You know that makes me hot, that wasn't fair when I'm not going to be seeing you all night," I whispered, shaking my head in mock disapproval.

He laughed and wrapped his arms around my waist. "Well maybe you'll have to call me, and we can do something about it over the phone if you're that hot," he teased, flicking my nose.

I giggled and blushed knowing what he meant. "Maybe I will," I replied, raising one eyebrow at him suggestively.

He gulped loudly. The smile fell off of his face; he obviously thought I would react differently to that little suggestion. "Really?" he asked, his voice shocked.

I nodded and shrugged easily. I was up for anything he wanted to try, a little dirty talk should be all right, he wouldn't be able to see my burning face from the other end of the phone anyway, and who knows, we might just enjoy it. "Sure," I breathed, watching as his eyes widened. I smirked, knowing that I'd won; he was unquestionably more shocked than I was. "I'd better go. Thank you so much for making my night so special. I love you," I promised, gripping my hand in the back of his hair and pulling his mouth down to mine again. He kissed me for a few minutes. The kiss was scorching hot, and my breathing was practically in pants with excitement. *If we weren't in school right now then I so would have been tearing his clothes off of him!*

A loud and insistent banging on the door had him jumping away from me like I had the plague. We both looked at the door with wide eyes wondering who it would be. "I don't care if you're in the middle of something nasty; if you don't let Chloe get dressed and send her out here in ten seconds, then I'm coming to join in!" Sam shouted, laughing from the other side of the door.

I burst into a fit of giggles as Will blew out a big breath and closed his eyes, running a hand through his hair. I kissed him lightly on the lips again. "Want me to help you put out the candles? We could wait for you and you could come get a pizza with us," I offered, looking around at the twenty or so candles he'd set around the room.

He shook his head. "Nah, I got it. You should go, I've got to reset all the fire alarms in here anyway and then I'm tidying up the gym. Call me tomorrow?" he asked, stroking the side of my face.

I slapped his ass and stepped to the door. "I'm calling you tonight, remember?" I winked at him and laughed as I pulled the door open and headed out to the hall to see Sam leaning against the wall waiting for me.

"Your dress is on inside out, Foxy," he teased, smirking at me.

"Ha-ha. Come on let's go get some food before you take me home. I'm buying considering you helped set all this up for me," I insisted, linking my arm through his and heading off through the hallways to the waiting limos. I looked down at the little charm on my bracelet and sighed dreamily. I really was one lucky girl.

Chapter Forty-One

I stood there with an uneasy excitement in the pit of my stomach. This was it; this was the day we had been waiting for. This was the day that my whole school life had been building up to. Graduation.

Today I would leaving this school, graduating with honours, and finally all of the hiding, the being careful, the worrying, would all be over. Will and I could be together without looking over our shoulders all of the time. Once this ceremony was over, it was no longer illegal for me to be in love with my teacher. Sure, it would probably still be frowned upon a little, but people would get over it eventually, and I didn't care anyway.

I smiled as I scanned over the crowd of people. I saw my parents sitting there; my mom was crying happy tears, with a big smile on her face. Sitting a couple of rows away from them was Sam, Angela, and William. They had insisted that they wanted to come today too and watch me graduate, though they would be staying clear of my parents for now. The time would come for them to meet, but that day wasn't quite yet.

I spotted the teachers sitting off to one side. Will was watching me with a proud smile on his face; I felt the goofy smile stretch onto my face so I quickly looked away before I made anything obvious. I frowned a little. I hadn't seen him much recently; I'd been studying and working hard so that I could graduate so we hadn't spent much time together lately.

Also, even when I did spend time with him, he'd been a little distant recently, making phone calls, sending emails, talking to Sam and then stopping when I walked into the room. I didn't know what it was about, but I was hoping it was something as simple as he was buying me a graduation present or something. My mind started wandering to horrible things, like maybe he didn't want to be with me anymore; maybe now that the excitement of a forbidden relationship was over he didn't want me. I'd been worrying about that for the last couple of weeks when he started going away for the weekends with Sam, and turning his cell phone off so I couldn't call him. He said it was nothing, that Sam needed to let loose, and he was just having 'boy bonding time'. So I'd let it go, just praying that he wasn't cheating on me or something.

I forced myself to stop thinking about it. Today wasn't about that; today was about finally being thrust into society as an adult. I'd speak to Will later and find out what was going on, but for now, I needed to worry about nothing more important than tripping on the bottom of my robes and falling on my face in front of everyone. Sam would love that.

I absentmindedly traced my hand over my wrist, catching my charm bracelet and worrying the little charms between my fingers trying to calm my nerves. There had been a couple more additions to my bracelet recently, the one that he gave me on prom night - the tulip - had also been joined by a horseshoe that he bought me when I had my exams, and the one that he gave me this morning, the little silver scroll charm that was for my graduation.

Chewing on my lip I waited for my name to be called. I watched as Amy skipped up to get hers, doing a dramatic bow which made people cheer and clap. I laughed and flicked my eyes back to Will again, watching as he clapped and grinned. Amy and Will got on great, in fact, he got on great with all of my friends, we hung out quite a lot. Everything was easier now that people thought I was with Sam. We were allowed to hang out as a group with no one wondering why a teacher was with us, as far as other people were concerned he was just hanging with his brother, so nothing more was said about it.

When Erika floated onto the stage, the boys all hollered and whistled as she sauntered on, shaking her ass and flicking her hair over her shoulder, looking like a supermodel. She was the only girl here that pulled off the sunshine yellow ceremonial robes, and still managed to look like a goddess while wearing them. I smiled. She hadn't hassled me at all since that lie I had told her, when I told her I had recorded her threatening me. She had kept out of my way and I had kept out of hers. Sure, she was still bitchy to me and Amy, I was pretty sure that would never change; it was just part of her personality. From what I heard though, Erika was going to be moving to England in a couple of weeks. Her family were uprooting and moving there for her dad's business, so I wouldn't even have contact with her after today was over with.

Nick got his turn on stage too; fist pumping the air which made his dad whoop and stand up to do the same thing. Someone nudged me in the back and I looked around to see a girl from my year, frowning and looking at me like I was crazy. "Are you going to go on?" she asked, nodding at the stage.

I looked at her quizzically until I realised what she was talking about. It was my turn to get my certificate. I gulped and gripped my bracelet tightly as I walked onto the stage, trying to appear confident even though I was secretly counting the steps in my head and praying I didn't fall and embarrass myself. I could vaguely hear my dad shouting something along the lines of "Yeah, go pumpkin!" I blushed and kept my eyes focused on the Principal who was smiling at me and watching me walk over to him.

When I stopped in front of him he grinned and held out his hand. "Congratulations," he stated. I laughed and shook his hand taking the little scroll with my other hand, feeling a burst of accomplishment rush over me. *I've done it. I've graduated. Now I'm free to get on with my life, my life with Will.*

346

"Thanks, Principal Sherman," I replied, practically skipping off of the stage while Sam hollered and chanted "Go, Foxy!" over and over. I shot him a warning look which just made him laugh and wink at me.

When I got to the other side of the stage I grabbed Amy and hugged her tightly before pouncing on Nick who span me around in a little circle, laughing. We watched as the rest of our year got their certificates, then, as per tradition, we all threw up our little hats. After that I was swept into an embarrassing display of affection by both of my parents. They were gushing over my robe, my hat, my certificate, telling me how proud they were. I posed for hundreds of photos; it would be a miracle if I could see right after this considering how many times the flash went off in my face.

I waved to Sam, Angela, and William. They made a swift and discreet exit right after the ceremony. My parents still hadn't met Sam, and I didn't want them to. I couldn't exactly introduce them to Sam and then tell them after that I was dating his brother, the teacher. So we just kept them all away from each other for now.

I felt my cell phone vibrate in my pocket so I pulled it out to see I had a new message from Will.

'Meet me around the back of the gym.'

I didn't bother to reply. He knew I would meet him, I didn't need to confirm. I smiled at my parents who were happily chatting with Nick's dad and Amy's parents. We were all going out now for a celebration dinner, it would be fun because all of our parents got on well too.

"Guys, I just need the bathroom before we leave," I lied.

My dad kissed the side of my head, smiling at me proudly. "Okay, pumpkin, we'll wait here." I smiled and skipped off to see Will and get my celebration hug from him.

As I headed around the side of the gym, there was no one there. I frowned and headed a little further up, deciding to wait here for him. *Maybe he's been caught up talking to someone.*

Before I knew what happened someone grabbed me and dragged me around the last corner, behind a bush so we were out of sight. I squealed from shock, but I knew it was Will because of his laugh.

I turned around in his arms and smiled. "Hi," I breathed.

He grinned and pressed me against the wall. "Hi," he replied, kissing me softly. I moaned into his mouth, just praying that we were completely out of sight because we really shouldn't be doing this here. He was obviously excited I was now graduated. He broke the kiss trailed little kisses across my cheek to my ear. "I'm so proud of you, Cutie."

"Will, we should probably go somewhere a little more private," I suggested breathlessly as he kissed down the side of my neck.

He sighed dramatically and pulled away from me, taking my hand, his other hand moving up to cup the side of my face. "I need to talk to you about something," he whispered, kissing my lips again lightly. "Can we go somewhere? I don't want to take you away from your family or anything, but this is important."

I gulped nervously. *Is this something bad? Why does he look so serious?* "Um… okay. We're supposed to be going for dinner, but I could cancel them," I stated, wincing. My parents would be annoyed with me, but I guess if it was important then I needed to.

He shook his head in rejection. "Don't cancel. This can wait, but I need to talk to you today, so maybe we could meet up after dinner?" he suggested, cocking his head to the side, looking at me hopefully.

I nodded and gripped the front of his shirt, pulling him closer to me. I didn't want to let him go, I was actually a little terrified. *Is he going to be break up with me? Is he going to tell me that he wants someone else? Or more space? Am I crowding him?*

He smiled and brushed his thumb over the line of my cheekbone. "You look beautiful in your robes, just like an angel," he complimented, kissing me softly.

I felt my eyes filling with tears; I didn't want my time with him to end. I would never get over this guy; never in my life would I ever be able to find someone that made me as happy as he made me. He was the one for me and I would never recover from this if he broke it off. How had I let this guy have so much power over me? How had I let him so far inside me that it was going to be like sheer agony to watch him walk out of my life?

"Have I done something wrong?" I whispered, trying desperately not to let the tears fall.

He frowned and looked at me like I was crazy. "Something wrong? No, why would you think that?"

"You've been so distant lately, you've been busy, and we've not really seen each other that much. Are you having second thoughts about me? Do you want to… to…" I couldn't say the words, I couldn't force the two words out of my mouth, they tasted so bitter, so repugnant that I didn't want to say them.

"You think I'm going to break up with you?" he asked incredulously. I nodded, chewing on my lip, waiting for him to say the words and for my world to collapse into the pits of hell. He frowned angrily and shook his head. "Cutie, why do you always assume the worst? Why do you doubt my love for you all the time?" he asked, shaking his head sadly.

"I'm not good enough for you. One of these days you'll realise it," I mumbled.

He closed his eyes and blew out a big breath, pressing his body against mine. "Cutie, I'm the one that's not good enough for you, not the other way around. I love you. I love you more than anything in the world and I'm always going to love you. You need to stop doubting yourself and stop doubting me. You're stuck with me now. You're wearing my promise ring for goodness sake, doesn't that tell you how I feel about you won't change?" he asked, pressing his forehead to mine.

I swallowed noisily. "So what's the thing we need to talk about?" I asked, wrapping my arms around his neck, pulling him closer to me, letting his sweet words wash over me. I felt my body calm down and relax. I was being stupid and he was right, I really needed to stop doubting him, I should have known that he loved me, I shouldn't have questioned that. I was just still so insecure because I would never feel worthy of his attention.

He smiled. "We'll talk later. It's important, but not bad. Don't start stressing that beautiful head about it, okay?" I nodded and pulled his mouth back to mine, kissing him deeply, showing him with that kiss how much I loved him, needed him, and appreciated him. He pulled back after a minute or so. "You should go; your parents are probably looking for you. Call me after and we'll meet somewhere."

I sighed; I didn't want to leave him here at the school. I wanted to take him with me, introduce him to my parents and have him come to dinner with everyone else. It felt so wrong to go off on this momentous occasion without the love of my life.

"Okay. I love you, Will." I kissed him again softly, before turning and moving away from him. I only got one step away before he slapped my behind as I walked off.

"You rock that robe, Cutie," he complimented, winking at me. I blushed and did a little curtsy before walking off quickly towards where my parents were waiting and talking to Trevor, Nick's dad.

Dinner was good. Our parents were all sharing stories about when we were kids, talking about how time whizzes past and before you know it that little baby that you gave birth to, was now graduated from high school. Nick, Amy and I just laughed at them as they reminisced. It was good, but in the back of my mind I couldn't stop thinking about Will. I constantly wished he was here and that he was part of this. He was the only thing missing from this picture.

When we'd finished with dinner, I text Will to tell him I was done, and we arranged to meet in half an hour. I skipped into the house to change. When it was finally time, I made my excuses to my parents and headed out of the house to go and meet him and find out what this 'important thing' was that we needed to talk about.

I jogged over to his car that was parked down the road from my house. I tried desperately not to stress about what it was, he said I shouldn't worry, and I was trying my hardest not to, but I must be more of a pessimist than I thought I was because the fear of what this was about had been eating away at me.

As I slipped into the passenger side he smiled happily. "Well hi there, long time no see," he chirped.

I smiled and rolled my eyes playfully. It had actually felt like a long time to me, even though it had only been a few hours. "Yeah it's been ages. How have you been? Keeping okay?" I replied, playing along. I raked my eyes over him; he looked so handsome in black jeans and a white T-shirt.

"Yeah, good thanks. You're looking well," he answered.

I grinned and scooted over in my seat and pressed my lips to his to silence him. "Enough of the playing around. Let's go somewhere and talk because the anticipation of what this is about is actually killing me slowly," I complained, pouting at him.

He smiled and started the car, driving to the children's play park that wasn't too far away from my house. We both climbed out and walked into the deserted park. He headed over to the bench and sat down so I followed suit and sat next to him, waiting for him to spit it out.

He turned to me, looking a little nervous. "So I'll just get to it then," he stated. "You're dead set on staying here to go to college, right? You definitely don't want to go to your dream school in New York?"

Okay, I wasn't expecting this conversation to be along these lines! I nodded in confirmation. He knew the answer to that; we'd spoken about it at great lengths over the last few weeks. I wasn't leaving to go there; I was staying here with him because I didn't want to leave him. We'd made the decision together, as a couple, what was better for both of us. We had both decided that staying together was what was important; location didn't matter as long as I was with him. I'd already told my family and friends, I'd told Amy that I wasn't going with her, I'd turned down my places at the other colleges. I was staying here with him. So why was he asking me this now?

He nodded. "Okay, so, you said I'd been distant and busy lately, so I thought I should tell you what I've been doing."

My heart stuttered in my chest. I knew something had been up with him lately. He'd seemed stressed, and always preoccupied on the internet. "Right, okay," I said uneasily, thinking he was going to tell me that he'd been seeing someone else.

He took a deep breath. "I got a new job."

I gasped, shocked. "You did? What job?" I asked, looking at him curiously. I still wasn't sure if this was a good thing or a bad thing.

He nodded. "Yeah I did. It's another teaching position, but it's not in this area," he replied, raising one eyebrow and watching for my reaction.

He's moving away? "Oh."

He smiled. "I've already accepted the position. I have to be there in a few weeks so I'll be moving away from here."

I could feel the horror building in my chest; the hysteria was threatening to crush me. *Will is moving away from me? I've turned down all of my college offers to stay here with him, but yet he's accepted a job somewhere else? How could he do that to me? Why would he?*

He nodded, seeming oblivious to my internal freak out that I was starting to have. "Yeah, I've been a little busy lately with interviews and things like that. But I was offered this really good opportunity that I just couldn't turn down," he continued.

"Oh," I mumbled again, not really able to form any coherent thoughts other than the fact that Will was leaving me. It was over.

He cocked his head to the side, looking at me expectantly. "Not going to ask me where I'm moving to?"

Can I speak? If I open my mouth will I just start screaming? Will any words actually come out if I try to form a sentence? My mouth was so dry I could barely even swallow. I licked my lips. "Where?" I whispered, fighting the sadness that was trying to consume me. This started off one of the happiest days of my life, and it was going to end one of the worst.

A smile twitched at the corners of his mouth. "There you go, doubting my love for you again," he whispered, kissing me softly. I didn't know how to respond. *Of course I'm doubting your love for me, stupid! I gave up my dream school to stay here with you and you're just up and leaving me here? How freaking selfish is that?*

"Will... just-" I didn't know what I wanted to say. Part of me wanted to cry, part of me wanted to shout at him, part of me wanted to hold him tight and never let him go.

"The job is in New York," he said, pulling back and looking at me waiting for my reaction.

New York? He's moving to New York? "Is that some kind of sick joke?" I asked, shaking my head, just not understanding this boy's humour. *He knew that I wanted to go there, yet he let me turn down my college place, but now he's moving there anyway? What the hell is up with that?* I jumped to my feet, looking at him angrily.

He laughed and gripped my hand, pulling me down to the bench again. "Yeah, I'm moving to New York. I have a great job lined up there, it's pretty close to your dream school actually," he commented, looking at me happily.

I pushed him away from me angrily. "What the hell? I turned down my place there! Why would you do this? Will, for goodness sake, this is just-" I groaned in frustration and shook my head at him.

He grinned. "You didn't turn down your place there actually. You accepted it. Well, that's not strictly true, Amy accepted it, pretending to be you," he said, shrugging.

What the? "She did what?" I mumbled, suddenly getting even more confused as to where this conversation was going.

He sighed happily. "Stop being angry with me, I can see you're angry by your expression. This is a good thing, I promise." He took my hand and turned in his seat so he was full on facing me. "Before you spoke to Amy and told her that you were staying here and not going to New York, I spoke to her. I told her that you were going to tell her that," he explained. "For the last couple of months I've been scrambling trying to find a new job close to your school that you wanted. It's been hard because I'm young and not a lot of schools want to take a chance on a guy that has only one year of teaching experience. But I found one eventually. I just got offered the place last week. It's only a half an hour drive from your dream school," he explained.

Holy crud, I did not see any of this coming! Is he being serious? "So, you have a job in New York, and Amy accepted my place at college when I thought that I'd turned it down?" I asked, needing conformation.

He nodded. "Yeah, it was pretty easy, she confirmed over the internet using your laptop, and I kind of intercepted your place rejection letter that you mailed," he agreed, grinning sheepishly.

I closed my eyes, still unsure what to think about any of this. "You would move to New York with me?" I whispered.

He laughed. "I'd move to Antarctica with you, Cutie."

"We're going to New York?" I gasped, the reality of it suddenly washing over me.

He nodded. A smile stretched across his face. "Yep. Me, you, and Amy."

How the hell did I get this guy? I seriously don't deserve him at all. He's willing to leave his family, and move half way across the country, just for me? "Will, what the hell? Seriously?" I cried, jumping off of the bench and covering my mouth as I started laughing.

He nodded, stretching his arms out across the back of the bench, looking the epitome of ease as he smiled up at me. "Seriously," he confirmed, shrugging casually as if this was no big deal.

I squealed and jumped on his lap, making him grunt before he laughed too. "Oh my God, thank you. Thank you! You're just... I don't the words to describe you. You're just perfect," I gushed, looking at him in awe.

He shook his head. "I'm not perfect, I'm a messy math nerd," he joked.

"Correction, you're *my* messy math nerd," I countered, grinning at him.

He smirked at me and gripped his hand around the back of my head, pulling my mouth closer to his. "And you're my Lucky Charm eating, Cutie," he whispered, before pressing his lips to mine and kissing me tenderly.

I smiled against his lips, feeling so happy that I could burst into song at any second. Then it hit me. I pulled back and winced. "I told my parents I was staying here now. How am I going to them that I'm not?"

He smiled. "I thought we could do that together." He looked a little nervous about it as he stroked my hair softly.

"You finally worked up the nerve to want to meet my dad?" I teased, knowing he'd wanted to do it for months now, but we couldn't until I'd graduated.

He nodded. "Finally yeah," he agreed, playing along. "Not only am I meeting the guy, but I'm also about to tell him that I'm taking his only daughter to live in sin, miles away from home. I can see this night ending badly."

I laughed and pressed my lips to his, kissing him fiercely. "Don't worry, we'll get through it together," I promised.

He nodded. "That's why I'm not freaking out. Whatever happens after this, I know it'll be fine, because I'll be with you." He kissed me again, ending the conversation.

I melted against him, my heart crashing in my chest as I wondered just how it was that I got so freaking lucky. I now had my dream guy, and we were moving together so that I could go to my dream school. Life couldn't get much better than this. No matter how my parents reacted, it wouldn't matter, Will and I would get through it, we'd get through anything. Together.

Epilogue

"I'm so nervous that I feel sick," Will muttered, shaking his head, gripping my hand tightly.

I smiled and tried to pretend that I was confident, that this would all be fine, when in reality I knew it wouldn't be. We were about to tell my parents that he was my teacher, that we got together last summer, and that we were moving to New York together. This was not going to end well at all.

"Would you rather me tell them on my own and then introduce you tomorrow? Maybe that would be a better idea," I suggested, wincing. *Maybe they won't go as crazy if it isn't all thrown in their faces in one go.* I knew my dad would be angry about it. He would be seriously annoyed that I'd been keeping it secret; he would be even more annoyed that Will was older, but he was going to be seething mad that he was my teacher.

Will shook his head and frowned. "I'm not letting you do that on your own," he protested. He nodded towards the door. "Come on, Cutie. Let's get this done."

I took a deep breath and jammed my key in the lock, opening the door, feeling my heart sink as I heard the click. The TV was on in the lounge, my parents were laughing at some show they were watching. I tugged Will into the house with me and closed the door quietly behind us. I smiled tentatively at him before going up on tiptoes and pressing my lips to his, kissing him softly.

"I love you. If they kick me out can I stay at yours?" I whispered, looking at him hopefully.

He smiled. "Of course you can. It really is wrong for me to hope that they do kick you out, isn't it?" he countered, winking at me. I giggled and slapped his chest with the back of my hand, nodding towards the lounge. He smiled and kissed my forehead softly. "I love you too by the way."

I closed my eyes and took a couple of deep breaths before heading into the lounge, seeing my parents sitting there watching TV, cuddled up on the sofa, sharing a bowl of popcorn. My mom noticed us first. She smiled happily, but then her eyes took in Will who was standing slightly behind me, still holding my hand in the death grip. Her smile turned into more of a polite, bemused expression as she looked at him curiously, as if trying to work out if she knew him or not.

"Er, hey guys," I mumbled, noticing how my voice shook with nerves as I spoke.

My dad looked up from the TV then and frowned, his expression turning into the bad cop that happened whenever he met a guy I brought home to meet them. "Hey, pumpkin," he replied, his voice tight, his eyes locked on Will.

I was sweating. I could feel it forming on my top lip where I was so nervous. "Er, okay so I have someone I want you to meet," I started, unsure how I was going to kick off this conversation. "This is Will Morris." I tugged him forward a little, nodding in his direction. "Will, these are my parents."

Will smiled and stepped forward with his hand out. Both my parents stood up too, my mom's eyes flicking to my dad worriedly. She obviously knew what he was like too. "It's nice to meet you, Mr and Mrs Henderson. I've heard a lot about you," Will said confidently.

My dad raised one eyebrow as he took Will's offered hand and shook it. "Really? Well we've heard absolutely nothing about you," he replied, his voice harsh.

Oh God, please let the ground open up and swallow me!

Will laughed nervously. "Yeah I know. Sorry about that, that was a small complication." He shook my mom's hand too; she was watching me curiously, probably wondering why I was just standing there with my teeth gritted and my hands in tight fists. "Chloe and I have a few things we need to explain to you. I'm not quite sure how to say it really," Will continued.

Jeez, is he oblivious to the death glare my father is shooting him right now? Does he just not care that my dad looks like he wants to rip his head off?

My dad's hard stare turned on me. "Who is this then, Chloe?" he asked. I flinched; I knew he was already mad because he hardly ever called me Chloe, always pumpkin.

I cleared my throat. "This is my boyfriend," I answered, trying to sound confident.

My dad's eyebrow rose even further. "Little old for you, isn't he?" he countered, his eyes not leaving mine.

"Not in my opinion, but I'm sure in yours he will be," I agreed, slipping my hand back into Will's, squeezing gently. "We need to talk about some stuff. I'm sure you're not going to like it, but just hear us out. Please?" I asked, looking at him pleadingly.

"Why don't we all sit down?" my mom suggested cheerfully. I smiled gratefully. She was obviously trying to help me out and keep my dad calm.

I nodded and tugged Will over to the other sofa, sitting down and pulling him down next to me, pressing into his side, wishing I could hide behind him or something. My parents were both looking at me curiously so I knew I needed to get the conversation going and explain.

I swallowed loudly. "Okay, so remember I told you that I was dating a guy last summer but we broke up?" I inquired, wincing.

My dad nodded. "Yeah, some guy called," his eyes flicked to the love of my life, "Will," he finished. Understanding crossed his features before his eyes narrowed. "A year? Seriously, you've been dating for almost a year and have only just brought him home?" he cried, shaking his head angrily.

"There were some other things, it was impossible," I countered. *This is not going well.*

"What other things? You know I like to meet your boyfriends, Chloe. Why are we only just meeting now?" Dad asked, glaring at Will again.

Will shifted on his seat, and I knew he was about to take over this conversation. Hopefully my part was over now and I would just have to add into the conversation a little here and there. Will would take care of everything and make this all right, he always did.

"Mr Henderson, I met your daughter last summer and I didn't know how old she was. I thought she was older than she was. We started dating and getting on great. But then at the end of the summer Chloe went back to school and... well, we found out that Chloe was actually my," he took a deep breath before finishing his sentence, "student."

A frown crossed my dad's face as he took in what Will said. "Your student? What does that mean? I don't understand. Student in what?"

Will shifted on the sofa, his hand tightening on mine. "I finished college and was offered a job at Chloe's school. I'm her calculus teacher. Well, I was, she's obviously graduated now," he explained.

My mom's eyes widened, but my dad still looked confused. His eyes flicked to me again. "What's he talking about, Chloe?" he asked.

I winced and blew out the breath that I didn't even realise I was holding. "When I met Will last summer I didn't tell him how old I was, and he assumed I was older than seventeen. When I went back to school at the start of senior year, Will was there too, but he was... my teacher," I explained, just repeating what Will had said. This time my dad understood though.

His face turned from confused to murderously angry as he sprung out of his chair. His eyes were hard and accusing as they latched onto Will. "Get your goddamn hands off of my daughter!" he shouted warningly.

Will nodded and let go of my hand immediately, holding up his hands innocently. "Mr Henderson, it's not as bad as it sounds. I love your daughter very much, more than anything," he said quickly, obviously trying to calm my dad down.

"You've been using your position at her school to date my daughter like some kind of sicko paedophile?" my dad spat. He pointed over to the other couch where my mom was sat with her eyes and mouth wide, looking like she was in shock. "Get over there and sit with your mother, Chloe. I'll talk to you later!"

I gulped and shook my head. "No. Dad, seriously, calm down! I love Will, it's not like that! It's not some seedy thing," I cried, looking at him in astonishment. I was expecting him to freak out and be angry but he looked like if I moved away from Will, that he would tear him to shreds.

"Move next to your mother!" my dad repeated, his eyes still locked on Will.

I stood up and shook my head. I wasn't letting this end in a fight, sure I could understand he was angry, but I wouldn't let him talk to Will like that. "You have no right to be looking at him the way you are. He's an incredible person, yet you're looking at him like he's scum!" I cried angrily.

My dad's jaw tightened as his face turned a darker shade of red. "He *is* scum! Please tell me you two haven't been..." he trailed off, his frown deepening.

Oh God.

"We waited until I was eighteen," I lied, wincing, hoping he wouldn't see through me. I was a terrible liar. My mom shifted uncomfortably on her feet, and I knew she could tell I was lying. My dad, however, nodded and seemed satisfied with my answer. I begged my mom with my eyes not to say anything; if she chimed in right now there would be no stopping my dad's fist from flying into Will's face.

"Well, that's one good thing I guess," my dad admitted somewhat grudgingly.

"That was what Will wanted," I said quickly, trying to get across to my dad that he was a good guy. We were all on our feet now. I knew I needed to add in the other stuff, the college stuff and get it all out in the open. "Will and I have decided that I should go to the school that I always wanted to, the one in New York," I stated.

A smile twitched at the corners of my dad's lips. "I think that's a good idea. Put some distance between you two and then if you are still intent on being together then in the future the age difference wouldn't seem so bad. How old are you anyway, you look about twenty-four," my dad questioned, looking at Will expectantly.

"I'm twenty-two, sir. I'll be twenty-three next month," Will answered. "Um, Mr Henderson, I think you have the wrong impression about Chloe's school," he added uncomfortably.

I frowned. *Maybe we just shouldn't tell them. I can just pretend that I'm going with Amy and that Will is staying here. When they come to visit me in New York I could just make Will stay in a hotel or something the whole time, they'll never know any different. At least then we won't have to deal with this again for four years, hopefully my dad would have mellowed by then.*

"What does that mean?" my mom asked, looking between the two of us for confirmation as she moved closer to my dad's side. He slipped an arm around her and watched us curiously.

"I'm going to New York with Chloe. I've secured another teaching position at a high school near there. We're going together," Will explained.

My dad's shoulders stiffened. "Not a cat in hells chance of that happening!" he roared, making my ears ring where it was so loud.

I elbowed Will in the ribs. *Why couldn't he just shut up and leave it as I was going on my own? Jeez, we should have discussed this plan at the park earlier!* He slipped his arm around my waist, pulling me closer to him. "Sir," Will started, by my dad cut him off.

"No way, Chloe. I'm not allowing you to move half way across the country with a pervert!" he cried.

Rage boiled in my stomach. "Will is not a damn pervert!" I shouted angrily. "I won't let you keep talking about him like that. I love him. If you can't see how happy he makes me then that's your problem, not mine. I'm going with him to New York, and that's the end of it, no discussion is needed here!" I ranted, my fists tightening in anger. I wanted to punch something. *Where's Erika when I need her? I would certainly like to take my frustrations out on her.*

My dad looked at me incredulously. "So you're choosing him, over us?" he shouted, making my mom flinch because he'd probably yelled in her ear.

I swallowed loudly. I really didn't want to answer that question. "I'm really hoping you won't make me choose. I love Will, I'm going to be with him whether you like it or not. I don't want to choose between a guy I'm in love with and my family, please, please don't make me, Dad, please," I begged, starting to cry as I felt my lip tremble.

Will's arm tightened around my waist supportively. I watched my father struggle to calm himself down, to accept what we were telling him. I just prayed that he would give him a chance. I didn't want to have this happen, but I knew with every bone in my body that if they forced me to make a decision, then it wouldn't go in their favour.

"So you're saying you're going to be with him, and move away with him, no matter what?" my dad asked, his voice breaking as he looked at me. His emotion was clear on his face even though he was obviously trying to hold it together.

"Yes," I whispered.

He closed his eyes and spoke, "I could have him arrested; it's illegal for a teacher to date a student. It doesn't matter that you're graduated, I could still report him," he stated, still not opening his eyes.

I gasped. "Don't," I begged.

"Mr Henderson, you would be perfectly within your rights to do so. If that's the way you want to go, then Chloe and I will respect that," Will stated, shrugging.

I looked and him and frowned. "What the hell? *I* won't respect that! I'll be seriously pissed," I snapped. I turned to my dad and glared. "Don't you dare!"

Will smiled sadly. "Cutie, we both knew this was wrong. If your dad feels like he needs to do that, then fair enough. We'll both respect his decision," he said, looking at me sternly.

"What happens if you get sent to jail?" my dad asked.

I felt my body tighten at the word jail and my hands gripped fistfuls of Will's shirt as if that could somehow keep him with me. Will shrugged. "Then I'd hope that she'd still want to be with me when I got released," he replied.

"So if I was to threaten to call the police if you didn't leave her alone, then you'd still be standing there by the time I got to my phone?" my dad asked incredulously.

Will stood tall and confident as he nodded. "Yes, sir, I love your daughter. How we met was unfortunate but I wouldn't take it back for the world. I'm here for as long as she wants me here for," he answered, his eyes locked on my dad's, his sincerity clear in the tone of his voice.

My dad looked at my mom who shook her head fiercely. I saw his jaw tighten as he seemed to make his decision. "If you hurt her I swear to God, I'm gonna bring a whole heap of shit down on you, you'll regret the day you ever heard of the name Chloe Henderson," he warned, his voice menacing and full of promise.

Will smiled. "Sir, I'll never regret it, she's the best thing that ever happened to me. I give you my word that I'll never hurt her," he vowed as he held out his hand for my dad as a kind of peace offering.

My dad looked down at Will's outstretched hand. "You're word means nothing to me. I don't even know you."

"And I have a long time to change that fact, sir. I plan on being here for a very long time. I'll earn your trust eventually," Will replied.

"Cutie?" I could vaguely hear it, my mind was like a fog, I had no idea what was going on. "Cutie?" Will said a little louder. His voice cut through the fog, slowly bringing me back to reality. I groaned and cracked my stinging eyes open, looking towards the voice. "Cutie, you need to wake up, we have visitors," Will cooed, stroking the side of my face.

"I'm still tired," I grumbled, yawning. I closed my eyes again; wanting just another hour of sleep, maybe even just ten more minutes would suffice. I felt his lips press against mine; I smiled against his lips and kissed him back tiredly. I wasn't, however, too tired to notice the little shiver that ran down the length of my spine, or the tingling in my stomach, or how the hair on the back of my neck seemed to prickle. His kisses never ceased to amaze me, though I should have been used to them by now.

I wrapped my arms around his neck and pulled him closer to me, making him fall down beside me onto the bed. He laughed and pulled back a little as I slipped my hand up the back of his T-shirt, digging my fingers into his skin. "Not too tired for that, huh?" he teased, kissing me again lightly.

I giggled and shook my head. "Never too tired for that, you know that." I winked at him suggestively, and he smirked at me. I'd never get used to this happiness, this elation that I felt in his presence. Will was, and would always be, the best thing that ever happened to me. Well, actually, maybe he was the second best thing…

"I was dreaming about you," I mumbled, pressing my face into the side of his neck as I snuggled closer to him.

He laughed. "Oh really and what were we doing? Something dirty?" he asked, ticking me lightly.

I grinned and pulled back to look at him. "No actually, I was just dreaming about the day that we told my parents about us," I replied.

He winced and hissed through his teeth. "You had a nightmare then," he said, cupping the side of my face.

I laughed and gripped his T-shirt, rolling onto my back, pulling him on top of me but he immediately lifted his weight and hovered above me. "Yeah I had a nightmare, want to make me feel better?" I purred suggestively.

He groaned. "Cutie, we have visitors. I'll have to take a rain check," he replied, bending and kissing across the side of my face. I tangled my hand into the back of his hair as his lips travelled across my skin, making me moan quietly. His hand slipped down my body, making me bite my lip and arch into him.

Suddenly the bedroom door opened and I heard little footsteps running across the room, the mattress dipped, and I heard a giggling sound. I smiled as Will sighed and moved off of me, looking somewhat reluctant; my guess was that he'd forgotten we had visitors.

I smiled and sat up; grinning at the little four year old boy that was jumping on the foot of my bed like it was a trampoline. He was so handsome, just like his dad, brown hair, and brown eyes. "Logan Morris, you stop jumping on my bed and come and give me a hug," I ordered, pointing to myself, pouting.

He squealed and dropped down onto his bum, making the bedsprings groan in protest. He smiled and crawled over to me, wrapping his little arms around my neck, hugging me tightly. "Auntie Foxy, I missed you!" he chirped.

I rolled my eyes. *That damn boy still hadn't told his son to stop calling me that!* "You too, Logan. Where's your dad?" I asked, kissing his forehead, making him squirm and wipe it roughly. He didn't like being kissed by girls. *Not like his dad...*

"Daddy's in the kitchen eating the cake already," he replied.

I gasped and looked at Will who immediately jumped off of the bed and ran for the door, shouting for Sam to leave the birthday cake until everyone else got here. I smiled back down at my nephew; he looked really cute today in his Generator Rex T-shirt that I'd bought for him last week. "Shirt fits then?" I teased, fingering the sleeve of it.

He grinned and nodded. "Did you see yesterday's show? It was so good, Rex was..." I smiled and nodded as he proceeded to tell me everything that happened yesterday in his favourite show. The kid talked so much that it was almost unreal, but I loved him dearly.

I pushed myself up from the bed and groaned. I hadn't slept very well last night again. I'd only just gone for a lie down an hour ago before everyone got here. I could actually do with sleeping all day today just to make up for it. I changed my shirt with Logan bouncing on my bed, telling me about this new toy he'd seen that he desperately wanted for Christmas. Logan and I were close, probably because for the last year, I'd looked after him while Sam was at work. He kind of felt like my kid in a way too, I certainly loved him like my own.

"Come on then, chicken, let's go to see everyone," I suggested, holding out my hand for him to take when I was dressed and had brushed my hair. He took my hand and skipped along at my side as I walked out of the bedroom and down the stairs to where I could hear voices. A lot of voices. *Sounds like everyone's here already.*

As soon as I stepped into the kitchen I was engulfed into a hug by Angela. "Chloe! Are you feeling all right? Will said you had a bad night?" she asked, looking at me worriedly.

I waved my hand dismissively. "I'm fine, don't worry about it."

I turned to see my parents laughing and talking to William and Sam. They all got on great; the Hendersons and the Morris' were like one big extended family. Everything settled down between Will and my parents pretty quickly. They saw how good he was for me, and what he was doing for me by moving to New York and letting me go to my dream school. They actually treated him like the son they never had now. It was incredibly sweet to watch how they fussed over him and joked around with him. My dad and Will even played racquetball together every Saturday. It was nice.

When my four years of college had finished, we'd moved back here to be closer to our families. That had worked out pretty well too considering that Sam had gotten a girl pregnant on a one night stand. The girl had told him that she was going to get an abortion because she didn't want to be tied down with a kid, but he'd managed to convince her not to. As soon as she gave birth, she signed over full custody to Sam, she hadn't even been back to see him in four years. It was so sad because Logan was incredible; she was missing out on an awesome kid.

Sam was so totally opposite to what I thought he would be. I would have never pictured him as a single dad, but he totally pulled it off. Hopefully one day he'd meet a nice girl. Logan had told me last week that his daddy liked another kid's mom at pre-school. Sam refused to comment, but I was pretty sure Logan was right, he definitely liked her. If she was a single parent too then they'd probably be well suited. Sam deserved a happy ending too, so I really hoped he'd get one. Any girl would be lucky to nab a Morris brother so she'd be crazy not to give him a shot.

Someone grabbed my shoulders and span me around so fast that I actually felt a little dizzy. I looked up to see Nick and his wife, Julia. I smiled and hugged him tightly. "Hey guys, thanks for coming!" I chirped.

Nick smiled and looked at me like I was crazy. "I wouldn't miss this for the world, it's tradition," he replied. I laughed and hugged Julia too. She was great. They had met at college, and were very happy together. They'd gotten married about three months ago; it was so nice to see Nick so happy.

Amy couldn't come today; she was off travelling the world at the moment. Her and Ryan hadn't made it. The long distance of college kind of ruined their relationship, but it all worked out for the best because she'd met this incredible guy who was a travel writer. He was actually paid to travel the world and write reviews of hotels, places, tourist attractions and things like that. Of course he wouldn't go without her, so she was usually gone for months at a time with him. I got emails all the time keeping me up to date on where she was, and all the fun she was having.

A cheer erupted around me, so I turned in the direction of the door to see Will walk in. I smiled happily, my heart aching with love for him and the little thing he had in his arms.

"Mom-mom-mom-mom-mom!" she chirped, holding out her chubby arms for me.

I smiled and took her into my arms, grinning. My baby. She was so beautiful. She had Will's grey eyes, but her hair was a dark blonde like mine. She was incredible and was the very centre of my world. I would do anything for my little girl, absolutely anything. I would even stay up with her practically all night because she had a cough, and I didn't even feel the need to complain.

"Hey there, beautiful," I cooed, stroking her hair down. She'd been to sleep too, that was why I went for a quick nap, because we'd both been up all night and when I put her down to sleep, I went too before everyone arrived.

Elise wasn't planned; she was a total accident, but that was the best freaking accident that had ever happened to me. She was one year old today, and as per the Henderson tradition, we were having lunch here at our house. Sure, we weren't exactly Henderson's anymore, Will and I had gotten married a long time before Elise was born, but the tradition still carried on.

Will saddled up beside me, wrapping his arms around me and kissing the side of my head as Elise buried her face into my hair, her little chubby arms wrapped around my neck as people started singing happy birthday to her.

I smiled and kissed the top of her head. She didn't really understand what was going on today, she was too young, but that wouldn't stop the adults - and Logan - from eating as much dessert as possible in her honour.

I settled her into her highchair as my mom and Angela started taking off the coverings of all of the desserts on the countertop, passing out bowls and spoons to everyone. Everyone had brought something with them so that Will and I didn't have to make it all. I spotted a slightly burnt cake that was lopsided and decorated with Generator Rex edible stickers; the icing had a couple of finger prints in it where they'd started eating it already.

I smiled at Logan as Will lifted him onto a stool at the counter and passed him a bowl. "Did you make Elise a birthday cake?" I asked, smiling at him gratefully. He was such a sweet kid.

Sam laughed sheepishly. "Yeah we did, but we didn't have enough sugar like the recipe said, so I don't know what it'll taste like. The icing's good though," he stated, tracing his finger across the top getting another blob on his finger and eating it.

Logan gasped, pushing Sam's hand away from the cake as he went to get another blob. "Daddy, stop touching my cake, you maked prints!" he scolded, shaking his head. Sam just laughed harder and got another blob, wiping it on the tip of his son's nose, sticking his tongue at him. They were always like this, they were well suited.

"Right then, I'm going for three years in a row!" Will stated, grinning proudly as he smirked in my dad's direction. This competition got fiercer every year. Will had taken over as leader. Him and Nick were the only ones that really stood a chance. Will would suffer for it all afternoon though, he'd be lying on the couch groaning and whining about it, but that didn't stop him from eating more on the following Henderson's birthday.

Nick snorted distastefully. "In your dreams, nerd-boy."

Sam laughed and high fived Logan. "We're working as a team this year," Sam stated, grinning confidently.

My dad decided to chime in at the same time as William did. "No chance, age wins it this year," William chirped, patting his stomach, at the same time as my dad said, "You boys got nothing, I haven't eaten for two days!"

I held up my hands to silence everyone. "Guys, guys, just cut out the trash talk. You all seem to have forgotten something," I said. They all looked at me curiously. I smirked and slipped my hands down to my swollen tummy. "I'm six months pregnant, I'm eating for two. I'm *so* kicking ass this year!"

Made in the USA
Lexington, KY
09 April 2017